ROMANCE SHALVIS
Shalvis, Jill, author.
The summer deal : a novel

JUL - - 2020

W9-BLK-751

PRAISE FOR JILL SHALVIS

"Believable, realistic characters are at the heart of this novel. Shalvis will immediately grab the reader's attention with a strong heroine and caring connection between two wounded souls."

—*Publishers Weekly* on *Almost Just Friends*

"Fans of the TV drama series *This Is Us* as well as love stories ripe with secrets waiting to be spilled will devour Shalvis's latest in the series."

—*Library Journal* on *Almost Just Friends*

"Sisterhood takes center stage in this utterly absorbing novel. Jill Shalvis balances her trademark sunny optimism and humor with unforgettable real-life drama. A book to savor—and share."

—Susan Wiggs, *New York Times* bestselling author, on *The Lemon Sisters*

"Jill Shalvis's books are funny, warm, charming. and unforgettable."

—RaeAnne Thayne, *New York Times* bestselling author, on *The Lemon Sisters*

"The love story you need to read this summer isn't what you expect: it's about the love between sisters. Jill Shalvis has written something totally different for your beach read this year—and you're going to love it."

—Bustle on *Lost and Found Sisters*

"Readers will be utterly charmed by Shalvis's latest, and will be eager to visit Wildstone again."

—Bookish on *Lost and Found Sisters*

"I love everything about this book, the family dynamics, the humor, and the amazing romance. Just amazing!"

—Lori Foster on *Lost and Found Sisters*

"Shalvis's rich cast of characters add just the right dose of color and sage advice, while she spins yet another sexy contemporary tale that showcases her indelible wit and eye for sweet, compulsively readable romance."

—*Entertainment Weekly*

"Romance . . . you can lose yourself in."

—*USA Today*

"Hot, sweet, fun, and romantic! Pure pleasure!"

—Robyn Carr

"Jill Shalvis will make you laugh and fall in love."

—Rachel Gibson

The

Summer
Deal

ALSO BY JILL SHALVIS

WOMEN'S FICTION NOVELS

Almost Just Friends
The Lemon Sisters
Rainy Day Friends
The Good Luck Sister (novella)
Lost and Found Sisters

HEARTBREAKER BAY NOVELS

Wrapped Up in You
Playing for Keeps
Hot Winter Nights
About That Kiss
Chasing Christmas Eve
Accidentally on Purpose
The Trouble with Mistletoe
Sweet Little Lies

LUCKY HARBOR NOVELS

One in a Million
He's So Fine
It's in His Kiss
Once in a Lifetime
Always on My Mind
It Had to Be You
Forever and a Day
At Last
Lucky in Love
Head Over Heels
The Sweetest Thing
Simply Irresistible

ANIMAL MAGNETISM NOVELS

Still the One
All I Want
Then Came You
Rumor Has It
Rescue My Heart
Animal Attraction
Animal Magnetism

The Summer Deal

A Novel

JILL SHALVIS

Bookmobile
Fountaindale Public Library
Bolingbrook, IL
(630) 759-2102

WILLIAM MORROW
An Imprint of HarperCollins*Publishers*

This is a work of fiction. Names, characters, places, and incidents are products of the author's imagination or are used fictitiously and are not to be construed as real. Any resemblance to actual events, locales, organizations, or persons, living or dead, is entirely coincidental.

P.S.™ is a trademark of HarperCollins Publishers.

THE SUMMER DEAL. Copyright © 2020 by Jill Shalvis. Excerpt from THE FOREVER GIRL copyright © 2021 by Jill Shalvis. All rights reserved. Printed in the United States of America. No part of this book may be used or reproduced in any manner whatsoever without written permission except in the case of brief quotations embodied in critical articles and reviews. For information, address HarperCollins Publishers, 195 Broadway, New York, NY 10007.

HarperCollins books may be purchased for educational, business, or sales promotional use. For information, please email the Special Markets Department at SPsales@harpercollins.com.

FIRST EDITION

Designed by Diahann Sturge

Title page and chapter opener art © globe_design_studio / Shutterstock, Inc.

Library of Congress Cataloging-in-Publication Data has been applied for.

ISBN 978-0-06-289791-6
ISBN 978-0-06-300711-6 (library edition)

20 21 22 23 24   LSC   10 9 8 7 6 5 4 3 2 1

The
Summer
Deal

 CHAPTER 1

Brynn Turner had always wanted to be the girl who had her life together, but so far her talents hadn't led her in that direction—although not for lack of trying.

Mentally recapping the week she'd just endured, she let out a stuttered breath. Okay, so her life skills needed some serious work, but as far as she was concerned, that was Future Brynn's problem. Present Brynn had other things on her mind.

Like surviving the rest of the day.

With that goal in mind, she kept her eyes on the road, and three hours and two 7-Eleven hot dogs after leaving Long Beach in her rearview mirror, she pulled into Wildstone. The place that reinvented itself many times over since it'd been an 1800s California wild, wild West town complete with wooden sidewalks, saloons, haunted silver mines, and a brothel. Sandwiched between the Pacific Ocean and green rolling hills filled with wineries and ranches, Wildstone had once been her favorite place on earth.

Parking in the driveway of her childhood home, she took a

minute. It'd been a decade since she'd lived here. She'd gone off to attend college and to conquer the world, though only one of those things had happened. She'd been back for visits, but even that had been a while. Six months, in fact. She'd stood in this very spot and had asked both of her well-meaning moms to butt out of her life, saying that she knew what she was doing.

She'd had no idea *what she was doing.*

Note to self: You still don't.

With a sigh, she pulled down her visor and glanced in the mirror, hoping that a miracle had occurred and she'd see the reflection of someone who had their shit together. Her hair was knotted on top of her head with the string tie from her hoodie because she'd lost her scrunchie. She was wearing her old glasses because she'd lost her newer pair. Her face was pale and her eyes were puffy and red from a bad combo of crying and not sleeping. She wore yoga pants that hadn't seen a yoga class since . . . well, ever, and in spite of being nearly thirty, she had a big, fat zit on her chin.

In short, she looked about as far away from having her shit together as she was from solving world hunger.

Knowing her moms—sweet and loving *and* nosy as hell—were going to see right through her, she pawed through her purse for a miracle. She found some lip gloss that she also dabbed on each cheek for badly needed color. As a bonus, she found two peanut M&Ms. Couldn't waste those, could she? She shook her purse looking for more, but nope, she was out of luck.

The theme of her life.

With a sigh, she once again met her own gaze in the mirror. "Okay, here's the drill. You're okay. You're good. You're happy to be home. You're absolutely *not* crawling back with your tail between your legs to admit to your moms that they were right about Asshole Ashton."

Swallowing hard, she got out of her hunk-o-junk and grabbed her duffel bag and purse. She'd barely made it to the porch before the front door was flung open and there stood her moms in the doorway, some deep maternal instinct letting them know their sole offspring was within smothering distance.

Both in their mid-fifties, their similarities stopped there. Olive was pragmatic and stoic, and God help the person who tried to get anything by her. She was perfectly coifed as always, hair cut in a chic bob, pants and blazer fitted, giving her the look of someone who'd just walked out of a Wall Street meeting. In sharp comparison, Raina's sundress was loose and flowery and flowing, and she wore beads around her neck and wrists that made her jingle pleasantly. She was soft and loving, and quite possibly the kindest soul on earth. And where Olive was economical with her movements, Raina was in constant motion.

Opposites attract . . .

But actually, her moms did have something in common beyond their age—their warm, loving smiles, both directed at Brynn. It was her own personal miracle that they loved her madly, no matter how many times she'd messed up and driven them crazy with worry.

And there'd been a lot of times. Too many to count.

"Sweetheart," Raina said, jingling as always, bringing forth welcome memories: growing vegetables in the back garden, taking long walks on the beach to chase seagulls, and late-night snuggles. Raina opened her arms and Brynn walked right into them, smiling when Olive embraced her from behind.

The three of them stood there for a long beat, wrapped up in each other. Catherine the Great Cat showed up, her appearance forewarned by the bell around her neck. She might be twelve and seemingly frail and delicate, but as with Brynn's moms, looks were deceiving. Just beneath Cat's skin lived the soul of an ancient prized hunter—hence the bell. No one blamed her for her instinctual drive to do this, but Raina did object to Cat dropping "presents" at her feet in the form of cricket heads and various other pieces of dead insects. Which made Cat the most adorable murderer who ever lived. She rubbed her furry face against Brynn's ankles. Once. Twice.

And then bit.

"Ouch!"

"You know her rules," Olive said. "A little love, a little hate. It's how she is. Now tell us why you're home unannounced, looking like something not even Catherine would've dragged inside."

"*I* think she looks wonderful," Raina said.

Olive's eyes never left Brynn. "She hasn't been sleeping or eating."

"Trust me, Mom, I've been eating plenty."

"Okay, then you aren't sleeping enough or eating the *right* food. You're as pale as . . . well, me."

Olive indeed had the pale skin of her English ancestry. In

contrast, Raina was Puerto Rican, and golden brown. Being a product of Raina's egg and an unknown sperm donor, Brynn's skin was a few shades lighter than Raina's. Unless she was trying not to hyperventilate, of course. Like now. In which case she was probably even whiter than Olive.

"We can fix the eating right and sleeping, for a start," Raina said with determination. She slipped her hand into Brynn's, and as she'd been doing for as long as Brynn could remember, she took over. She settled Brynn onto the couch with one of her handmade throws, and in less than five minutes had a tray on Brynn's lap with her famous vegan chickpea noodle soup and steaming gingerroot tea.

"Truth serum?" Brynn asked, only half joking. Raina was magic in the kitchen—*and* at getting people to spill their guts.

"I don't need truth serum." Raina sat next to her. "You're going to tell me everything."

"How do you know?"

"Because I made almond-butter cups for dessert and you love almond-butter cups."

"You'd withhold dessert from your only child?"

"She wouldn't, she's far too kind," Olive said. "But I would. In a heartbeat." She sat on the coffee table facing Brynn. "Talk."

"How do you know I've got anything to talk about?"

"A mom knows."

This was . . . mostly true. Her moms loved and adored her; they'd never made any secret of that. They'd had her back whenever she'd needed them, with the exception of the times that she'd managed to keep her need a secret. Such as in her younger years when she'd been mercilessly bullied for having two moms . . .

She loved them madly, but it was a lot of pressure to be their only child, especially given how long and hard they'd fought for the right to have a baby at all. Sometimes she could admit to herself it was hard to live up to their expectations. And she often didn't. She tended to skate through life—she knew this. But if she didn't dig too deep into anything, if she kept her life surface only, it was safe there. Her house of cards couldn't fall down.

Cat jumped onto her lap, and Brynn gave her a long look. "You going to play nice?"

Cat gave her a gentle headbutt to the belly, and then tried to put her face in Brynn's soup. The bowl amplified the raspy, old-lady purr so that it sounded like a misfiring engine.

"Welcome home," Olive said dryly, scooping up Catherine before she got any soup, gently depositing her onto the floor. "Now, let's hear it. Not that we're not thrilled to see you, but what's going on? You've brought a pretty big duffel bag for a weekend visit. Thought Long Beach was working out for you? You were substitute teaching and living with Aaron—"

"Ashton," Brynn corrected, and managed a casual shrug while ignoring the tightness in her chest, the tightness that had been there the whole drive. The whole past week. *Months.* She was really hoping it was a warning sign of an upcoming zombie apocalypse and not a panic attack. When she'd been young, she'd had them a lot. Like every day at summer camp over the course of the nine years she'd gone, something else she'd managed to keep from her moms. The attacks were infrequent now, but at the thought of the conversation she was going to have to have, she could feel one building. She'd rather face zombies than worry them. They'd been through enough in their lives. "Just thought I'd come home for a bit," she finally said.

"You know we love having you." Raina put her hand over Olive's when her wife opened her mouth again. "But we also know that you're a fierce protector of those you love. You'd keel over before worrying us. Something's wrong." She softened her voice. "Did . . . something happen?"

Brynn started shoveling in the soup, even though she hated vegan chickpea noodle soup. "Mmm. Yum."

Olive hadn't taken her eyes off Brynn. "It was Adam, wasn't it? Somehow this is all connected to that asshole."

Brynn pushed her glasses farther up her nose. "Ashton."

"Whatever. And you only push your glasses up like that when you're upset."

"Olive," Raina said softly. "Back up, give her a little breathing space." She turned to Brynn. "Honey, you need to exhale."

This was true. She was holding her breath. She let it out and gasped in some air. "I'm fine."

"No, you're not." Raina sounded and looked deeply worried. "You're breathing too heavily and your pulse is racing."

Right, because she was in the throes of a good old-fashioned panic attack, her first since last month when she'd realized she'd lost her great-grandma's necklace, the one Olive had told her to take the utmost care of as it wasn't just of sentimental value, but also worth a small fortune. But that wasn't the only thing causing this attack. It'd been the unrelenting suspicion that Ashton had taken the necklace.

He'd sworn he hadn't, and had been so hurt and devastated at the accusation that Brynn had started to doubt herself. Maybe she had really lost it. Now she tried to suck in some more air and failed. "It's just allergies. I'm fine."

"See? She says she's fine," Olive said.

"I *am*," Brynn said, rubbing her chest and the impending freight train in it. "Totally fine."

Olive slowly shook her head. "You're right, Raina. She's not okay. She's not working and her promise ring is no longer on her finger, which means that after their eight months together, Alan was a huge ass-plant and she's moving back in."

"*Ashton*," Brynn whispered.

"None of those things came out of her mouth," Raina said, sounding distressed.

"They would, if she'd talk."

Raina frowned. "She's clutching her chest and looking like she's going to hyperventilate. Honey, are you in pain?"

If by pain she meant the feeling that her ribs were being cracked open by a sledge hammer, then yeah. She was in pain.

Raina crouched in front of her. "On a pain scale of one to ten, where are you at?"

Fifteen sounded about right.

Raina whirled to Olive. "Oh my God, I think she's having a heart attack!"

"No, I'm not." Brynn pulled off her glasses and dropped her face into her hands. "But everything else is all true. The not working thing. The coming home to stay for a bit thing. The leaving the asshole boyfriend thing."

"I'm going to kill Ashton," Olive murmured.

Brynn managed a mirthless laugh at her mom finally getting his name right.

"Oh, honey," Raina whispered. "I'm so sorry."

"The school I was working at closed its doors. And the Ashton thing, it's for the best." An understatement . . . Brynn shook her head. "But I'm okay. Really. I'm just"—*bonkers*. Completely unhinged. Homeless—"A-okay."

"She's whiter than you," Raina told Olive. "And clammy, but also chilled."

"I see it. Sweetheart, breathe," Olive said calmly to Brynn. To Raina, she said, "Call 911."

"No!" Brynn said. Or tried to. But of course now she really *was* hyperventilating.

Raina was on the phone with 911. "Hi, yes, my daughter's having a heart attack."

"I'm not!" Brynn wheezed, as little black dots danced behind her eyelids.

Olive held both of Brynn's hands. "Breathe," she said again. "Breathe with me."

She was trying. But she couldn't seem to draw air into her lungs, which was now intensifying the sharp throbbing in her chest. Ripping her hands from Olive's, she pressed them against her rib cage, trying to ease the pain.

"Oh my goddess," Raina whispered helplessly, and ran to the door. "What's keeping EMS?"

A few minutes later, two uniforms stood over Brynn, now on a gurney, putting an oxygen mask over her face. She no longer had her glasses on and couldn't see past her own nose.

"Honey," Raina yelled, as Brynn was stuffed into the back of an ambulance. "We're going to be right behind you, okay? I've got your glasses."

Brynn held out her hand, but couldn't reach them.

"Just relax," one of the paramedics said. "Your only job here is to keep breathing."

"I'm fine!" Brynn tried to yell through the mask.

But no one was listening. So she gave up and stared up at the interior roof of the rig that was a blur and did the only thing she could. She breathed.

Forty-five minutes later at the hospital, a doctor and nurse were standing at her cot.

"Looks like it was a panic attack," the doctor said.

Brynn sighed. "That's what I tried to tell everyone."

"We had to be sure. Your moms were adamant you were having a heart attack."

This was true. They'd been unbudgeable. Brynn had finally made them go to the waiting room because they'd been driving the hospital staff nuts. She sighed. "It doesn't matter. They needed an excuse to cry because I'm home and they missed me."

"It'd have been a lot cheaper to just say that to you," the doctor said.

"Yeah." Like the entire five grand of her insurance deductible cheaper . . .

Half an hour later, she was cleared from her little cubicle in the ER. Her moms had been told the good news and were still in the waiting room while she changed back into her clothes. Winding her way down the white hallways toward the waiting room, she stopped in front of a vending machine, catching sight of her reflection in the glass.

She was clutching the bag the nurse had provided for her to stow her personal belongings. Everything was pretty blurry, but even she could see that she was indeed very pale, and her light-brown eyes seemed huge in her face. Embarrassment and humiliation did that to a person.

A freaking panic attack . . . *Gah.* She now needed a chocolate bar more than she needed her next breath, and considering she'd almost died from lack of oxygen due to panic, that was saying something.

A tall, leanly muscled guy stood in front of the machine, hands on either side of it as he gave the thing a hard shake.

A candy bar shook loose and he caught it, shoving it into one of his cargo pants pockets.

Pockets that looked already quite full.

She couldn't see well enough to know which kind of candy bar he got, but it didn't matter, because she liked *all* the candy bars in all the land. "Hey," she said. "Save some for the paying customers."

He turned to face her, his brown, wavy hair falling into his eyes, and . . . something made her fumble around in her plastic bag for her glasses. Self-preservation, maybe, because her instincts were screaming. Clearly not a common occurrence for her, or she wouldn't always be able to detonate her life so thoroughly. When she got her glasses on, the world came into focus again and she breathed a short-lived sigh of relief.

Short-lived because though she hadn't seen Eli Thomas since they were both fifteen, she did indeed know him.

"I did put money into the machine." His expression was tight, as if he was highly stressed. And given where they were, in the hallway to the waiting room for both the ER and surgery, he in all likelihood *was* highly stressed. "Lots of money, in fact—" Stopping, he cocked his head, recognition crossing his face. His eyes softened and he smiled, flashing white teeth and a dimple in his left cheek. "Hey." His voice was different now. Lower, quiet, like the one you used with people you knew. It was also filled with emotion. "It's been a while."

True story. It *had* been a while. But not long enough. And in the bad-news department, the dimple and smile were still attractive and charismatic as hell, but the good news was that she'd learned how to shut off her heart. She gave him a vague smile, implying she didn't remember him. He hadn't chased her after their kiss, and yeah, it was a zillion years ago, but hey, a girl had pride.

He arched a brow.

Ignoring this, because they *so* weren't going there, she gestured that he should stand back because it was her turn at the vending machine. She pulled a wrinkled dollar from her pocket and tried to shove it into the slot, extremely aware of the weight of his stare. He wanted her to recognize him. She was still going with *no thank you.*

The machine spit her dollar back at her.

"You have to straighten it out first," Eli said.

Grinding her teeth, she slapped the dollar against her thigh and ironed it flat with her hand before once again attempting to thread it into the machine.

And . . . once again, the machine immediately refused it.

Seriously, was it a Monday? Was the universe out to get her? *What?*

Eli gestured to her dollar bill. "Can I . . . ?"

When she nodded, he took it and calmly fed it into the machine.

And, of course, it was accepted.

Eli started to say something, but she held up a finger to stop him, then punched in the corresponding letter and number for the candy bar she wanted.

Nothing happened.

Oh, for God's sake— Gripping the machine the same way Eli had, she shook it.

Nothing.

So she kicked it.

Her audience of one smirked. "Missy Judgerson goes to the dark side."

Brynn shocked herself by laughing. It was her first laugh in . . . well, she couldn't remember. Life hadn't exactly been a pocket full of pilfered goodies lately.

"Here." Her *pretend* stranger pulled two fistfuls of goods from his pockets. "You look far more desperate than me. Take your pick."

She took a candy bar. And then on second thought snatched a bag of gummy bears as well.

He gave her a look.

"Hey, I'm a pint low, okay?" She stretched out her arm, revealing the Band-Aid in the crook of her elbow where they'd taken blood.

His smile faded. "You okay?"

Physically, yes. Mentally, the vote was still out. She tore into the candy bar. "I will be."

His eyes were still the most unusual shade of gray, which should have meant they were cold, but they weren't. They were actually very warm, and curious. And maybe she'd feel warm and curious about him too, if she hadn't made a fool of herself with him by sporting a big, fat crush that clearly had not been returned. Add to that, he'd fooled her into thinking they were friends when they'd been nothing of the kind because he'd been part of a group with Kinsey Davis—Brynn's arch nemesis.

Yes, apparently she *could* hold a grudge for years. Maybe it'd stuck with her because she'd written about the two of them often enough in her long-ago camp journal. They'd all had to write in one every night. She actually still had hers, shoved somewhere deep in her duffel bag. She used it as a reminder of the her she used to be, Past Brynn, who'd been too gullible, too loyal, too forgiving . . . She'd practically been a golden retriever.

But she'd learned. She was tougher now. Present Brynn was a German shepherd.

Eli's phone pinged. He grabbed for it, stared at the screen, and looked stricken. "Gotta go." He took the extra few seconds to empty his pockets, shoving his entire loot into Brynn's arms. "In case you need another fix."

And then he was gone, leaving her torn between the humiliating memories of the past and the hope that whomever he was here for would be okay. She started with the pilfered gummy bears. The sugar began to work its way through her system, giving her the courage she needed to go out and face her moms with the truth.

That, once again, she'd failed at life and let down the people she loved.

 CHAPTER 2

K insey hated hospitals with the passion of a thousand suns. No, make that ten thousand suns. Yet here she sat in a hospital bed, wearing a washed-so-many-times-it-was-practically-sheer hospital gown.

Damn, some days life sucked more than others. She'd received the call late last night. There was a kidney, and she needed to be at the hospital by five A.M.

She'd gotten here at four thirty, because she was a lot of things, most of them not especially complimentary, but she was never late.

Especially for her own kidney transplant.

It was now late afternoon, and she was tired of cooling her jets, tired of hearing "the doctor will be here shortly to fill you in" but getting no further explanation.

If there was one thing she knew from years and years of waiting on a kidney, with a whole bunch of false starts and even more false hopes, it was that if it didn't happen when she was told it would, it wasn't going to happen at all.

But since that was a far too depressing thought to contemplate, she focused on things she *could* control. She was so hungry that it felt as if her organs were starting to eat each other. Hopefully not her one working—barely—kidney, though. She'd received it fourteen years ago at age fifteen, and her body had decided it wasn't a good fit and was slowly but surely rejecting it.

A nurse entered the room and smiled as she began to check Kinsey's vitals. "How are you feeling?"

"Oh, just peachy—" She broke off as the only person she trusted more than herself rushed back into her room.

"Where were you?" she asked.

"Moving the car," Eli said.

He'd been doing this every hour or so all day long and it was driving her nuts. To be honest, life was driving her nuts. "I told you not to park in the drop-off area or you'd get a ticket. Did you get a ticket?"

He smiled. "Nope."

She narrowed her eyes. "Why do I feel like you're lying?"

"I'm not. I got there just in time."

"Let me guess," Kinsey said. "A female cop was about to write you up and you flashed that annoyingly charming smile and got out of it, even though I've never once managed to talk anyone out of giving me a ticket."

"Because you don't even try to use charm. Ever."

This was true. "It's false advertising."

He smiled. "Not in my case."

Also true.

"And I'd park in the visitors lot if there were any open spots, but there aren't."

The nurse looked up from the chart to eye Kinsey. "Your husband reminded me that you haven't eaten anything today. Is that correct?"

"Yes, during the preop, I was asked not to eat twelve hours before surgery. And Eli's not my husband. He's my . . ." She hesitated, because it was hard to describe the person you loved like a best friend, but also often wanted to smother with a pillow in his sleep.

Eli raised a brow.

She rolled her eyes. "Annoying-as-crap life mate."

He'd been her best friend since third grade, from the day Kinsey had pushed bitchy Donna Morgan into the mud for saying that Kinsey was trailer trash. Eli had taken the blame so she wouldn't get in trouble, and they'd been BFFs ever since. Actually, more like brother and sister, because it truly was a sibling-like relationship, right down to bickering being their favorite pastime. Together, they'd been through thick and thin, and there'd been a helluva lot of thin. Her health issues. His family issues. Her utter failure to let people into her life. His inability to trust people to love him. And so on.

Though they were both pretty messed up, they'd become a family of sorts, and she knew no one had her back like he did. Just as she also knew she'd do anything to protect him.

Still, he managed to drive her insane on a daily basis. Like right now. "Why do you smell like chocolate?"

"Because I made a pit stop at the vending machine."

She sniffed him like a police dog on the scent of drugs, and her stomach growled. She might've growled too. "Oh my God, you had a Snickers," she accused.

"Yep."

She wanted to kill him on sight, and was glad to see the nurse step out of the cubicle so there wouldn't be any witnesses. "Are you kidding me?"

He didn't even have the good grace to look guilty as he came to the side of her bed and took her hand. His eyes were guarded. Worried. "What did the doctor say?"

"Haven't seen him yet."

Eli let out a breath. "Your text scared me. I rushed back."

"Sorry. I didn't mean to scare you." She paused. "Were you really just moving the car and getting a snack?"

"What else would I be doing?"

"Calling Deck."

There was a beat of disbelief, during which Eli apparently absorbed the fact that she *hadn't* called Deck.

Deck, short for Deckard Scott, was the guy Kinsey let into her bed on the nights they were both free. He was big and built, tough as nails, sexy as hell, and best of all, didn't have any need to fill a silence with words. She could love him for that alone— if she was free to love anyone.

She wasn't.

She'd grown up with chronic renal failure, and after her first transplant at age fifteen, her body had switched things up for shits and giggles to a new problem—transplant rejection. This meant she was literally a walking, talking expiration date. She didn't know when, but she knew it *would* happen. Eventually she'd run out of luck and her kidney would give out. So falling in love and letting someone fall for her in return was selfish. And she might be a whole bunch of things she wished she wasn't, but selfish wasn't going to be one of them.

"You should've called him," Eli said finally, clearly trying to keep his tone even, but also just as clearly thinking she was an idiot. "He'd want to be here."

Yeah, but . . . Deck was supposed to be just her fun-time guy. A year ago, he'd agreed on that term with a rough laugh and a dirty gleam in his eye.

She loved when he had dirty thoughts. It always worked to her benefit. But she'd never imagined him sticking around for a whole year with no sign of wanting to kick her to the curb. Which meant *she'd* have to be the one to kick *him* to the curb. "Don't start."

Eli shook his head, but after all these years, he knew how to pick his battles. "Fine. So what's the news?"

"The nurse said the doctor will be in anytime."

"They've been saying that for eight hours."

"Oh, I'm sorry," she said, as her stomach growled again. "Has it been hard on you eating your favorite food group all day while I sit here in a stupid hospital gown with nothing to eat but ice chips?"

He scooted his chair closer and took her hand, and she had no idea how the hell he did it, but he eased her blood pressure with every single economic movement he made.

"You're going to get through this," he said, his voice quiet steel. Everything about him was quiet steel. If Deck was a bull, Eli was a cat. A feral mountain lion, deceptively playful, strong inside and out, intelligent and capable of getting shit done with quiet and deadly finesse. Sometimes she thought maybe he'd kept her alive with nothing more than the sheer force of his personality.

But she'd leaned on him enough. His face was drawn. His hair was even more wild than usual around his face, framing those stormy gray eyes that could be cold as slate when he was pissed, or warm as a summer storm. "Go home," she said softly. "I'll call you when I know what's up."

"I'm not leaving you," he said.

"Eli—"

"You going to call Deck? Cuz unless you do—and you know you damn well should—I'm not leaving."

"Okay, then, how about a favor?"

"Anything," he said, so easily she knew it was true. He'd proven it over and over again. But . . . she needed him gone to ask the doctor the kind of questions she wanted to ask. "Go home and get me my favorite comfy wrap, the soft black one? And a couple magazines to read?"

His eyes narrowed. "You're trying to get rid of me."

"No, I'm cold and tired of my ass hanging out."

He sighed and nodded. Bending over her, he brushed a kiss to her forehead and vanished.

Not five minutes later, her doctor finally strode into her room, his expression inscrutable. But in that moment, Kinsey knew the answers to all her questions and she closed her eyes.

"I'm sorry," he said quietly.

"It wasn't viable."

This was what, the fourth time? The fifth time? God, she was tired of this. So tired . . .

Her doctor was still talking, giving her the usual spiel, not to give up, *blah blah blah* . . . when Eli walked back in.

He had his head down, reading a *Cosmo* magazine. "Hey, did you know there's a hundred and one ways to jack a guy off?"

At the awkward silence, he lifted his head and shut the magazine when he saw the doc.

"Interesting," the doctor said with a small smile. "The benefits of staying well read, I suppose."

"Thought you were going home to get my stuff," Kinsey said tightly.

"Saw the nurse on my way out, she said your doctor was heading in, so I came back." He studied Kinsey's expression and then the doctor's, as always sharply intuitive. "Someone needs to tell me right now that today wasn't another false alarm."

Kinsey looked into his eyes, and even though she knew that *she* was losing hope, he never had. But he had to eventually realize the thing she was slowly coming to terms with—that she wasn't going to get a kidney in time.

 CHAPTER 3

From nine-year-old Brynn's summer camp journal:

Dear Moms,

I'm supposed to be writing in this journal for my-self, but that seems dumb, so I'm writing to you. I miss you.

Wish you could come get me.

It's very dark here. Everyone goes for a long walk before bed, but I had to stay because I can't see good at night. Which I get is hereditary, but it's annoying. Why couldn't I get something good passed down, like pretty hair?

Also, they make us eat our veggies. Peas, gag. I al-most threw up on the mean girl sitting next to me. She yelled at me. She's also in my cabin. She didn't feel good and had to stay in from the hike too. She told everyone that I lied about having two moms.

I don't like her.
COME GET ME!!!!!!!!!!!!!

                     Love,
                     Brynn

ELI FOUND HIMSELF in the waiting room, his gut in knots, while Kinsey dressed and was discharged to go home. Realizing he was still holding the stupid magazine, he tossed it down onto a pile of others on a side table. In what world did people think a magazine could offer hope to anyone in this place? Hope was elusive, and a total bitch.

His phone buzzed with an incoming text from work, asking if he was going to make it in today. He was a marine scientist for a nonprofit out of Morro Bay, and on most days it was the best job in the world. He got paid to study and report on sea life, which involved a lot of boating, scuba diving, endless studies, and meetings. But today his job was the last thing on his mind. He returned the text, saying he'd be in as soon as he could. His stomach growled loud enough to rival Kinsey's, making him regret handing over everything he'd had in his pockets to a woman who hadn't even remembered him.

But damn. He'd seen her standing there and his heart had actually lightened in his chest. Fate, he thought. It *had* to be fate that Brynn Turner had shown up now, today of all days, and for a minute he'd felt such relief he'd nearly hugged her.

But she hadn't remembered him.

The story of his life.

Shaking his head at himself, he pulled out his phone and

googled black market kidneys for what had to be the millionth time in the past decade. There was actually a horrifying array of opportunities to buy an illegal kidney. Yeah, he'd have to mortgage himself to his eyeballs, not to mention break the law, but he'd do it in a heartbeat.

Except that Kinsey flat out refused to let him—or *anyone*— buy her a kidney. No one was allowed to get tested for a match either. And he got it, she'd already taken a kidney from someone, and to say that hadn't gone well was the understatement of the year.

So he kept googling.

The last false alarm had been eighteen months ago, and it had nearly broken her. This time, she'd seemed . . . resigned.

That scared the shit out of him. He didn't have many fears. Growing up the way he had, he'd conquered just about everything bad that could happen to a person and was still alive. As a result, he had only a precious few people in his life who mattered to him, and Kinsey was one of them.

He refused to lose her.

Slowly, he became aware of sounds outside his own thoughts. A quiet murmur, and someone crying nearby. He lifted his head. There were two women, mid-fifties, one dressed as if she were about to attend a board meeting, the other looking like the original flower-power girl. She was sobbing into the other's arms.

"Raina, honey, this isn't helping."

"Our baby could've had a heart attack, Olive!"

"But she didn't. You heard the doctor. He said it was a panic attack, that she'd be out shortly and we can take her home."

Raina let out a long, purposeful breath, bracelets jingling as she straightened. "Clearly something terrible happened to her in Long Beach," she said tearfully. "If he hurt her—"

"Then we'll kill him together."

Raina sat back in her own chair. "I'm sorry. I just had to let that all out. I can't hold it inside or it eats me up."

"I know."

"You should let it out too."

"I have," Olive said.

"No, you haven't. You're sucking it all in and holding on to it, and next time it could be you in there."

Olive shook her head. "I'm too stubborn."

This got her a snort from Raina, who wiped her eyes and looked around, her gaze landing on Eli.

"Raina," Olive said softly. "Stop staring at him."

"I can't," Raina whispered. "I can feel his sad energy."

"I can hear, you know," Eli said. And what the hell? He didn't have a damn "sad energy," but Raina was already scooting over several chairs until she was only two away from Eli.

"Hi," she said.

Terrific. "Hi."

She gave him a small smile. "Do you want to talk about it?"

He didn't answer, although his stomach grumbled again, speaking for him. The woman nodded, like this made perfect sense to her. "I always need to eat before I talk about things too. I'm an emotional eater." She pulled something from a purse that was the size of the state of California. "You're not allergic to walnuts, are you?"

He was about to back away from the crazy lady, but then the scent of something delicious teased him.

"Carrot cake muffins," she said.

He'd have preferred brownies, but he folded like a cheap suitcase and took one.

In each hand.

"They're gluten-, dairy-, and sugar-free."

And . . . he froze. *Well, shit.*

With a smile, Raina brought one of his hands up to his mouth, and he forced himself to take a bite. But then, suddenly, he had his mouth full of the most amazing carrot cake muffin he'd ever eaten, and was in fact fighting back a moan when she pulled something else from her bag.

"Dab this at the pulse points on your wrists and rub it in," she said. "It's a mix of essential oils meant for calming. Bergamot, ylang ylang, lemon, and a few others." And because he hadn't moved, she leaned in and did it for him.

"Oh, for God's sake," Olive muttered, and came close as well. "Feel free to ignore her. I find a good shot of something in the Jim Beam family usually works just as well as the oils." She pulled a small flask from her bag.

Eli felt like he'd walked onto a *Mary-Poppins*-meets-*Twilight-Zone* set.

Raina smiled. "My wife doesn't like to admit it, thinks it makes her a softie, but she's a worrier too. It's why we're a good fit." She held out the flask.

He was just about to give in and take a quick swig when the double doors opened. He stood, thinking it would be Kinsey.

It wasn't.

Brynn came out, looking wan and tired, and he realized she was the one these two women had been waiting for. She'd had the panic attack, the one that had presented like a heart attack.

Raina and Olive were also on their feet, moving toward her, engulfing her in hugs and kisses, along with relieved laughter and tears.

Brynn wasn't laughing or crying. Her eyes were closed and she was hugging her moms back tightly, but Eli couldn't get a bead on her emotions. It was fascinating, actually. Her quietness. The people in his life—his brother, Max, friends, even Kinsey, all of them, himself included—were not quiet. Not even close. They had sarcasm and bickering down to a fine art, much like a real family. Or so he assumed.

His phone buzzed in his pocket, and he pulled it out.

"What's the update?" his brother asked in lieu of a greeting.

"Kidney arrived unviable."

Max let out an audible breath. "Shit. Goddamn. Fuck."

"Yeah." In the background, Eli could hear excited barking. Max had probably just come in from surfing. He was probably standing in the kitchen dripping water all over the floor along with their rescue dog, Mini.

"She all right?" Max asked.

"What do you think?"

"That she's devastated."

"While pretending not to be," Eli agreed.

"Need me?"

"I'm okay." He and Max shared a dad, who'd dumped Eli's mom to have a baby with the eighteen-year-old babysitter—Max's mom.

Eli's mom, a British college professor who'd never really enjoyed children, including her own, had taken the opportunity to leave her cheating husband and ten-year-old son to go back to England and teach there. And with his dad far more interested in his new trophy wife and baby, Eli had been out in left field.

But in spite of the ten-year age difference, he and Max had forged a relationship that remained strong to this day. "There's something else," he said, eyes on the three women hugging in front of him. "Brynn's here. At the hospital."

"Brynn," Max repeated, sounding confused. "You don't mean—"

"Yeah."

"Holy shit. Did Kinsey see her? Did they talk? Maybe—"

"No, Kinsey didn't see her."

"Did you tell her how hard you crushed on her all those years ago?"

Eli scrubbed a hand down his face. "I should never have told you that story. And how do you even remember it anyway? That was forever ago."

"You'd lost a dare and had to admit your most idiotic crush, which fascinated me because you don't tend to do idiotic. Plus, I never forget anything. Did you talk to her?"

"Not really."

"Why not?"

Hell. "She didn't recognize me."

There was a stunned silence from Max, then a very amused laugh. "Sorry, but shit, that's funny."

"Is it though?"

"Oh, yeah." Max had just turned twenty-one. He was a beach bum and surfer at heart. He worked two part-time jobs: as an assistant to Eli at the marine life nonprofit, and also cooking at the local bar and grill. He cooked better than he surfed, which was saying something. And he very much enjoyed lording stuff over Eli whenever possible.

"Bring our girl home," Max said. "I'll have food waiting for you guys." Then, still laughing, his brother hung up.

Shoving away his phone, Eli went back to watching Brynn. Wondering how to get this to play out the way it needed to. He had a couple of choices. One, keep his mouth shut, and in doing so, let go of a connection that Kinsey desperately needed.

Or two, bring them together.

Or back together . . .

None of them had known during all those years they'd spent together at summer camp that Kinsey and Brynn were related. That hadn't come to light until Kinsey had taken one of those ancestry tests to try to find a blood relative other than her mother and good-for-very-little con artist of a father. She'd actually gotten lucky. At some point in the past, Brynn had apparently gone looking for relatives as well. She'd uploaded her DNA and a picture. So when Kinsey had come along several years later, she'd been able to follow the bread crumbs. Once she'd found the shocking connection, she'd given Eli a second surprise—she had no intention of telling Brynn they were half sisters.

Clearly Brynn had never gone back to her own relative hunt, or she'd have found Kinsey. And by then, Kinsey was too sick to go back to camp anyway, so they'd not seen Brynn again.

Until now, when Brynn was currently being smothered by her moms. She pushed her glasses up farther on her nose as she rolled her eyes, but she wasn't trying to get away. She was comfortable with the easy affection and the way they were holding on to her like she was the very best part of their entire world. Eli tried to remember his parents holding him like that, but couldn't. He had no idea what it must be like, but thought it was sweet.

Brynn had been a tiny thing, undersized like him. She hadn't had asthma like he'd had, but she'd stuck to herself, especially whenever there'd been sports involved. She didn't have a single athletic bone in her body. That, combined with her quirkiness, had made her different.

Eli liked different, always had, but the other kids hadn't, and he knew camp had been a lonely place for her.

Raina was sniffing at Brynn. "Baby, why do you smell like chocolate and trans fats and sugar?"

"You don't want to know."

"I do."

"I had a candy bar."

Raina gasped, horrified, and clapped a hand to her heart, bracelets jingling. "From that death distributor in the hallway?"

Brynn looked amused. "You mean the vending machine?"

"Oh my God. Have I taught you nothing?"

"It fell right into my mouth."

"That stuff will kill you!"

"Raina, not now," Olive murmured. "Remember? Pick your battles."

"You're right." Raina cupped Brynn's face lovingly and then kissed each cheek. "You're really okay?"

"Yes."

"I'm pretty sure you're fibbing, but you *will* be okay. How can you not be? You've got us."

Brynn gave a soft snort and hugged them again, her expression clear now: half-amused and half-annoyed affection. There was an energy about her. Part Raina, with the warm and quirky spirit, and part Olive, with the cool, dry wit. But what Eli liked most was that it was clear she genuinely loved her moms, and they loved her back.

That's when he realized Brynn was looking at him. Noticing him as a man, while still not recognizing him.

But he called bullshit on that. Maybe if they'd never become friends back then. Maybe if he hadn't been the one she'd come to with that long-ago summer deal—she'd wanted her first kiss, the deal being that they never talk about it. Sold. It'd been his first kiss too, although he'd never told her that.

She was *pretending* not to remember him. Annoying, but this wasn't about him. It was about Kinsey, and having her run into Brynn could be the very best thing to ever happen to her.

Brynn pulled free of her moms, her gaze still on him. "So, um . . . this is Eli, the very kind stranger who gave me the candy bar."

Ha. *Gotcha.* "Not a stranger," he said.

She actually stood there and tried to sell him on pretending to not understand. "Excuse me?" she asked.

Oh, she was good. But he was better. And there was no way in hell he was going to make this easy on her. "You introduced me by name."

"No, I didn't."

"Actually, honey, you did," Raina said helpfully.

Brynn froze for a beat. Then winced before smoothing out her expression from *oh, shit* to *dammit.* "You told me what it was at the vending machine," she said.

"No, I didn't."

"Fine. So I knew who you were." She looked at her moms. "He's from summer camp."

"Oh, so he's *that* Eli," Olive said.

"Mom."

That Eli. What did that mean, he wondered.

"It's been a long time," Brynn told him.

It had been. Fourteen years, in fact. He wasn't big on coincidences, but if he had been, this one was too big to ignore. After all these years, to see her again, today of all days. It was surely a sign meant for Kinsey. Although he had zero idea how to get Kinsey that sign, except to stall. How long could it take her to get discharged and dressed? A long time, he knew. "So . . . what are you up to these days?" he asked, doing his part.

"Oh." She shrugged. "A little of this and that. I just got back into town."

"To stay?"

"I'm hoping." She eyed her two moms, both of whom looked elated at this news. "I'll need a teaching job and a place to live, but if that all pans out, then, yeah. To stay."

"Honey, you don't need a place to live," Raina said. "We've still got your room."

"What you've got is a shrine to a girl who doesn't exist anymore. And I thought you were going to make it into an office slash workout room."

"Well, it's good we didn't," Olive said. "Or your bed would be a yoga mat."

Eli laughed. He thought her family was . . . well, adorable. But Brynn didn't seem amused. Instead, her eyes seemed oddly haunted, and it reached something inside him that he didn't want it to. But it wasn't that that made him speak. It was the fact that, if he couldn't give Kinsey a kidney, he could do this. He could bring the two of them back into each other's orbits, which might just be the thing to spark some life back into Kinsey or, at the very least, serve as a reminder that she wasn't as alone as she thought. "I've got a room for rent," he said.

Everyone stared at him. Raina, looking like she was sorry she'd been so nice. Olive, appraising him with cool eyes.

And Brynn . . . she bit her lower lip. "Here in Wildstone?"

Clearly he wasn't getting enough oxygen to his brain, because manipulating Kinsey into this situation meant certain death. But that didn't stop him. "Just outside of town, actually. Right off Beach Drive."

"You live on the beach?" she asked.

"Across the street."

"What do you mean exactly, a room for rent?" Olive wanted to know. "Are you looking for a roommate . . . with benefits?"

"*Mom,*" Brynn said, but then turned back to Eli. "Okay, yeah. What's the catch?"

"No catch," he said. "I've got a big, old house that costs a fortune to keep up." It was the usual spiel when someone wanted to know something personal and he didn't want to give it. Because the personal was . . . a little too personal. "So I have roommates."

Brynn's eyes held his, like she was searching for the real reason he'd offer such a thing.

"Honey." Raina shook her head. "You need to be home, with us. You need some TLC, some good food, and rest."

"Mom," Brynn said softly, taking Raina's hand and putting it to her own chest. "I love you. I love you both to the moon and back, but what I really need right now is to stand on my own two feet." She looked at Eli. "But it's also something I need to figure out how to do on my own. Thanks, though."

"Just think about it," he said.

She held his gaze for a long beat and then nodded.

He gave her his contact info, and, having no idea if he'd done the right thing or if he'd just made everything worse, he watched her walk out with her moms. He wanted this more than he should, but if he knew one thing about life, it was that what he wanted rarely mattered.

 CHAPTER 4

From nine-year-old Kinsey's summer camp journal:

Dear Journal,

> *I was told today that I need to write home at least once this week, but I hate home more than I hate you. My mom's dumb. My mom's boyfriend is dumb.*
> *I wish a journal could drive so you could come get me.*
> *I wish you were a real person.*
> *Tonight we were given some writing time. I told the counselor I don't see good at night, which my mom says is a genetic thing, but no one cares. Writing in a journal is dumb. So is the girl who sleeps next to me. She can't see at night either, and pretends she has two moms. Who'd want two? Anyway, they send her presents, like food! It's all dumb. Eli thinks I should stop saying everything's dumb. He's my best friend, but he's*

*also a boy, so he's dumb too. Except he's nice to me
because his family is even awfuler than mine.*

Kinsey

BRYNN SPENT THE next day attempting to get her life together. This involved applying for jobs—a good decision—and reliving all her recent mistakes—a bad decision. She held a brief pity party for one at McDonald's, involving a Big Mac, large fries, and an M&Ms McFlurry. But then she forced herself to get on with it.

Except it turned out that rent in Wildstone was high and jobs were scarce. The only good thing was that the biggest employer in the county happened to be the school district. There were no openings at the moment, so she'd applied to be a substitute teacher. There were only four schools in the district: a high school, a middle school, and two elementary schools. She wanted high school. She'd suffer middle school if she had to, but in her mind, elementary school was out.

So, of course, that's who called her, offering a position as a long-term kindergarten sub for a teacher going on maternity leave.

Pros: a paycheck.

Cons: good God . . . kindergarteners.

The paycheck won. For one thing, Brynn had fewer than zero pennies to her name, because along with losing all her self-esteem and self-trust, she'd also let Ashton rob her blind.

So . . . she was going to make a deal with herself. No rash decisions. Actually, no decisions on the fly at all. She knew some might call this deal something else. Say, avoidance. But she'd thought it through carefully, and it was definitely the best way to avoid future mistakes and screwups. She didn't need any more of those in her life.

Even better, it would protect the people she cared about. Like her moms. No one's life would be disturbed by any bad decisions or choices she made. No one's emotions would be at risk. The deal allowed everyone, including herself, to continue walking down their chosen path, without interference or distraction.

Theoretically, following this plan would be easy. After all, the basis of it was a *lack* of action. There was nothing difficult in taking no action, in not involving her heartstrings or tugging on anyone else's. Sure, sometimes she'd have to walk away when she wanted to step closer. Sometimes she'd have to make a lighthearted remark when she wanted to reveal her soul. But all she had to do was hold her heart captive instead of letting it lead her on wild goose chases. No more freeing it into someone else's hands.

It was the right thing to do, for all involved.

Having committed to this deal, having convinced herself this was the only way to go, she came home from her pity party, aka carb-loading.

Her moms were waiting. They knew the value of working as a team. They'd spent the day trying to follow along with her everywhere she went, constantly shoving food at her, continuously asking how she was doing with twin worried looks on their faces.

So she'd asked them very nicely to give her a few hours. But those hours were apparently up.

"Please tell us what happened to you in Long Beach," Raina said.

They meant well, and she understood she was their whole life. She also loved them more than anything, but if she didn't find a way to get out of this house, she was going to die here.

Which—not for the first time, or even the hundredth—brought her thoughts back to Eli. To what she knew about him, which admittedly wasn't much. Back then, he'd been funny and easygoing, and not in the least bit shy. Lean to the point of too skinny, as well as asthmatic, he'd still managed to hold his own with the other boys and somehow also seem older than all of them.

In sharp contrast, Brynn had been a quirky, awkward kid, not funny, not easygoing, and terribly shy. She hadn't exactly fit in, and the kids hadn't liked her because of that.

Eli, in spite of being BFFs with the meanest of the mean girls, had been nice to Brynn.

And on one memorable occasion, more than nice—because sometimes a girl needed someone to help her try new things. She'd been fourteen and dying to know what it felt like to kiss a boy. She wanted to make sure she knew what to do when the time came.

So she'd scrounged up enough courage to ask, and Eli had been more than willing to make a summer camp deal with her. A single kiss, no expectations.

She could still remember how nervous she'd been, but Eli

had just stood there quietly against the cabin in the woods, letting her take the lead. She'd gone up on tiptoe to kiss him. His lips had been warm and soft, and he'd tasted like the chocolate chip cookies he'd had for snack that day, and smelled like sunshine and lake and cute boy. He'd closed his eyes, and his eyelashes had been longer than hers. She'd never even noticed that boys had eyelashes before.

It had been the only time she'd ever been happy at summer camp, and when she'd dropped down from her tiptoes and stared at him, he'd grinned.

She'd pulled a typical Brynn Turner and run like the wind.

They'd never spoken of it.

Just as well. He'd been tight with a group headed by Kinsey, the one who'd single-handedly ruined camp for Brynn for a lot of years. In her eyes, his affiliation with Kinsey had put him in the Mean Kids Club. But he was an adult now, and he'd treated her moms with a patient kindness that was hard to fake.

That went a long way with her.

As would having a neutral place to live. Not with a boyfriend, not with her moms.

But on her own for the first time in her life.

Well, relatively on her own anyway. At Eli's, she'd have roommates. But no emotional ties, she reminded herself, and she felt like she needed that. She needed to find herself, needed to learn to trust herself and figure out who the hell she was.

It was a big decision, and she'd just made that deal with herself—no rash decisions. Think about it, he'd suggested. And that was exactly what she planned to do.

On the couch, she patted the cushions for her moms to sit as well, and took a deep breath.

"It's okay," Olive said. "Whatever it is, baby, it's going to be okay."

Raina nodded. The two of them were holding hands, watching Brynn with love and acceptance.

Which was a big part of what made this hard. On the outside, she was relieved to have them on her side, loving and nurturing her whenever she needed it. But on the inside, she still didn't feel like she deserved it.

"And there are no wrong answers here," Raina assured her. "We just want to know what we can do to help. You're holding stuff in, and it's not healthy. Plus, there's no need. There's no judgment here, you know that. Not ever."

That was the thing. She *deserved* judgment on this.

"It's just us here," Olive said. "Tell us what happened, why you're here, and what your plans are, and how we can help."

"Also, we love you," Raina said, giving Olive some side-eye.

Olive gave her a look right back. "That part was implied."

"But sometimes people need the words," Raina said.

Olive sighed. "I love you, Raina. And I love you, Brynn. There. *Now* can we get to what's going on?"

"Okay, okay," Brynn said, wanting to stop them before they could get traction on a fight. "I went to the school district office today and got a substitute teaching job. There's a long-term sub needed at the elementary school for a kindergarten class." She tried not to grimace at the "kindergarten" part. "It's a year-round system, and I'll be working there starting Monday."

Both of her moms smiled in surprise. Raina was a high school English teacher. Olive was a professor at the city college. Teaching ran in their blood.

"That's wonderful," Olive said. "We're so proud of you, but we could've put in a good word for you at the district and smoothed the way."

"Thanks, and I know, but I wanted to do this on my own." Needed to. "Also, there's some not-great news too." She took off her glasses, swiped them on the hem of her shirt, and put them back on. "You already know that Ashton and I broke up. But what you don't know is that the apartment was in his name and he gave notice. Months ago." She left off the part about how he'd not told her he'd done that. He'd emptied their bank account, run up her credit card, and vanished, also skipping out on the last two months of rent that he'd told her he'd paid. When she'd come home from work, she'd found herself locked out. She'd tried to talk to the landlord. He'd told her that Ashton had given three months' advance notice, and then moved out earlier in the day.

While she'd been at work at her substitute teaching job.

The landlord had felt sorry for her, letting her know that there'd been some things Ashton hadn't packed up, stuff that looked like it might all be hers, and he had it locked in the basement. He could get there the next day to let her in.

But Brynn hadn't been able to stomach the thought of staying in town for one more minute, much less another day, so she'd left without her stuff. "And you guys were right, he's an asshole."

"Oh, Brynn," Raina said softly. "We didn't want to be right."

"It's okay. I was too trusting."

"Baby, that's nothing new," Olive said. "You're sweet and kind to everyone."

"You make it sound like I'm perfect," Brynn said.

Olive smiled. "I love you, Brynn, more than life itself, but perfect you are not. When someone finally does push your buttons too hard, you walk away and cut them out of your life."

"That's not true."

"Middle school, CeeCee Stone," Olive went on. "She stole your clothes from your locker in gym class when you were in the shower. She was suspended, and even though she lived right down the street, you never spoke to her again."

Brynn sat up straighter, with a frown. "Does she still live down the street?"

"No, they moved away years ago."

Good. And of course she'd never forgiven her. She'd ended up naked in front of the entire class because CeeCee had wanted to see if she "looked gay like her moms."

Not that she'd ever tell them that part. Ever. They'd never forgive themselves. They'd been through enough.

"And then there was summer camp," Olive said. "You had some problems with a girl there for years."

True. And Kinsey hadn't been like the other bullies she'd come across. Nothing with Kinsey had been personal, which almost made it worse. She'd discounted Brynn without any apparent reason, leaving her out, completely ignoring her, as if she hadn't existed.

For a girl who'd felt invisible for most of her life, it had cut Brynn to the core. "What's the point of this walk down Brynn's Bad History?" she asked. "Are you saying I should make up with Ashton?"

"Absolutely not," Olive said.

"But for people who don't actually cause you real, long-lasting harm, maybe you can find room in your heart to forgive them," Raina suggested softly. "Just a little. Just enough to let go of some of the anger and resentment you carry around."

"I'm not full of anger and resentment," Brynn said in automatic defense.

"Just think about it," Raina said. Then they each kissed her and went into the kitchen to cook dinner.

Find room in your heart to forgive . . .

Okay, Brynn was self-aware enough to know that might actually be a thing she should try. And maybe she'd work on that. But first— She reached for her cellphone, bringing up the contact info Eli had given her at the hospital.

BRYNN: If the room's still available, I'm in.

 CHAPTER 5

From ten-year-old Brynn's summer camp journal:

Dear Moms,

OMG, this camp does like only one veggie a year or something. This year it's canned green beans. I'm going to die and I'm NOT KIDDING. Don't they know they can drive to the grocery store and buy fresh stuff?

Also, my glasses are missing. I think Kinsey hid them, because when I stubbed my toe, she laughed.

She's still mean.

Eli said he'd help me find the glasses, but he's good friends with Kinsey so I don't trust him.

I'm not going to tell you any of this in my real letter to you, you'd be upset for me.

Love you,
Brynn

KINSEY WOKE UP the next morning wrapped around a huge, tattooed, badass body made of pure muscle, sinew, alluring heat, and strength. She lifted her head and found melting dark-chocolate eyes on her, making her breath catch. Funny that such a tough guy had a soft side. Even funnier that *she* was his soft side.

"Deck," she murmured, closing her eyes again. "We talked about this. You can't just break in and climb into my bed. You have to wait to be invited."

He lifted a big hand and pushed her hair back from her eyes. "Am I unwanted?"

She realized he was flat on his back on one side of the bed, and that she'd curled herself up against him, a leg and arm thrown over his body, her head smooshed into the meat of his shoulder. Her body felt sated and boneless, and memories of the things he'd done to her in the middle of the night had her going damp for him again.

He was waiting for an answer, his eyes still warm, a slight smile curving his lips. She shook her head at him. "You know just how *not* unwanted you are. I proved that a time or two last night, I think."

"Four. Four times."

She snorted and pushed him.

He didn't budge. One of the things she loved about him. He was as badass as they came, but he was also laid-back and easy-going. And best of all . . . he didn't fuss over her like everyone else tended to, even though he was a head nurse at the dialysis center. He was pragmatic and never shied from reality. But he was also the best distraction from the hell of her life there ever was. "I've gotta get up," she said. "I've got"—she squinted at the clock—"only thirty minutes to get ready."

"Good thing, then, that you only need twenty." Rolling her flat onto her back, he pressed her into the mattress, holding her there with his deliciously warm body.

"Yes, but that leaves you only ten minutes to do your thing," she managed, already breathless. "And we both know you like to take your time."

"I can make do with ten."

God, his gravelly voice. It never failed to make her forget all her problems. He was the best "friends with benefits minus the friends part" that she'd ever had, and he knew it too. "What if I need more than ten?" she asked.

"You won't."

And then he went on to prove it.

Hours later, she was at her desk at the local school district office playing catch-up. She was a school psychologist for each of the schools in the district. Her job was what they called a three-quarter position, meaning she worked thirty flex hours a week but was allowed to pay in for benefits, like her insurance and a 401(k) plan.

It was a whole lot less generous than it sounded, but the freedom of setting her own hours was vital, since she spent four hours three times a week in dialysis, and a whole lot more hours feeling like she had the flu, when what she really had was transplant rejection.

Today had been a long day. As the district counselor, she

had a lot of ground to cover each week. Today she'd been at the high school dealing with a situation where several teachers had thought a female student was being taken advantage of by some male athletes. After talking to the girl, it'd come out that she wasn't being taken advantage of at all. She'd been running a homework ring for cash. She was doing the homework of ten different athletes and charging them big bucks for it too. Kinsey hated to be the one to squash such entrepreneurial brilliance in one so young; maybe it was the fact that her own job paid like shit, but she felt pride that the girl had figured a way around a cash shortage. If only Kinsey could find such a way, she'd be less stressed.

In any case, the day had been full and long even without the homework scandal. She'd seen her doctor to check on her immunosuppressive therapy, had gone to a district-wide board meeting that had lasted an hour and a half when it could've been a single email, and though she had a stack of files on her desk, all she wanted to do was go home and be alone. When she heard her phone buzzing with an incoming text, she dug it out of her purse.

ELI: How are you?

KINSEY: I feel like my body's "check engine" light's on but I'm still driving it anyway.

ELI: Did you take your meds? Drink water?

KINSEY: Yes, Mom.

ELI: New roommate coming in tonight.

Resisting the urge to *thunk* her head on her desk repeatedly, she shoved her phone back into the bag rather than respond.

A new roommate. Just what she didn't want: another person in her life to look at her like she was broken or needed to be felt sorry for.

When she'd been little, she'd actually dreamed of living alone in a mansion. She'd dreamed of being a billionaire CEO of some really great corporation, wearing fancy designer duds and to-die-for shoes, and driving fast cars. She'd dreamed of being able to travel on a whim, and having wild, fun adventures. She'd dreamed of having tons of good people in her life. She'd dreamed of being beloved.

Instead, she was up to her eyeballs in medical debt, unable to travel to exotic lands because of her weakened immune system, and drove a POS. She did have great shoes because . . . well, a girl needed one vice, didn't she? But she lived in her best friend's house, which was admittedly huge, but not hers, and had . . . sigh . . . *roommates*. She didn't have a ton of people in her life, and she was definitely *not* widely beloved.

And yeah, that last part was her own doing, because she didn't like people all that much, but, hey, she couldn't help it. People sucked.

And now she was going to have to go home and meet a new roommate, which would require smiling and playing nice. Hell, who was she kidding? She didn't play nice. She'd just give the canned greeting Eli had taught her long ago—"Nice to meet you"—and then head to her own room and go to bed.

She loved her room. Loved the whole house, actually. It was big and old, and had lots of character and quirks. It didn't hurt that it was directly across the street from the beach. Eli had bought it as a dump five years ago when he'd gotten hired out of grad school straight into his dream job as a marine biologist. He'd been slowly fixing the place up with help from his brother, Max.

"Slowly" being the key word. Because six months after Eli had signed the deed, his grandma, the woman who'd raised him from the age of ten, had gotten pancreatic cancer. It'd been a brutal five-year fight, and Eli had taken on the bulk of her medical costs. Months after her death, he was still paying them off and would be for a very long time.

So he filled the house with roommates to offset some of the house expenses. Kinsey had been there since the beginning because of her perpetual money problems. Same for Max. Max wasn't sick like Kinsey. He just put surfing above all else, including a decent paying job.

It was a good thing Eli liked to gather the losers he loved ridiculously and keep them close.

There were two additional bedrooms that Eli rented out as well. One was a long-term lease to a guy who worked six months out of the year in Paris, and that's where he was now. The other room was currently open. The last roommate had been Max's lover. Until she'd wanted more and he hadn't. Mostly because Max wasn't capable of loving anything as much as his surfboard.

Kinsey had known it'd be only a matter of time before Eli filled the room. She didn't bother to speculate on who it might be. Whoever it was, they wouldn't last long. Max would seduce them, then eventually piss them off, and onward they'd move.

So really, she had nothing to worry about.

She got home before anyone else and breathed a sigh of relief at the empty driveway. Perfect. She opened the door and immediately heard paws scrabbling on the wood floor, bracing herself as Mini came barreling around the corner.

There was nothing mini about Mini. She was a one-year-old, eighty-five-pound yellow lab puppy. Emphasis on eighty-five pounds and puppy, which meant that even though Kinsey braced to greet her, she still ended up on her ass being loved on by a whole lot of exuberant dog.

"Dammit, woman, control yourself."

But Mini had no self-control at all. She whined excitedly and "woo wooed" while giving a ridiculously adorable grin, beyond thrilled to have one of her humans on the floor with her. She went on like she'd been alone for decades instead of a few hours, her entire hind end wriggling while she licked Kinsey from chin to forehead.

"You're the only one I let do this," she murmured, knowing it was a big, fancy lie. Just last night Deck had taken his tongue on a tour of every inch of her body. "Well, *one* of the only ones I let do this," she corrected.

Managing to get to her feet, she walked through the creaky old beach house, heading up the stairs and down the hallway to her bedroom with Mini shadowing her. Stripping out of her clothes, she let out a sigh because her pants had been cutting into her waist all day.

Side effects of the meds she was on . . . bloating.

Her bra hit the floor next, and she sighed again. *Bliss.*

So was her bath, even if Mini sat there watching with her huge eyes, just waiting for an invite into the tub. "No," Kinsey said firmly.

Mini huffed out a sigh and set her head on the edge of the tub. But Kinsey remained firm, because the last time she'd forgotten to set boundaries, Mini had jumped in with her. It'd taken all the towels in the house to clean up that disaster.

After her bath, she pulled on a soft T-shirt dress and her favorite, way-too-expensive new work sandals, before piling her hair on top of her head and heading down the stairs. She'd say hi to whoever was home, grab food, and vanish. Because that was all she had in her.

She was standing in the kitchen eating leftover Chinese out of the container when she heard the front door open. And then voices.

Eli and a woman. Her first thought was, Good for him, because it'd been a while. Her second thought brought a sigh— it was probably just the new roommate.

"Oh, it's beautiful," the woman said. "Have you lived here long?"

"Bought it about five years ago," Eli answered. "Couldn't resist the location. We're fixing it up slowly as we get the time."

"We?"

"My brother and I. There's one bedroom downstairs—which is rented out to the roommate who's in Paris for four more months—and then four more bedrooms upstairs. Two with their own bath, which are mine and Max's. The other two bed-rooms have a bathroom between them, so you'll have to share. That's why the rent's so cheap."

"You had me at cheap," the woman said, and Kinsey cocked her head.

Wait. Why did that voice sound familiar?

"The woodwork in this house is beautiful. Reminds me of the cabins we used to stay in at summer camp."

Kinsey froze. Oh, *hell* no. No way Eli would do that to her. Except . . . shit, this was *exactly* something he'd do to her, be-cause that's what he did. Interfered in her life, doing whatever he thought best for her. She set the Chinese food down and cau-tiously peered out the kitchen doorway.

Eli was in his usual work uniform of faded jeans and a button-down, his sleeves shoved up to his elbows. The woman with him wore a cute strappy denim sundress that Kinsey could never wear because all the bruising around her biceps from the three days a week of dialysis made other people uncomfortable.

And, yeah, Kinsey knew her.

Dammit.

Pretty ballsy of Eli not to give her a head's up—though, actu-ally, it was undoubtedly the smartest way for him to have gone about this, because she'd have refused. She took one step into the living room and glared at Eli. "Can I talk to you a sec?" Mov-ing back into the kitchen without looking at the new roommate, she then sent daggers at Eli as he entered, thankfully alone.

He looked at her.

She looked at him right back.

He leaned against the counter, casual as you please, and raised a brow.

Fine. She'd go first. "Why the hell is *she* standing in our front room?"

"Take a wild guess."

Because Kinsey had been promising to get in touch with her half sister for years now. She'd also promised to tell said half sister that she *was* a half sister. "How did you even find her?"

"She was in the ER when you were in the OR, but the waiting area is the same for both. We ran into each other at the vending machine."

She crossed her arms, feeling bitter and defensive. "Right."

"It's true," came Brynn's voice from the other room. "And hey, I'm totally okay, thanks for asking! Also, are you? Because I'll need a yes to that question before I go back to not missing you in my life. P.S., you've got very thin walls."

Eli gave Kinsey a long look, like *Say something.*

She'd say something approximately never.

"Fine," Brynn called out from the other room. "I should've known this was too good to be true. Thanks anyway, Eli, and no offense, but you both still suck!"

Then the front door slammed.

Eli looked at Kinsey. "Go get her."

Kinsey blew out a sigh. *"Why?"*

"You've talked about finding her. When I saw her at the hospital, it felt like more than a coincidence. It felt like fate."

Kinsey scoffed through an aching heart, because she only

wished it could be that easy. "You know I don't believe in fate. And even if I did, fate's a bitch."

"Brynn would be the perfect roommate for you," he said quietly.

"Except she hates me."

"Who's fault is that?"

Kinsey looked away. "You can't really believe that my long-lost sister, who doesn't even know she's my sister, is the perfect roommate for me. Did you hit your head on your surfboard again?"

"Hey, that happened one time. And I was fine."

"You gave yourself a concussion."

Eli waited until she turned back to him. "If you don't want her in your life," he said, "just say so."

She closed her eyes, because she couldn't say that. It'd be a lie.

"Just talk to her, Kins. You need to."

He was right, of course. He almost always was. Not that *that* fact made it any easier to take. And she *wanted* to tell Brynn. She did. But it wouldn't be easy. She tended to scare people away, and she'd rather have the possibility of a relationship in front of her than a failure behind her.

Eli's irritated expression suddenly vanished, and he gave her a very small smile.

"What? What do you *possibly* have to be smiling about right now?" she demanded to know.

"You're flushed. You're biting your lower lip, which you do whenever you're feeling hopeful but don't want anyone to know it. I haven't seen you this excited about anything in years."

Damn. She didn't like being so transparent. But maybe deep, deep, deep down she was a little excited. And also very scared. "That's not true," she said. "Max cooked homemade brownies last week. *That* was the most excited I've been in years."

"Kinsey." His voice was quiet. Serious. "Admit it. This feels right."

Dammit. It did. And she *hated* that it did. "I don't know her anymore—it's been years."

"Kids that you get to know when you're young . . . no one will ever know you in that same way," he said. "This relationship with her, good or bad, it's got a built-in history to it that most don't ever get to have. She knows you at a core level."

Yeah, and that was what Kinsey was afraid of. It's not like she'd ever shown Brynn her kind side. Not once. If she was Brynn, she'd hate her, and for good reason. "This is ridiculous. She's already gone."

"Who's fault is that? Maybe she'll come back. If she does, will you admit then that it was meant to be?"

"Sure," Kinsey said, knowing hell would freeze over before Brynn would come back.

The front door opened.

Eli slid a triumphant look at Kinsey.

"Don't get excited," Brynn yelled. "I'm only back because I left my purse in the foyer."

"Brynn," Eli said, eyes on Kinsey. "Wait."

"Are you kidding me? If you two argue this loud, I sure as hell don't want to be living here and hear you have sex that loud."

Kinsey rolled her eyes. "We're not having sex! We're platonic life partners!"

"And bad ones at that," Eli muttered, as the front door slammed once again.

Kinsey pushed her glasses farther up on her nose. She hated wearing her glasses, but she'd run out of contacts.

Eli looked amused.

"What?"

"Your sister does that too. Pushes up her glasses when she's uncertain. I saw her do it at the hospital and also today."

"I'm not uncertain!"

"Go get her," Eli repeated. "You promised me. Don't lose out on having a sister because of your damn pride. Or worse, fear."

She felt her heart squeeze. She knew that for the first ten years of Max's life, Eli had resisted getting attached to his baby brother out of resentment and anger. He'd nearly lost his shot, but he'd turned things around. Now he and Max couldn't be closer. She knew Eli wanted that for her, with Brynn. God, she really hated when he was right.

"Look," he said. "If it helps, I get the feeling she needs you every bit as much as you need her."

She shook her head. "I don't even know what I'd say to her. I was such an asshole."

"Keep it simple and honest and from the heart. Say that you're sorry, but that you're working on yourself, and you'd like the chance to make it up to her, to get to know her."

"That's good stuff," she admitted, not really surprised, because Eli always knew what to say. He was a rock.

"Not my first time," he said softly, and gently tugged a lock of her hair. "Now go make it *true* stuff."

Rolling her eyes, Kinsey headed toward the front door, having zero idea what she was doing. Oh, wait, yes she did. She was about to ruin Brynn's life. She wasn't sure how, but she was sure it would happen. Because that's how it went in her life—she always managed to mess everything up.

Every single time.

 CHAPTER 6

From ten-year-old Kinsey's summer camp journal:

Dear Journal,

Ugh. Everyone looks at me weird here because I take a lot of medicines, and because the counselors let me sit on the sidelines when the other campers have to exercise. I hate the stares. So I stare back. I'm getting good at it. Someone stole my medical bracelet but no one would confess, so I stole something from everyone in my cabin. I hate them all.

I'd run away, but I don't feel good enough to walk home. Also, I can't leave Eli. He's the only person here who's nice to me. Okay, so he's nice to everyone, but he's the nicest to me. When I told him I was sad because I didn't have family to write to, he told me he'd be my brother for life, and I could write to him. But he's right here, so that's stupid.

There'd better be ice cream for dessert tonight. Chocolate *ice cream.*

Kinsey

p.s. I still hate you.

"Stupid, you're so, so, *so* stupid," Brynn muttered to herself, taking herself and her duffel bag back down the walkway toward her car. How could she have just blindly agreed to move in? Had she learned nothing? Had she already forgotten the deal she'd made with herself to protect the people she cared about, the one where she was going to lay off rash decisions and let everyone continue to walk their chosen path without interference or distraction from her?

She shook her head. A temporary setback, that was all. A "two steps forward, one step back" sort of thing. She could fix that. And she'd make it easier on herself—the hell with no rash decisions. No more decisions *at all*, at least until she grew the hell up.

Behind her, she heard the front door open, but she refused to stop. "Sorry, Eli," she said without looking. "But you should've told me that you're still a member of the Kinsey Davis Mean Kids Club."

"The Kinsey Davis Mean Kids Club?"

Brynn closed her eyes. Shit. Not Eli. Kinsey herself, the president of the club, the Kinsey who'd grown from a moody, surly teen into a moody, surly woman. And that she was also stunningly beautiful with great taste in shoes really chapped Brynn's hide. "Never mind," Brynn said. "Forget it. Forget all of it, I shouldn't have come."

"Yeah, well, you did, so . . ." Then Kinsey surprised her by grabbing the strap on Brynn's duffel bag and tugging on it.

Brynn turned to face her. "What the hell?"

"You're not leaving."

"Oh, yes, I am." Brynn tugged back, and—perfect—now they were in a full-out tug-of-war with her bag.

"Stop." Kinsey won the wrestle-for-the-bag contest. Damn, she was stronger than she looked. "You gave Eli a verbal agreement," the mean girl had the balls to say. "You're our new roommate, for better or worse."

"I gave that verbal agreement under false assumptions. No way am I going to live here with you."

"Okay. I get that. But consider this—if you didn't want this too, you wouldn't be yelling at me. And you wouldn't be all red-faced and sweaty."

That *that* might actually be true really fried Brynn's ass. Enough that her mouth bypassed her brain and ran free. "Seriously, you're like . . . a Disney villain."

Kinsey's eyes narrowed. "Take that back."

"Fine," Brynn said. "'Villain' is a little strong. Deep, *deep* down, you've got some good qualities. Probably."

"I meant the Disney part."

Brynn rolled her eyes. For the past year, she'd slowly gotten into a bad headspace where she had clearly forgotten how to stand up for herself. Ashton had done that, and she was ashamed of herself because she'd let him. But it was a cycle she hadn't known how to break.

Until now.

Suddenly, she felt strong and willing to be vocal and fight for herself. "You and I both know this would never work out, and frankly, I'm not even sure why you'd want it to." She let her bag drop to the ground. "You don't want me here."

"You don't know me."

"I know you like to be mean to little kids just because they're different."

Kinsey stilled, then closed her eyes. "Yeah. So about that . . ."

"I'm listening."

Kinsey grimaced. "You have no idea how badly I feel about what a big asshole I used to be."

"*Used* to be?"

Kinsey's eyes flew open, flashing something Brynn couldn't get a bead on. Maybe slight humor and approval that Brynn was standing up to her. "People change," she finally said.

Not buying it, Brynn shook her head. "Come on. I know you don't want me here either." Some of what she'd overheard hadn't computed, but she'd understood that much.

"I just had a really shit day, okay?" Kinsey paused. "But I'm okay. Thanks for asking back there, about the hospital thing. It was a false alarm. I'm sorry for taking all of that out on you."

Brynn supposed she could understand that, given her own situation and the whole string of really bad days she'd had . . .

Kinsey met her gaze. "I'm also sorry I was so unwelcoming,

but I'm like that. Ignore me, but don't go. Don't take my bad behavior out on Eli. He needs to fill that room."

"The house is great. It's right across the street from the beach. He could get another roommate without even trying."

"It's not that easy."

"Why?"

Kinsey looked away. "It's . . . complicated."

"Because . . . ?"

Kinsey didn't answer.

"Oh my God. Tell me it's not something kinky, like you and Eli need a third."

Kinsey blinked and then laughed, and by the rusty sound of it, it wasn't something she did often. "I told you, it's not like that between Eli and me, but nice one on making me laugh. Just . . . stay."

Brynn narrowed her eyes. "I still haven't heard why it has to be me."

Kinsey looked down at her very pretty, very expensive sandals, which Brynn recognized as the latest "in" brand, costing over a hundred dollars. She knew this because she'd been coveting a pair and unable to justify the price.

After a deep breath, Kinsey lifted her gaze to Brynn's. "I'm sorry," she said. "About a lot of things."

"Like?"

"Like how I treated you all those years ago at camp. I'm"— she paused as if trying to remember what she'd preplanned to say—"working on myself. I'd like the chance to make it up to you, and to get to know you."

Well, damn. Those were some good words. And truthfully, Brynn was working on herself too. She'd made plenty of mistakes, not the least of which was that apparently she wasn't exactly the most forgiving sort. "I'll think about it."

"What's there to think about?"

"Well, I'm not used to this side of you, for one thing," Brynn said.

"My sweet side, you mean?"

Brynn's brows went up.

Kinsey nodded. "Yeah, okay. 'Sweet' might be a stretch."

Brynn snorted. "Look, it's not personal. It's that I just made a deal with myself—no more decisions until further notice, because I'm bad at them. I really do just want to think it through."

"I guess I can respect that," Kinsey said, sounding as though maybe the words were like cut glass on her tongue, which made Brynn snort again.

"Was that painful?" she asked.

Kinsey made a face. "Little bit. Listen . . . Just think about it. Maybe you'll see that this wouldn't be a bad decision to add onto a string of other bad decisions."

Brynn froze. "I didn't say I'd made a string of bad decisions."

"You said you'd given up decisions. That was brought on by something, the most obvious choice being a string of bad decisions. Plus, it's all in your eyes."

"Our eyes are nearly the exact same color of light brown," Brynn said.

"Yeah," Kinsey said, giving her an odd look. "But mine are

good at hiding shit. You should work on *that* instead of the no-decision thing. Think about the room, okay?"

THE NEXT DAY, Brynn stood in her moms' kitchen at the very end of her proverbial rope. Whoever had said you couldn't go home again had been right. She was slowly going insane. Raina had tried to take her to a shaman to heal all her "inner wounds." Olive had signed her up for karate classes, like the ones she'd taken at age ten—before breaking her hand on day one, proving she had zero athletic ability. Raina cooked and cooked, leaving labeled containers in the fridge such as *For If Brynn's Constipated, For Brynn's Peckish Mood.*

They meant well, but she'd gone back to the drawing board, looking for a place to rent. She'd looked at three places. Two were completely out of her budget, and one was an hour drive to work. Now, scarily enough, she was actually reconsidering going back to Eli's. Neither Eli nor Kinsey had pushed. She'd asked for time, and it was apparently being granted.

She had to admit that was a first, for someone to listen to her, really listen, and give her what she asked for, and how sad was that?

The problem was her own. Her shaky self-esteem. It'd already taken a beating just being back in Wildstone. The last thing she wanted to do was make things harder on herself. She was inhaling some contraband donuts she'd picked up on her way home from filling out all the school district's paperwork when she heard her moms. She quickly took her half-dozen donuts into her room and shut the door.

And then nearly screamed.

Someone—two certain busybody someones—had taken it upon themselves while she'd been gone to repaint her bedroom. It wasn't hard to tell who'd done which walls. Olive had done two in a muted, understated cream, and then had put up pictures of the three of them from over the years. Like hundreds of pictures, from when she'd been missing her four front teeth all at the same time, to that time she'd gotten a bad perm and resembled a circus clown.

Raina had done her two walls Raina style. One was a rainbow, the other a corkboard, upon which she'd hung every single one of Brynn's questionable achievements over the years, including all her "participation" awards for everything she'd ever failed at, and there'd been many, *many* things.

Brynn did an about-face and headed back out to the living room. Olive was standing on the couch rearranging the pictures above it according to Raina, who stood in the middle of the living room giving instructions.

"And we're doing this again why?" Olive asked, removing the last picture from the wall.

"You know why. I promised my sixteen Instagram followers." Raina flicked a red reflector light on the now bare wall so Catherine could chase it. "Start recording, please."

Olive pulled out her phone to capture a video of Catherine the Great Cat chasing the light.

For Raina's sixteen Instagram followers.

Love was very strange.

Backing out of the living room unseen, Brynn was in her

bedroom again, halfway through a buttermilk glazed, when she caught a shadow moving in the space between the bottom of her door and the hardwood floor.

Four feet. Two bare, two in heels.

She chomped on her donut, hoping the sugar would miraculously lower the blood pressure that her moms were keeping at stroke levels.

"Hello?" Raina called out.

Brynn bit her lower lip.

"Darling?" This from Olive.

Never alone . . .

Sure, she'd promised herself no more decisions, especially any life-altering ones, but this seemed like an emergency situation as it affected her mental health. Setting the donut down, she pulled out her phone and sent a text.

BRYNN: So here's the thing. I recently promised myself no more life-altering decisions until I grew the hell up and could stop ruining my own life. So I need a life-altering decision-making committee.

ELI: What are the requirements?

BRYNN: They have to have my best interests at heart.

ELI: I could do that.

BRYNN: You think you can make decisions for me that will only be in my best interests?

ELI: Try me.

BRYNN: First of all, why did you not tell me your roommate was Kinsey? Were you being manipulative, or an asshole?

ELI: I deserve that. And I'm sorry I blindsided you. I didn't think you'd even give it a shot if you knew. She doesn't exactly present well. Can we still be friends?

BRYNN: To be determined.

ELI: Fair. And second of all?

BRYNN: I need out of my moms' house before I lose the rest of my marbles. I've searched and searched, but there's nothing I can afford. Except . . .

ELI: Here. If it helps, I can tell you it's the right decision.

BRYNN: How do I know that?

ELI: Because your life-altering decision-making committee can one hundred percent assure you it is. Do we have a deal?

Brynn eyed the box of donuts.

ELI: If it makes you feel better, we could pinky swear on it.

In summer camp, pinky swearing had been a big thing. If you broke a pinky swear, you were never trusted again. And she had to admit, Eli had never broken a pinky swear. She looked at her phone. Once again, he was being patient, allowing her time, something that she had to admit was very new and very welcome.

BRYNN: Okay. I'm in.

ELI: Great. What do you need?

BRYNN: A lobotomy.

BRYNN SHOOK HER head at herself the entire drive through Wildstone and down the highway a few miles to the beach exit. She was still shaking her head at herself when she parked in front of the house she hadn't imagined she'd ever see again.

It was a classic New England style, in ocean blue with white trim around the windows and a large deck that held a grill and a porch swing, along with a table and Adirondack chairs, all looking well lived in and loved.

It was dusk, and she knew there was nowhere prettier on earth than Wildstone at dusk. The sun was a huge, bright-red ball low on the horizon, flirting with the water's edge, a few streaky clouds teasing the sun, the water's whitecaps sparkling like diamonds.

She stood there at the end of the driveway staring at the gorgeous view and actually felt her blood pressure lower just a little bit. Not her pulse, though. Nope, that was still kicking from nerves.

Then she felt a hand slide under the strap of her duffel bag and remove it from her shoulder. She whipped around and Eli smiled.

"Sorry," he said, and shouldered her bag. "It looked heavy."

"What's heavy is my life."

He nodded like he understood that all too well, and she let her eyes wander over him, taking in the battered work boots, the faded and ripped jeans riding low on his hips, and the thin, olive drab cotton of the T-shirt with some complicated science formula on it stretched over broad shoulders. His hair was wet, like he'd just showered, but the sexy stubble on his jaw said he hadn't shaved. He was barefoot and wearing a pair of reading glasses. Be still her heart. A sexy nerd.

A bark sounded, followed by paws scrabbling for purchase against the floor.

"Brace yourself," Eli warned mildly.

What looked like a huge yellow polar bear came barreling out of the house. Mini. She gave another happy bark and started to jump on Brynn, but Eli stopped her with a calm but firm "Down."

Mini sat, ears flapping, tongue lolling, an actual smile curving her canine mouth, which adorably wrinkled her face.

"If you remind her not to jump before she gets to you, you've got a better shot at not getting knocked flat on your ass," he said. "Also beware of sitting on the ground to pet her. She'll plant herself on you like you're a dog bed."

"Anything else?"

"Don't leave anything where she can get it. She prefers to chew high-quality stuff too, like AirPods and expensive shoes."

They both looked at Mini, whose tail was sweeping the ground. Brynn patted her on the head. "But she looks so cute."

"Yeah, don't let that face fool you. She's just on a break between bouts of destruction."

Suddenly Mini jumped up, snapping her jaw at thin air.

"Sky raisin," Eli said.

"What?"

He lifted a shoulder. "She loves flies, thinks they're a delicacy."

Brynn gave a shudder. "That's gross."

"Agreed. That's why we call them sky raisins—not as disgusting sounding. Also, FYI, she's allergic to the jalapeño sky raisins, so we have to keep an eye on her when she's outside."

"Jalapeño sky raisins?"

"Bees and wasps."

She laughed as Mini moved to Eli, the clear love of her life, leaning against him, knocking him back a step. With a laugh, he crouched low and gave her a hug. Mini melted to the ground, a puddle of love, where Eli obliged her with a full belly rub before looking up at Brynn. "Welcome home, by the way."

She bit her lower lip. "I still have reservations." Not the least of which were her conflicting emotions about the man now straightening back up to his full height and, at just over six feet, also looking like the sexiest welcoming committee she'd ever seen.

"I get it," he said, and for a moment Brynn freaked, thinking she'd spoken out loud. "Your reservations are founded," he said quietly, "but I hope you'll be happy here. Come on in. Max is home. Kinsey's on a date."

"She dates?"

Eli laughed. "She wouldn't call it a date. But the guy she's with, Deck, absolutely would. They've been doing their thing for nearly a year now, and no one, not even Deck, has got the balls to tell Kinsey she's in a relationship."

"Huh," she said, processing something else, something she hadn't really thought she needed to know until right that minute. "So you two really aren't a thing."

Their eyes met and held. "Nope."

And again her mouth disconnected from her brain and acted independently. "Do you date?"

"Other than my dog?" He shrugged. "When the stars align. You?"

"Same," she said softly.

He smiled. "What's an ideal date for you?"

Someone who doesn't con me out of my things and my self-esteem . . . "Anything that involves food, *real* food, and hopefully dessert, where my date's impressed by my ability to eat an entire cake and not at all disgusted."

He laughed, and Mini barked in excitement. Then, from a house down the street, a woman and a little girl came out. The little girl went skipping down the sidewalk and Mini froze, whined, and then leapt right into Eli's arms.

"Aw, I've got you," he murmured. "You're okay."

"I thought you're supposed to tell her 'down.'"

"She's scared. Today at the dog park, another little girl—and I mean *tiny*, like she was *maybe* two years old—chased her, and now she wants to be carried whenever she sees a little kid."

"But the girl's not even looking this way."

"Tell that to Mini."

Brynn looked into the most devastatingly sweet brown eyes she'd ever seen and stepped closer. "Aw, it's okay," she whispered, cupping that incredibly expressive face in her hands. "I'm scared of little kids too."

"Aren't you a kindergarten teacher?" Eli asked, sounding amused.

"Yeah. And your point?" Smiling, she lifted her head and

froze, because she hadn't realized how close to him she'd moved. They were toe to toe, and if he dipped his head, they'd be nose to nose.

He didn't look perturbed by the nearness in the slightest. Just smiled, bent to kiss his dog on the top of her head, and then set her down. "Listen up," he told Mini as he led them into the house. "Brynn's one of us now, so if you could refrain from eating her food, making yourself at home on her bed, or farting when she's in the room, that'd be great."

"Does she do all those things?"

From the vicinity of Mini's hindquarters came an unmistakable sound.

Brynn laughed.

"I assume that answers your question," Eli said, fanning the air. "Just don't feed her any human food. Hard to believe, but it gets worse when you do."

The room she'd rented had a window that looked out onto a side yard. Lots of wild grass, but beyond that she could see the cliffs and the ocean. She'd have stayed here for the view alone, but then Eli dropped her duffel bag onto the bed and pointed to the attached bathroom, which held a big, fat, porcelain self-standing tub between the shower and the sink.

"Oh my God," she whispered reverently, and moved closer, running her fingers along the edge. "I just fell in love."

"That was easy."

She slid him a look. "With your tub."

He grinned, and gestured to the closed door at the other end of the tub. "That leads to another bedroom."

Her eyes went to the door. Oh, boy. "Kinsey's, I presume."

"She loves baths too." Eli rubbed a hand over his scruffy jaw. "Maybe we should write up a schedule."

"We're grown-ups," Brynn heard herself say. "I'm sure we can figure it out." But actually, she wasn't really sure at all.

"Where's the rest of your stuff?"

She hesitated, not wanting to admit it was still in Long Beach. She didn't want to tell him any of that story for lots of reasons. "In my trunk," she finally said.

"Need help unloading it?"

"No, but thanks." Even if her things had been in her trunk, she'd want to leave them there for now. No sense rushing into something that might not work out.

Especially when nothing else ever had.

That was what happened when one fell for a con artist; you lost your perspective and self-trust. Because everything felt like a mirage now. Her relationships, her sense of home, her sense of security and well-being. *Everything.*

Eli looked like maybe he wanted to say more, but he didn't. He just gave her a nod and headed out of her room, stopping to look back. "Want dinner?"

"Oh. Um, I don't want to intrude . . ."

"You're not. Max does most of the cooking. He's got the barbeque going. Burgers or hot dogs?"

Her stomach rumbled. *A burger. No, a hot dog. Wait. Maybe both?* But that would mean she was mooching too much food. God, look at her. Such an easy decision, and she couldn't even make it. "I don't know."

"We've also got vegan burgers in the freezer, left over from someone Max was dating, but fair warning, they suck."

"No, it's not that."

He studied her for a moment. "Maybe choosing between a burger and a hot dog is one of those . . . life-altering decisions you need your committee for."

She let out the breath she'd been holding, because she didn't know how he possibly could, but he seemed to understand. "Maybe."

"I get low blood sugar when I don't eat," he said. "And once that happens, hanger sets in and it's hard to recover."

"Hanger?"

"Hunger plus anger."

She laughed.

Smiling, he said, "Just give me a little hint and your committee will take it from here."

"I like both burgers and hot dogs."

He nodded. "Both it is, then."

That got another smile out of her. He'd made it easy. But she had no such illusions about any of the rest of this being so easy.

 CHAPTER 7

From eleven-year-old Brynn's summer camp journal:

Dear Moms (it's really just you, dear journal, because this can't go to my moms, they'll worry about me),

This year's veggie of choice is creamed spinach. Yeah, it's as disgusting as it sounds. I tried to tell the counselors that you like me to eat only fresh vegetables, but they didn't care. I tried to tell them how much sodium we were consuming, and that it canceled out the goodness, but deaf ears . . .

I still get picked last for teams, in case you were wondering. It was Eli who picked me this time, and he apologized, but I'm still mad.

Oh, and don't you worry, Kinsey is still mean. She didn't hide my glasses this time, but she still can't do any of the night activities, so we're the only two stuck in the cabin.

She pretends I don't exist.

Works for me.

Eli sneaked me a candy bar. I think he really is sorry, but I'm not going to forgive him until tomorrow so I can have another candy bar.

Oh, and I still want to come home.

Love,
Brynn

BRYNN FOLLOWED THE scent of barbeque through the warm, cozy house, loving the feel of the creaking wood floors beneath her feet. She ended up in the kitchen, where Eli introduced her to his brother.

Max took one look at her and smiled at her the same way Eli had when they'd first seen each other again. Like it was incredibly amazing and touching to see her, and she realized he knew about her, while she knew nothing about him.

"Nice to have you," Max said genuinely.

Mini was sitting on a dog bed in the corner, chewing on a bone, but stopped chewing to greet Brynn with wild enthusiasm, including a chin-to-forehead lick, even though she'd just seen her five minutes ago.

"Sign of approval," Eli said.

She sensed the brothers staring at each other over her head, but when she pulled back, she couldn't tell what was going on.

Mini was head-butting Brynn's hand, trying to get more pets, and Brynn laughed. "I'm getting the feeling she loves everyone."

Max touched his finger to his nose in confirmation. "Grab a plate, darlin'."

The master of pretending everything was fine and normal, she did. They ate on the porch. She consumed both a burger and a hot dog, and found herself laughing and relaxing with the brothers in a way she hadn't let herself in . . . well, forever.

After, she insisted on helping clean up. "I like a woman who can eat," Max said appreciatively, drying the dishes she washed while Eli cleaned the grill.

Max looked a lot like his brother. Matching searing gray eyes, sun-kissed brown hair that seemed to have no interest in anything other than doing its own thing in a sexily mussed kind of way, a fit body that said he spent a lot of time doing physical things, and a smile that could stop hearts. He was also very young, though that mischief in his eyes said he could compensate for his age with plenty of experience.

Eli came back into the kitchen and pointed at his younger brother. "Stop that."

"Stop what?" Max asked with a mock innocence that had Eli shaking his head.

"You know what. Don't flirt with her. Roommates are off-limits."

"Since when?" Max wanted to know.

"Since the last three roommates you single-handedly chased away once you broke their hearts. No more. Besides, Brynn is smarter than you are, she can see right through you."

Max looked at Brynn.

Brynn nodded sagely.

Max laughed. "Okay, I'll give you that much. But it would've been fun."

Brynn had no doubt.

When they'd finished cleaning up, Brynn headed out of the kitchen. Knowing she was starting a new job tomorrow had put butterflies in her tummy. "Thanks for dinner, but I've got to get some sleep."

"Let me help you bring the rest of your stuff in first," Eli said.

She shook her head. "Thanks, but that's okay, it's not important."

Those fascinating gray eyes seemed to be able to see inside her, but she just smiled and made her way to her new bedroom to avoid more talk.

And a little bit to avoid Kinsey, as well, who presumably was in the car she'd just heard pull into the driveway.

She used their bathroom quickly, and then turned off her light and got into bed.

Two hours later, she was still staring up at the ceiling. She couldn't sleep, and she didn't want to think about why. When her stomach growled, she sat up and listened.

The house was quiet.

Assuming the coast was clear, she slipped on her favorite baggy sweats and tiptoed out.

Mini was sleeping in yet another dog bed at the top of the stairs. The sweet dog lifted a sleepy head and gave her a smile, and Brynn choked out a laugh. Someone had hung a small sign around her neck that said:

Zero days since the last toilet paper massacre.

"You're my favorite roommate," she whispered, and hugged her before heading down the stairs and into the kitchen. She hadn't had a chance to go food shopping for herself yet, but Eli had said to make herself at home. She'd just take a peek and see if there was anything she could snack on and replace tomorrow. But the view out the window had her stepping out onto the back porch. Staring up at a gorgeous full moon high above the water, she sank into the porch swing in the far corner to take it all in. She was still there a few minutes later when she heard voices.

Eli and Max.

They were coming up the back porch steps wearing wet suits, leaning their surfboards against the house at the bottom of the stairs.

They'd been surfing in the dark. At midnight, by moonlight. She didn't know if that was the coolest thing she'd ever heard of, or the most stupidly dangerous.

The guys unzipped their wet suits and peeled them down to their lean hips, and she quickly sat up to make herself known, but Max spoke first. "She's cute."

Eli just slid him a look.

"What? She is. And I know you know it because I caught you looking at her ass."

Eli reached into a cooler. He cracked open a bottle of water, drank for a long moment, and then said, "I just remembered you owe me that favor from when I got you the job at the marina. You said it could be *anything*."

"That was a year ago."

"Well, I've finally decided. You're going to clean out the garage this weekend and make room for our new renter to park in it."

Max grinned.

"What?"

"Man, it's been a long time since you resorted to dickhead threats to change the subject. Just admit it, you've got a thing for her."

Brynn stilled. Well, everything except her good parts. Those tingled. Eli couldn't possibly have a thing for her. If he had, it would've happened after their long-ago kiss. Or any of the summers after that, until he'd stopped going to camp. Or even the other day at the hospital.

When you'd pretended not to remember him . . .

She sighed silently. She was such an idiot, compounding her errors. Because she should've made herself known the minute they'd appeared on the porch, but now it was too late. So she sat very still and hoped they didn't say anything else she couldn't unhear.

"You going to do anything about it?" Max asked. "Or are you going to tell me I'm full of shit, that you feel nothing, the same nothing you've been feeling for way too long? And you need to be careful here, bro, because if you say that, it means she's up for grabs. Think she likes younger guys?"

"Try anything on her and no one will ever find your body."

Max grinned. "See, I *knew* it. You *do* still like her." He leaned forward to catch Eli's response.

Brynn leaned forward too. Because . . . *still?*

Eli pressed a finger to an eye, like maybe it was twitching. "She's not here for that," he said. "I think she's been hurt. She's . . . trying to heal."

Brynn froze, shocked to realize she'd broadcasted that with body language alone.

Max lost both his smile and teasing tone. "Do we need to go teach some guy his manners?"

"Only if she wants us to," Eli said, and Brynn felt something warm inside her, in a place where she'd shoved deep the things that made her cold and scared.

"I see you, you know," Max said.

Brynn froze, feeling her face flush. She'd been found out, and she opened her mouth to apologize, but Max spoke again.

"I know you're still struggling with your grandma's death."

Brynn blinked, because he was talking to Eli, not her.

Without a word, Eli set his water aside and went back to the cooler for a beer.

He'd lost a grandparent, one he'd clearly been very close to. Brynn knew what that felt like; it was an actual hole in your life. Not having ever had a dad, she'd always been aware of what she was missing, the grief of it. But since she was lucky enough to have two moms, she'd kept that grief to herself.

But that didn't make the feeling go away.

"I'm okay," Eli said.

"You spent a lot of time with her, from age ten on," Max said. "She left a void."

"Of course she did. She was my only parent after Dad . . ."

"Boned the babysitter?" Max's voice was dry and sounded

much older than he was. "You don't have to dance around that for me. My mom was never shy about how she stole him from your mom. I was always jealous as hell that you got to go live with your grandma. She sent you to that great summer camp for a bunch of years."

Eli smiled. "She did."

"Did you ever hear back from your mom on what she's going to do with your grandma's ashes?"

The soft snort from Eli didn't sound like amusement. "No. I called the funeral home, but unless she gets back to them, aka pays for their services, Grandma will end up in a grave where all the unclaimed remains go."

"Not what she wanted."

"No, she wanted to be buried, not cremated, with a proper funeral," Eli said. "And blessed by her priest before being laid to rest next to her husband. But Mom did the cremation without a care for any of that. Now the best I can do is get the funeral home to hold off on the unmarked grave until I can get the paperwork for the right to make the decisions."

"And how are you going to get the paperwork?"

"I don't know," Eli said. "I was counting on at least one of my parents calling me back so I could try to talk them into letting me do the right thing."

Max shook his head. "You're going to offer to pay for everything, aren't you?"

Eli took a long pull on his beer.

"That's such bullshit, man. You already mortgaged the house for her long-term care and medical bills."

"This isn't about me."

"No, but it should be. Seriously, you're the most stubborn person on the planet."

Eli shrugged. Apparently he already knew that.

Max sighed. "I heard your mom was in Singapore," he said quietly.

Eli looked at him in surprise. "What's she doing there?"

"She bought a house there." Max turned a disbelieving look on Eli. "She really didn't tell you?" He paused and shook his head with obvious disgust. "Of course she didn't. The only reason I even know is because my mom found out."

"She still stalking her via Instagram and Snapchat?"

It was Max's turn to snort. "Yeah, and has ever since she was that eighteen-year-old babysitter screwing her paycheck. She'd cooled it for a while, but someone called her the trophy wife a few weeks ago and it sort of renewed her obsession."

Brynn felt a tug at her heart at the expression on Eli's face, which she could only see in profile. Hurt. Angry.

"I'm sorry," Max said. "You deserve better."

"It doesn't matter."

"Dude, it fucking matters, okay? It was your birthday last week and neither of them even called you. Now you're just trying to give your grandma the burial she wanted. It's not rocket science. Our parents, *all* of them, suck ass."

Brynn realized she was rubbing a hand across her chest, aching, feeling a connection to Eli that she hadn't expected. She couldn't imagine either of her moms ghosting her. Or avoiding her at all, for any reason. And if one of them were to die—

even the thought hurt madly—the other would do whatever her wife had wanted, no matter what. So it was incredible to Brynn that Eli was burdened with this. Fighting his mom to give his grandma the burial she'd wanted.

Max stirred. "I'm going to bed, man, and you should do the same."

"Yeah."

They both began to—oh, shit—peel their wet suits the rest of the way off right there on the porch. Brynn had long ago lost her moment to announce herself, and she knew it, but . . .

Good.

Lord.

They weren't wearing *anything* beneath. Their backs were to her and she knew it was wrong, but her feet wouldn't move and her eyes couldn't seem to help themselves.

Eli had the best butt on the entire planet.

And then he turned around and, sweet baby Jesus, even in the chilly night he was impressive.

At that very moment, Mini pushed her way out the screen door, looking sweet and sleepy, tail going a mile a minute, happy to see her guys.

But she didn't go to her guys, because Brynn's luck didn't run that way. Nope. The big yellow lab headed right for Brynn on the porch swing, letting out a welcoming snort.

Shaking her head, she held out her hands, trying to ward the dog off.

But Mini didn't have any sense of boundaries. She snorted again right before she jumped onto her lap.

Brynn gasped and automatically wrapped her arms around the dog to keep them both from tipping off the porch swing.

And failed.

"What the hell?" Eli said, just as Brynn and Mini landed on the floor in a tangle of limbs.

Someone hit the porch light. Eyes trying to adjust to the sudden glare, Brynn blinked like an owl.

Or a peeping Tom.

Mini helpfully licked her face.

Finally, Brynn managed to crane her neck out of licking range, and from flat on her back, looked up at two naked men.

"I think we made her speechless," Max said, and grabbed the two towels slung over the railing.

Eli held out his hand for one of them, but Max flashed a grin and, still holding both towels, walked into the house, passing right by Brynn to do so.

"Nice," Eli said sarcastically to his brother's ass, but just shook his head and turned to Brynn. "Remember to tell Mini 'down,'" he reminded her, offering her a hand up.

She took it, sucking in a breath at the odd bombardment of sensations. His hand was warm and slightly rough with calluses. As for the rest of him, she did her best not to look.

Much.

As soon as she was upright, their gazes met for a single beat, during which he gave her a look she couldn't quite interpret before he turned away. "Mini, come."

And then man and dog followed after Max, into the house.

With a grimace, Brynn headed in as well. Mini turned three

circles in her huge dog bed and plopped down with a groan, closing her eyes. In two seconds she was snoring at shocking decibels.

Max was leaning against the kitchen counter, covered by one of the towels, sipping a beer. Eli snatched the other and wrapped it around himself. It was a Day-Glo pink and read, I'M HOT, all in bright-white letters. He should've looked ridiculous.

He did not.

"Beer?" Max asked her.

"No, thank you." She was trying not to stare at Eli, she really was. But he had a drop of water on his collar bone, slowly sliding down his pec and heading south, south, south, past his abs and still moving. It was absorbed by the towel sitting low on his hips, and good God, she was *still* staring, so she jerked her eyes up to the ceiling.

Her first reaction had been decidedly female. Her second reaction, right on its heels, was different, and all amusement fled. Because the last time she'd had a naked roommate, he'd ended up robbing her blind. She cleared her throat. "First of all, I'm really sorry," she managed. "I know I should've told you I was there. And second"—she looked at them both—"I'm wondering if it's okay if we make a roommate rule."

Max stopped with his beer halfway to his mouth and looked at her. "Roommate rule?"

"Such as 'eavesdropping is rude'?" Eli asked mildly.

Brynn blushed. "Yes. Absolutely, yes. But also . . . maybe something about roommates walking around naked and stuff."

"Good idea," Max said. "How about if one of us is naked, we should *all* be naked." He laughed, clearly amused by himself.

Eli didn't laugh. He frowned at his brother. "Max."

Max looked at Brynn's face, and his own smile faded. "Sorry. I'm just kidding. I wouldn't—"

"Go to bed, Max," Eli said.

Max looked at Brynn again, all teasing and joking gone. "Sorry," he repeated. "I didn't mean to upset you."

She thought maybe she managed a reassuring smile before he tossed his beer into the trash and ambled off down the hall, but she wasn't sure. She was still somewhat frozen in place. It'd been wrong of her, very wrong, to stay on the porch like she had. All of it—hearing a conversation she shouldn't have, seeing them strip out of their wet suits—that was all on her, and she felt awful about it. But she hadn't felt . . . *uncomfortable* until right now, because they hadn't done anything wrong. *She'd* given them the wrong idea.

Eli had set down his own beer after only a sip and was now looking at her, gaze weighted.

"I really am sorry," she said quietly, feeling nervous and sick. "I should've announced myself."

"Why didn't you?"

Good question. And when she didn't, couldn't, answer, he turned and vanished into the laundry room.

 CHAPTER 8

From eleven-year-old Kinsey's summer camp journal:

Dear Journal,

Never fear, I still hate you. But other than Eli, you're my only friend at camp. I don't want to be here, but my mom's got a new boyfriend—yeah, another one—and they're on a stupid trip.

I'm tired, but they keep making us do stuff. We walked up a mountain in the rain and got muddy. I hate muddy. All the boys took off their shoes and socks because they got blisters and then . . . bare boy feet! Gross.

We also had to play dodgeball—worst game on the planet. One of the obnoxious boys kicked Eli "by accident" so I "accidentally" kicked him back. I told Eli that's what sisters do. But I actually don't know what sisters do because I don't have one.

Brynn's in my cabin. Again. She gets packages from
home with special food and letters. I hate her.
And I hate you, Journal. But not as much as I used to.
                                                   Kinsey

ELI OPENED THE dryer and pawed through his clothes for a pair
of jeans and a T-shirt. It was a little like closing the barn door
after the horses had escaped, but he pulled the denim on anyway and went back into the kitchen.

Brynn had moved to the sink and was staring out the window
into the night, her profile somber. "I thought you left," she said.

He looked at her in surprise. "I just wanted to put on some
clothes. Thought it might not seem like it because Max's a tod-
dler, but making you uncomfortable was the last thing either of
us wanted to do."

She bit her lower lip, still looking exactly that, uncomfortable.

"Also, for future reference," he said quietly, "I don't walk
away when there's an issue."

"That makes one of us, then." Her smile was a little self-
conscious, and he remembered when he'd asked her if he could
help her move her things into the house. She'd said it wasn't
important. As if she was used to being unimportant. He hated
that for her.

She turned to face him, eyes going to his jeans. On the porch,
she'd soaked up the unintended view of him buck-ass naked and
appeared to appreciate the sight. But then Max had opened his
big mouth and made an inappropriate comment about everyone
getting naked, and her amusement had been gone in a blink.

Rightfully so. "Max's young and an idiot," he said. "He won't say anything like that to you again."

She nodded, but he could tell from her carefully hooded gaze that she wasn't big on promises. Maybe she'd had too many broken in her life, something he understood all too well. A fact that only made him all the more determined to never break a promise to her.

Not easy when he was holding Kinsey's secrets. And his own. Such as the fact that, long after their summer camp deal, she'd had a starring role in his teenage fantasies.

"Tonight wasn't Max's fault. It was mine. I . . . had a bad experience with a previous roommate." She broke eye contact. "That was *also* my fault, and it didn't end well. And while I'm being honest, he wasn't just a roommate, he was a boyfriend for four months and then a live-in boyfriend for two months, which is maybe why it's sticking with me." She shook her head. "It's not important. I'm not upset with either you or Max. I'm upset with myself. Also, I'm super tired, so I'm just going back to bed and—"

"Brynn." He very gently reached out for her hand, catching her. "You live here now. You're part of us. Which means you, and everything about you, are very important."

Again her gaze skittered away. She wasn't ready to believe that, which he understood. How long had he himself gone feeling unimportant? For him, family and a sense of belonging came from where he *made* them, which was why he'd gathered Max and Kinsey here, with him. But if he was being honest with himself, there was still a part of him that secretly yearned . . . to be the one picked. "Did he hurt you, Brynn?"

"He never laid a hand on me, if that's what you mean."

"There's more than one way to hurt someone."

She nodded. "Yeah. So . . . I fell for his charm and charisma, and he . . ." She shook her head. "It doesn't matter. My point is that I can't trust my own decisions right now because I was stupid."

"We've all made stupid decisions. It's part of life. A sucky part, but still. Do you want to talk about it?"

"No."

His smile was wry. "As the master of shoving things deep so I don't have to deal, I get that."

"What do you shove deep?"

"Oh, you know, the usual. Boy grows up with disinterested, divorced parents and then goes on to choose poorly in love as well." He shrugged. "Just your everyday, typical abandonment issues."

"I'm sorry," she said softly.

"It happens. And I've got a nice life here, with people I care about. We have each other's back, including yours. And on that note, do you need help with your past?"

"No. And I'm in a good place now too. I learned the lesson I was supposed to."

"And what was that?"

"That I'm too trusting. I'm not going to be walked on, not ever again." She paused, took a deep breath. "And I really am sorry about tonight. That was all on me. I just was embarrassed, but that was no excuse not to let you know I was there. I'm also sorry about your grandma. What you're doing, trying to make sure she gets the burial she wanted—you're a good person."

"You sound surprised."

"No. *No*," she said again on a small laugh when his brows went up. "I knew you were a good person. I just . . . didn't know I liked you."

"Same." He thought he'd had her pegged. A bird with a broken wing who needed a little help. He was good with that scenario. He was good at helping. It was what he did. And it made her a good roommate for him, because he could tell himself he wasn't in any way attracted to her.

But he hadn't counted on those sweet brown eyes and how she looked at things, including him. He hadn't counted on her adorably sexy smile, the one that seemed to reach right inside his chest and warm him when he hadn't even realized he was cold.

She gave him another one of those smiles now. The window was open and they could hear the surf pounding the shore. The salty ocean air, one of his favorite things, drifted over them. And though the only things touching were their elbows as they both leaned against the granite countertop, it was one of the most intimate moments he'd had in a long time.

"You're a marine biologist, right?" she asked. "Cool job."

"It's not as glamorous as it sounds. Mostly I spend a whole bunch of time in scuba gear freezing my bits off, or searching for funds so that we can continue to protect and report on the marine life in the bay."

"Explains your comfort in a wet suit." She raised a brow. "You always go commando under it?"

He laughed. "Not at work. And only if it's like a week past laundry day."

"Is it dangerous work?"

"Laundry? Yes, deadly dangerous. It's why I procrastinate."

She laughed. "Your job. You ever run into a shark?"

"It's the jellyfish that are terrifying. I've been stung twice, which hurts like a bitch. How about you?"

"Nope." She smiled. "I've never been stung by a jellyfish."

"Smart-ass." He liked that. A lot. "I meant about your work."

"I start a new job tomorrow, so I'm nervous. It'll be the first time I've ever taught kindergarteners. I'd maybe prefer to get stung by a jellyfish."

"Trust me, you wouldn't. What did you teach before this?"

"High school English. Before that I tutored middle schoolers and high schoolers at a tutoring academy. Before that I was a nanny and a waitress, along with a few other odd jobs while I was in college."

"If you could teach and tutor middle and high schoolers, you can teach kindergarteners. They're kind of the same thing. Plus, you're bringing a lot of experience to the table. You'll do great."

She stared at him like maybe no one had ever said anything like that to her before. "Thanks," she said softly.

One of their stomachs growled. His this time, and he began to move around the kitchen, pulling out what he needed, oddly reluctant to call it a night in spite of the late hour.

"What are you doing?" she asked. "Didn't we just eat?"

"*Hours* ago. Do you like pancakes?"

She laughed. "I love pancakes. Especially at midnight."

He grinned. "Midnight pancakes taste better."

"So you do this a lot?"

"Yeah. Surfing burns a lot of calories."

"Then maybe I should try it."

"I could teach you," he said, stirring the ingredients together.

"Be careful what you offer me," she said. "I like to try new things. I'm just not usually any good at them."

"You'll be good at this."

"You know I'm a klutz," she said.

He turned and looked at her. She looked at him right back. "Trust me," he said.

She busied herself with moving around the kitchen. "You also know I'm not very good with trust either. Are you as good at pancakes as you are at surfing?"

"Better."

"Hmm." She hopped up onto the counter. "Then consider me as hopeful as Mini."

The dog had showed up with hopeful eyes, padding over to the stove to sit and watch Eli.

Brynn didn't just sit. She always seemed to be in motion, legs moving, talking with her hands. Her hair was a riot of loose waves and she didn't seem to care, which he found refreshing and—*damn*—extremely attractive.

She was intriguing.

More than.

He added an ingredient that had Mini sitting up straight.

Brynn too. "Chocolate chip pancakes?"

"Is there any other kind?"

She grinned, and something deep inside him . . . warmed. His cold, dead heart, he realized with surprise, and he flipped the first pancake with a flick of his wrist.

Brynn clapped in delight sitting there on his countertop, legs now crossed and tucked beneath her.

"You look like you're sixteen and in high school," he said with a smile.

"I didn't go to high school. I was homeschooled by then."

"Why?"

She shrugged, looking at the pan, not him. "I was moving at a faster pace."

He knew by her body language that there was a whole bunch more to that story than she was willing to tell him. Something he understood. "So why kindergarten?" he asked.

"It was all that was open. I'm hoping for the best. Kindergarten's a really hard time for kids. They're away from their moms and scared to be different. Maybe I can help them see that they're unique and special just the way they are."

He thought that statement was more revealing than anything she'd said up to that point. "I don't think you have anything to be nervous about," he said quietly.

Their gazes met and held.

Max reappeared, breaking the moment. He'd dressed, Eli was happy to see, wearing loose basketball shorts and a T-shirt, looking rumpled, like maybe he'd gone to bed but had just rolled out of it again. "I smell chocolate chip pancakes." He spied what Eli was doing and pumped a triumphant fist. "Yes!" He went to the fridge and unwrapped what looked like a pancake, stuck it on a plate, and set it down for Mini.

"Chicken and rice and carrot pancake," Eli told Brynn. "Max makes a batch for her once a week or so. She likes to eat with us."

Max pulled out more plates, handing them to Eli, who loaded them up with *not* chicken and rice and carrot pancakes just as Kinsey walked in, nose wriggling.

Eli nodded at her and said what he always said. "You're alive."

She returned it with her usual, "Not for lack of trying."

This had been going on since they'd been teenagers and she'd almost died after her surgery. It sounded macabre, but truthfully it was a release and a relief to repeat those words to each other. Sort of like taking the burden off her of trying to stay alive, when sometimes he knew she wasn't one hundred percent sure it was worth the effort.

"Gimme," Kinsey said, grabbing a plate. She nodded at Brynn, then turned to Max and froze. "You're barefoot in the house again."

"I was born with bare feet," he said.

"Yes," Kinsey said, "But we've been over this. Bare feet are not allowed."

Eli looked at Brynn. "She's got a phobia of men's feet."

"It's not a phobia," Kinsey said. "Men's feet are gross."

"*Phobia*," Eli repeated. "Along with people throwing up and getting dirty."

Kinsey tossed up her free hand. "Well, why don't you just throw all my crazy out there at once and scare off the new room-mate again?"

Eli scooped two pancakes onto her plate. She was wearing flip-flops and a huge black T-shirt that fell to her knees and had slipped off one of her shoulders. It read: I LIKE MY WATER FROZEN INTO ICE CUBES AND SURROUNDED BY VODKA.

"Deck's shirt?" he asked.

"No. *I* love vodka."

"Liar," he said. "You hate vodka—you love bourbon. But I know why you're lying. It's because you told me if I ever saw you in anything of Deck's, I should shoot you on sight because you'd deserve it for being so sappy as to wear your man's clothing."

She pointed at him. "Don't piss me off and get on my shit list."

"I'm always on your shit list. I just move up and down on it."

"Yeah, well, you just moved to the number one spot."

Eli laughed as he turned to Brynn and dropped two big, fluffy pancakes onto her plate. "Butter? Marshmallow spread? Syrup? Whatever you want."

Kinsey's eyes narrowed, and she stopped in the act of grab-bing the syrup from the fridge. "How come you didn't offer the 'anything you want' to me?"

"Because you're mean."

She flipped him off, then took her first bite and murmured, "Oh my God." She swallowed and gave him a thumbs-up.

Mixed signals. The story of his life from all the women in it.

 CHAPTER 9

From twelve-year-old Brynn's summer camp journal:

Dear Moms,

Omg, this year's veggie is WILTED SPINACH! I don't even think they mean for it to be wilted, but it is. And it's disgusting!

I'm not even going to bother telling you how much I hate it here, or that I want to come home, since I know you're on your dream cruise this week and I don't want you to worry about me. I'm fine. UGH! But if you come home early, come get me.

Also, guess what? Someone—I'm sure it was Kinsey, because hello!—stole my glasses again. But when I fell into the creek and got all muddy and scraped both knees, Eli brought me my glasses. He said he found them, but I know he stole them back from Kinsey. He seems really quiet this year. I heard someone say

*his dad ran away with the babysitter. I'm glad I don't
have a dad.*

Also, I still hate everyone here but him.

Love,

Brynn

BRYNN WAS WORKING her way through her stack of chocolate chip pancakes, trying not to moan with pleasure with every single bite. How in the world had she lived her entire life without midnight chocolate chip pancakes? When she finished, she nearly licked her plate, and would have . . . except a guy came into the room.

He was massive. Six and a half feet of solid muscle. Clearly just out of bed, dark hair sticking up in an oddly endearing fashion, dark eyes at half-mast, and a whole bunch of dark skin covered only by a pair of basketball shorts, tats, and nipple piercings. He had a T-shirt in one big hand, which he shrugged into as he entered the kitchen, sniffing the pancake-laden air appreciatively. He came up behind Kinsey, where she was eating standing up at the island. Got right into her space, his chest to her back, and rubbed his jaw to hers. Then he swatted her playfully on the ass, ending with a palm squeeze.

Deck, she presumed.

"Hey," Kinsey said. "Hands off the merchandise."

"That's not what you were saying a few minutes ago." He took her fork and helped himself to a bite. "Were you seriously not going to wake me for Eli's pancakes?"

Kinsey snatched her fork back.

Brynn goggled at this domestic display.

Max didn't. "Wouldn't mind having my ass slapped," he said a little woefully.

Deck slapped his ass.

Max grinned at him. "Thanks."

"Anytime."

"This here is Deck," Eli told Brynn. "He's Kinsey's—" He broke off and looked at Deck.

"Don't look at me," the guy said, accepting a stack of pancakes on his own plate from Eli that was so tall, surely no single human could eat it. "You know she gets hives if you put a label on it."

"I do not," Kinsey said.

"Yeah?" Deck took a big bite, chewed, swallowed. "Then label me. Boy Toy? Best Lover You've Ever Had?"

"How about Pain in My Ass."

"Aw," Deck said with a grin, not appearing the least bit insulted. "Sweet."

Kinsey rolled her eyes and went to the fridge, grabbing a cranberry juice before going still. "Hey, there's a piece missing from my chocolate lava cake."

Eli raised his hand.

"That cake's mine," she said.

"She's cranky when she's not getting her beauty sleep," Eli said to Deck.

"No shit," Deck said.

Kinsey's eyes were narrowed. "A mom of one of the kids at the middle school made that cake for me."

"It's massive," Eli said. "You're not sharing?"

"Let me repeat. *Chocolate lava cake.*"

"Thought I was your best friend," Eli said.

"You are, but touch my chocolate lava cake again and I'll murder you in your sleep."

"I remember like six months ago coming home with that whole big basket of mini muffins," Eli said. "I went to bed, and when I woke up, you'd mowed through all the good ones."

"Hey, that basket came to you by way of some rando chick at a work party. You didn't even know her name. She could've been a stalker for all you know. I was merely taste-testing for you. You're welcome."

"Wow." Eli flipped some more pancakes. "Just when you think you know someone . . ."

"Just stay out of my cake," Kinsey said.

Brynn was fascinated by the easy comradery between them all. They were close and comfortable with each other in a way she couldn't say she'd ever been with anyone. Thinking about that, she pushed her glasses up farther on her nose . . . at the exact moment that Kinsey did the same thing.

Max snorted.

Kinsey glared at him.

Max just shook his head.

Okay, there was either an odd dynamic going on, or Brynn was missing a whole bunch. Like take Deck and Kinsey. If Brynn went off just their words to each other, she'd have said they were a one-night stand. But Kinsey was wearing Deck's shirt, and Deck clearly liked that. And then there was the way they looked at each other. Or at least the way Deck looked at Kinsey, with warmth and genuine affection.

But she realized that Kinsey was looking at Deck too, but only when she thought no one was watching.

Brynn had no idea why she'd hide it. If she had someone as into her as Deck appeared to be, she'd . . . well, she'd probably screw things up like she always did.

"How's the arm?" Deck asked Max.

Max flexed his arm, rolled his shoulder. "Better."

"Max wiped out on his surfboard a few weeks back," Eli explained to Brynn. "Tore some ligaments. Deck's a nurse at the hospital and was on the night I dragged Max's whiney ass in."

Deck grinned. "That was a fun night."

"Hey." Max pointed a fork at both of the other men. "I did *not* whine."

"Ah, man, you *so* whined," Deck said. "And then you passed out when you got a steroid injection. Bounced your head off the floor and gave yourself a concussion. We admitted you for the night, and then you mooned all the nurses when you got up in the morning."

Max sighed. "Those hospitals gowns suck, man. You try dragging an IV stand around and holding the back of the stupid gown together at the same time."

"I only moon people who *want* to see my ass." Deck flashed a grin at Kinsey.

She pointed at him. "Finish your damn pancakes and get out."

Deck just laughed. He'd cleaned his plate. But he grabbed one more pancake, rolled it, and took a bite. He winked at

Kinsey, bent for a quick but hot-looking kiss, and then walked out the back door, eating his pancake.

Kinsey watched him go. Well, she watched his butt go, and Brynn got it. The guy had an exceptional butt.

"You kicked him out of bed?" Max asked.

"He takes up all the space."

"And?"

"And *I* like to take up all the space."

Max just shook his head and ambled off, presumably back to his room.

Brynn hopped off the counter to do the same, but stopped at the sink to wash dishes.

"What are you doing?" Eli asked.

"You cooked—again—so I'm washing."

Eli looked at Kinsey. "You see that? *That's* a good roommate."

"Hey, you explicitly forbade me to do the dishes ever again."

"That's because you throw away the silverware instead of washing them."

"That was an accident." Kinsey yawned and pushed away from the island, wobbling for a minute. Eli quickly set down the pan he was carrying to the sink and grabbed her, sliding an arm around her.

"I'm fine." But for a single beat Kinsey set her head on his shoulder and accepted the hug. Then she pushed away and walked out of the room.

Brynn sent a silent question Eli's way, but he just shook his head.

"She gets vertigo."

They all had a role here, she realized. And Eli's role was the glue. He nudged Brynn over and took on the dishwasher role, letting her dry, directing her where to put everything away.

It was a comfortable silence between them, but there was something underlying the ease, she realized, watching him efficiently wash the dishes. He had a way of moving, his muscles bunching and releasing beneath his T-shirt, that sent a zing through her body, putting it on high alert. The good kind of high alert.

Which was not good at all, but bad.

Not making any decisions right now, remember?

"Deep thoughts?" he asked.

"No. Ignore me."

His gaze held hers. "That's going to be hard to do."

She stared back at him. "I . . . should tell you something."

"Besides the fact that you're not allowing yourself to make any decisions right now?"

"I think I should also be off men."

"Forever?"

"I don't know." She grimaced, because she knew herself. "No. Not forever."

He gave a single nod. "Noted."

She nodded too. "All righty, then." *All righty, then?* What the hell was wrong with her? "Good night."

"'Night. Oh, and, Brynn?"

She turned back to him.

His eyes were no longer just amused, but also heated. "You'll let me know if that changes."

"The decision-making thing?"

He smiled. "The 'off men' part."

BRYNN SPENT THE remaining hours of the night tossing rest-lessly, and not sure why. She loved this big, old, creaky house. Loved having her window open so she could hear the waves rhythmically hitting the beach. Loved that her roommates sometimes ate chocolate chip pancakes at midnight.

Loved that she'd been brave enough to agree to staying here, even if she worried that, like most of her other recent decisions, it would turn out to be a bad one.

She remembered how Eli had looked at her in the kitchen when they'd been alone, and how just that had changed the rhythm of her heart . . . Yeah. She was worried that he'd gotten under her skin in the very best of ways.

When her alarm went off, she groaned and got out of bed to get ready for day one of the rest of her life. Thanks to her open window, the room was chilly, but she liked that. Nothing in here belonged to her other than the duffel bag on the chair in the corner, but somehow she felt more at home than she had in a long time. She grabbed a sundress and cropped cardigan from the duffel, showered and dressed, and then left the room.

Kinsey stood in the kitchen in front of the opened fridge, frowning.

"Morning," Brynn said.

Kinsey grabbed some juice before turning to eyeball Brynn, then immediately squeezing her eyes shut with a pained look. "Jeez, I need sunglasses just to look at you."

Brynn looked down. Okay, so her dress was a very bright and sunshiny yellow, but she thought it'd seem cheery to the kids. "Should I change?"

Kinsey shut the fridge and sighed. "Like kicking a puppy," she muttered. Then she shook her head. "No, you shouldn't change. You should tell me to go to hell, that you're wearing what you damn well want to wear and you don't care what I think."

Brynn's backbone snapped straight. "You're right." And oh, how she hated that. "Go to hell. I'm wearing what I want to wear and I don't care what you think. And you know what else? Roommate rule number two—you have to say something nice for every *not* nice thing you say."

Kinsey blinked. "What's roommate rule number one?"

"No walking around naked."

Kinsey blinked again. Then she tossed what looked like a palmful of pills into her mouth and chased it with a glass of water.

"Vitamins?"

"They're my superpower pills," Kinsey said.

"Fine." Brynn shook her head. "Not sure why I thought things might be different." She headed to the door.

"Different how?" Kinsey asked.

"I don't know, maybe with you being sweeter and kinder."

Kinsey stared at her for a beat. "Those traits aren't exactly in my wheelhouse."

"No kidding."

Kinsey took in Brynn's outfit and appeared to squelch a grimace. "Um, okay. So . . . I like your bracelet."

Brynn was wearing a thin leather cord with a silver charm that said: BE STRONGER THAN THE STORM. "Thanks," she said, surprised at the compliment.

"So are you really going to wear sneakers to work?" Kinsey asked, and when Brynn just stared at her, she shrugged, palms up. "What? You said I have to say something nice first, so I did. I said I liked your bracelet."

Brynn sighed and looked down at her adorable favorite white sneaks. She started to second-guess her choice, but then narrowed her eyes. "I'm wearing what I want to wear and I don't care what you think."

Kinsey lifted her glass of water in a toast—granted it was also with a cynical smirk—and Brynn yanked open the door.

"Oh, and who walks around naked?" Kinsey wanted to know.

"Your roommates."

Kinsey's jaw dropped. "You saw Max and Eli naked?"

Brynn just shut the door on her, pleased with herself for once having the last word. Or lack of the last word . . .

At the school, Brynn was given the keys to her classroom and sent on her way without much fanfare. Two minutes later, she stood at the front of her classroom—*gulp*—staring at thirty-two little five-year-olds. She had them sit in a semicircle facing her and asked them to take turns telling her their name and a fun fact. She pointed to the girl on her left wearing a bunch of ponytails to go first.

"I'm Cindy," she said, jumping to her feet. "My dad thinks farting is funny, but my mom doesn't."

"Okay," Brynn said, biting back a laugh. "Thank you."

The girl in glasses next to Cindy was bouncing in place with excitement.

"I'm Tabitha. Sometimes in the middle of the night, my mommy yells at my daddy to go faster."

Brynn chewed on the inside of her mouth. "Interesting. Thank you."

Next was a little boy missing both front teeth. "I'm Toby. The tooth fairy gives me different amounts of money depending on whether I'm at my mom's or at my dad's house. Why would that happen?"

"Uh . . ." Brynn racked her brain. "Maybe the tooth fairy sells the teeth and demand fluctuates depending on which house it comes from?"

Toby processed this answer and put his hand down.

Huh. That actually worked.

Just then, Kinsey popped her head into the classroom, and there was an immediate chorus of "Hi, Ms. Davis!" telling Brynn that as unsociable as Kinsey had been with her, she was the opposite with the kids, who all genuinely appeared to love her.

Toby ran to Kinsey and hugged her tight before racing back to the circle.

"Deck's kid," Kinsey explained.

Brynn moved to the door for privacy. "I'm boggled."

"What, that I'd stop by and see you?"

"That the kids adore you."

Kinsey actually laughed. *Note to self: All you have to do to keep the new roommate in line is out-bitch the bitch.* "Thought we had to say something nice for every not nice thing."

"You're right," Brynn said. "Your clothes are amazing." She paused, let a beat of time go by. "But *why* do the kids adore you?"

Kinsey shrugged. "Maybe they know something you don't."

Yeah, and that was what was bugging her. How was it that she brought out the worst in this woman, someone others clearly loved and adored? There was no point in asking. Kinsey wouldn't answer. Hell, she probably didn't know the answer. "What can I do for you, Ms. Davis?"

"Nothing. Just wanted to see if you were drowning."

"Sorry to disappoint."

Kinsey blew a kiss at the kids and walked off.

"You and Ms. Davis kinda look alike," Tabitha said when Brynn moved back to the share circle.

Brynn glanced at the window to catch her reflection. Stilled. Then pushed her glasses up. They did sort of look alike. How annoying was that?

 CHAPTER 10

From twelve-year-old Kinsey's summer camp journal:

Dear Journal,

Ugh. Sometimes I wonder if you hate our times together as much as I do. I've got a fever, so I'm stuck in the nurse's cabin and not allowed to be near any of the others in case I'm contagious. The counselor said she called my mom to come get me. Good luck, lady. She's with her latest dumbass at some music festival. No way she's going to give that up.

Eli snuck in last night after dark. He's got every girl here stupid over him, but I decided to forgive him for that because he had forbidden snacks with him.

Hate you,
Kinsey

"Breathe, Kinsey."

She did, but not because Deck was telling her to. She breathed because she needed air to tell him exactly what she thought of him right then. "You suck."

"That's it," he said in his low, gravelly voice, the one she found so sexy. He stroked a big, callused hand up and down her arm. "Only one more poke."

"I hate this," she gritted out.

"I know."

"And right now I hate you."

"I know that too."

She sighed and kept her eyes squeezed shut while Deck hooked her up for dialysis.

"Find a good memory to replay," he said.

That was his trick, teaching her to pretend she was somewhere else.

"Remember the bluffs," he said.

A few weeks ago, he'd driven her to the beach. Most people parked there and went to the sand. But there were walking trails all over the hills, one leading straight to the top.

Kinsey got winded too quickly to use the trails, and for what had seemed like forever now, she'd felt like she had the flu. Tired. Nauseous. Off.

There was no way she could get to the top under her own steam. So Deck had four-wheeled her up in his off-road vehicle. Without saying a word or making her feel incapable, he'd carefully buckled her in, checked her helmet, made sure her face mask was in place to keep out dust.

And then he'd given her a hell of a ride. But not the ride of her life. That had come later that night when they'd been in his bed.

She grinned at the memory. Deck had always made a point of spending their time doing things that thrilled her. It was glorious.

He was glorious.

But he wasn't hers. Not to keep anyway.

"Done," Deck said calmly. "You can open your eyes now."

Little-known fact: She had a needle phobia, which made dialysis a form of torture. She had a fistula implanted just beneath the skin on the inside of her left biceps, which made things a lot easier, but it still required two needle pokes each time, one for incoming blood, one for outgoing.

She wasn't a fan.

She was currently sitting on her usual corner cot of the dialysis clinic, which was attached to the small but efficient Wildstone hospital. She was grateful for both the clinic and the staff, as without them, she'd have to drive a hundred miles each way to the next-closest dialysis center.

So maybe she didn't hate the procedure as much as she wished things were different. A wish she'd been wishing for fourteen years.

Friends was playing on the small screen hanging on the wall. Season five, the episode where drunk Rachel and drunk Ross accidentally get drunk married in Vegas.

Deck had put it on. He wasn't a fan of sitcoms, much less ones from the '90s, but knew she loved them, so he always had something good playing for her.

"Okay?" he murmured, squeezing her hand, his dark eyes on hers.

"Yeah." She managed a smile. "Thanks. I don't really hate you."

"Oh, I know."

She blushed. Like actually *blushed*. To hide that, she rolled her eyes. She was the only patient in the clinic today, which she liked. It gave her some alone time, which she needed. It also meant that she had one hundred percent of Deck's attention, which she also liked. He was the first and only person in her life who could make her feel like she was an amazing person. Yes, she had Max and Eli, and they'd do anything for her, she knew this, but they also had each other.

She had no one. But being with Deck made her feel far less . . . alone. She squeezed his fingers.

With a grin, he leaned over her and brushed his sexy mouth to her temple. The feel of his thick stubble gave her a cheap thrill.

"You haven't even asked me what today's reward for being a good girl is," he rumbled into her ear.

"It better be a chocolate bar."

"Aim higher."

"An entire case of chocolate bars."

Deck shook his head. "Higher."

She met those dark, heated eyes, doing her best to ignore the feeling that the dialysis machine was slowly taking over her body. That wasn't what was really happening, of course, but the sensation remained. "Is this a present for me, or you?"

He grinned. "Getting closer." He leaned in again and nipped

her earlobe. "You get to go first." He kissed the spot he'd just bitten. "And last."

She smiled, because they both knew she always got hers first and last—he made sure of it.

"You've been scarce this week," he said.

"Well, not totally scarce . . ."

They both smiled now, remembering the other night before the midnight pancakes.

"Want to have a late lunch with me?" she asked. "I've got half an hour between afternoon meetings."

"Wanna have you for lunch."

Her good parts quivered. "It'd have to be . . . *fast* food."

His smile was slow and dirty. "I do some of my best work under pressure."

As she well knew.

He crouched at her side, checking the lines and the machine. "So . . . tell me what you're not telling me."

She stared at him. "How do you always know?"

He shrugged. "Just do."

She could fool everyone but him. Which was annoying, but also . . . a secret thrill. "Just busy with work."

"Why are you lying to me? That's against the rules."

Yes, they had rules. Hers being simple. They were friends with benefits minus the friends part, because he wasn't allowed to fall in love with her. He was just the good-time guy.

His rules weren't nearly as simple. She wasn't to hide from him, not how she felt, or what was happening with her health, nothing. And then there was the doozy—she wasn't to lie to him. Ever. "I'm not lying," she said.

"You're omitting then. Something's wrong, something's bugging you. Is it your new roommate? Is it because you two used to go to the same summer camp?"

She drew a deep breath. "No. But Brynn's not just my old summer camp cabin mate and new roommate. She's also . . . my half sister."

Deck raised a pierced brow.

"Yeah," she said. "Shock, right?"

"I thought you were an only child. It was just you and your mom, and the myriad of assholes she brought into your life, the ones you won't give me their names so I can go beat the shit out of them for what they did to you."

"Okay, first, only one of them ever bothered with me, and it's not like he laid a hand on me. He was just mean with his words. Big deal."

"Not all wounds are physical, Kins."

She closed her eyes. He was right. Way too right. But she didn't want to think about it, much less talk about it. "Brynn's not my mom's daughter. She's my father's."

"The con artist guy who lived with you and your mom on and off until she found out he'd been cheating on her?"

"That's the one."

He took this in for a stunned beat. "How long have you known?"

She squirmed. "Since I was fifteen and went looking for my dad's relatives."

He absorbed that and shook his head. "How long has Brynn known?"

"She doesn't."

He arched a brow. "Are you serious right now? You never told her."

"No."

"How is that fair to her?" he asked quietly.

"Obviously, it's not."

"Kins."

She met his dark eyes, filled with things that hurt. But also hope, for her.

"You've got a half sister," he said. "You know what that means."

"That there's a good shot she's every bit as charming and gracious as I am?"

He snorted. "Don't forgot obstinate and impossible."

He never held back, another thing she loved. "I'm not going to tell her, Deck."

He frowned. "Why the hell not?"

"Because I don't want her to think I want her kidney."

"Not want. *Need.*"

"Not going to happen."

"Kins—"

"Ever, Deck. *Never* ever."

He stroked her arm in the way he did when he wanted her to calm herself, lower her blood pressure and heart rate, giving absolutely zero indication that he was disappointed in her.

But she knew he was.

Deck was a man who marched to his own beat, and though

he played fast and loose with things like rules and expectations, he had a strong moral code. He was as badass as they came, and yet he was an amazing dad to his son, Toby, took care of other people for a living, and believed in the truth, *always*.

"You're quiet," she said. "Which means you've got things to say."

He gave a single shake of his head. "If you don't tell her and she finds out some other way . . ."

She winced. "You think I don't know that?"

"Then why not just put it out there? You're too stubborn to take her kidney, so there's no reason *not* to tell her."

"I hate it when you're more reasonable and logical than me." She rubbed her temples. "Eli's on me about it too. Plus, he likes her."

"*Likes* her likes her?"

"I think so, yeah."

He studied her face. "And you have a problem with that. Are you . . . jealous?"

"No." She put her hand in his. "No," she repeated more softly. "You know I'm not. I've never felt that way toward Eli, nor does he feel that way for me. Besides, I've got you." She smiled. "And frankly, you're more than I can handle on most days."

He laughed that sexy laugh and squeezed her hand.

"I just worry about him falling for someone who isn't necessarily sticking here. What if this is just a pit stop for her, a rebound?"

"You don't like her," he said.

"Actually, I think she's fucking adorable, and adventurous, and exactly the right person to break through Eli's walls. As well as the exact right person to break his heart. He's had enough of that for a lifetime, Deck."

He nodded and fell quiet for a minute, giving her hope that he'd leave it alone. She should've known better.

"I didn't know my mom and dad," he finally said.

Her heart clutched. He'd been adopted by an elderly couple who both passed away when he was a teen. A troubled teen. He'd then had a very rough, very short-lived marriage with Toby's mom, and by some miracle he'd managed to make joint custody work. He'd not had an easy go of things ever, and she knew that was because he'd felt like he had no one who wanted to claim him as their own.

"If I found a sibling," he went on quietly, "I'd move heaven and earth to keep them in my life."

She sighed. "I'm going to tell her."

"Before she runs off on you because she doesn't know she has ties here? Come on, Kins, she deserves to know."

"I get that. Eli's been all over my case as well. I'm . . . working my way up to it."

"I call bullshit on that. When you want something, you make it happen. Which means you just plain don't want to make this happen. But for the life of me, I don't get why."

"Hey," she said. "Eli's the one who brought her home like a lost puppy. I was fine not having her in my life."

"Now you're actually lying right to my face." He stood and

turned to walk away. He had other things to do, she got that. They overworked everyone here because they were so under-staffed. "Seriously?" she said to his back. "I thought you'd be on my side."

"Maybe I only side with people who let me spend the night."

Ah. Their age-old argument. She narrowed her eyes. "What about people who give you all the orgasms?"

"You know what? Don't bring me into this. We're just friends with benefits minus the friends part. I'm just the good-time guy for you, remember?" And when she just stared at him, he shook his head and vanished.

She was still brooding when Eli walked in a few minutes later. "See you've managed to piss off the un-boyfriend."

"Don't you start." She let her head fall back so she could stare up at the ceiling. There was a divot in the far-left ceiling tile, and for longer than she could remember, she'd wondered how it'd gotten there. Had someone levitated? Or thrown their annoying-as-shit nurse? Or their so-called un-boyfriend, perhaps?

"It's been days and you still haven't talked to her," Eli said.

She turned her head and slid him a look. "What, are you and Deck a gang now?"

Eli didn't let her derail the conversation. "*Why* haven't you told her?"

"I don't know, Eli, why haven't you told her that you've got a hard-on for her?"

"Stop," he said quietly.

"Stop what?"

"You always try to shove people away when you're frustrated."

"And yet it rarely works, because here you still are," she said wearily.

He ran a hand down her arm. "Go to sleep, Kinsey. You look exhausted."

"*You* look exhausted," she muttered, knowing she sounded like a three-year-old, but she was so tired of her life being beyond her own control that she couldn't stop herself.

When she opened her eyes, she realized by the daylight slanting into the room that a few hours had gone by. She'd actually slept, no bad dreams about dying and floating in gray matter for the rest of eternity—she wasn't sure what she believed about the afterlife, though she *was* one hundred percent certain she'd find out far before she wanted to—no waking up to a panic attack and not being able to put her finger on which of her problems had caused it. No shakiness, no urge to throw up.

"What are you smiling about?"

She realized Eli was still sitting there next to her. "I like napping," she said. "It's like being dead without the commitment."

He didn't smile. He always smiled at her commentary, so she now lost her grin. "What?"

"*Tell her.*"

She sighed. "You do realize that when I do, she's going to get mad at both of us and leave, right? Then who will you moon after?"

Eli stood up and then bent low to brush a kiss to her cheek. "You're so brave, Kinsey. Don't run from this, one of the really great things to happen to you." And then he was gone.

BEING WITH KINDERGARTENERS all day every day was teaching Brynn a lot. Such as the importance of tightening the lids on all the paint bottles when they put them away, so that the next day, when they shook them, they didn't spray the entire room. Or how five-year-olds felt every emotion loudly and publicly.

And that patience was nothing more than an illusion.

Or a delusion.

She'd also learned that no matter how careful she was, by the end of the day she'd be covered in at least *some* of that paint and food, and a whole bunch of disturbing other things, making her a walking, talking germ vestibule.

But mostly she'd learned . . . she loved teaching little kids.

They looked at the world differently. They were marveled by everything, curious, happy . . . honest.

It was the end of her first week back in Wildstone and still early morning. She went downstairs to the kitchen to grab the breakfast and lunch she'd made herself ahead of time so she could sleep an extra ten minutes—yes, she'd finally gone grocery shopping—and found the entire gang.

They'd all shared a few dinners, and had spent a couple of evenings together, one playing a vicious game of Pictionary on the porch, which had ended with Kinsey throwing her pad of paper at Max; the other, they'd all sat on the beach watching the sunset.

Since that first night, Max had been a perfect gentleman. Kinsey had been . . . muted, but pretty much her usual sarcastic self. And Eli . . . well, if anything, the days had only ramped up the tension between the two of them. A sexual tension, one she had absolutely no idea what to do with. And since nothing had happened, she could only assume he didn't either. Except . . . that didn't feel right. Eli wasn't an unsure man. He was confident, capable, and strong-willed. If he wanted her, there was a reason he was holding back.

She wasn't sure what to make of that.

Now Max stood at the coffee maker in nothing but board shorts, pushing buttons on the machine and swearing. Kinsey was eating a piece of toast and speaking in a professional work voice into her phone, dressed to perfection as always in a suit dress and strappy heels that Brynn would die for—if she had a shoe budget. Which she did not.

Eli stood in front of the opened fridge in a suit, orange juice in one hand, a tie fisted in the other. She'd seen him in everyday clothes and she'd seen him in nothing. And now she'd seen him in a suit, so she felt uniquely qualified to say he *always* looked good.

He didn't move or speak, just cut his eyes to her.

Max looked up from the coffee machine and laughed. "Dilemma, bro?"

Brynn felt confused until Kinsey, who'd finished her call, looked over. "Whenever you see him standing blankly in front of the fridge like that, he's dealing with low blood sugar. It dulls his thought processes and slows him down. I'm pretty sure he was just about to drink right out of the OJ bottle for a quick sugar fix, but now that you're here, he can't. His manners have kicked in."

"Wait," Brynn said. "So it's okay to drink from the container if I'm *not* looking?"

Kinsey snorted. "No one ever told you that you had normal roommates. With two of them being of the male species, you had to know the odds were stacked against you."

"Yeah, *we're* the not-normal ones," Max muttered as Eli put the OJ back on the fridge shelf.

"Don't hold yourself back on my account," Brynn said. "I don't drink OJ."

He pulled the OJ off the shelf and tipped his head back for a long drink. She watched him swallow, thinking it should be illegal for a guy to look that good in everything. *And nothing.* "It's going to be hard to go scuba diving in that, isn't it?" she asked.

He grinned at her. He was the first guy to actually like her smart-ass side. "I've got to testify in court today on a case about a gas leak into the marina by a service station."

"Our local expert," Max said proudly.

"Don't be impressed," Eli told Brynn. "I'm just the only one in my department who owns a suit."

Kinsey gave a rare laugh. "And don't be impressed by that either. He can't tie his own tie. So . . . settle a bet for us. You haven't unpacked your duffel bag. Why?"

Brynn's heart skipped a beat. She'd assumed no one had noticed. "It's only been a few days."

"A week, but yeah, *exactly*," Kinsey muttered oddly to both Max and Eli. Then to Brynn, she said, "Also, where's all your other stuff?"

Her pulse kicked into gear at the thought of her secret shame. Her palms began to sweat, but with some hard-won effort, she left her expression dialed to neutral. "How do you know I even have other things? Maybe I just live light."

"Doubtful, since you used to come to summer camp with two huge suitcases filled to the brim."

"Things change." Brynn's hands went onto her hips and she looked around. "Do we have a problem?"

"We've got a bet," Kinsey said. "There's twenty bucks on the line and I want it."

Brynn looked at Eli.

"Not me," he said, and eyed the others, looking pissed off. "Leave her alone."

Max lifted his hands. "Hey, I just thought it'd be an easy twenty bucks."

Brynn felt irritated, but she knew that was her shame at what she'd allowed to happen to her. Didn't stop her from saying, "Maybe I have *lots* of stuff. Maybe I just haven't fully decided on you guys, that's all."

"Aha! I win!" Max held out his hand, palm up, to Kinsey. "Pay up."

"No way," Kinsey said, and looked at Brynn. "And hey, we're a delight."

Eli laughed, and the weird tension was defused. Brynn even laughed too, but that was because Eli's laugh was contagious.

"Look, it's no big mystery," she said. *Such a fib.* "I've just been busy this week. My driver's license needed renewing, and my moms had stuff they needed me to do, and the teacher I'm subbing for didn't leave me a lesson plan, which means I'm creating a curriculum as I go, and it's taking a lot of time."

Max wiggled his fingers at Kinsey, who sighed and grabbed her purse off the counter.

"Hey," Brynn said.

They all looked at her.

"I want in on the next bet."

Eli grinned like he was proud of her, flashing a dimple and everything. And she might be a strong, independent woman— or at least she was working on it—which meant she didn't need his or anyone's approval, but it also didn't mean it couldn't feel good to get it.

"You need to get going," Kinsey reminded Eli.

They all looked at the tie crumpled in his hand.

"Shit," he said. "I'd rather get stung by a jellyfish again than wear this."

"Pretty please try to tie it on again," Kinsey said. "That was a fun show to watch."

Brynn set down her things and took the tie. Going up on her tiptoes to get it around his neck, she dropped the ends of the tie to lift his shirt collar. When her fingers touched his throat and encountered warm skin, she went still and forgot to breathe.

He was watching her from all of two inches away, and it was . . . shockingly arousing. Enough to fog her glasses. He hadn't shaved and his scruff scraped at her knuckles, and also at a few other body parts that were thankfully hidden away. She had to take off her fogged glasses, but somehow she still managed to button the top two buttons of his shirt and then work on the tie, keeping her eyes studiously on her own fingers and what she was doing, all while incredibly aware of the way she could feel his warm breath against her temple. They were toe to toe, and nearly chest to chest. If she so much as breathed deeply, there'd be contact.

Please let there be contact, her body whispered to her brain.

Her brain, clearly not on the same no-decision moratorium, approved, and she took a deep breath, her breasts leading the way, gently bumping into him.

"Sorry," she whispered.

His hands went to her hips and he shook his head, maybe meaning no need for the apology. She felt drunk from inhaling his clean, sexy scent, all of which somehow made the moment even more memorable than that long-ago kiss they still hadn't talked about.

"There," she croaked, finally finishing the knot on the tie, giving it a pat.

Eli's eyes held hers and warmed. And then Kinsey of course had to ruin it.

"Jesus," she said. "Get a room."

 CHAPTER 11

From thirteen-year-old Brynn's summer camp journal:

Dear Moms,

This year's veggie is carrots and they're candied, so the good news is that I'm going to live. The bad news is that I'm ONCE AGAIN in the same cabin as Kinsey. They say it's coincidence, but I know it's because I can't see at night and she's always sick, and they put us together so only one counselor has to miss the fun nighttime stuff.
AND IT GETS WORSE!
There's this cute guy named Sam, and he asked me to sit next to him at dinner. I did my hair in that cute braid you guys taught me. But then he didn't even show up. So rude! I went back to the cabin and guess what? Kinsey was there, all pissy too.
Turns out, he told us both he'd sit with us, and then didn't show for either of us! She was crying. I wasn't.

Okay, I was.

I hate boys.

And before you ask, Kinsey told me I wasn't Sam's type, she was, *so I still hate her too. I'd say come get me, but I know you're in Santa Barbara taking that art class, so just send food.*

Love you,
Brynn

THE NEXT MORNING Brynn showered, dressed, and then sat on her bed, taking care of a little business on her phone. She hadn't been kidding when she'd told Eli she'd had a bunch of odd jobs in college. One of them had been working the front desk at a funeral parlor. It'd been a little macabre for her, but she'd made enough money to keep her in peanut butter and jelly sandwiches. Plus she'd gained a good friend in one of her coworkers. She'd texted Jenny the day after she'd learned about Eli's grandma and how the poor woman's remains were stuck in limbo. It'd hurt to hear the story, so she could only imagine how badly Eli hurt.

Jenny had finally gotten back to her with the information Brynn hoped could help her fix the problem. Thanking her via text, she then made the phone call she needed to make, and hoped it would work. Then she headed into the kitchen, and found the usual crowd—plus one. Eli, Max, Kinsey, Deck, and . . . little five-year-old Toby from her class.

They were all watching while Toby gave a demonstration of his shoe-tying skills—something she'd taught him in class yesterday. He was squatted low over his foot, dark head bent, tongue in the space where his two front teeth had been, as he concentrated, whispering the steps she'd taught him beneath his breath—"Bunny ears, bunny ears, jumped into the hole"— his fingers moving with awkward slowness.

A painful two full minutes later, Toby finally tightened his lopsided bow and jumped up. "See? I did it!"

"Nice going, little man," Deck said, and scooped up Toby into his beefy arms. He was wearing gym shorts and a T-shirt, both revealing a lot of his body art. "You've had a full morning. A gym workout *and* a new skill." He mouthed a "thanks" to Brynn and then turned to Kinsey. "Ready, babe?"

Kinsey sighed and grabbed her bag. "I told you Eli could have driven me today. You and the cutie pie didn't have to swing by and get me."

"*We* wanted to," Deck said, looking at Kinsey with the same amount of love and affection as when he looked at his son.

"See you at school, Ms. Turner!" Toby yelled, and then the three of them were gone.

"I'm hitting the shower," Max said.

And then it was just her and Eli. His hair still wet from his shower, he was in another suit, looking far too good for her mental health. His expression was unreadable, but warming at the sight of her.

And something within her did the same. Whenever she was with him, she felt the odd and opposing emotions of safety and . . . danger.

"Morning," he said.

Just one word, and yet it felt like a lot more.

She smiled, moved to the fridge, and eyed the contents. Mini sat at Eli's feet, mirroring his stance while also staring intently into the fridge.

His tie was draped uselessly around his neck, and since wondering what was happening between them wasn't getting her anywhere, she closed the gap. Shut the fridge. Lifting her hands to the tie, she accidentally locked eyes with him and then couldn't tear herself away. His hands came up to her waist, every bit as heated as his gaze as he squeezed and . . . tickled her.

The squeal was utterly involuntary, and she was laughing when she shoved his hands away and knotted his tie, at the last minute snugging it up to his throat tighter than necessary.

"Feeling playful?" he asked, voice low and husky.

Well, she was most definitely feeling *something*. And to prove it, she tightened the tie a little bit more. "Maybe," she murmured. "You?"

He stepped into her, and she found herself back against the fridge, held there by a hundred and eighty pounds of outrageously sexy male, both of her arms imprisoned between their bodies, her hands still holding on to his tie.

Not his hands though. They were free, and he slid them up her arms and playfully encircled her neck, his thumbs gently gliding over the hollow of her throat. "Maybe 'playful' isn't the right word."

"No?" she asked a little breathlessly. "What is?"

He smiled a very naughty smile, and she was grateful he was holding her up.

"Brynn?"

"Yeah?"

"There's something I've been wanting to do all week."

"Oh? What's that?"

"First, a question."

Her heart had already started pounding, but now it skipped a beat. "Okay."

"I want to kiss you."

She stared at his mouth. "That's not a question."

Those warm, callused hands of his slowly cupped her jaw now, and the pad of a work-roughened thumb rasped over her lower lip. "May I?"

She felt a smile curve her lips. Because that's exactly how she'd asked him once upon a time when she'd wanted her first kiss. "I'm getting déjà vu," she said.

He smiled. "So you do remember."

"The kiss? Yes. It was nice."

He choked. *"Nice?"*

"Well, it was a long time ago," she said demurely.

"Hmm. Let me refresh your memory." He slid his fingers into her hair and she moaned softly. "Is that a yes, Brynn?"

For a single beat, she tried to remember the deal she'd made with herself. To avoid screwups and mistakes and hurting the people she cared about, she wasn't going to make any decisions. No interfering in anyone's life; she was going to let them continue down their own path.

But it's just a kiss, a little voice deep inside her head said.

Eli was waiting for her answer; he was steady, quiet, but also giving off enough testosterone and pheromones to make her light-headed. As did the way he was looking at her like her answer mattered to him. *She* mattered. *"Yes,"* she whispered, overriding her own good sense, her fingers curling into the material of his shirt.

His hands were making slow, sensual passes up and down her back. "You're sure?"

In answer, she tugged his head down and planted one on him. No slouch, his arms tightened around her and he deepened the kiss, making her instantly forget everything but this, him. With the cool fridge at her back and a very hot man at her front, she lost herself in the hungry kiss, in the way his mouth on hers felt both rough and tender. She heard a moan and was startled to realize it was her. "Okay, so still pretty nice," she managed when he lifted his head.

He gave a rough laugh of agreement.

She looked down, surprised to find that their clothes were still on, that they hadn't gone up in smoke, and that only a few moments had gone by. She had a hand cupping his butt and another stroking the curve of his jaw, his stubble scraping against the pads of her fingers. She pulled her hands back and swallowed hard. "You've got some new moves."

"Better than 'nice.'"

She let out a shaky laugh. "Just a little bit."

"I don't know how you do this to me." He rested his forehead on hers while they both steadied their breath. "Make me forget everything but you."

"I thought it was you doing that to me," she said.

She felt his warm exhale on her temple as he pressed a kiss to her brow. "I'm sending you to work now," he said.

"Because you don't know what to do with me?"

"Trust me," he said, eyes hot. "I know *exactly* what I want to do with you." His mouth made its way up her jaw to her ear. "It's just that unless you're willing to call in sick, we don't have nearly enough time. Because I've got plans for you, Brynn, and I'm going to need hours."

Her knees got a little wobbly at that. No one had ever spent hours on her pleasure. She herself only needed about twelve minutes . . . "I'm not sure we should go there."

"Because you're off men."

She took a deep breath. "It's more that every time I'm . . . with someone I like, my life ends up imploding."

"So . . . you like me."

She laughed. "Listen to what I'm saying. You should be running from the inevitable implosion that *this* would cause you."

"Define 'this.'"

She shook her head. "You just want me to say the words."

"Yes. Use the words. Use the dirtiest words possible."

She laughed again. "Be serious. We're not going to be stupid."

"You're not even close to stupid, and neither am I. We're two smart adults who have an insane attraction to each other, while at the same time having pasts that make *this* terrifying." He cocked his head. "How am I doing?"

"Nailed it."

Again he cupped her face. "I'm trying to respect the fact that you've put yourself in a time-out," he said softly. "You haven't unpacked, or brought in more than a single duffel bag."

She started to open her mouth, then shut it.

He watched her for a beat. "I know you've been hurt, and I hate that for you, but no one's going to hurt you here. I hope you get that. You're safe here, Brynn."

She bit her lower lip. "I know." And she was getting more than that as well. The other night while watching the sunset with everyone on the beach, Max had made the joke that the three of them—him, Eli, and Kinsey—were wounded birds, watching one another's backs, being one another's family because family was who you let in, not who you were born to. "You're a gatherer. But I don't need to be gathered. I'm okay, Eli."

"I know. But I want you to be comfortable here. I want that a whole lot." He pulled her in for a hug, and she was surprised to find herself wrapping her arms around him, pressing her face into the crook of his neck—an addictive spot, she was discovering—and holding on, taking solace in his warmth and easy strength.

It comforted her that he was just as attracted to her as she was to him. As did the way he was taking things slowly and cautiously, which she knew was for *her* sake.

His phone beeped, and he looked at it and swore. "I'm sorry, I've really gotta go." He kissed her again, lightly, the appetizer on Eli Thomas's menu, before meeting her gaze. "Have a good day."

Oh, she would. "You too, Eli."

When she was alone, she let out a shaky breath. She felt . . . She didn't even know. She was still standing there, lips tingling, body quivering with an anticipation of something that *wasn't* going to happen, when her cell buzzed with an incoming text.

> **KINSEY:** I forgot my lunch box. It's in the fridge. Bring it to work with you? I'll swing by and pick it up from your classroom after my 11:00 a.m. meeting.
>
> **BRYNN:** Please?
>
> **KINSEY:** Please what?
>
> **BRYNN:** *Please* bring the lunch box.
>
> **KINSEY:** I'm not one of your students, but okay, sure. PLEASE bring my lunch box.

Rolling her eyes, Brynn opened the fridge and pulled out Kinsey's black lunch box. Because she was completely discombobulated—that kiss!—the lunch box slipped from her fingers, hit the floor, and spilled open.

There was no lunch. But there were meds, lots of them, none pronounceable, all prescribed to one McKinsey Davis.

Brynn scooped them all back inside and worried about it the entire drive to school.

Mornings in her classroom were always a fine balance between teaching and managing behaviors, so naturally there were a lot of various behaviors today, thanks to kids not sleeping for whatever reason, or eating a bowl of pure sugar cereal for breakfast, or maybe just plain being five years old.

All of which meant that Brynn didn't get a spare second to

look up any of Kinsey's prescriptions until circle time. This twenty minutes before lunch was used for sharing and talking about bad feelings in a healthy way, aided by a talking stick. "Okay, bring it in for circle time," she called out.

Because this always took them a few minutes, she quickly pulled out her phone and googled a couple of the meds she'd seen. Her heart stopped. They were all related to transplant rejection.

"Ms. Turner! Cindy's touching me!"

"Ms. Turner! Ethan's looking at me!"

"Ms. Turner! I have to go potty!"

Brynn let out a breath, her mind racing. Transplant rejection. That was . . . serious. Really serious. Potentially life-threateningly serious. And even though she and Kinsey had been frenemies for years, more actual enemies than friends, Brynn felt . . . heartsick. Because she wouldn't wish something like this on her worst enemy, and Kinsey wasn't that. Not even close.

"Ms. Turner, can I go first?"

Brynn shoved her phone away and pasted on a smile as she joined the circle with the kids, bringing the coveted talking stick she'd bought after her first day of teaching. You couldn't talk without the stick.

The stick was genius.

With it, the kids could—one at a time—talk about their feelings, good or bad, and help each other learn to get along.

Huh. Maybe she should bring the talking stick home with her . . . "Okay, let's get started," she said, just as Kinsey popped into the classroom.

"Ms. Davis!" Toby called out. "Sit next to me for circle time!"

Kinsey's eyes met Brynn's, and Brynn could see she wanted to refuse, which made Brynn say with perverse amusement, "Yes, Ms. Davis, join us for circle time, where we talk about our bad feelings in a calm, healthy way."

Kinsey shot her a look that said maybe she shouldn't close her eyes tonight when she went to sleep, but smiled sweetly at the kids.

Brynn hadn't even realized she could do that.

Then she very carefully kicked off her pretty nude, strappy high heels and sat on one of the folders she'd been holding, still smiling at the kids like she genuinely loved them.

Brynn handed the stick to Suzie, the student on her right.

Suzie sucked in a deep breath and spit out her words really quickly. "Carly told me that her brother has the same shirt as me and that hurt my feelings."

"My brother does have that shirt!" Carly said.

"Remember," Brynn said gently. "We can only talk if we're holding the stick."

Carly's hand shot up in the air for the stick, and Suzie reluctantly passed it to her.

"My brother has that exact same shirt," Carly repeated. "And I'm going to borrow it after my mom washes it, because my brother gets dirty all the time and I just wanted to know if you'd wear yours the same day so we can be twins."

Suzie blinked, and then beamed. "Okay!"

Carly handed the stick to Matt, the boy sitting next to her.

"River wouldn't let me have a turn at the water fountain."

"Because you wouldn't let me have a turn yesterday!" River yelled.

"River, you need the stick," Brynn repeated quietly, having discovered that a quiet voice forced everyone to zip it in order to hear her.

Matt handed River the stick.

"You were mean to me yesterday," River said. "And you hurt my feelings."

Matt just crossed his arms.

"Matt," Brynn said. "Do you want the stick?"

Matt shook his head and glared at River.

River glared back.

"Matt, are you sure?" Brynn asked.

Matt held his hand out for the stick. "I hurt your feelings because you hurt mine first. You didn't pick me for your kickball team."

"Because you told Trevor, who told Harrison, that you didn't want to be on my team!"

This went back and forth for several minutes, during which it was discovered that Matt had said he *did* want to be on River's team. A little detail that had been left off the gossip train. They apologized to each other and resumed their BFF status.

Brynn picked up the forgotten stick. "Anyone else have something they'd like to share and get off their chest? Remember, sharing is caring, and holding on to bad feelings isn't good for you."

"Ms. Turner always shares," River noted.

Brynn grimaced inwardly and took a quick look at Kinsey.

Kinsey took a sip of the drink she'd brought with her while giving Brynn a look that said, *Don't you dare.* And damn if that didn't make her *dare*. "Actually, I do have a grievance to air. A friend of mine is sick and I want to help, but I don't know how."

Kinsey choked on her iced tea, then, with a long look at Brynn, took the stick. "She's not your friend and she doesn't need your help. Now for *my* problem. Someone from my summer camp days thinks I don't remember how awful *she* also was."

Brynn gaped at her and snatched back the stick. "At *my* summer camp, there was a mean girl who always stole my glasses, even though she *also* wore glasses and knew how hard it was to see without them."

There was a collective gasp from the kids. Kinsey didn't gasp, but once again she choked on her tea.

The kids were watching them like they were at a ping-pong match.

"What happened, what did you do?" Suzie asked Brynn.

Kinsey snatched the stick right out of Brynn's hand. "She tattled, even though the other girl was younger and none of the girls were nice to her." She paused. "Probably."

"You're supposed to ask nicely for the stick, not just take it," Brynn said through her teeth. And younger, her ass. There were only two months between them.

"My point is, that other girl's . . ." Kinsey paused, like she was working on chewing something extremely distasteful. "Sorry. Okay? She's sorry for taking the glasses, but honestly? She was just tired of all the drama."

"Drama," Brynn said, shocked.

"Ms. Turner, you have to wait for the talking stick."

Kinsey tossed the stick at her and rose to her feet. "I have a meeting." She grabbed her heels and the lunch box from Brynn's desk before heading to the door.

Oh no she didn't. "Kids, let's talk about something good that happened today. My something good is that I feel very lucky to have such sweet, well-behaved students who always keep themselves in line when I have to step outside the classroom." She handed the stick to Toby. "I'll be outside the door for a minute, and then *right* back."

"*I was drama?*" she asked Kinsey's back in the hall. "Are you kidding me?"

"No." Kinsey turned to her. "Everything had to be about you, and everyone thought you were amazing."

Brynn gaped at her. "You made fun of me when I cried because I was homesick. You made fun of me for those completely vegan, weird-looking homemade packages I got from home. *No one* thought I was amazing, least of all you." She shook her head and took a deep breath. Dammit, she'd let Kinsey distract her. "Look, forget camp. Forget all of this. You're *sick*?"

"Nope, not me. I had my flu shot."

Brynn crossed her arms and narrowed her eyes.

Kinsey blew out a sigh and looked around. They were still alone in the hallway. "Yeah, okay, fine. So I've got a little situation going on."

"Really? You call kidney failure a little situation?"

"It's not kidney failure." She paused. "Exactly. It's transplant rejection. And I don't want to talk about it."

Brynn crossed her arms. "When?"

"When what?"

"When did you get a transplant?"

"See, normally, 'don't want to talk about it' means no talking about it."

Brynn shook her head. She was horrified and sad and . . . *sad*. She'd been here over a week now and no one had mentioned it. Which meant she was literally just the roommate, not friends like she'd hoped they were all becoming. Which also meant that she was still way too trusting and naive.

But none of that mattered even a tiny bit because Kinsey was in trouble. Life-threatening trouble. Which put a pretty damn big damper on hating her.

 CHAPTER 12

From thirteen-year-old Kinsey's summer camp journal:

Dear Journal,

So . . . I'm back, even though I don't want to be. I almost got out of coming to camp this year altogether because I—shock—got sick. Really sick. Ended up in the hospital, but of course I recovered in time for my mom to ship me off. And I found out why—she gets a scholarship for me to come here. She doesn't pay a penny of the cost.

She's in Hawaii, by the way.

While I'm in hell.

Eli likes girls even more than last year, and he's having the time of his life. I hate him. I hate you, journal. And I hate life.

Kinsey

ELI GOT HOME from work and followed the most amazing scent of food into the kitchen. Max had lasagna going and was working on garlic bread while telling Kinsey she was cutting up the veggies for the salad all wrong.

"If I'm doing it wrong, then maybe you should do it yourself."

"No, because you're doing it wrong to get *out* of doing it," Max said. "Do it the way I taught you, or no lasagna for you."

Kinsey looked at Eli. "Your brother's mean."

Max laughed.

Eli didn't even try to get in the middle of the two, who'd been bickering bickersons since the day they'd met years and years ago. He snagged a piece of the cucumber Kinsey was currently mangling. "Where's Brynn? Usually the scent of something cooking lures her into the kitchen with the rest of us."

"She's not home yet," Max said.

Eli looked at the time. Six o'clock. "She wouldn't still be at school this late, would she?"

This got him a double shrug from the bickering bickersons. He headed to his room to change but stopped in the doorway of Brynn's room.

Her duffel bag, which had sat on the chair since day one, was gone. The bed was neatly made, odd only because, though Brynn was a lot of really great things, a good bed-maker wasn't one of them. In fact, there were none of the usual signs of her presence. No sneakers on the floor, no sweater tossed over the back of the chair.

Concerned, he stepped into the bathroom and found her

things gone from there too. No toothbrush and toothpaste, no hairbrush, none of her lotions or makeup . . . nothing.

He went back to the kitchen and looked directly at Max. "She's gone. Did you say something stupid again?"

"Dude," Max said. "I swear to God I didn't. I mean, okay, yeah, I might've checked out her ass because, well, you've seen it, right? But I swear I didn't say anything or touch her. I've been a fucking angel."

Eli looked at Kinsey, who was now cutting carrots with chef-like precision while remaining uncharacteristically quiet and sarcasm-free. "Kinsey."

She stopped cutting. "Okay, maybe it had something to do with me."

"What did you do?"

"I forgot my lunch box and asked her to bring it to me. She snooped and found my meds, and then we were in the share circle and she got upset with me."

"Explain."

"Turns out, she's still mad at me for how I treated her at camp. I mean, talk about holding a grudge."

"Aren't you still mad at Kendall, that chick you used to be good friends with at work, because she made fun of how much you spend on shoes?" Max asked.

Kinsey flipped him the bird.

Eli didn't take his eyes off Kinsey. "So you apologized for summer camp and told her why you were the way you were, and also that you two share a sperm donor for a father. Right?"

"Wrong," Kinsey said.

"Us guys are *always* the ones in the wrong," Max said.

Eli glared at him and his brother held up his hands in sur-render.

Brynn was gone. And he wasn't quite ready to examine why he was so bugged by that fact. Or why he felt every bit as protective over her as he did about Kinsey, albeit in a very different way. He loved Kinsey like a sister.

Nothing he felt for Brynn was sister-like.

Kinsey was back to cutting carrots. She now had a pile of them in front of her that would take them a week to eat, a rare tell from her, and he felt anger bubble up. "Let me get this straight. You had the opportunity to tell her everything and you didn't."

"Don't." Kinsey pointed at him with her knife. "You weren't there. And anyway, what did you expect me to do? Tell her that my dad's a dick who, by the way, cheated on my mom and do-nated sperm for cash, which makes us sisters? That in spite of what it might look like, no worries, I'm not telling her now so that she'll give me a kidney? Come on, Eli. She's not going to buy any of that. Plus, it's sort of frowned upon to discuss that sort of thing in front of children. 'Sperm' isn't exactly on the spelling list."

"Wait, you think Brynn's *gone* gone?" Max asked, sounding disappointed. "As in not coming back?"

"Would you?" Kinsey asked.

"Hell no," Max said. "You're scary as fuck."

Eli took the knife from Kinsey's hand before someone got stabbed with it. Like Max. And then he waited until she met his gaze. "You messed this up because you're afraid to get close to her."

Her eyes went shiny. "That wouldn't make me a very good person."

He let out a breath. "You are a good person. You're one of the best people I know. You're just afraid to love even one more person, because you think you're a walking expiration date, and you don't want anyone to hurt other than you. Fix this, Kinsey. Fix it for yourself."

"I can't," she whispered.

"Why?"

"Hi, have you met me?"

He looked at her. She looked at him right back, letting him see what she rarely let anyone else see. Regrets. Sadness. Fear. It was the last that squeezed his damn heart and had him shaking his head. Because he knew she wouldn't make a move toward fixing things with Brynn. He could tell she felt . . . frozen, like it'd been *her* who'd put a decision-making moratorium on herself, and not Brynn—who appeared to be making decisions just fine.

BRYNN WAS SITTING in her moms' kitchen, slowly being smothered to death. It was her own fault, of course. She'd told them she was coming back because the house hadn't worked out, which had sent them into private-investigator mode.

"Did someone hurt you?"

"Was someone mean to you?"

"Do we need to call the police?"

"No!" Brynn said. "Look, I know I told you that I thought

Kinsey and I could make peace and become friends. And I thought the same thing of Eli."

"But . . . ?" Olive asked.

"But . . . now I'm not so sure on either."

"Is it because you like Eli?" Raina asked.

Just when she thought she might be smarter than them . . . "I don't know." She paused. "Maybe. A little."

"And that's bad?" Raina asked.

"I'm not sure I'm ready to feel . . . things again. I need to clear my head."

Olive didn't want to let it go. "But—"

She held up her hands to ward them off. "Look, I'm going to be fine, no one's done anything to me. I just don't want to discuss it right now, okay?"

So they switched tactics.

"Try this, baby." Olive handed her a mug.

"Wait," Raina protested. "*I'm* making her a special tea blend."

"Trust me. She'll want mine," Olive said.

Brynn sipped from the mug. It was a hot toddy with a whole bunch more alcohol than hot water.

"Don't tell your mom," Olive whispered.

Twenty minutes later, as she was sitting on the couch, with Catherine the Great claiming her lap, Raina handed her a napkin with two small cookies in it.

Never one to turn down cookies, Brynn still hesitated. "They're not . . . *special* cookies, are they?"

"Just a little bit special. For your anxiety, baby. *Don't tell your mom.*"

So that was how Brynn ended up a little toasted and also a little high. But the joke was on her moms, because now she was too sleepy to spill her guts and admit she'd actually been delusional enough to think she'd become a part of the Kinsey, Max, and Eli gang, that she meant something to them, that she belonged. That she was embarrassed it wasn't like any of that. She was nothing more than a paying renter, filling a spot.

But more than any of that—much, much more—she'd come home because Kinsey didn't need the complication of Brynn being there upsetting her.

The doorbell startled Brynn awake and Cat into hissing. She figured her moms would get it, but oddly, they'd made themselves scarce. So she got up and looked out the peephole, and suddenly she knew where her moms were.

Hiding out at the top of the stairs, straining to eavesdrop.

Because Eli stood on the porch, hands braced on either side of the doorjamb, head down, studying his shoes. When she'd swallowed her heart out of her throat and back into her chest, she opened the door.

He lifted his head. He'd lost the suit jacket, loosened his tie, and unbuttoned the top two buttons on his shirt. The sleeves were shoved up his forearms, his hair was mussed, and the dark lenses on his sunglasses were a nice finishing touch to the whole Frustrated Male look he had going on.

She lifted her chin. "If you're here to tell me I need to apologize to Kinsey, don't worry. I figure me being gone was apology enough."

He tugged off the sunglasses and shoved his fingers through

his hair, solving the mystery of the tousled look. "How about *I* apologize to you," he said.

She stared at him. "Go on."

"I'm sorry." He drew a deep breath. "I'm sorry one of my roommates is a compilation of every cliché of a surfer there ever was. I'm sorry the other roommate's always on edge and irritable and . . . well, downright mean as a snake. And I'm sorry if not knowing about Kinsey's condition made you feel like you weren't a genuine part of the household."

She sucked in some air. "How did you know?"

"Because you're kind and caring, and you attach easily, even when you don't want to. I can imagine how you felt when you saw inside Kinsey's lunch box."

"Yeah? How did I feel?"

"Sick, probably, with worry and concern, like the rest of us are. She's dealing with a lot, always has been, but this isn't about her. It's about you, and no one meant to make you feel left out."

She gave him a long look.

"Okay, neither me nor Max meant for that. Kinsey is . . . well, Kinsey. Please come back, Brynn. Give us another chance."

Hating that she was tempted, she started to shake her head.

"Wait, before you say no, maybe just think about it?"

Like she'd be able to do anything else.

Taking her hand in his, he squeezed it gently and lifted it to his mouth, kissing her palm.

A skitter of awareness went through her.

"Maybe you'll think about that too," he said quietly.

She did nothing but, all night long.

 CHAPTER 13

F rom fourteen-year-old Brynn's summer camp journal:

Dear Moms,

OMG, it's asparagus this year. And whenever a girl eats any, the boys yell, "Don't eat the stinky tinkle sticks!"

Boys are so dumb. Why didn't you ever tell me that?

And why do we only get one veggie for the whole camp?

Also, everyone's got boobs but me. I know you said it would happen, but WHEN? Kinsey's boobs arrived. Everyone's boobs arrived.

Except mine.

Kinsey said, and let me quote, "Nice mosquito bites."

I'm not going to put on my bathing suit. I'm not going swimming. Which, because it's a million degrees, means I'm going to die. Good-bye, Moms, we had a good run.

Love,
Your thoroughly dead daughter

THE NEXT DAY after work, Kinsey was frustrated. She'd tried to see Brynn at school, but her sister had refused to talk to her during class and then had sneaked out at the final bell before Kinsey could catch her.

Both Max and Eli gave her a wide berth until she finally tossed up her hands. "Look, it's not my fault she's gone."

"Actually, it kinda is," Max said.

Eli didn't say anything, just leveled her with those steel-gray eyes that never failed to reach into her soul and remind her that she wanted to be a better person than she really was.

Dammit.

She spun on her heel and left. Using the GPS to get to Brynn's moms' place, she parked on the street and eyed the small, modest but well-kept home. The grass was a little long, but vibrant green. The two oaks were thick and lush. Gorgeous, colorful flowers lined the walk and filled planters along the porch railing. She had no idea what kind of flowers, because she'd never been impressed by flowers before. And she'd certainly never grown any.

One of the moms—Kinsey didn't know which one— answered her knock. She was petite and wore a long, flowy, whimsical sundress covered in bright sunflowers. "Can I help you?" she asked Kinsey with a sweet smile.

"I'm looking for Brynn. I'm Kinsey Davis. Her . . . room-mate."

Her mom looked interested in this information. "I thought she wasn't taking the room after all."

"There was a . . . miscommunication. We very much want her to."

Brynn's mom's smile warmed. "I'm Raina. And I remember you, you know. I haven't seen you in years and years, not since Parents' Day at summer camp in . . . goodness, eighth grade, I think. Come in."

"No, don't let her in." This was from Brynn, who was suddenly standing behind her mom.

Raina shook her head at her daughter. "Hiding from your feelings is never a healthy choice, baby. And it plugs you up, remember?"

Brynn banged her head against the doorjamb a few times.

Kinsey smiled at her sweetly. "We wouldn't want you to get plugged up," she said.

Brynn rolled her eyes, gently nudged her mom aside, and said, "We'll be outside talking. Do *not* listen in." She then shut the door.

Kinsey opened her mouth to say something, but Brynn held up a finger and cocked her head at the closed front door. "Mom, I can still hear you breathing," she called out.

"Dammit," came Raina's voice. "It's my allergies. There's a lot of pollen today. I'm going to go sit in front of the humidifier."

Again, Kinsey opened her mouth, but Brynn shook her head. "Not yet," she whispered, then said loudly, "Let's go to

McDonald's for a Big Mac and fries, the extra-large order with extra fat."

Nothing from the other side of the door.

"Okay," Brynn said with what looked like relief. "She's really gone." She eyed Kinsey coolly. "What are you doing here?"

Kinsey paused. "You, um, have nice toenail polish."

Brynn looked down at her sparkly purple toes. "You came here to say that?"

"No, I came here to say you suck at fighting. But we have that deal where I have to say something nice to every not-so-nice thing." She drew a deep breath. "You're not supposed to go away when you get mad. You're supposed to fight back. Didn't anyone ever tell you that?"

"No," Brynn said.

"Well, it's true."

"Okay," Brynn said. "So let's fight. You're sick. Like really sick."

Kinsey sighed. "Yes, but don't you *dare* look at me with pity."

Brynn let out a choked laugh. "Are you kidding me?"

The front door opened. It was the other mom, or so Kinsey assumed. This one was wearing a suit dress and heels that Kinsey drooled over.

"Honey," this mom said to Brynn. "Even I don't leave friends out on the porch." She smiled at Kinsey. "Hi, I'm Olive."

"She's not a friend," Brynn said. "This is Kinsey, from summer camp. You remember, the one I complained about every time I got to call home."

"Ah," Olive said, and looked Kinsey over for a long beat.

Kinsey squirmed a little bit. Embarrassed, she realized, at what a shithead kid she'd been. She gave a little wave and a grimace. "Camp was a long time ago."

"True," Olive said, and stepped back, gesturing for them both to come inside the house.

Brynn hesitated, but not Kinsey. She took the only "in" she was likely to get and entered the living room.

"Raina's making tea," Olive said. "She also has homemade cookies."

"Don't eat the cookies," Brynn said quickly to Kinsey.

"Not *those* cookies." Olive shook her head. "I made her throw those out. You can eat the new ones and still pass a drug test."

Kinsey blinked and looked at Brynn. "Your mom makes pot cookies?"

"Don't ask."

Okay, then. She smiled at Brynn, surprised. "You get more and more interesting."

Brynn rolled her eyes. "Mom, we need a moment."

"Understood." Olive moved to the kitchen.

Again, Brynn shook her head when Kinsey began to speak. She gestured for Kinsey to follow her and led her down a hallway to a bedroom that appeared to be a shrine to Brynn's entire life, between the corkboard wall covered with pictures and the shelves filled with trophies.

"Who did you steal all the athletic awards from?" Kinsey asked.

"They're participation awards. I sucked at all sports, as you well know."

"And the Backstreet Boys poster on the back of your door?"

"It was a phase." She swiped her forehead. "You're making me crazy anxious."

Kinsey let out a low laugh.

"You think this is funny?"

"No," Kinsey said. "I just thought I was the nervous one. And I don't even do nervous anymore. I've learned that being anxious about shit ahead of time just means I've got to be anxious twice. I'm no Miss Merry Sunshine, but sometimes it helps to just think as positively as possible."

Brynn slid her a look. "That's . . . surprisingly astute."

"Yeah, yeah. But since my natural state is to be Eeyore, sometimes it's a process." She looked at her sister standing in the middle of her childhood bedroom, a grown woman surrounded by her past, which by all accounts had been happy and sweet. Still, she had her arms crossed, her expression pissy.

Like her life had been so hard. It was a bunch of BS really. Yes, she'd come over here with the intention of opening up, but having watched Brynn with her awesome, loving, weird moms, suddenly she didn't want to.

Because what did Kinsey have? Let's see. She had a con artist for a dad, a mom who was only around when she needed something, and a messed-up kidney.

"So?" Brynn asked. "Why are you here? You made it pretty clear we're not friends."

"Maybe I want to be. Friends."

Brynn laughed.

Annoying, even if she deserved that. "You've had things pretty good, you know that? Good health, even if you're constipated."

Brynn sighed.

"Hell, even my best friend likes you."

Brynn met her gaze. "Does that bother you?"

"Not even a little. I like seeing Eli open his heart. He doesn't do that, you know. Like . . . ever. His relationships with women are superficial at best. It's because he thinks he's faulty."

"We're *all* faulty."

Kinsey gave a grim smile. "True, but some more than others. Although Eli's only fault is seeing the best in people like me, even though he's had it rough. Did you know he was pretty much rejected by both parents and then sent away at age ten because they didn't have time to be bothered with him? That scars a kid, Brynn, big time, and yet he's still a great guy. He deserves a really great woman, but the one time he allowed himself a serious relationship, she tossed him aside for a promotion on the other side of the country. That was five years ago," Kinsey said. "And now he doesn't commit his heart because he sees himself as disposable."

Brynn was standing there, arms still crossed. "Is there a reason you're telling me all of this?"

"Yes. If you hurt him, I'll have to kill you."

"I'm going to pretend you're joking, but I get it. Everything I know about Eli tells me he deserves the moon."

"Damn right," Kinsey said. "But this isn't about Eli. Or you and Eli, even though he thinks you have a good ass, which is annoying because it's true."

Brynn blinked. "Then what is it about?"

"It's about just you. Your life's all put together."

Brynn's jaw nearly hit the floor. "Are you kidding me?" Shaking her head, she laughed. Then she kept laughing, eventually having to bend over and put her hands on her knees.

Pissed off, Kinsey turned toward the door.

"Wait." Her sister seemed to make an effort to get herself under control. "Look, I'm sorry, okay? I'm sorry you're sick. I really wish you'd tell me more. I'm also sorry that you didn't get good parents. And that I fell into a fun job and you didn't. Your job's hard, because you mostly only get to hear about problems and have to help people fix them. That's got to be draining. But you need to know that my life is about as far from put together as it can be." Brynn spread her arms, gesturing to her shrine. "I mean, yes, my moms are amazing, but they can also be a bit smothering. I can't find myself to save my life, and my résumé makes me look like a ping-pong ball."

"Yeah, well." Kinsey drew a deep breath. "It's all subjective, I guess. You've got two moms who care, good health, and a very annoying way of being sweet and kind—two things I can't manage on my best day."

Brynn came toward her. "You know, my moms have far more love to give than they have children. Feel free to take some of it. You'd be doing me a favor. They're . . . a lot."

"Hey, we heard that!" came Olive's disembodied voice. "And

we're not smothering in the least! Also, can you ask Kinsey where she got her heels? They're fabulous."

Kinsey blinked at Brynn. "Are they right outside the door?"

"That or they still have the kid monitor in here somewhere."

Kinsey was . . . boggled. Still staring at Brynn, she said, "I buy my shoes online at a discount outlet. They're still ridiculously priced, but I search the internet for coupons and wait for the four-for-the-price-of-three sales."

"Nice," Olive said. "I'll need the website when you get a chance, honey."

"Oh, and dinner's ready," Raina said. "I set the table for four."

Brynn looked at Kinsey. "I warned you not to come in. It's not my fault now—this is all on you. Let's go."

Which was how Kinsey found herself seated at the dining room table, where there were napkins—stolen from Taco Bell, but still—and everyone sat at the same time and ate together, talking, laughing, and talking some more.

The food was amazing. "I want to marry your enchiladas," she told Raina.

Brynn's mom smiled sweetly. "Everyone does. Do you cook?"

Kinsey laughed. "My culinary talents run in the direction of ordering takeout."

They all laughed, and then Raina dished out small tins to each of the three of them.

Olive and Brynn stared at theirs with twin expressions of dread.

"What is it?" Kinsey asked.

"It's my summer dry-skin balm," Raina said. "Olive and Brynn have really dry skin, and I didn't want to leave you out. It'll fix you right up."

Kinsey opened the salve, smelled it, and coughed. *Yow.*

"*Never* smell it," Olive whispered.

When Raina moved into the kitchen to clear some dishes, Kinsey leaned into Brynn. "The salve smells like dirt."

"It's turmeric. Just smile and bear it."

Raina came back, and everyone smiled at her. Somehow they started telling stories. Olive told them about the time Brynn's grandma got arrested for trying to bring CBD oil onto a plane and ended up as a headline: *Granny Arrested at LAX for Carrying Illegal Substances.* "I had to drive to LA in the middle of the night and bail her out," Olive said.

Raina shook her head. "You know I can beat that. Remember the year Brynn called from summer camp, sobbing because someone had taken her wubbie?"

"Yes," Olive said. "You got in your car and headed right up there."

"Yes, and as you know, halfway there, I got stopped by a cop for speeding. When I told him I was racing to summer camp to save a traumatized child, he said I was a nice grandma and should have a nice day." She lifted her chin. "So I told him I was no one's grandma, that I was in fact thirty-five years old, and he *laughed.*"

"Because you were forty-five," Olive said.

"*Forty!*" Raina shot back.

"Right, and those five years were so important to you that

you threw your soda at him and got arrested for assaulting an officer, and then resisting arrest."

"Well, he wouldn't listen to me!"

Brynn turned to Kinsey and gave her a look that said, *Still think my life is all put together?*

Yes, she did. She was smiling. In fact, her face hurt from smiling. She was still smiling when after dinner Brynn walked her out.

"You're coming home with me, right?" Kinsey asked her.

"No."

Her smile faded. "So then why did I sit through dinner?"

"Because you liked my mom's enchiladas so much you moaned while eating them, and then nearly licked your plate. Plus, you laughed your ass off."

Yeah, she had. At least until she'd realized that *she'd* been the bully at summer camp who'd stolen Brynn's . . . "wubbie," which had been a very old, ragged stuffed teddy bear. Her stomach still hurt thinking about it. "Look, about summer camp—"

"I don't want to talk about it."

"Fine." Because neither did Kinsey. "But here's the thing. If I don't bring you back, Eli and Max are probably going to change the locks on me."

Brynn huffed out a dramatic sigh. "Well, I wouldn't want you out on the streets."

Kinsey paused and took a good look at her, narrowing her eyes in suspicion. "Hold on. You had every intention of agreeing to come back. You just wanted to see me beg. You need out of this house as badly as I need you in Eli's."

Brynn grimaced. "Maybe."

Kinsey laughed. "You know what? You actually suck less than most people."

"Good to know."

"And . . ." Kinsey said, giving her a "let's hear it" gesture.

"And what?"

"And I suck less than most people too," Kinsey said.

"No, actually you suck way *more* than most people."

Kinsey thought about it and nodded. "Yeah, probably. But you're still going to come back, right?"

Raina opened the front door and smiled at them. "This weekend I'm making another batch of enchiladas. I'll expect both of you and your other two roommates as well." She beamed. "And, Kinsey, bring your parents, too."

Kinsey looked at Brynn.

Brynn shrugged.

Okay, so Kinsey was on her own with this. "That all sounds nice," she said carefully. "But it's just my mom and she's usually busy, *very* busy."

Raina brushed this off with a sound that said, *Don't be silly*. "Who's too busy to meet their daughter's new roommate? Oh, and don't worry about bringing anything, we've got it all covered." She smiled. "I'm so excited to meet all of Brynn's new peeps."

"Brynn asked you not to say 'peeps' anymore," Olive called out from the living room.

"She knows what I mean. Don't you?" Raina asked Kinsey, looking at her with eyes that were far sharper than her easy smile let on.

She was definitely being summed up, and normally she wouldn't give a single crap about what people thought of her. But she found herself nodding.

"So you'll come?" Raina asked.

"Yes."

"And bring everyone?"

"I'll invite them," Kinsey said. "Whether they come or not is up to them."

"Tell them I make the world's *best* enchiladas. Tell her, Brynn."

Brynn smiled with love and affection, not even a little embarrassed that her mom was basically bribing Kinsey to be Brynn's friend. "It's true," Brynn said. "You do make the world's best enchiladas."

Raina beamed. "Good girl." And then the front door shut.

Kinsey looked at Brynn. "Wow."

Brynn narrowed her gaze. "Wow *what*?"

Kinsey lifted her hands. "Nothing."

They both stared at each other, and for the first time in a long time, Kinsey wanted something, and she wanted it bad too. She couldn't have said why or how, but she wanted Brynn in her life, and hell, she also wanted her moms. "I'll come if you do," she said softly.

Brynn nodded. "Then we have a deal."

It was what Kinsey had wanted, but . . . "That seemed too easy."

"Trust issues much?"

Kinsey blew out a breath. "Just tell me. You've got a stipulation, I can feel it."

"Actually, no. I don't."

"Everyone's got a stipulation."

"Fine," Brynn said. "I get that your health issues are your own business, but if we're going to really be friends, then you have to let me in a little. Tell me things."

Like the fact that you're my sister? "Such as . . . ?" she asked carefully.

"Such as, what's the trick to getting the kids at school to love me as much as they do you?"

Kinsey felt herself go warm with the unexpected compliment. "You just have to be real."

Brynn met her gaze. "You should try that with me sometime. When you do, I'll know you meant it about being friends."

Normally when people were snippy with Kinsey, she wrote them off. *She* was the only one allowed to be bitchy, because, hello, look at her damn life. But something weird happened with every prickly response Brynn gave. Kinsey's tension lessoned. It was like Brynn was the perfect antidote. Dammit. "You're a very strange woman."

"Takes one to know one."

Kinsey drove home, still a little stunned that she'd actually—hopefully—talked Brynn into coming back. Her sister was different from anyone she'd known, which left her feeling a little off-kilter and confused. She had no idea why, but she liked bickering with her. And laughing with her.

Oh, boy. *Please don't let it be that sister thing Eli had always told her was there.* Because that would mean Eli was right about something, just like he almost always was.

But whatever was happening with her and Brynn, it felt . . . sibling-like. She'd seen it with Eli and Max. Yeah, they were brothers, but they were also more. They argued, they fought— hell, just two weeks ago Max had pushed Eli through the hall-way wall. But they'd made up, laughed, and then had played a video game, all within a ten-minute span. Then Max had taped up a huge poster of the beach over the hole in the wall, the one Eli told him he had to fix before summer was over.

They were so annoying, and yet . . . and yet she wanted *that*. Desperately. And she wanted it with Brynn, even though she didn't deserve it.

 CHAPTER 14

From fourteen-year-old Kinsey's summer camp journal:

Dear Journal,

Do you know how sucky it is to find out your best friend got his first kiss before you did? Yeah. And of course Eli kissed Brynn, and he smiled for the rest of the night.

Annoying.

So I went after my own first kiss. His name is Jack and it took me almost all damn week to get his attention by completely ignoring him. But in the moment, I got sick and almost puked on his shoes.

I mean, I missed. But not by a lot, and he was really grossed out. Now he's ignoring me.

I hate everything. I'd list it all out, but I'm too tired.

Also, I'm tossing you in the lake.

Good-bye, Journal.

BRYNN DIDN'T LEAVE her moms' house when Kinsey did. She needed a minute.

Or a bunch of minutes.

So she and her moms spent the next few hours marathoning *Bachelor in Paradise.* When Brynn's eyelids got too heavy, she knew it was time to go.

"Here, baby." Raina had packed her up a bunch of leftovers.

Olive handed over her duffel bag.

"Are you guys giving me the bum's rush out?" she asked, amused.

They exchanged a look that had Brynn putting hands on hips. "Okay, spit it out. What are you up to?"

"Nothing," Raina said. "We just really think you should go back."

"So you don't want me here?"

"No," Olive said gently, reaching for her. "Well, yes. We want you here, but we also want what's best for you."

"And that's being back in Wildstone," Raina said. "We're so happy you're back, you have no idea. But . . ."

"But we think you'll be happier at the house with your friends," Olive finished.

Except they weren't her friends, not really. She didn't know what they were yet. Well, okay, she adored Max like she would a younger brother. As for how she felt for Eli . . . well, that was distinctly un-brother-like. Kinsey she mostly wanted to strangle. But she looked into her moms' sweet, hopeful faces and it was like being a kid all over again.

All they'd ever wanted for her was to be happy and safe.

Except the only time she'd been those things had been when she was here, in this house. But as she'd always done, she simply hugged them tight and said as she always did, "I'm happy, I'm fine, you don't have to worry about me."

Then she kissed them good night and drove back to Eli's place. Which, she supposed, for now at least, was hers as well.

ELI SHUFFLED THE deck and dealt. It was midnight. He, Deck, and Max had gone surfing, and they now sat on porch chairs around a makeshift coffee table of an old wooden surfboard laid flat on two stumps of wood.

They were playing Cards Against Humanity. Or at least their version of it, which involved betting cash.

Eli tossed down a card. All three men looked at it.

"What do old people smell like?" Deck read out loud. "Heh." He tossed one of his cards down.

Max grimaced and read it out loud. "The ball-slapping sex your parents are having right now."

Eli winced.

Deck grinned. "Once in a while, it pays to have dead parents."

At the sound of soft footsteps, they all turned toward the stairs. No one.

Then came Brynn's voice: "And once in a while, it pays to have a place to live where you don't have to know if your parents are having sex, ball-slapping or otherwise."

Eli quickly craned his neck and found her standing just outside of the reach of the porch's light, and felt relief go through him. "Hey."

"Hey, yourself," she said, coming up the steps and into the light. She was wearing her strappy denim sundress and white sneakers, her hair piled on top of her head.

Just looking at her stirred something deep inside him, and it wasn't anything as simple as hunger or affection. But what had him standing and reaching for her duffel bag was the sheer exhaustion and stress on her face. He shouldered her bag and smiled at her. "Want to play a round?"

He got a very small smile in return. "Of drunken Cards Against Humanity?"

"Hey," Max said. "And also, only one of us is drunk." Max pointed to himself. He shot Brynn a welcoming smile as he shuffled the cards. "You in, sweetness? Got plenty of beer."

"Another time."

"Don't blame you." Deck tossed down his entire hand and stood. "I've gotta hit the road." He nodded to Brynn. "Good to see you back," he said quietly, and with a gentle tug on her ponytail and a genuine smile, he vanished into the night.

Brynn watched him go. "So he sleeps with Kinsey, but doesn't *sleep* with her?"

Max shook his head. "Don't even try to understand it. It'll just give you a headache. I'm actually thinking of enrolling the both of them in an English as a second language class." He stood too and stretched. "The waves wore me out tonight. This guy"—he pointed to Eli—"kicked my ass out there. I'm going in." He gave Brynn a quick hug. "Don't you kids do anything I wouldn't do."

"There's nothing you wouldn't do," Eli said.

"Exactly." And with a laugh, he was gone.

Eli looked at Brynn. "Seems like this is our time. Late at night."

"I want to know how sick Kinsey really is."

Okay, so she wasn't feeling playful. "She didn't tell you?"

"Come on. You've met her. After I found the meds, she told me she had transplant rejection, not much more. She wouldn't even if the sky was falling."

He took in the seriousness of her gaze and cursed Kinsey for being so closemouthed and secretive. Not to mention difficult. But he was done playing by her rules. She needed this, needed her sister, whether she wanted to admit it or not.

And he thought maybe Brynn needed Kinsey too.

"She was born with chronic renal disease. She got a transplant when she was fifteen, but the kidney's slowly failing."

Brynn stared at him for a long beat. "That's why you guys stopped coming to summer camp that year. She got sick."

He nodded. "She had a hard time with the recovery and several bad infections, and I didn't want to go away, because she needed me. We didn't know until later that it probably was because the kidney was far from an ideal match. She's back on dialysis, which means sitting still for four hours, three times a week. We all rotate sitting with her so she doesn't lose it. The rejection disorder is low grade. She's not in immediate danger of it failing, but it gives her flu-like symptoms, stuff like fatigue and a faint nausea."

"And grumpiness and irritability."

Eli gave a small smile. "Nope, those are all Kinsey. Just a special bonus for the people she cares most about."

Brynn stared at him some more, still looking upset. But instead of telling him how awful Kinsey had been to her, which he knew was true, she took the conversation in a direction that surprised him.

"You're a good friend," she said.

He shrugged. "I know it's hard to imagine, but she's a good friend right back. She's fiercely loyal and protective of the people in her life. When she joked that we were platonic life mates, she meant it. She's as much a sister to me as Max's a brother."

"And you take care of both of them."

Uncomfortable with that, he changed the subject. "I'm glad you're back."

"You knew I'd come. You sent Kinsey to apologize."

"Did she actually apologize?"

That got him a small smile. "Almost," she said. "Also, side question. You think I've got a good ass?"

He stared at her. "Sorry. She's got a strange sense of humor."

"Yeah. But just for the record, I think you've got a good ass too."

Eli felt a smile crease his face, and she pointed at him.

"But don't tell your ass, okay? Because I don't know how I feel about the rest of you yet, and I've got no idea what to do with it."

"Understood," he said, and then paused. "Would it help if I told you I know *exactly* what I want to do with you?"

"Stop." She gave a short laugh. "Actually, no. To be honest, I know what I want to do to the rest of you too. But . . ."

"I know." He ran a finger along the side of her face, tucking a strand of hair behind her ear. "There's no pressure here, Brynn."

"Yeah, well, that's just great." She groaned and surprised him by dropping her forehead onto his chest. "Because I work really great under no pressure. There are parts of me already working under no pressure as I speak."

He stroked a hand down her hair. "I need it to be unanimous."

She lifted her head.

"I pressured you to come back," he said. "I won't pressure you for more."

He could see the emotions going through her, some of the same ones that were going through him. Affection, and a hunger, which was gratifying. But she was worrying her bottom lip, and not only did he not want her to feel any anxiety over this, over them, *he* wanted to be the one nibbling on that sexy lip of hers.

"Eli?"

"Yeah?"

"You said you wouldn't pressure me, but what if I pressure you?"

And then her mouth was on his. Pulling her in was instinctive. So was kissing her back, and he soaked up the hungry sound that escaped her, before forcing himself not to take it to the next level.

"I'm going to walk away now," he said softly against her lips when they were both breathless. "Before we rush this."

She made the sound again, and he nearly lost his resolve. But his past was littered with pieces of his heart shattered and broken, and not even Brynn could put them back together again. Getting laid was all well and good when he wasn't emotionally invested.

But that wasn't the case with Brynn. He'd been emotionally invested in her from day one. Hell, if he was being honest, he'd been emotionally invested since summer camp. For the first time in a very long time, he'd found someone who called to him on a far deeper level than just physical, and he had no idea what to do with that.

Liar. You know exactly what you want to do. You want to be buried deep inside her . . . But that couldn't happen, because he'd brought her home for Kinsey.

Not for himself . . .

Brynn stepped closer. "Maybe I'm more ready than I thought."

He shook his head. "Always go with your first instinct."

Taking a step back from him, she stared up into his face as his smile slowly faded. "Sorry." She headed for the kitchen door.

"Brynn."

"No, I get it."

"I'm not sure you do." He caught her hand and turned her to face him before hauling her in close. Lowering his head, he kissed her until neither of them could breathe. "I had a crush on you when we were kids," he murmured. "And that crush is still in play."

She just stared up at him, clearly shocked.

"That's so surprising?" he asked.

"Yes, actually. You never let on. After the kiss, we kind of ignored each other."

"You mean you ignored me."

She bit her lower lip. "I put you in the I Don't Know What to Do with You file."

He cocked his head. "Do you lump all the people in your life into categories?"

"Yep. My moms are in the Love Me to Death file. My ex is in the Men Are Assholes file. Kinsey's in the Bully Mean Girl file, although I might have to move her to just the Pain in My Ass file."

"And where am I now, in the Men Are Assholes file?"

She held his gaze. "No. I don't think of you as being anything like Ashton."

"So what file do you have me in?"

"The I Don't Know Where to File You file."

He gave a wry smile and had to nod in agreement. "Fair enough."

 CHAPTER 15

From fifteen-year-old Brynn's summer camp journal:

Dear Moms,

Guess what?????? Kinsey isn't here this year. No one knows why. I'd ask Eli, but he isn't here either.

Guess what else? A boy asked me to hold his hand on the walk to the campfire. He said it was because he knew I couldn't see at night, but he didn't let go, not even once we got there. No, I'm not going to tell you his name. I'm not stupid. I love you both, but you'll pester me about him forever if you know his name.

Love,
Brynn

p.s. But he's cute!

Brynn jerked awake at her alarm blaring and then groaned as she reached for her glasses on the nightstand.

They weren't there.

She'd left them on the bathroom counter last night when she'd brushed her teeth. Damn. She rolled out of bed and made the sound her grandma used to make when trying to move too fast. She wasn't even thirty, and staying up until midnight made her feel ancient. When had that happened?

Hands out because her eyesight was always worst first thing in the morning, she tentatively made her way across the room, tripping over her own shoes and then something that let out an "oomph."

"Mini!" she gasped. "Are you okay?" She bent to pet the dog, who rolled onto her back for more love.

Brynn gave the obligatory belly rub and got a sweet morning kiss. "I don't suppose you'd go get my glasses?"

Mini licked her face again.

"Close enough." Brynn straightened and headed toward the bathroom. Feeling for the handle, she opened the door, belatedly realizing that in her morning fog, she hadn't caught onto the fact that the shower was running and the mirror was steamed.

"Hey!" Kinsey stuck her head out from behind the shower curtain. "What the—"

"Sorry!" Brynn whirled to leave, only to freeze in place when she saw a brown hairy . . . *thing* on the floor that—dear God—looked like a *huge*, massive spider. "Oh, shit!" she said. Actually, she might've screamed it. Acting on impulse fueled by sheer panic, she opened the vanity cabinet under the sink, grabbed the small bucket sitting directly beneath the pipes, and—while yelling "omigod, omigod, omigod" like a mantra—dropped the bucket over the biggest spider she'd ever seen.

"What the hell are you doing?" Kinsey yelled.

"Saving you from a mutant spider attack!" Brynn, heart still throwing itself against her ribs with every beat, slapped her hands down on the counter, looking for her glasses. Finally finding them, she shoved them onto her face just as Max and Eli rushed through the doorway. Max was in boxers and carrying a baseball bat, Eli in jeans that he was buttoning up as he entered. Levi's, sitting dangerously low on his hips. He didn't have a weapon, at least not in his hands, and although his expression was calm, his body language suggested he was ready and able to fight whatever monster had dared come after her and Kinsey.

Unable to form words, she pointed to the bucket.

Eli stepped into the bathroom and tilted the bucket to look beneath.

"Careful!" she said quickly. "It's a mutant spider."

To her horror, Eli lifted the bucket and revealed . . . her own hairbrush.

Max burst out laughing.

Eli looked like he wanted to do the same, but managed to control himself. "Attack of the killer hairbrush," he said.

"Wow," Kinsey said. "You really can't see shit, can you?" Shaking her head, she vanished behind the curtain again. "If you could all get out of here, that'd be great. And, Brynn, you might want to start wearing your glasses around your neck on a granny string."

"Hey," Brynn said to the shower curtain. "Those things aren't just for grannies!"

Kinsey shrieked.

"Oh my God, a real spider this time?" Brynn asked, stepping closer to the shower to help.

"No, I just ran out of hot water. Get the hell out!"

Max went back to bed.

Brynn and Eli retreated into the hallway.

"Thanks for the early morning adventure," he said with a smile in his voice.

She sighed. "Maybe I need to try contacts again."

His smile was warm. Affectionate. Not at all mocking, and she felt an answering smile curve her lips. "You remember that whole thing about not knowing where to file you?" she asked.

"Yeah."

"I've been working on that."

His smile went from affectionate to hot. "Good to know. And since we're sharing, you should know that I like your pj's."

She looked down at herself. She was wearing men's plaid knit boxers and a faded old tee. Very schlubby. Very not sexy.

"It actually isn't the pj's," he said. "It's you."

She had no idea what to say to that. He had a way of warming her up from the inside out.

"I also like your sundresses," he said. "And that pair of jeans you've got with the hole in the right thigh. Oh, and those army-green cargo capris with all the pockets, the ones you wear with your soft white T-shirt."

He'd just described all of her clothing, but she went still, because she knew where this was going.

"I'm just wondering if you're still leery of moving more stuff in, and how I can help you get . . . un-leery."

"It's complicated."

"Or . . . you don't want to talk about it."

"Or that." She looked away from those all-seeing eyes of his, the ones that made her talk too much. "The thing is, I didn't leave Ashton. He left me. And since he turned out to be a bad guy, that's embarrassing. I was stupid."

"No, that's not how it works. You're not to blame for what he did. And I'd really like to know what that was."

"He stole stuff from me." She closed her eyes. "I mean, if this had happened to someone I know, I'd wonder how they missed the signs." She grimaced and shook her head. "I was weak. Dumb. I practically asked for it."

"No one asks for that. What happened wasn't your fault. Will you look at me?"

"No. Because if you've got any pity in your eyes, I'm going to want to scream."

"I'm feeling a lot of things, but pity isn't one of them."

She opened her eyes a teeny little bit and pushed her glasses farther up her nose to see better. He was still just standing there in his jeans, looking his usual calm. But there was a tightness in his mouth and in the faint lines around his eyes that gave him away. He was angry, but not at her.

"Did you get the police involved?" he asked.

"I did. I wasn't the first, and until he's caught, I won't be the last. And I do have a few boxes of things."

"In your trunk," he said.

She nearly told him the whole truth, but didn't. *Couldn't.* "Look, I've not been good at navigating the path of my life. There's been some detours, some really bad decisions. I tend to disappoint the people I care about. I rush in too fast."

"And now you're taking your time. I get that."

"Because you've been through a rough time too."

He looked at her for a long moment and nodded. "Yeah. And I'm not convinced anyone's great at navigating life. Making wrong turns, taking detours, figuring it all out by trial and error . . . that's kind of the whole point."

"Maybe, but I've trusted when I shouldn't."

"So now you're going to trust no one?"

"Something like that," she said as lightly as she could.

His eyes remained serious. He didn't want her to joke this away. "I've been there, Brynn. I was with someone I thought was all the way in, but as it turned out, she was only in until something better came along. And when that was a job on the East Coast, she was gone in a blink."

"I'm sorry."

"Don't be. It was a pit stop."

"I'm not sure I'm as brave as you about putting myself back out there," she admitted.

"I'm not. Or at least I wasn't."

She stared up at him as his meaning sank in. Until her. He wasn't putting himself out there . . . until she'd come along.

"Maybe you just need someone to watch your back," he said quietly.

"I'm watching my own back now."

He shrugged. "Never hurts to have backup."

Was he offering? And why did the thought of that reach deep down and stir up all the good feels? It'd been a long time since she'd had someone at her back. Someone willing to protect her and keep her safe. Well, that wasn't *exactly* true. She had her moms, and she loved them with all her heart. But she'd been really good at hiding when she'd needed help.

And she suspected Eli was cut from the same cloth. "You've got a lot on your plate," she said. "People you take care of."

"Those people might argue that they don't need any such thing."

"I agree. You're really good at being sneaky about it."

He smiled. "You think so?"

"I know so. You trying to add me to your plate, Eli?"

He stepped closer, gently pushing her up against the wall, tilting her face up to his. "Do I want to add you to my life? Yes. But I'm not feeling altruistic about you, Brynn. I'm not feeling the need to take care of you either. You're doing a damn good job of that on your own. Do you want to guess what I *am* feeling?"

He was hard against her, so it didn't take a genius. Her hands went to his chest and headed north—even if they wanted to go south—and wound their way into his hair. "Are we going to sleep together?" she whispered.

He lowered his head and kissed her. Lightly at first, a query almost, which she answered with her tongue, making him groan as he wrapped his arms around her and took the kiss to a very serious place, putting her in an equally very serious state.

"Yes," he finally said against her lips, voice gravelly. "But I'm not sure there will be any sleeping involved, and it won't be tonight."

Disappointment chased arousal through her veins. "No?"

"I want you, Brynn. I can't even begin to hide that, but I'm not going to be another mistake or disappointment. I want to be one of the very best things in your life."

Given how she felt when he kissed her, she could guarantee he would be. Standing there, sandwiched between the lean hard muscles of his body and the cool wood of the door, she felt some of her bones go squishy. She could feel the heat pulse from him, enclosing her in a cocoon of warmth and desire. "Maybe," she said, "we should just jump in with both feet."

"Yeah?"

Before she could say hell yeah, Kinsey yelled from behind the bathroom door. "Oh, for God's sake! Either go fuck each other blind or shut up and go to work!"

Ignoring her, Eli kissed Brynn again, then reluctantly pulled back. "We'll finish this later."

She hoped that was a promise.

 CHAPTER 16

From fifteen-year-old Kinsey's summer camp journal:

Dear Journal,

Okay, so I never did throw you in the lake. But if you tell anyone, I'll dump you into the hazardous waste bucket in my hospital room.

Yeah, I'm back in the hospital. Had a kidney transplant. From what I overhead, I guess it didn't come a day too soon. There was a community fund-raiser, which brought a lot of people to the clinic to get tested to see if they were a match for me. Eli got himself tested again. He hates that he isn't a match, but he doesn't understand how much it means to me that he tried. Or that he won't go to camp without me.

A kid at my school was a match. I can't believe someone I barely know is willing to do this for me. It's kind of a miracle, the first really great thing to ever happen to me.

Maybe I'll stop being sick all the time now . . .

Also, I don't hate you anymore.

Kinsey

ELI GOT HOME from work and was jumped by an exuberant Mini, who was thrilled to see him. Because no one else was home, he exchanged his clothes for board shorts and went for a long swim. When he was too exhausted to go another stroke, he floated on his back in the tide, staring up at the sky.

Thanks to spider-gate and the ensuing hot make-out sesh in the hall with Brynn that morning, the day had started out with a lot promise. But it'd gone to hell pretty quickly. A coalition of environmental groups, including the one he worked for, had sued the state for granting permits to seismic-mapping companies. The permits allowed the companies to harass and harm marine animals while blasting deafening sounds underwater in the Pacific Ocean in search of oil and gas deposits.

The court battle was tying up most of his days lately, making him crazy. And today he had missed a call from the funeral home. He'd been calling them every few days for months to no avail, and then the one time they try to get in touch with him, he'd missed the call. They hadn't left a message and had closed by the time he called back.

He'd tried everything he could think of to track down his mom over the past few weeks. He'd left messages, DMed her, snail mailed her, made Max try as well, and . . . nothing. Not even his dad had been able to help.

His mom was really going to just let his grandma's ashes remain at the funeral home indefinitely. He couldn't quite wrap his head around that fact. So he swam. And swam.

When his legs began to tremble with fatigue, he headed in, surprised to find Brynn sitting on the beach at the water's edge, Mini at her side, clearly waiting for him.

When she saw him coming out of the water, she stood, shook out the towel she'd been sitting on, and handed it to him.

"Thanks." He swiped it over his face and bent low to love up on Mini, who'd melted into a puddle at his touch, wriggling on her back in the sand like she was the happiest dog on the planet.

"Rough day?" Brynn asked quietly.

From his crouched position at her feet, he looked up and took in the very welcome sight of her in a candy-apple-red sundress and no shoes. "It's getting better now."

She gave him a look.

"Seriously," he said. "You're the best thing I've seen all day."

She smiled, but it was pensive, and then suddenly she thrust a piece of paper into his hands.

"What's this?" He skimmed the document and stilled.

"Remember when I told you that I'd worked some odd jobs during college?" she asked quietly. "Well, one of them was at a funeral home."

Without taking his eyes off the document, the one that said his mother had granted permission for him to handle his grandma's remains provided she was clear of financial obligation, he let out a shaky exhale.

"It was a temp thing," Brynn said. "But I've still got a friend who works there. I called in a favor. She called the funeral home where your grandma's remains are and got the contact information your mom had left them. Then I, um . . . made contact."

He looked at her. "She picked up your call?"

"She did."

"You . . . called my mom and she picked up."

"I called her as an employee of a funeral home . . ." She grimaced and started talking, getting faster and faster as she went, like she was really nervous. "And I'm hearing my own words and realizing what a huge invasion of privacy this was, but I just wanted to help. I knew you weren't getting through to her. When I called, I sort of left out the fact that I'm really an ex-employee . . . and apparently she also spaced out on the name of the funeral home being different from the one where your grandma's cremated remains are. Anyway, I got her to digitally sign the release. Which means you can arrange for your grandma's remains to be blessed by her priest—which I get isn't exactly how she wanted it, but I figured it was better than nothing, and then she can be put in her church's cemetery."

He was boggled. "She really agreed, no problems?"

"No problems."

"*Why?*" he asked.

"It's simple, really. The longer you wait to decide, the more the cost. There's now additional storage and administration fees . . ."

He didn't care about that. He was . . . overwhelmed and

humbled by what she'd done, and almost unbearably touched. He felt her hand slip into his as she stood at his side, waiting for him to get a hold of himself.

It wasn't easy. For one thing, he still couldn't believe that she'd pulled it off. And for another, he was just starting to realize how deep his feelings for her had gone. No one had ever done anything like this for him. He started to speak but found he couldn't. Literally couldn't, because there was a big, huge ball of emotion stuck in his throat, leaving him too choked up.

So instead, he stared some more at the paper, which was now blurry. And because his legs were wobbly—something he decided to attribute to his swim rather than emotion—he sank onto the sand and sat.

"Hey." She dropped to her knees at his side. "You okay?"

The nod was automatic, because he was always okay. He'd made sure of it. If he wasn't okay, his entire world would tumble down, and he had people in it that relied on him.

Brynn cupped his jaw and tipped his face to hers, studying him with a worried frown. "You're trembling."

"No." But he was, and it was his own damn fault. He'd skipped lunch and then swam for an hour. His tank was empty and his blood sugar way too low.

Brynn got to her feet and moved off, and he nodded again, because her walking away was definitely the best thing for her. He'd promised her she was safe with him as a roommate, and all he wanted to do was take her home to his bed and do some very *not* roommate-like things to her.

She was smart to walk away.

But then suddenly she was back, once again on her knees at his side, handing him a soda and a fully loaded hot dog she'd just purchased from the food stand. She nudged the soda at him, and he took a long pull and then grimaced when the sugar hit his system.

"Nothing like a quick sugar rush, right?" she quipped, but her eyes were serious as she watched him carefully. "Now the hot dog."

Already just from the soda, the cobwebs left his vision and his brain cleared. And he was able to remind himself he was an idiot. But because she was looking so worried, he obediently took a bite of the hot dog and made a face. "Pickles."

"My favorite," she said. "Another bite."

"Is that your teacher voice?"

"Yes, is it working?"

He gently reached out and pushed her glasses farther up her nose from where they'd been slipping. His fantasy life was as rich as the next guy's, but he'd never had any particular fantasies regarding a teacher—until now. He stared into her eyes, slightly magnified behind her lenses, her wild hair piled on top of her head with tendrils slipping loose and framing her face. "Yes," he said. "It's working. Keep talking."

She narrowed her eyes, as if unsure if he was kidding or not. She must have decided it was a combo of both, because she said, "Eat some more or you'll get detention."

Oh, yeah, most *definitely* working. It was one of those seemingly innocuous moments in time, but this one felt . . . different. He was somehow aware that he'd remember it forever: the feel of the salty ocean air brushing over him, the sound of the waves rhythmically hitting the shore, Brynn's breath warm against his skin. How sweet she looked feeding Mini a bite of the hot dog, then her hands back on him, and that inexplicable magnetic pull he felt whenever she was close. He smiled and she stared at his mouth, reassuring him he wasn't alone in this. He took another bite of the hot dog, and then held it out for her.

"It's for you," she said.

"Pretend it's share time."

She rolled her eyes, but opened her mouth.

He fed her, laughing softly when she tried to nip his finger along with the hot dog.

She chewed and then her tongue darted out to catch a dollop of wayward ketchup on her lower lip, making him smile. "I'm going to share something else," he murmured. "I'm having a serious teacher fantasy."

She looked intrigued. "Yeah?"

"Oh, yeah."

"Do I give you detention in this fantasy?"

"Among other things."

She laughed, just as Mini yelped and began pawing frantically at her own nose.

Brynn moved toward Mini but Eli beat her there, dropping to his knees. "Shit. Again, girl?" He opened Mini's mouth, but when he found nothing, he swore and then scooped the dog up against him and stood.

"What's wrong?" Brynn asked, worried as Mini lay unusually still in Eli's arms.

"She ate a jalapeño sky raisin." He strode toward the house at a pace that required Brynn to run to keep up with him.

"Did you forget to tell her she's allergic?"

"She's a lab. She lives to eat shit."

They rushed into the house. In the kitchen, Eli lay Mini on her bed and pulled a bottle of Benadryl from the top drawer. He shook out a pill and held it out to the dog. "A trick from my vet, designed to save me a bazillion dollars since Mini's done this four times already this year."

Mini sniffed at the pill and then turned up her nose at it.

"Oh, sure, yesterday you ate the neighbor's week-old trash, but now you're going to be picky," Eli muttered.

Mini whined and began scratching herself with her hind foot. Her fur was now raised in spots all over her.

"Hives," Eli said. He went to the fridge, liberally coated the small pink pill in enough cream cheese for a dozen bagels, and offered it to Mini.

Mini gobbled up the entire blob and . . . spit out the pill.

"Are you kidding me?" Eli asked.

Mini whimpered.

"Dammit." He went to the cabinets and pulled out the peanut butter, once again liberally coating the pill.

Mini ate the peanut butter and . . . spit out the pill.

Eli, on his knees, shook his head. "We both know that if this was cat poop, you'd eat it so fast I'd be dizzy."

Mini's tail thumped against the floor.

He stood, turned back to the fridge, and took out some deli meat, carefully wrapping up the pill.

Mini nearly took off Eli's finger to get at the meat.

Both Eli and Brynn watched a long moment, but no pill reappeared.

Eli, on his knees in front of the dog, sagged in relief. "She's going to be the death of me."

Mini lifted her head and licked his face.

"Yeah, yeah," he murmured, stroking the dog. "You love me. I love you back, you crazy girl."

Brynn would swear that Mini grinned at him. "You do realize she just conned you for high-quality deli meat, right?"

"Yep."

"What now?"

"She sleeps it off. She'll be okay." He rose to his feet and came toward her. "Why do all the women in my life play hard to get?" Gently, he pulled her in and kissed her. "I told myself I wasn't going to get emotionally attached to you, but the truth is I've been emotionally attached since we were nine years old."

She was stunned, and a warmth rolled through her, a warmth she hadn't felt in a while. "No one's home," she whispered. "Right?"

"Right."

"Take me to your room?"

He raised a brow.

"Share time isn't over," she said.

He was smiling when he kissed her again, sending shivers down her body. They kissed their way out of the kitchen. They kissed as they staggered up the stairs. They were still kissing when halfway up, she tripped and went down, bringing him with her.

They laughed, and Mini appeared, trying to join the fun. Eli gently nudged the dog away just before she pounced on them. "Go to your bed," he said.

"Yes, sir," Brynn quipped.

His mouth twitched. "That's another fantasy all together," he murmured, kissing her again, cupping the back of her head so she didn't hurt it against the wood floor.

Somehow they got back to their feet, this time getting as far as the hallway before she couldn't help herself. She pressed *him* up against the wall, slid her hands beneath his shirt, and nibbled his lower lip.

With a groan, he reversed their positions, running his hands down the backs of her thighs, encouraging her to wrap her legs around him.

Her dress rode up. Eli took in the sight of her itty-bitty sky-blue panties and smiled. "Pretty." His hands cupped her ass as he ground against her, kissing her again, taking his sweet time about it too, dragging sounds from deep in her throat that she'd never made before.

"Thought we were headed to your bed," she managed on a gasp, as his fingers slowly stroked the damp silk between her legs.

"This first." He was beneath the silk now, and doing something cleverly diabolical that had her head back against the wall, her mouth open to just breathe, and some seriously needy little whimpering pants coming from her lips. He scrambled all her brain cells, surrounded her with his warmth and muscle.

"Eli," she whispered, her toes beginning to curl, and she was mere seconds away from dragging him to the floor, needing him inside her. "You—I—I'm going to—"

"Good," he murmured, using his teeth to tug down the strap her sundress, then her bra, and from there it was a nudge of his jaw to reveal a bare breast. He sucked her into his mouth at the exact same time as his fingers slid into her and she came in wild shudders, completely losing herself.

When she could hear and see again, Eli was still holding her up, watching her, eyes hot, his body thrumming with an erotic tension that eradicated any embarrassment she might have had about how quickly he'd managed to get her there. "Um." She bit her lower lip. "Hi."

He smiled. "Hi."

"I hope there's more."

"Me too," he said fervently. "Just wanted to make sure you were still with me before I get you beneath me."

"Maybe I want *you* beneath *me*," she said.

His smile went Big Bad Wolf, and he got her to his room and on his bed so fast, her head spun. He lay on his back and encouraged her to straddle him, smiling up at her, eyes hot. "Have at me, babe. Whatever you want."

She started with her hands, then added her mouth, which had him alternately swearing and groaning out her name in a rough voice that gave her a secret thrill. She could tell when he got close. He'd had his head back, throat bared, body gorgeous and tense, his hands in her hair. Then suddenly, he moved so stealthily she never saw it coming. Pressing her into the mattress, his mouth moved down her body, his lips and tongue forging a path that had her crying out again, her hands fisted in his hair as stars exploded behind her eyes.

Before she'd caught her breath, he was inside her. "Brynn," he said huskily. "Look at me."

She managed to open her eyes. His own were filled with heat and affection and desire.

"You're so beautiful."

And then his mouth found hers again and she couldn't think; all she could do was feel as their bodies strained against each other. They moved together like this was a dance, but there was nothing practiced about it. It was shockingly powerful and primal, and she loved it, even as it overwhelmed her. This time he came with her, shuddering in her arms as they gasped for breath, savoring every last second.

After, he tucked his face into the crook of her neck, where she could feel the heat of his breath against her skin as he slowly regained control. When he finally lifted his head and looked at her, she knew.

This wasn't a playful, casual hookup between friends.

This wasn't a friends with benefits situation.

Something was happening between them, something intangible and yet more real than anything else in her life.

Everything was going to be different now, she knew that. What she didn't know was how. She stared into his eyes, not quite knowing if their tentative friendship would survive this . . . until he smiled at her. Relief flooded her as he leaned in and pressed his lips to her damp temple.

"It's okay, Brynn. We're okay."

Good thing, as she was rag-doll floppy and still making contented, purring noises. All she could do was bask in the glow and the way his hands were slowly moving over her body, soothing, calming, comforting as he headed south. She got her hands involved in the action, and the next thing she knew, she was moaning and rocking up into him again, needing more. "Aren't you tired after all that hard work you just did getting us here?"

He laughed softly and looked up at her from between her thighs. "If you think this is work, then I'm doing it wrong."

She arched into him without conscious thought, her body wanting more of him. And for once, her body and her brain were in accord. "Trust me," she gasped. "You're not doing *anything* wrong."

He smiled and rubbed his stubbled cheek against her belly, his warm breath on the underside of her breast as he moved up her body toward her mouth.

"Again?" she whispered hopefully.

"Unless you'd rather sleep?"

She slid her fingers into his hair and tightened, bringing his mouth to hers. "There's no sleeping in detention."

 CHAPTER 17

From sixteen-year-old Brynn's summer camp journal:

Dear Moms,

   Okay, so this year is . . . SO MUCH FUN! I know, shock, right? I bet you never thought you'd get this letter. ☺ But now that I'm a junior camp counselor, we get to stay up late, and there's a TV they let us use, AND . . . there're cute guys!
   Still no Kinsey. Or Eli. BUT get this. Kinsey called me. Wanted to know if I'd see her. I was like, yeah, right. And then she hung up on me! I immediately felt bad, so I called her right back, but she sent me to voice mail. I feel like such a jerk, but I also feel like that stupid little kid again, you know? Why does she make me so crazy?
   Gotta run. We're going to make s'mores.

Love you both!
Brynn

BRYNN WOKE UP wrapped around her own personal heater. Eli was on his back; she was pressed up against him, her face smashed into his armpit, her arm and leg holding him down. Her body couldn't have said "mine" any more clearly than if she'd crawled inside him.

It was light outside and she froze. She'd slept with him, here in his bed, all night. *How had that happened?*

Okay, so she knew how it'd happened. He'd pleasured her into a near coma. But now it was morning, and she was really great at making mornings awkward, so, holding her breath, she tried to disentangle herself without waking him up. But just being this close to the body that had given her such pleasure throughout the night had her body getting . . . ideas.

No. You've got morning breath and God knows what your hair looks like. Plus you have to pee, and— Her stomach growled loud enough to wake the dead.

"Hungry?"

Her gaze flew to Eli's, which was sleepy, sated, and . . . sexy as hell.

And also amused.

Her stomach growled again, and he laughed softly.

Okay, so *he* wasn't feeling awkward. No emotional conflict for him as he stopped her attempted escape by tucking her beneath him. Pushing her hair from her eyes, he got serious. "You okay with everything that happened last night?"

She blinked. "Are you asking me if you were good?"

He smiled. *Right.* He knew he'd been good. He probably

still had the nail indentions in his ass to prove it. "I'm asking if you're okay," he clarified.

"I'm pretty sure I'm better than okay."

"Glad to hear it." He kissed her softly. "Going to try to keep you that way."

"It's not your responsibility."

"I know. I just like seeing you happy. And if I can be the cause of it, even better."

She bit her lower lip.

"What?"

"So for you, last night was . . . okay?"

He laughed sexily, then tightened his grip on her when she tried to wriggle free. "Brynn, last night was . . . amazing. If you'd held out on me for even another second, I'd have started begging. Go out with me tonight."

Any lingering awkwardness vanished as she smiled. "I don't know, I might need some convincing. After all, I apparently agreed to sleep with you too readily, seeing as I missed out on making you beg for me—"

She was cut off by his kiss, a very hot kiss. "Careful what you wish for," he warned softly, his lips brushing hers. "You'll find I can be *very* persuasive when forced to beg."

The innuendo in his tone set her blood on fire. Definitely out of her league. "I've gotta . . ." She gestured vaguely to the door. "I'll use my bathroom, since I know you've got to get up too . . ." And then she slid out of bed and shoved herself back into her dress and retreated to her room. Okay, so clearly she'd failed spectacularly on her own personal deal about not involving her heartstrings or tugging on anyone else's. She'd promised herself she'd step away when she wanted to step closer, that she'd keep things light when she wanted to reveal her soul.

Now, not only had she revealed her heart and soul, but she'd given it away. To a man who had no idea. But . . . she wouldn't take it back. Not when it felt so good. So right. Which meant it was time to make a new deal with herself. And it needed to be far less complicated than the last, since apparently she couldn't think in Eli's presence. This time, she was going to do the *opposite*. She would take action when she was moved to action.

And she planned to be moved to action often.

In Eli's bed.

She was tired of pushing feelings aside. If given the chance, she'd embrace every emotion he stirred up in her. She had no illusions of keeping him forever, but she trusted him enough to give her what she wanted. At least for now, since their wants—and needs—seemed to be aligned.

And, oh, how they aligned . . .

She smiled all through her shower, thinking, hoping that this could actually work. Up until now, everything lacking in her life had been her own doing. She'd been wary of getting involved with anyone because she'd chosen poorly in the past. But Eli gave her his time and his affection, all freely. He didn't hold back from her. He didn't ask for anything in return. He only seemed to want one thing—her, just as she was.

And that was something she could actually offer.

She dressed for work—still smiling—and finally told her reflection in the mirror to stop thinking about last night because right now she needed caffeine and her keys. This meant leaving the safety of her bedroom, but there was also another really good reason to do so. Because she was missing her bra from last night. It hadn't been in Eli's sheets or on his floor. Which meant she'd lost it earlier than that. Like on the stairs.

Not good.

And wherever it'd landed, it wasn't visible. Maybe it'd sailed over the railing. At the bottom of the stairs, she turned into the reading nook and began to search the loveseat there. She got down on all fours and peered under it.

"Looking for this?"

Brynn jerked upright and hit her head. Swearing, she straightened, and holding on to the top of her head, which hurt like a son of a bitch, she stared past the great shoes to the bra dangling from Kinsey's finger.

Brynn snatched it from her and shoved it into her oversized bag.

"Sleeping with a roommate seems a little risky," Kinsey said lightly.

Also stupid, but hey, that ship had sailed.

Kinsey looked at her for a beat. "Do we need to have a talk?"

"I'm not going to hurt him. And he's a big boy." In more ways than one . . .

"Actually," Kinsey said. "It was you I was worried about."

Brynn laughed. "Okay."

"Hey," Kinsey said, looking a little insulted. Then she blew out a sigh. "Look, I'm a bitch. I know that. I'm also a pit bull about those I care about."

"And suddenly I'm one of those people?"

"Yes. I told you I wanted to be friends. I don't lie. I don't want you to get hurt again."

"And how do you know I've been hurt?"

"Am I wrong?" Kinsey gave her a "get real" look. "You showed up here with only a duffel bag, looking like a kicked puppy. How dumb do you think I am? Your last boyfriend was an asshole, right?"

Brynn crossed her arms over herself. "Everyone makes mistakes."

"And some of us make more than others," she said, raising her own hand. "All I'm saying is that even though Eli's one of the best guys I know, someone I'm also worried that you're going to inadvertently hurt, you have to look out for yourself."

Brynn was about to laugh again, but Kinsey wasn't laughing. And she wasn't being a smart-ass either. "Let me get this straight. Even though you're worried I'm going to hurt your best friend, you're warning me off him . . . for *my* sake?"

"I'm just saying you need to protect yourself. Wear a shield."

"Is that what you do?"

Kinsey's smile faded. "Yes. And mine's permanent."

"Maybe I'm not built like that."

"Nothing in life lasts, Brynn. I hope you know that, and what you're doing."

Ditto.

Eli surfaced from a dive on the job next to Demi, his work and dive partner. He hung back so she could get on board the work boat first, watching as Max assisted her.

Eli was . . . exhausted. His ass was seriously dragging. That's what happened when one stayed up all night worshipping a woman's body. He had zero regrets, but damn, he'd pay big money for a burger and fries and then eight hours of shut eye.

He and Demi had gotten a late start on the day's dive because he'd made a stop at the funeral home, where he'd finally been able to deal with his grandma's remains.

Thanks to Brynn.

His grandma would now be buried next to her husband, just as she'd always wanted. She hadn't gotten blessed by her priest and she'd been cremated, and Eli would forever blame his mom for going against her mom's wishes, but the priest had said he'd be honored to bless the remains before burial. It was the best Eli could do, and he had to take his peace from that.

Now he was treading water in the ocean on a day so clear that there was barely a line where the sky and the sea met.

Demi was boarded. So, pulling off his mask, he reached for the swim platform on the back of the boat. Demi was already all the way to the bow of the boat, out of hearing range, drying off.

"Cutting it close," Max noted quietly, eyeing his phone and the timer app he had going. "I asked Demi about it and she said you wanted to get the last of some measurement I didn't understand. A stupid measurement."

Eli tossed his mask on board. "It wasn't just some stupid measurement."

Max shook his head and reached out, grabbing Eli's gear while Eli rolled onto the swim platform and onto his back. "Don't do that again."

Eli heard the tremor in his brother's voice and lost the smile. "You okay?"

"People drop out of our life like fleas, man. I'm not going to lose you too, especially not over some microbes or organisms or whatever the fuck you're doing down there."

Eli set a hand on Max's arm, but Max shoved it off.

While he put both Eli's and Demi's equipment where it went, Max's movements were jerky and very unlike his usually easy-going gait.

Eli stood in his way and waited until Max looked at him. "*What?*"

"You're right, and I'm sorry," Eli said. "I won't do that again."

Max glared at him, then, seeing the honesty in Eli's gaze, slowly lost the hostility and nodded.

Eli pulled him in to give him a full-body—and very wet—hug.

"You're such an asshole," Max muttered, trying to pull free.

The kid might have an inch on him, but Eli had the muscle. He grinned and held tight. "Not until you say you love me."

Max was laughing now, struggling to free himself. "You're such a dumbass."

"Say it."

"Fuck off."

"Say it. Say you love me."

"You love me."

Eli shook his head. "Not letting go until you say I love you."

"I said it. You love me."

"I swear I'll dump you right over the edge."

"We're at work," Max said. "Demi's looking at us like we're a pair of idiots."

"Ask me if I give a shit. I love you, and I want to hear you say it back."

Max let out a rough laugh. "I love you, you crazy-ass idiot. Now let me go. And I'm using your towel."

Eli let him go and watched as he indeed grabbed Eli's towel and moved off to finish taking care of the equipment while still watching the boat's controls as he'd been hired to. He got everything in order and then squatted low at Eli's side, looking him over with careful eyes, which he *hadn't* been hired to do.

"You're exhausted," Max said. "You should never have gone out in this condition."

"I'm good."

Max looked him over again and shook his head. "You're wrecked."

More like an empty husk of a man. Literally. He wasn't sure how many times he'd had Brynn, but he'd depleted all bodily fluids, plus any reserves he'd had in the tank.

And . . . he was lying to himself. He knew exactly how many times he'd had her last night, and it still hadn't been enough. He forced himself to sit up to get the rest of his gear off. Then he needed to get back to the marina and to his desk to make notes on today's findings.

"You know it's stupid dangerous to dive when you're so distracted, right?"

"Again, thanks, Mom."

"Shit." Max pushed his ballcap off, ran his fingers through his hair, then shoved the hat back on his head, backward this time. He pointed at Eli. "Something's up with you."

"I'm fine."

Max lifted a single brow. They didn't keep secrets from each other. "Then I'll tell you what's up," he said. "You slept with her."

"You don't know that."

"I was with Kinsey when she found Brynn's bra dangling from the stair railing."

Shit.

"Yeah." Max laughed. "Definitely a rookie mistake."

Eli started to strip off his wet suit.

"I mean, who does that, sleeps with their roommate?" Max asked casually.

"You," Eli said. "Usually it's you."

Max pointed at him. "Exactly. And if memory serves, you warned me off hitting on her. And then you did it instead."

"We're not talking about this."

"So should I be upset that I missed out?"

Eli rose to his feet and took a step toward Max, who immediately put his hands up, but instead of an apologetic look on his face, he laughed.

Eli turned his back on his idiot brother and stared out at the water. He purposely let out a long breath, counting in his head until he lost the urge to put his fist through Max's know-ing smile. It took a minute. Or ten. When he turned back to Max, his brother offered him a bottle of water, his smug-ass smile gone.

"So you didn't just tap that," Max said quietly. "You fell for that. And hard." He nodded and tipped his bottle of water to Eli's. "About time, man. You deserve it."

Eli shook his head. "What am I doing? She hasn't even brought her boxes into the house from her trunk. Her job's temporary. She's probably got one foot out the door."

Max shook his head. "She's scared. I'm guessing she's been given the short end of the stick so many times she's convinced herself temporary everything is the only way to go. She's shak-ing in her boots over getting attached to us, but most especially to you."

"So what do I do?"

Max shrugged. "Give her a reason to grow roots."

Eli just looked at him.

His brother looked right back, steadily, a slow smile curving his lips. "Even though you don't know you're doing it yet, it's really good to see you engaging in some feels, man."

Didn't feel nice. Felt scary as fuck.

He got home, planning on taking Brynn out wherever she wanted to go. Getting out of his car, he caught sight of some-thing on the beach that had him walking across the street to the sand. Because to his utter shock, Kinsey and Brynn were at one of the three volleyball courts, throwing down in a game that looked very serious for the two most uncoordinated, unathletic people he'd ever met.

Brynn had the ball. She served and got Kinsey right in the center of the forehead. Brynn gasped in horror and went running toward Kinsey, yelling, "I'm so sorry, I'm so sorry!"

Kinsey touched the spot on her head and pointed at Brynn, eyes narrowed. "Don't you dare come over here and ask me if I'm okay, like I'm some fragile little snowflake." She then snatched the ball and got in position to serve.

With a squeak, Brynn whirled and ran back to her spot.

Kinsey was in shorts and a fitted tank that read, PEOPLE, NOT A BIG FAN. She had sand stuck to her—everywhere. Her face was red and sweaty, her hair piled on top of her head as she pointed at Brynn.

Brynn was in shorts and a tank as well—hers had a smiley face on it. She was also hot and sweaty, but she was grinning, and as Kinsey pointed at her, Brynn gave her a double-handed, universal "bring it on" gesture.

Deck stood on the sidelines, his son, Toby, on his shoulders, the both of them cheering the girls on.

"Get her, Ms. Davis," Toby yelled.

"Just don't kill her, Kins," Deck called out.

Kinsey served, and since she sucked at it—Eli should know, he'd made the mistake of being in a league with her and she'd lost them every game they'd played—the ball hit the net.

This year, he and Max had switched from a three-man team to a two-man team, cutting Kinsey out.

She still hadn't forgiven him.

She swore impressively and waited for Brynn to serve. Brynn's body moved more easily than Kinsey's, who'd spent most of her life feeling sick. He could tell Brynn didn't feel off, but she also had zero idea of the power of her own body. She moved with a slight awkwardness that told him she wasn't one hundred percent convinced her limbs were her own. And yet that smile . . . that girl-next-door smile slayed him every time.

She missed the net by a mile and shrugged. "Don't want to beat you too fast," she called out.

Okay, so the girl-next-door—with an edge.

Adorable.

And sexy as hell.

Suddenly, standing there watching the sisters beating the shit out of each other, yearning for Brynn in ways that went far deeper than their animal attraction, everything Max had said sunk in and clicked, and the epiphany punched him in the face.

He was tired of standing on the sidelines, tired of letting life, love pass him by. He wanted Brynn. He wanted her in his bed, but also in his heart, where truthfully, she'd already made a home for herself.

Definitely one of the scariest thoughts he'd had in a long time. But with a deep breath, he stepped off the sidelines, both emotionally and physically.

The women looked over at him. Both hot and sweaty, while at the same time using the civilities of the game to go at each other, both giving him very different looks.

Kinsey was in competitive mode and didn't want to be interrupted. Nothing new. He often irritated her just by breathing. But she also loved him, so she gave him a thumbs-up and then a "go away" gesture.

Brynn was in competitive mode as well, a mode he hadn't realized she even had, but she didn't mind the interruption. She didn't love him, at least not yet, but he hoped to change that.

And *that* was truly the scariest thought he'd had in a long time.

CHAPTER 18

From sixteen-year-old Kinsey's summer camp journal:

Dear Journal,

I'm in the hospital again, an infection this time. A shrink came to talk to me. He told me I needed to write down my feelings. I guess people are worried, but whatever, I told him I don't care.

He said I should care, but that until I could care for myself, others would for me. He said I should consider the journal my homework. I hate homework.

But here goes nothing. One week after I had the surgery last year, the kid who gave me his kidney . . .

Died.

Because of me.

It was an infection from the surgery. Rare, they said, but whatever. He's gone and it's my fault. He wouldn't be dead if he hadn't donated a kidney.

And that's not even the worst part. My body is rejecting his kidney. So I now officially hate my body more than I hate you. How's that for irony, dear journal?

I caught Eli searching for black-market kidneys on the internet and I made him SWEAR to me he'd stop. I refuse to take another kidney from another breathing soul. Which I get only leaves me one option, an option I don't wanna think about.

Whatever.

Kinsey

IT WAS SATURDAY, Kinsey's favorite day of the week. She had her eyes closed, her face tilted upward to the sun as she inhaled the salty sea air, smiling as a few drops of ocean hit her skin. Sitting with her legs crossed, she raised her arms out at her sides and tilted her face back. "This is better than sex."

"I'm going to make you take that back later," Deck said from behind her, where he stood manning the paddleboard that she was sitting on like a queen.

"And I'll enjoy you trying to make me take that back."

His bark of laughter had a smile crossing her face, and she was glad he couldn't see her. Deck didn't have a confidence problem. No sense in giving his ego even more room in that sexy brain of his.

"Faster," she said.

"Yep, you're going to say that later too."

She grinned and opened her eyes to take in the glorious

sight of nothing but azure-blue Pacific Ocean in front of her. They'd left land behind, and also, it seemed, the entire world.

She loved paddleboarding. She loved the minimalism of it. There was no gear required other than the paddle. Just her and the board—and the sexy guy behind her. There was something about being out here, no set plan, surrounded by nothing but water as far as the eye could see, that thrilled and exhilarated her. Maybe it was because her life was always so structured, and completely orbited around her treatments and dialysis, that made this so incredibly freeing.

She didn't do meditation. She didn't have a Zen bone in her body. But being on the water with the gentle sway of the swells beneath them and the light spray of saltwater hitting her body and the warm sun on her face was . . . life changing. This was her church.

She had a bucket list, comprised of things she couldn't do. Walking the Great Wall of China. Skydiving. Running a marathon.

Okay, so running a marathon wasn't really on her list. Even if she could run without feeling like complete shit, she wouldn't want to. But maybe that's why she had it on there. Because, dammit, she wanted to be able to pick her own limitations and not have them decided for her.

"I want to paddle," she said. "I want to stand up and paddle."

"Okay."

That simple. It always was with Deck. He didn't buy into her living her life around her disability. Unlike everyone else, who'd wrap her up in bubble wrap if they could, Deck expected her to live her life exactly how she wanted to, on her terms. If she felt like she could stand up, keep her balance, and use the paddle, he was going to support her doing that. Because he thought of her as an adult capable of making her own decisions.

She could love him for that alone.

If she believed she could love at all.

Or be loved . . .

But not even Deck could ignore the very real fact that she had an expiration date. Which meant that no matter how much she might be tempted, she couldn't allow him to fall for her.

The problem was, she'd forgotten to remind herself not to fall for him. But loving him was her own private burden, and she wasn't sorry about it. She was just sorry she couldn't say it. Holding those three words back had only gotten more and more difficult as time went on.

She struggled from her seated position onto her knees. Sitting on the paddleboard while having a big, strong guy stand behind you and do all the work of paddling was one thing. It was another entirely to stand up, hold her balance, and not knock them both into the water.

When she finally rose a bit unsteadily to her feet, Deck immediately wrapped an arm around her waist to anchor her. Grateful, she backed up a few inches so that her back was plastered to his front. He ran warm anyway, but all that skin and sinew was deliciously heated from the sun. Seeing as he wore only a pair of black board shorts, slung low on his hips, there was a lot to rub up against. "Mmm," she murmured.

With a low laugh, he lifted the long paddle over her head

and held it out in front of her. The minute she took it, his hands went to her hips. One palm slid to her belly.

"Kins."

"Hmm?"

His mouth was at her ear. "You gotta put the paddle in the water, babe, or that swell is going to take us down."

She blinked away the sexual haze he always put her in so effortlessly and put the paddle into the ocean, trying to plow it through the water.

"It's backward."

She shifted the paddle the other way and still could barely force the paddle through the water. "How in the hell do you make this look so easy?"

With his left hand still on her belly, giving her goose bumps, his right hand traced its way down her right arm, better positioning her hands on the paddle. "Loose knees," he said, bending his a little, which forced her to do the same. "Now stroke like you mean business."

"I know how to stroke."

His laugh rumbled from his chest into hers. "Yeah, you do. You're doing great."

She was. Thanks to his hand on hers, guiding the paddle through the water. They were parallel to the shore, at least a hundred yards out. If she'd been on her own, she'd have been terrified. But when she was with him like this, she could do anything. "Deck?"

"Yeah?"

"Take the paddle."

When he took the paddle, she carefully turned to face him.

Deck, quiet, tough, practical, resilient, self-sufficient . . . stood there with all his tats and muscles looking like a pagan god as he gazed down at her, one brow raised like he was thinking, *Now what are you up to, woman?*

She kissed the part of him she could reach. A pec, right above a pierced nipple. Then his throat. God, his body was a work of art. He ran most mornings. He lifted weights at least three times a week. His body was a temple, and she was always ready to worship it. With a little tiptoe action and some careful balancing, she fisted her hands in his thick, wavy hair that was weeks, maybe months past needing a cut, and tugged his face down so she could kiss him.

She felt his muscles bunch and shift as he adjusted, since she'd basically abandoned her post, leaving it up to him to keep them upright.

"Thought you wanted to do this," he said.

"Yes, but what I really wanted to do was see you all wet and gorgeous."

He grinned down at her. "That's *my* line." He ran a callused finger over the bruise in the center of her forehead, the one her sister had given to her in their volleyball game.

She'd never admit it, but she'd loved every moment of that game. Nipping Deck's lower lip to distract him, she stuck both of her very cold hands down the front of his board shorts, taking hold of his very favorite body part.

This had him going still while sucking in a breath, carefully hissing it out through his teeth.

She smiled and gave him a playful tug.

"You're a cruel, heartless woman."

This had her laughing out loud. His words didn't match the reaction she'd gotten out of him.

At her smile, his expression softened—unlike what was in her hand!—and he bent his head and nuzzled his face in her hair. "Love it when you laugh." He stopped paddling and one hand slid down her back to her butt, which he squeezed.

"Deck—"

"You started this, babe."

"We're going to fall."

"Trust me, I've got you."

Trust him . . . That was the thing. She did. So much it was terrifying. "Pretty full of yourself."

"Maybe I just know I'm right for you."

That had her heart squeezing painfully hard. Because he was right. But *she* wasn't right for *him*. "Remember what you promised me."

A look of pain and frustration crossed his face. "Kins."

"You promised me, Deck. You did. On our third date, when I tried to cancel on you. You came and got me anyway and then took me up in your friend's helicopter, letting me sit in the co-pilot seat so I could be on top of the world. I made you promise not to fall in love with me."

He wasn't paddling now. They were drifting freely, the two of them staring at each other, inches apart.

"Tell me you won't break your promise," she said softly.

"You made me an oath as well," he reminded her instead.

"That one doesn't count."

"Bullshit."

On their fourth date, they'd gone horseback riding in the green, rolling hills that backed Wildstone. They'd had a picnic for dinner and watched the sunset, and she'd had the time of her life. Seriously. The time of her life. And she'd known then that she'd never be able to protect her heart from him. So afterward, when he'd taken her to a friend's pub, she'd gotten drunk. It'd been a rare misstep, something she wasn't supposed to do, but she'd needed the escape. And somehow he'd gotten her to promise that she wouldn't die before she was old and gray. "Promises made under the influence don't count."

He let out a rough breath. "Fine. We'll drop it. For now."

"There's something else I'd like to drop."

"What?"

"You," she said sweetly, and then she shoved him into the water. Only she didn't count on him grabbing her as he went, so that they both flew off the board.

She was laughing when she surfaced and hooked an arm on the board to hold her upright. Which didn't turn out to be necessary since Deck surfaced with her, keeping one arm tight around her, and one hand on the board as well.

"You fight dirty," he said, but he was looking amused.

Relieved to see that tortured look in his eyes gone, she pressed herself up against him and kissed him, long and deep. "Dirty is the only way to fight," she murmured when they broke free to breathe. "Wanna go have a late lunch with me?"

"Wanna have you for lunch."

She laughed, because he always said that, but . . . this lunch turned out to be the best in recent memory.

BRYNN GOT TO her moms' house by midday, knowing they'd be in full company mode about the night's "family" enchilada dinner. Brynn herself was still thinking about the previous night's dinner. After her and Kinsey's impromptu volleyball game, Eli had taken her out. They'd had dinner on the water, then gone for a sunset hike to the top of the bluffs. And after . . . after, back in his bed by moonlight had been her favorite part.

Her moms were rushing around the house. "Don't go to any trouble," Brynn told them for the millionth time as she dug in to help.

"Of course we're going to trouble," Raina said.

"We want to get to know your friends," Olive said from her perch at the table, where she sat with her laptop and a stack of bills.

"They're all coming, right?" Raina asked Brynn.

"I think so. But, Mom, don't read too much into this, okay? You know I'm a really crappy judge of character. I don't really know them all that well."

A fib, of course. Whoever had said that childhood relationships were the deepest relationships a person could ever have had been onto something. She and Kinsey and Eli were forever linked from all those years they'd spent at summer camp. Whether the three of them had *liked* each other or not back then no longer mattered.

Even after this short amount of time of being back in each

other's orbits, they now *knew* each other better than she did just about anyone else.

And then there were the current relationships. The adult ones. A few of them more adult than others. She'd slept with Eli now. They'd done things to each other that she'd only read about. Their chemistry was so far off the charts, she couldn't even see the chart.

Terrifying.

Raina's gaze softened and she cupped Brynn's face. "You've known two of them forever, and you've made peace with your past. I'm sure they love you. You're so lovable, how could they not?"

Brynn laughed and shook her head. And then spent the next hour running around doing Raina's bidding. The food was just about ready and she'd set the table, *twice*—"The *good* silverware, Brynn, honey, what's wrong with you?"—when the doorbell rang.

Raina clapped her hands with glee.

"Mom," Brynn implored. "Please don't get your hopes up."

"I'm just saying . . ."

Brynn gave up and headed to the door, looking through the peephole. Eli stood there holding a bottle of wine and looking delectable in a pair of sexy faded jeans and an untucked Henley the exact color of his slate eyes.

Kinsey stood on the step behind him with Max, who was holding a small bouquet of flowers. Suddenly nervous as hell to have her two worlds collide, Brynn did a turnabout and rushed back to the kitchen.

Both of her moms stared at her as if she'd grown a second head.

"You're not going to let them in for family dinner night?" Olive asked.

"I'm trying to decide."

"Oh, no," Raina said. "I made some seriously kick-ass enchiladas and I need an audience to fawn over them."

"*I'll* fawn over them," Brynn promised.

Raina pointed to the door.

With a sigh, Brynn headed back to the door, hoping she wasn't making a big mistake.

AFTER RINGING THE bell, Eli took a deep breath.

"He feels really nervous to me," Max said to Kinsey.

Kinsey tugged on the back of Eli's shirt. He turned. "What?"

She looked him over. "Yeah," she said to Max. "You're right. He's nervous. Haven't seen that since . . . ever."

"I'm not nervous." He turned back to the door so as to not give himself away. Because he was nervous as hell, and it was ridiculous, because he didn't know why.

Except he did. He liked her. Too much. Way too much. He turned back to Kinsey. "You need to tell her. Why haven't you told her yet?"

"I'm working on making her like me first."

"But that could take forever."

"Hey," she said, pointing at him. "It's not my fault you're falling for my sister."

Eli slid Max a look.

Max lifted his hands in surrender. "Not me."

"Please," Kinsey said. "Like I couldn't see it for myself. She's giddy, and you're so mellow I nearly checked you for a pulse earlier."

"Which is why you *have* to tell her."

Kinsey stared at him. "You do realize that this is actually about me and *not* you, right?"

"Kins, *everything's* about you."

"So why haven't you told her yourself if you think I'm so bad for not doing so?"

"I almost did."

"Yeah? And what stopped you?"

He gave her a "get real" look. "We both know it needs to come from you. And besides, it's not about me, remember? It's actually not about you either, princess. It's about her right now. You need to step out of the center of your universe for a minute and see the bigger picture."

"The bigger picture is that you're falling for my sister."

"Guilty," he said, and knew he shocked her by admitting that because her eyes widened. And it was true. He wanted to stay up late and eat chocolate chip pancakes at midnight with her, talking about everything and nothing at all. He wanted to kiss that spot behind her ear, the one he knew drove her crazy, then work his way to her lips, watching them curve for him. He wanted to watch her sleep in his bed. She was a bed hog. She slept on her stomach spread out wide, and he didn't care. He wanted to kiss that spot along her tailbone where her shirt rode up in her sleep . . .

"You really are falling for her," Kinsey said again, slowly this time, not a question, but a statement of fact.

He nodded just as the front door opened.

Brynn stood there in her denim sundress with her beat-up white sneakers on her feet. She took in the three of them with one sweeping glance and then her eyes landed on Eli, and she smiled like maybe he was the best thing she'd seen all day.

She was certainly the best thing he'd seen all day.

"Hey," she said softly.

He smiled. "Hey."

Behind him, Kinsey made a sound that spoke volumes. He could almost hear her eyes roll as she brushed past him and headed inside. "Smooth," she whispered. "Real smooth."

Brynn's moms were sweet, easygoing hosts, taking everyone into the backyard, which was a wide, open grassy area, broken up by a tetherball and a bocce court. They plied everyone with drinks and set them all off to play a tournament.

Brynn shocked the hell out of Eli by beating him at bocce.

Olive beamed proudly. "She doesn't have an athletic bone in her body, my sweet baby, but she's got a lot of luck."

"Hey," Brynn said. "I've got plenty of athletic ability."

"Is that so, honey? In what?" Raina asked sweetly.

Brynn pointed at her with her drink. "I can play a mean game of volleyball."

Kinsey laughed.

"What?" Brynn said, looking offended. "I beat you, didn't I?"

"Barely."

Brynn narrowed her eyes. "If you're going to rewrite history, at least make it believable."

Raina stood to refill everyone's glass from the wine bottle, looking confused when she saw that Kinsey hadn't taken so much as a sip. "Honey, would you like a different kind? Red? I've also got vodka."

"No, I'm good, thanks." Kinsey shook her head. "I already had my quota of alcohol this week."

"Me too," Raina said. "But that's not stopping me."

"Mom, she's on dialysis."

"Oh, so sorry," Raina murmured. "I had no idea."

"I don't like to talk about it," Kinsey said, sending a glare at Brynn.

"I can understand that, but it's not good to hold these things in," Raina said. "It only makes things worse."

"No worries there," Kinsey said, and Raina looked relieved. But Eli knew that Kinsey had said that because she knew things couldn't get much worse.

A fact he hated.

BRYNN LOCKED HERSELF in the downstairs guest bathroom. She needed a few minutes. She hadn't meant to bring up Kinsey's illness, hadn't even realized that's what she'd done until she saw Kinsey's expression just before she masked it.

Anxiety.

Kinsey, who by all counts seemed on top of her world at all times, who wanted everyone to know she was in control and didn't give a single shit, was upset. Maybe scared.

And that killed Brynn.

Kinsey had never been her favorite person. But she'd been in Brynn's life far longer than most. Other than her moms and Eli, Kinsey was one of her oldest relationships. And whether she liked it or not, they *were* in a relationship.

She hadn't let herself understand or come to terms with what Kinsey was facing, but it hit her now, hard. Kinsey's life wasn't her own, not really. And the implications of that, realizing how much her own life would have to change if she were in Kinsey's shoes, was . . . well, terrifying and devastating.

Kinsey's health crisis was serious, and Brynn wanted to get tested to see if she was a match. If she could help, she wanted to. Needed to. Because the thought of Kinsey not beating this thing . . .

She put her hands on the counter and counted to ten. When that didn't work, she kept going. She'd gotten to a hundred when she heard Raina calling for her.

She swiped under her eyes and went into the kitchen.

"You okay, baby?" her mom asked.

"Sure. Of course."

Raina gave her a "get real" look and reached for Brynn's hand, pulling her closer. "Try again."

Brynn shook her head. "I feel . . . discombobulated."

"You care about Kinsey. And Max. And maybe especially Eli."

"Mom—"

"It's a good thing, Brynn. Such a good thing." Raina paused. "Look, I know something big happened with Albert."

Brynn opened her mouth to correct the name, but saw the light in Raina's eyes.

"I know his goddamn name," her mom said softly. "I just refuse to say it. Because he hurt you."

"Not like you think."

"Then tell me."

"Mom—"

"Baby, please. My imagination is killing me. I need to know all of it. What happened before you left him?"

Brynn looked away. "I . . . didn't leave him. He left me. Actually, he vanished, with everything. He ran up my credit card, withdrew my savings, and even cashed my bond from grandma. He took anything I had of value, including great-grandma's necklace. He was charming and charismatic and sweet, and I didn't see it coming or suspect a thing."

"Oh, honey. Did you call the police?"

"Yes. But Ashton had told me he was a financial planner, and I stupidly believed him. He was supposedly mobile and traveled to his clients, and didn't have an office. I never met any cowork-ers. No friends either, since he was so busy. So I didn't have much to give the cops to go on. He never left his laptop around. Never let me see his phone. There were a million red flags, and I didn't see a single one of them," she said bitterly. "One morn-ing, I kissed him good-bye to go to work, and when I came home, he was gone. With everything. The building manager had changed the locks because he'd been given notice that we were leaving—three months prior. All that's left is a few boxes of stuff to remind me of how stupid I was."

A sound from behind her had her going still and closing her eyes. *Crap. Shit. Dammit.* Taking a deep breath, she opened her eyes and turned around.

Everyone was crowded in the kitchen doorway. Max. Kinsey. Eli.

"I'm sorry," Kinsey said softly. "We came in to see if we could help get dinner ready."

Eli's gaze never wavered from Brynn's. "I'd like to help."

"Me too," Max said. "With my foot up that guy's ass."

Raina swiped at a few tears on her cheek, hugged her daughter tight, and then smiled brightly at everyone. "I'm so glad you're here for my girl."

"Always will be," Eli said in a voice of steel.

Raina hugged each of them in turn, then pulled back and looked at Kinsey. "Dinner's ready. When do you think your mom might arrive?"

Kinsey grimaced. "I'm sorry. She's always late. I called and left her a message, but she didn't get back to me. Please don't hold up dinner for her."

"Maybe she got caught in traffic. No mom wants to miss family night."

"Just don't hold your breath," Kinsey said with a smile that didn't quite meet her eyes. "She's usually too busy for stuff like this."

The doorbell rang.

"Look at that," Raina said, smiling at Kinsey before moving toward the door. "She surprised you."

"Oh, I'll get it," Kinsey said, trying to rush past Raina, but Raina was the ultimate hostess. She and she alone greeted the guests. "I've got this," she said to a worried-looking Kinsey. "You just relax."

A minute later, Raina was back, leading the way, with Kinsey's mom right behind her. "Everyone, Teresa's here."

Teresa looked like Kinsey plus a decade, which meant she either had great genes or she'd had work done. She breezed toward the group, all smiles.

"Sorry I'm late, I got here as soon as I could."

"She means she got here as soon as she wanted to," Kinsey muttered.

Teresa didn't appear to hear. She waved at everyone including Kinsey, but mother and daughter didn't share a hug, which Brynn thought was odd.

"Mom," Kinsey said. "I asked you to call me back about tonight. We didn't know if you were coming. Plus, I really needed to talk to you first. Can we go outside for a minute? Alone?"

"Sorry, darling. Busy week. We can talk later. I'll tell you all about Rick. He's why I was late—I was waiting on him. Turns out, he meant he was going to be permanently late. The asswipe dumped me by text, if you can believe it. Men, am I right?"

Olive nodded. "You are right."

"I honestly can't believe it," Teresa said. "A damn text."

"I can believe it," Kinsey murmured.

Teresa looked at her. "What does that mean?"

"It means it's the same pattern as always, so I don't under-stand why you're surprised. You let someone into your life, you let him hurt you, he leaves, then next comes you using it as an excuse to fall apart."

Teresa blinked.

So did Brynn. Because that was her pattern too. And that wasn't exactly a fun epiphany to have in front of a crowd.

"So," Olive said into the awkward silence. "How's it been renewing childhood friendships?"

Teresa looked around the group. "Childhood friendships?"

"Mom," Kinsey said, sounding a little panicked. "I *really* need to talk to you for a minute. In private."

"In a minute, darling." She was eyeing everyone curiously. "You've all known each other since you were kids?"

Raina beamed. "Eli, Brynn, and Kinsey were in summer camp together for years. Isn't that cute? There's nothing deeper and more meaningful than a childhood friendship, right?"

Teresa stilled, her mouth opened in a wide *O* as she set down her glass. Before she could say a word, Kinsey grabbed Brynn's arm and yanked her toward the hallway.

"What the—" Brynn started.

"Real quick," Kinsey called out to everyone with a smile that Brynn was sure Kinsey thought was pleasant and unassuming, but was brittle as hell.

In the hallway, Brynn yanked her arm free. "What's going on? What's the manhandling about?"

"Okay," Kinsey said, holding up her hands. "Don't freak."

Brynn narrowed her eyes. "I'm getting a bad feeling."

Kinsey blew out a breath. "Yeah. Warranted. So . . . there's another itty, bitty secret. We're sort of . . . half sisters."

Brynn blinked. "Say that again?"

"We share a sperm donor as a father."

Brynn's mind took a beat to process this, the meaning of the words hitting her like a Category 5 hurricane of sheer shock. She spun on her heel and strode back out to the other room, where everyone was sitting in awkward silence.

Teresa smiled. "They even walk alike."

Brynn realized Kinsey was right on her heels. Ignoring this, she looked at her moms. "Kinsey said that we have the same father. Is that possible?"

Her moms looked positively stunned, wide-eyed with the shock of it.

"Could that be true?" Brynn asked, needing to hear that no, it couldn't possibly in her wildest imagination be even close to possible.

"I don't know," Olive admitted, always truthful and upfront. "I mean the odds . . ."

"Not really as huge as you might think," Teresa said. "There weren't many fertility clinics with sperm banks back in the day. There's only one in this whole county. Guys came from all over to, you know, make deposits for extra cash."

"Not helping," Kinsey said tightly to her mom. "Brynn—"

"No, wait. Give me a second." Brynn put her hands to her temples, which were suddenly aching. "We're . . . *sisters*."

"I mean, all you really have to do is look in the mirror for confirmation," Teresa said. "You both have the same frown when you're pissy—"

"*Mom!*" Kinsey shook her head. "*Please, stop talking.*" She was pale. Looking sick.

Brynn figured she looked about the same at the moment. As far as worst-case scenarios went, this was pretty much numero uno—that she was related to the one person on earth who'd tortured her more than anyone else. And that *that* was probably the *real* definition of sisters wasn't lost on her.

Teresa was still staring at Brynn as if she was just a sight for sore eyes. "We tried contacting you when Kinsey was fifteen to ask if you'd be willing to get tested to see if you might be a good kidney match."

"Oh my God, Mom," Kinsey said, sounding near tears. "*Stop.*"

With her pulse beating in her ears, Brynn took a step back. "*No*, that's actually not true. You called and then hung up when I answered. And even though I tried repeatedly to call you back, you never picked up."

"Yes," Kinsey whispered, looking tortured.

"Why did you hang up? Why didn't you just tell me the truth, that you wanted one of my kidneys?"

Kinsey opened her mouth and then . . . shut it again.

Brynn could feel her eyes burning, but she refused to cry in front of an audience. She started to leave the room, but stopped. "No," she said. "I need to know. Was this"—she gestured between the two of them—"just a long con for my kidney?"

"No. *No*," Kinsey repeated when Brynn made a disgusted sound. "And *that's* the reason I didn't follow through with the phone call all those years ago. It's the reason I was upset when Eli ran into you at the hospital and offered you a room. It's the reason why I didn't tell you I was sick. Because I *don't* want your kidney."

Right. And she was supposed to believe that. God, she'd done it again. She'd let someone in and had gotten hurt. What was wrong with her? "You know, when I moved back here, I wasn't going to put up with bullshit from people anymore. And yet, here I am—" She cut herself off when her voice broke, because she refused to break down in front of Kinsey.

Her half sister . . .

Shaking her head in disbelief, she strode out of the room. She heard her moms calling after her, and Eli too, but she grabbed her purse and got the hell out of Dodge.

Because sometimes a girl just needed a pity party for one.

 CHAPTER 19

From seventeen-year-old Brynn's summer camp journal:

Dear Moms,

Now that I'm officially a counselor and they're pay-ing me, I'm actually having fun. There's a little girl here with thick glasses and out-of-control hair, and I love her. She's scared of . . . well, everything, just like I used to be. I hold her hand and read her stories.
I wish I'd had me at camp back then!

Love you guys,
Brynn

ELI STARTED TO go after Brynn, but Olive stopped him. "Honey, let's give her a moment. Trust me when I say she's stubborn and that she needs to come to terms with things in her own time. Hearing she has a sister will be a blessing once she thinks about it."

"Maybe I should go," Kinsey said. "She's my sister."

"Is she really your sister if she just walked away from you for being an idiot?" Max asked.

Kinsey glared at him. Everyone did.

Max tossed up his hands. "What? Kinsey should've told her sooner."

"Thank you, Einstein," Kinsey snapped. "I hadn't thought of that."

Eli shook his head and moved toward the door. He was going after Brynn and no one was going to stop him.

"Wait," Kinsey said. "You're just leaving me here?"

"Yeah, Kins. I'm going to leave you here. Your sister's out there thinking the only reason you befriended her was for her kidney. Even you can't be that selfish."

"She gets that from her father," Teresa said.

Eli gave the woman a long, hard look and then turned back to Kinsey. "I'm going to try to help her through this, for all of us." Not completely heartless or clueless to what this was costing Kinsey, he looked at Raina. "You got her?"

She nodded and came around to put an arm around Kinsey, also handing her a tissue.

Kinsey looked shocked to find herself with tears on her face, and Eli knew why. She never cried. The woman was a rock. A grumpy, sick rock that he understood and loved with all his irritated heart.

"We've got you, honey," Raina said, patting Kinsey's back.

Teresa shifted on her feet. "I should . . . go. I've got a thing . . ." She looked a little surprised when Olive opened the front door for her, before she'd even finished her sentence.

Kinsey started to make a move to go too, but Olive took her hand. "Stay, baby. I've got the most amazing flan de queso for dessert."

Eli watched Kinsey blink, looking touched and shocked that they'd want her to stay after what she'd done—or not done. With a grateful nod at Olive and Raina, Eli left.

Brynn had a few minutes' head start on him. But he'd find her. Maybe he wasn't crazy about how deep his feelings had developed for her, feelings he'd promised not to catch ever again, but that was him not wanting to get hurt. Brynn was a totally different kind of woman than he'd ever been with. She was warm and giving and open, and . . . well, everything. She didn't deserve this.

He found her sitting on the curb a few houses down with her head on her knees, gulping in air.

It broke his heart.

She broke his heart.

He sat beside her and put a hand on her back. She was trembling. "Brynn."

She burst into tears.

"Come here," he whispered, pulling her against him.

"I'm not falling apart. I just cry when I'm mad," she said, hiccupping through sobs. "And I'm really, *really* m-mad!"

"I know."

She scooted a little closer and lifted her head, giving him a glimpse of her tear-ravaged face before she pressed it into the crook of his neck. "I'm mad at you too," she said, voice muffled.

He closed his eyes and tightened his grip on her. "I know."

"*Really* mad, Eli."

"I know. I'm so sorry."

She rubbed her face on his shirt, getting it wet, and then sighed. "I mean, I get why she didn't tell me. She's emotionally bankrupt. But you. You knew and didn't tell me either. I didn't see that coming."

"She was going to tell you."

She snorted and then—he was pretty sure—used his shirt as a tissue. When she pulled free, she gave him a little push. "When exactly was she going to do that? Back when we were teenagers and she first found out—which, bee-tee-dub, would've been the right choice. But she didn't do that, which tells me that she didn't want to be sisters. Not then, and not anytime in the years since either. Not even when I moved into the house. Which also means that on top of not wanting to be sisters, she didn't even want to be friends. None of you did. Because you don't do that, keep this big a secret, not even to a perfect stranger, much less a friend."

"Brynn—"

"Don't. Please don't." She shook her head. "Let me give you some facts, okay? I'm not good at this stuff, at reading cues from people, cultivating relationships, and especially at keeping them. In fact, I'm a real failure at it. I'm a failure at a lot of things, actually. But I sure as hell don't want to talk about it, not with you." Standing, she looked down at him, eyes red-rimmed but fierce. "I promised myself I'd change things up this time, that I'd be in the driver's seat of my own life, that I'd choose myself if others wouldn't. I almost forgot that, but I'm remembering now." She turned from him, and he stood and reached for her hand.

"Don't run, Brynn. Let me take you home."

She pulled her hand free and crossed her arms. "Right now I don't know where home is."

"I'd like to think it's still at the house with me and Kinsey and Max. We screwed up, but we can fix this."

"Remember when you were all butthurt when you thought I lumped you in with my asshole ex? Well, guess what? You fit right in."

"No argument," he said softly, his chest hurting just looking at her. "Please, Brynn. Let me get you home."

"My grandma always said to never take home an asshole."

"And *my* grandma always said that when you make a mess, you need to fix it," he said.

"I'm not your mess."

"I'm not just leaving you out here, Brynn."

"Fine." She crossed her arms. "You can take me home, but you're still going into the asshole file with everyone else."

He was just relieved she was still willing to consider his house her home. "Understood."

WHEN KINSEY LEFT Brynn's moms' place, she wasn't sure what to do with herself. Olive and Raina had been wonderful to her, so kind and sweet even though she hadn't deserved it, but she couldn't stay forever. She had apologies to make and fences to mend. Only the minute she left the safe bubble of the house, her chest started hurting.

Okay, her heart. Her *heart* hurt.

Her mom, as always, had made the evening about her. Shock. But then *she'd* done the exact same thing. She was grateful Eli had gone after Brynn, and she hoped he'd caught up with her. She didn't want Brynn to be alone right now. Max had taken an Uber. Kinsey could do the same, but she didn't pull out her phone.

Instead, she started walking. It was pouring rain, but she liked the rain. It matched her mood, and within minutes, she was just about as wet as she could get.

And cold.

Fitting, since her heart was also cold.

Except that wasn't quite right. It didn't feel cold. It felt . . . broken. She still couldn't quite wrap her mind around how bad it had gone, and how fast. She felt really alone.

Also her own doing. She could've invited Deck to go with her tonight. He would've wanted to be here with her. But she hadn't asked him because she'd been trying to reinforce that they weren't like that. They were friends with benefits—minus the friends. And even though she knew that wasn't really true, she also knew she couldn't change the reality of her life.

Everything felt so wildly out of her control, and, oh, how she hated that.

She realized she'd been walking for half an hour and was shivering and soaked through only when she found herself in front of Deck's house.

The door opened and Deck stood there in jeans and nothing else except a five-year-old on his back. "Hey," he said, with a smile that failed when he caught sight of her face.

"Ms. Davis," Toby yelled. "You came to visit us!"

Deck gently set Toby down. "Hey, kiddo. It's almost bedtime. How about you go get started with getting on your pj's and brushing your teeth, and I'll be right there to tuck you in."

"But—"

"What did I say about buts?"

Toby sighed. "That they stink."

Deck ruffled his hair. "Go on now."

The kid turned his beautifully woeful eyes on Kinsey. "Sorry, Ms. Davis, you'll have to come visit me another time. I can't argue my bedtime, on account'a if I do, then I don't get to go fishing with Daddy tomorrow."

Somehow Kinsey managed to give a smile and a "no problem," and then she was alone with Deck.

He pulled her inside, peeled her out of her drenched sweater, and draped a throw blanket around her shoulders. Then he pulled her into him and wrapped her up in his arms.

She didn't even realize she was crying until he palmed the back of her head and soothed her with his low voice, murmuring things she couldn't hear over the sound of her sobs.

It was mortifying.

But seeing Brynn shut down with shock had just about gutted her. She hadn't expected that. Hadn't really even realized how much she wanted to be sisters with her, until she'd blown it. She didn't want to lose her, or her moms. They were amazing. But as usual, she'd put a match to all of it.

It wasn't like she enjoyed being the girl who everyone loved to hate. But no matter how hard she tried, she chased people away. She honestly had no idea why Eli, Max, and Deck still liked her, but she was grateful.

But it was only Deck she needed tonight.

He extracted himself briefly, then reappeared a few minutes later. "Wanted to make sure Tobes was settled okay. He's already out like a light." He then scooped her up and sat on the couch with her in his lap. Holding her against his big, warm body, he didn't press her to talk.

Which was probably why she did. "I screwed up," she whispered.

He stroked a big hand down her back and she snuggled in, wishing there weren't wet clothes and a thick blanket between her and his bare chest.

"What happened?" he finally asked.

"I was at family night at Brynn's tonight."

"By accident?"

She snorted, appreciating his dry sense of humor. "I know, right? Pretty unlike me. But Brynn's moms asked me to come, invited everyone. They said no one ever skips family night, so we all went."

He was quiet a minute. "By all, you mean who?"

"Eli, Max, me . . ."

"So . . . *everyone* got an invite."

She lifted her head. "My mom came too. I never thought she would. She never shows when she says she's going to. I only invited her in the first place because Olive and Raina insisted. And then, because she was about to spill my secret, I had to tell Brynn the truth."

Deck's brows raised. "The truth."

"About us being half sisters."

Another pause from Deck, probably wondering exactly how stupid she was to have let this happen. "How did Brynn take it?" he finally asked.

Kinsey winced. "Not great. She left."

"Remind me again why you didn't tell her until you were forced to?"

She blew out a breath. "I've always meant to. But . . . she's got this great life, you know? Awesome moms, and she's so loved . . ."

Deck stood up, set her back on the couch, and strode across the room to the sliding glass door, looking sightlessly out into the night.

"Deck?"

"You've got an option at that same so-called perfection that Brynn has. You know that, right? You've just chosen not to pick it. Over and over again."

She nodded, because this wasn't new information. Something else that wasn't new—she had a long history of not paying close enough attention to those she cared about. Having studied psychology for her job, she'd learned that was because she was selfish. The world revolved around her. She tried really hard to teach kids to stretch their wings beyond that selfish place. She'd been working on doing the same, but she'd clearly regressed big time. Because if she forced herself to look at tonight from the outside, it all came into sharp focus.

Deck was frustrated because she hadn't invited him to the dinner. "I should have brought you with me tonight," she said softly to his back.

He shrugged. "I don't ever want something from you that you don't want to give."

Somehow this only made her feel even worse. "I should've asked you." With a throat thick with emotion, she rose and walked to him. "Just as I should've told Brynn about me and her before she found out this way." She put her hands on his arms and turned him to face her. "I'm sorry I didn't ask you, Deck."

"Why didn't you?"

"I don't know."

Not buying this, he shook his head.

She sighed and admitted the truth. "I'm afraid to let you all the way in."

"Babe, you've already got me on my knees. All you've gotta do is unlock and open up." He gently tapped a finger over her heart.

She dropped her head onto his chest. "I'm just so tired."

His hands went to her hips and he pulled her in. "It's late. Stay. I'll make you grilled cheese."

She managed a smile. "You know I've got a soft spot for grilled cheese." She paused. "And for you."

He gave her a knowing look. "More than just friends with benefits minus the friends part."

Yes. It was on the tip of her tongue, which she bit to keep the words inside. Because she couldn't say them. She'd never be able to say them.

He stared at her for a beat. "Shit." He dropped his hands from her. "I'm such an idiot."

Her heart lurched and she stood up. "No. It's me. I'm the idiot. I . . . I'm attracted to you, Deck. You know that. And I need you. You're important to me. You know that too."

"Most guys would buy that and let you take the out because you've got kidney disease. But I'm not most guys, Kinsey. So stop bullshitting me. If stolen moments are all you're feeling for me, then fine. But if you're running scared, which I think you are, then you're also a hypocrite."

"Excuse me?"

"Isn't running scared what you object to about Brynn? You worry she's going to take off and hurt Eli? And you?"

"I—" She shook her head. How was it he always got to the heart of the matter, where she'd not even *seen* the heart of the matter? "Yes. Okay? Yes, I'm a hypocrite. But I'm afraid I'm going to get hurt. Somehow I always get hurt because I overestimate how much people like me. Or don't like me. I mean, most of the time, I don't know why anyone would feel anything for me at all. I mean, look at me, Deck. I'm a mess, all the time."

"I like you just as you are. Always have." He cupped her face, forcing her to look at him. "How could you not know how I feel about you?" he asked softly.

"Well, I try really hard not to dig too deep," she quipped,

heart pounding. "It's an art, really, and it's the one thing I'm really good at—"

"Stop." His voice was gruff but gentle. "Stop redirecting and avoiding. Just listen. Because I'm going to tell you *exactly* how I feel so that I know that you know, and then you know that I know that you know."

She gaped at him. "You've been watching *Friends*."

"Three times a week without fail. I'm in love with you, Kinsey."

Oh, God. Her heart stopped.

But Deck wasn't finished. "And I believe you love me too. But you're in denial, deep. I get that tonight was rough on you. I also get that this is about you and Brynn right now, so we can absolutely table this and discuss later, but at some point, we will circle back to it."

He was always there for her, always willing to set aside his own feelings and his own agenda for her. No one had ever done that, not even Eli. But all she could do was shake her head. "I can't do this. Any of it. Brynn probably hates me."

"Since when has it ever bothered you what anyone thought of you? Did you at least tell her all of it? That you also know where your dad is, the dad you two share?"

"Of course I didn't! Look, I didn't start off this story by saying I'd made smart decisions tonight! I realize I've kept three big secrets from her: the whole me being sick thing, us being sisters, and our dad. And for the record, I never intended to keep that last a secret. But I know the truth—that she'll hate me even more when she finds out about him, and my history with him, that he lived with us a few times on and off. So I have to swallow my urge to come clean, because that's for me. Not telling her . . . well, that's for her. Especially after hearing some of her story tonight. There's no way I'll *ever* let her meet that asshole. Her ex conned her, Deck. She has no idea how easily her father would do the same if given a chance."

Some of his irritation seemed to fade, replaced by concern. "I know you went and saw him for his birthday a few weeks ago," he said. "That it was the first time in years. But you said it went fine and you didn't want to talk about."

She plopped back onto the couch. "Still don't."

"Kins." He crouched at her side and looked into her face in that way he had of seeing her, really seeing her. "What did he do?"

She sighed. "I've told you about him. He comes off all sweet and affable and charming. But . . ." She shook her head. "Just like always, I let him fool me. He always does that and I think, hey, it's all going to be okay, and then . . ."

"*What did he do?*"

Instead of answering, she closed her eyes. "Am I really so difficult and hard to love?"

"Oh, Kinsey." He pulled her into him. "Loving you has been the easiest thing I've ever done. And I bet if you asked Eli or Max, or any of the kids you've taken care of at work, they'd say the same."

She drew in a deep breath of pure Deck. She hated to correct his emotional declaration with some cold, hard facts, but that's exactly what she had to do. "Everyone loves chocolate milk.

Until it expires, and then it's over. It doesn't matter how much people love it . . . it's still gone."

He wrapped a fist in her hair and tugged lightly, tipping her face up to his. "Are you comparing yourself to expired chocolate milk?"

"*Yes!*" She gave him a little push for emphasis. "I'm the expiring chocolate milk!"

He was looking pretty ticked off now. Quite the feat, making the man with infinite patience run out of that infinite patience. "I should be pretty fucking insulted that you think I'd actually walk away from you because you've got a medical condition that you can't control," he finally said. "But I get how you grew up, how the people who should've loved you let you down, so I know you're speaking from hard-earned experience, but let me say it again. None of that shit matters to me."

She shook her head. "You *have* to say that. You want to sleep with me."

His mouth tightened. "You're tired and upset, so I'm going to do us both a favor and pretend you didn't just say that. Tell me what your father did, Kinsey."

"He wanted to know the current going rate for one of his kidneys."

"Jesus." He dropped his head for a moment and studied his feet while the air crackled with tension. But as always, he got ahold of himself, and by the time he looked at her again, all she could see was steady, stoic Deck. "He's not a potential donor, you already knew that."

Yes, she'd known it since the day he'd actually shown up for one of *her* birthdays. Her fifteenth. He hadn't been around for a few years at that point, and he'd told her there at her party that he'd been out of rehab for only a few weeks. She'd had no idea at the time what he'd been addicted to—drugs or alcohol, it hadn't mattered. Either left him out of the running to give her a kidney, ever.

"I wish I was a match," Deck said with a fierce quiet, volumes of emotion behind those six words.

She shook her head, grateful he wasn't. "I've told you, I'm never again going to take a kidney from someone still using it."

"Why would you deny someone who wants to save your life?"

"You know why!" She jumped to her feet and paced the room, frustrated he didn't get it, that *no one* got it.

"Your donor's death wasn't on you."

Logically, she got that. But emotions weren't logical. And neither were hopes and dreams. All she'd ever wanted was a fix that wouldn't involve putting anyone else at risk. The only reason she'd allowed herself to be on a list for a kidney was because, in most of those cases, a kidney would come in because someone unfortunately no longer had a need for it. She knew that no one understood this, but she didn't care. Because what they also didn't understand was how it'd felt knowing that not only had she wasted someone's good kidney when her body had rejected it, but that the process of donating had killed him. "I've held a lot back from you," she said. "I admit that. It seems I'd rather choke on my words than let you see me vulnerable. But God, I'm so tired of being so vulnerable," she whispered.

"Ah, Kins." He pulled her back into him, pressed his jaw to the top of her head. "Being vulnerable isn't a sign of weakness. It's a sign of strength. But even if that wasn't true, you're not alone."

This was true. He was there. He was always there. And the thought suddenly made her panic, made her throat close up, which in turn made her feel hemmed in, claustrophobic. Because no matter how hard she tried to keep him at a distance for his own good, she failed. Stepping free, she turned away. "I've got to go."

"There it is." He let her get to the door. "While you're already freaked out," he said to her back, "you might as well know."

"Know what?"

"I want more than this."

She closed her eyes. Dropped her forehead to the door.

He came up behind her but didn't touch her. "I want to be more to you than just a booty call because you've had a rough time at a family dinner that you chose to go to alone rather than bring me."

"Don't you see?" she whispered, turning to face him. "Being with you . . . having you love me . . . you're already giving me so much more than I can ever give you."

"Maybe you've underestimated yourself."

"It's a gift I can never pay back, Deck. Ever."

"When it comes to love, there is no paying it back," he told her. "Real love goes to the ends of the earth with no regrets. It's there for you, Kins, and it's right in front of you. All you've got to do is hold on."

"I can't." She felt the tears leak from eyes and swiped at them angrily. "I've gotta go."

Shockingly, he reached around her to open the door for her.

And with nothing else to say—after all, this was a disaster of her own making—she walked away.

And he let her.

CHAPTER 20

From seventeen-year-old Kinsey's summer camp journal:

Dear Journal,

Surprise! I'm still around. Survived the infection from hell, and now I'm going to be living with transplant rejection, but, hey, breathing is breathing, right?

I'm weaning off the depression meds, and Eli is no longer watching me every second of the day like I might jump off a cliff. Fuck that. I want to live, just to prove I can.

But I've got a secret. When I was at rock bottom last year, I went looking for my dad. Sure, he walked away from his own daughter, so I don't know why I did this. Okay, that's a lie. Honestly? Just between you and me? I think I went looking to see if he'd offer to help me. I told myself I'd never accept his kidney, I just . . . Hell. I just wanted him to offer. My mom actually helped me, and we located him in Bakersfield, a hellhole about two and a half hours from Wildstone.

He was the same charismatic con man I remember. Oh, and he wanted to know what the going rate was for a kidney these days. Charming, right? But . . . when I was looking for more deets on him through one of those ancestry apps, I learned something shocking—he isn't my only blood relative. I've got a sibling, a half sibling, and with some more research, I found her.

Are you ready for this?

It's Brynn.

Yes, that annoying weirdo from summer camp, the one with the frizzy hair, the one who was even worse at sports than me, the one who also had bad night vision—although mine was less bad.

Mental head thunk here. Because how did I not see this sooner???????

I called her. I don't know why. I just thought that somehow we'd immediately feel like sisters. She was rude and I hung up. And that's the end of that story.

Thanks for being here for me, journal.

Kinsey

BRYNN WOKE UP slowly. Mornings always sucked, and this one sucked harder than most. Even lying there perfectly still while trying to fall back asleep, she couldn't. Because she knew what was waiting for her.

The memories of what had happened last night.

She was Kinsey's half sister, which had been kept from her.

Which also meant that any progress she and Kinsey had made toward a real friendship was null and void.

Rinse and repeat for Eli.

And if her heart hurt over Kinsey—and, oh, it did—it had actually broken over Eli.

But she'd never had the luxury of wallowing in heartbreak, and now was no exception. She had things to do. People to yell at. People being Kinsey.

Her sister.

Half sister, she reminded herself, trying make the "half" part matter more. But it didn't. All her life she'd wished for a sibling, and to find out she had one, but that it'd been kept from her—by that very sister, no less . . . *Gah.* Tired of playing dead, she opened her eyes. She was in her room at Eli's house. He'd brought her here, a quiet but solid, steady presence that on any other really bad night she would've appreciated. He'd tried to follow her into her room to talk, but she'd kicked him out.

He'd sent Mini in as his substitute, and the sweet, gentle dog was at her side, still sleeping.

And snoring. And drooling.

Her head was pounding courtesy of the bottle of wine she'd imbibed alone. And how had she forgotten how much wine made her head hurt the next morning?

With a groan, she sat up and blinked blearily. Mini lifted her head too, thumping her tail on the bed in greeting. Brynn hugged her, then froze at the sight of Eli fast asleep in the chair that usually lived in the corner. He'd pulled it closer. It wasn't big enough for a full-grown man, so his legs were sprawled out in front of him and his head was crooked to the side, his body loose and relaxed as only the dead asleep could manage. He wasn't snoring or drooling, which was annoying. He was a liar.

A liar who'd known her truth before she had.

A *long* time before she had.

She cleared her throat loudly, and he shot straight up. He had bedhead, wrinkled clothes, and eyes at half-mast, lazy with sleep as they landed on her. "You okay?" he asked.

Dammit. Why couldn't he just stay in the asshole file? This would be a whole lot easier on her if he did. And no, she wasn't okay, not by a long shot, but, hey, when was she ever really? "What are you doing in here?"

"Making sure you're okay."

"No, you were sleeping. And snoring and drooling."

"I don't snore."

"Like a buzz saw," she said. "I've got no idea how you even slept through it."

"Maybe you've got the two of us confused."

She narrowed her eyes. "I don't snore."

He gave her a small smile. "You sure?"

Shit. No. Because she did snore when she'd been drinking. With a huff, she tossed her covers aside and then stared down at herself. She was wearing her bra and panties. "Where are my clothes?"

"You threw them off just before climbing into bed. I tried to get you into pj's, but you threatened to hit me over the head with the bottle of wine you were hugging if I so much as touched you." He stretched and grimaced, rubbing the back of his neck; meanwhile, his shirt rose up and exposed a strip of tanned abs. Pretending not to notice, she started to stand up, swayed, and then sat back down.

He stood up and wrapped the blanket around her shoulders. "If I make you my famous hangover fix for breakfast, think you can keep it down?" he asked.

"I'm not hungover." Look at that. She could lie too. "But yes."

He looked at her for a moment, then sat on the edge of the mattress, leaning over her, and for a beat her body betrayed her, wanting to pull him down on top of her.

Bad body.

He ran a finger down the side of her face, his touch warm and gentle, and she closed her eyes.

He waited until she opened them again to speak. "You still haven't told me if you're okay."

"I'm fine."

"You're amazing and resilient, is what you are. But you're not fine, at least not yet."

She tossed up her hands. "Then why did you ask me?"

"To get you talking to me."

"You're a sneaky one." She looked away. "I'm . . . mad. Hurt. What happened last night cemented my shitty track record with trust."

He nodded solemnly. "I know. For the first time in my life, I nearly broke a promise and told you. But I knew it should come from Kinsey, who wanted to tell you."

"She's your family," she said. "I get it. But as it turns out, she's my family too." She shook her head. "Funny how I thought it would feel different."

"Family, real family, *is* different," he said. "And it has nothing to do with blood ties. I'm hoping you can eventually give me a chance to prove that to you."

"You, or all of you?"

He met her anger with regret and a grace she probably couldn't have managed. "All of us."

She made no comment on that. Because, unlike everyone else around here, she valued the truth. She also wanted answers. "Why didn't she tell me all those years ago?"

"She didn't want you to think she was calling only because she needed a kidney. She didn't want you to pay a price for a relationship with her."

"That wasn't for her to decide."

"True, but Kinsey's as stubborn as"—a small smile curved his mouth—"well, you, actually."

She stared at that mouth for a long beat, annoyed that all she could remember was how amazing it felt on hers.

"I screwed up," he said quietly. "And I'm sorry."

"Tell me the truth. Was I just a way to help Kinsey?"

"No." Eyes filled with sorrow and remorse, he bent his head and touched his forehead to hers. "Never. I wanted you and Kinsey to connect. I didn't realize it would be *me* feeling the connection. But that's exactly what happened." He cupped her face and her body reacted. Her hands went to his forearms and slid up to his biceps, then into his hair. She sucked in a shaky breath, but before she could speak, there came a single knock at her bedroom door as it opened—Kinsey doing her typical knock and enter at the same time, with utter disregard for anyone's privacy.

Brynn pulled back from Eli and crossed her arms. *"Does no one understand what a damn shut door means?!"*

Kinsey slapped her hand over her eyes. "Oh my God. You're in bed together. My life's falling apart and you're having sex? Seriously?"

Brynn rolled her eyes. "Go away, Kinsey."

Kinsey didn't, of course. "Are you dressed?" she asked, leaving her hands over her eyes, looking pained. "Tell me you're fully clothed."

Brynn sighed. *"Go. Away."*

Kinsey dropped her hand from her eyes and stared up at the ceiling. "Eli, I need to talk to my sister."

"Oh, look at that," Brynn said. "So you *can* say those words in the same sentence—'my' and 'sister.'"

"Look," Kinsey said. "We need to talk."

"No."

"I'm going to pretend you said yes. I'll be in the kitchen."

When Kinsey was gone, Eli looked at Brynn.

"No."

"Brynn—"

"Fine." Brynn blew out a sigh. "Whatever. I'll go out there, but only because I want to yell at her. A lot."

He brushed a kiss to her forehead. "I'll be close by if you need anything."

"I won't." But then she gripped his hand when he would have risen, and swallowed hard. "I don't know if I'm ready for this," she whispered.

He squeezed her hand. "This is what families do, Brynn. This is what siblings do. I'm not going to make any more excuses for her. I feel like shit you found out the way you did, which could've been avoided. Maybe you could just hear her out before you decide what to do." He bent and scooped up her sundress, handing it to her before heading to the door.

"One more thing," she said, and he turned back to look at her, those gray eyes dark and intense. "I don't know exactly what I think about all this, or how it affects my feelings for you."

"Understood," he said, his voice low and gruff with emotion. "But I'm not giving up. I won't hurt you, Brynn. Not ever again."

She knew he believed what he was saying, and she knew she wanted to believe what he was saying.

But she also knew that her history told her she couldn't. Her one-strike policy was in full force.

KINSEY WAS MAKING mimosas, her hands not quite steady when Brynn came into the kitchen wearing one of her cute sundresses, though she hadn't contained her hair or bothered with shoes. Kinsey took a deep breath and handed her a mimosa. "Even though you don't look of age."

Brynn looked into the glass. "Is this wise?"

"It contains thirty-two percent of the daily suggested dose of C, so consider it a vitamin."

Brynn nodded. "Good to know. But I was referring to us

drinking. At eight in the morning. When we're both looking for a fight."

"Ah." Kinsey nodded. Then shook her head. "I'm actually not looking for a fight," she said, filled with regret and remorse. Because she knew damn well that her actions didn't quite match up with her words. Everything she'd done with Brynn was fight inducing, especially her three secrets—the last of which she was taking to the grave if she had anything to say about it. At this point, she was a walking, talking ball of anxiety, deeply concerned about her relationship with her sister and how she'd sabotaged it by keeping things to herself. Doing so had led to the end of her and Deck. Maybe to the end of her and Eli—still to be determined, because she wasn't sure how mad at her he was. And now she was also in danger of losing her sister as well, before they'd even really found each other.

All of it her own fault.

And yet, she couldn't, wouldn't change a thing. She was in protection mode, and she would do this for Brynn, since she'd done so little else.

"Maybe *you're* not looking for a fight," Brynn said. "But I am."

Kinsey's heart tightened. Look at that, the poor organ was getting quite the beating this week. "You've found your backbone," she managed.

"Even slowpokes learn eventually. I've got a lot of questions."

Kinsey braced. "Fair. But first, I want you to know how sorry I am that you found out the way you did. It shouldn't have gone down like that. And I really wish I told you sooner. I should have."

"Why didn't you?"

"Didn't want you to think I wanted you only for your kidney."

"How long have you known?"

Kinsey winced. Okay, so they were diving right in. "I figured it out when I was fifteen. The year I stopped going to camp because I got really sick." She'd hated that. Camp had been an escape, a fantasy world where she could be whoever she wanted, and she'd not even realized it until she'd lost the option. "By that time, I needed a kidney and I needed it yesterday. I was on the donor list, but nothing was happening, so I got talked into looking for relatives on the off chance anyone might be willing to be tested to see if they were a match. I went through all the ancestry sites out there back then, and was amazed at the information available. I thought I'd find our dad and maybe siblings of his."

"But that's not who you found."

Holding Brynn's gaze, Kinsey reminded herself if she was going to save this relationship, she had to be brutally honest here. And she wanted that, desperately. So she shook her head. "No. I found another offspring."

"Me. Because I'd uploaded my DNA and a picture a while back in a moment of curiosity."

Kinsey nodded and took a big gulp of the mimosa.

"I've got a long history of letting things go," Brynn said. "Of just turning the other cheek, or better yet, walking away. But I'm done with that. This time I'm not leaving without answers."

"Lucky me," Kinsey quipped, and when Brynn didn't smile or break eye contact, she sighed. "Look, I have a problem with joking at inappropriate times. I also laugh when people fall down. I'm pretty messed up to be honest."

Brynn stared at her for a beat and then let out a low, mirthless snort. "I laugh when people fall too."

Middle ground. So they were both messed up. She'd take it. "I couldn't locate my dad." *At the time, anyway.*

"*Our* dad," Brynn said.

"Yeah." *Please don't ask me about him . . .* "Our dad."

Brynn appeared to think about that for a minute. "You called me. And okay, I was rude. But then when I called you back, you hung up. And then you wouldn't answer my return calls."

"I couldn't do it. I couldn't ask you for a kidney."

"How about just to let me know we were sisters so that I could make my own decisions on what I would or wouldn't give you?" Brynn shook her head. "But you didn't do any of that. You just decided for me."

"Guilty," Kinsey said softly.

"You could've died," Brynn said just as softly. "You would've preferred that to swallowing your pride?"

"I think you might be underestimating the size of my pride," Kinsey said, again trying to joke.

But apparently Brynn still wasn't playing. "Trust me, I know just how big it is. I knew it then and I know it now." Brynn shook her head. "So why are you telling me all of this? Why did you allow any of it to happen? You could have gone on as is, never saying a word, not letting me move in. I never would've known the difference."

"I thought about doing just that," Kinsey admitted.

Brynn didn't look impressed. In fact, she looked even more irritated. Kinsey wasn't surprised. She had that effect on a lot of people.

"Okay, so clearly you received a kidney."

"Yes." Kinsey hesitated, because this part sucked.

"If you want me to walk away, then by all means, please stop," Brynn said.

Kinsey drew a deep breath. "So my first kidney donor was a kid from my high school." She polished off her mimosa and turned away to set down the glass, staying where she was, staring out the kitchen window. "Our surgeries went well, but then complications happened."

"Complications?"

"Yeah. Big ones." Kinsey closed her eyes and took a deep breath. "He died."

"Oh my God. Kinsey." Brynn came up beside her. "I'm so sorry."

"Yeah, me too. So you can see why I've got an aversion to talking about this." She couldn't look at Brynn. So she went back to staring out the window. High tide, and surf was up. Max was most likely out there. Maybe even Eli by now too. No, Eli wouldn't have left. He was no doubt standing by somewhere close, making sure she and Brynn didn't kill each other.

"But you had complications too," Brynn said.

"Yes. My body's been trying to reject the kidney ever since."

Brynn looked sick. "Just how bad is it?"

"It's not as bad as you're thinking. I've got dialysis three times a week—that's just a part of life for me." She shrugged.

"I'm used to it. There're a few other annoying symptoms, but whatever. I'm alive. That kid isn't."

Brynn appeared to take this all in. "I assume Eli, Max, Deck . . . and everyone you know has already gotten tested and isn't a match. I'm getting tested ASAP."

Kinsey shook her head. "Don't bother. I'm not taking a kidney from anyone alive. *Especially* you."

Brynn blinked, looking shocked. "Kins—"

"I mean it."

Brynn's eyes narrowed. "You do realize you're not the boss of me, right?"

"This isn't a joke."

"Agreed," Brynn said. "And I'm not joking, I'm deadly serious. I'd give a stranger my kidney if they needed it. Why wouldn't I give my ex-frenemy turned sister the same?"

Kinsey's heart hitched. "So . . . we're not frenemies anymore?"

Brynn looked at her for a long beat, during which Kinsey tried to keep breathing.

"To be determined," Brynn finally said. "But whatever we are, we're also most definitely sisters. Which isn't the same thing as friends."

Kinsey absorbed that blow, but then Brynn said, "Sisters are better than friends. Hand me your phone."

Kinsey was completely turned inside out, dizzy from the emotional whiplash. "What?"

Brynn grabbed Kinsey's phone, then waved it in front of Kinsey's face to unlock it. She brought up the contacts and searched for something. "Where am I?" she finally asked.

Kinsey grimaced. "Under Pain in My Ass."

Brynn rolled her eyes, then changed it to Best Sister on the Planet before downloading an app called Find Your People.

"What are you doing now?" Kinsey asked.

"This app allows us to locate each other."

"What the hell for?"

"Because that's what sisters do."

Kinsey blinked.

"Look," Brynn said. "Other than your mom, I'm basically your only blood relative. I mean, since neither of us knows where our dad is, right?"

Kinsey hesitated, then forced herself to look Brynn right in the eyes as she nodded. She hadn't protected Brynn from much, but she could do this. Because God willing, Brynn would *never* know their father. "And you're *not* getting tested."

"*Yes, I am.*"

"*No.* I'm not budging on this, Brynn, not ever."

Brynn drew a deep breath. "If you're going to learn anything about me, even one thing, let it be this." She stepped closer and looked right into Kinsey's eyes. "I can't handle any more secrets or lies. I can't. I can't handle people keeping things from me. We have to agree to be honest from this point going forward, no matter what. And with that comes *my* honesty, my truth. I'm *going* to get tested, whether you like it or not. I'm telling you this because I know you don't like it, but for us to move forward, there can't be secrets. I'm forgiving you for the past, but now that you know me, you know my biggest fear is people keeping things from me, which *always* works out badly for me in the end."

Kinsey blinked. She was being forgiven . . . when she didn't deserve it. But she was also making the purposeful decision not to tell Brynn about their dad, which might come back to bite her in the ass. That would be her own problem. She was protecting Brynn. "I'm not an open book like you. I'm a private person."

"I respect your boundaries, but when it comes to things that impact our relationship, it's only going to work if we're honest."

"I don't want you to be tested," Kinsey said. "How's that for open book?"

Brynn gave her a tight smile. "And while I respect your feelings, it's my body, my choice, and I'm choosing to get tested."

Kinsey had to admit, Brynn playing loose and fancy-free with being an "open book" sure made it easier to hide their father from her.

"What you do with my info after we find out is a discussion for another day," Brynn said.

Kinsey just stared at her. "Are you always this obnoxious?"

Brynn actually laughed and threw her arms around Kinsey. "I'm your sister, aren't I? Deal with it." She pulled back. "I'm going to tell you one more thing. I'm going to find our dad. For you."

Oh, Jesus. Kinsey felt like she was on a Tilt-A-Whirl, going way too fast but unable to get off. When Brynn had smiled at her, her heart had squeezed. Then she'd hugged her too, and she'd felt a surge of emotion that was shockingly close to happiness. A cruel joke on her, because it wouldn't last. "I need you to listen to me very carefully. I don't want you to do that."

"Once again," Brynn said in her now-familiar stubborn

voice, the one that matched the stubborn light in her eyes, "I'm your sister, but you don't get to tell me what to do. I'm going to do this, and what you end up doing with the info is your choice. My choice will be to talk to him and get to know him."

Kinsey's stomach sunk to her toes, but Brynn shrugged. "Deal with it," she said. "I'm going to shower."

"Does that mean you're staying?"

Brynn met her gaze. "That's what family does."

And then she was gone.

A minute later, Eli came into the kitchen and looked at her.

Kinsey was horrified to find her eyes filling with tears. Her pulse was thundering and her heart hurt. "If you're here to yell at me, I don't want to hear it. I thought you were in my corner."

He gave a slow shake of his head. "Not even you can make me pick between someone I consider family and the woman I'm falling in love with."

Kinsey lost the battle with her tears. "I know. And she's . . ." She broke off, unable to find the words.

"Amazing?" he said. "Resilient? Strong? Yeah. All of the above."

Kinsey nodded, her throat thick.

Eli gave her a one-armed hug as he poured himself coffee. "Stubborn too."

Kinsey nodded again.

"And in that regard," Eli said, "you two are like twins."

She swiped at her eyes. "I'm sorry I keep messing everything up."

He leaned back against the counter. "You don't need to apologize to me. What I do need to hear is that you're going to get it together and stop detonating your life. Because there are people in it who love you, people who stand close to you, at your back, so when you blow yourself up, you blow us up with you."

She dropped her head onto his shoulder. "I know. If it helps, I'm done doing that."

He nudged her so that she straightened and he could look into her eyes. "Yeah?"

"Yeah. I want to fix it," she said. "All of it. Starting with you."

He shook his head. "We're okay, Kins."

"Are we?" she whispered past the huge lump in her throat.

"I know what you did, and I know why. I think you can't get out of your own way half the time, but I love you anyway. Just as you are."

Her eyes filled. "I don't deserve that."

"We all deserve that."

She knew he'd never been loved or accepted just as he was by his parents. Knew that was a deep-seated issue of his. She'd let him down, but that wouldn't happen again. She didn't want to ever be the one who hurt him.

As if he could read her mind, he shook his head. "It's not me you've hurt."

"I'm working on Brynn."

"And Deck?"

She bit her lower lip and shook her head. "That's . . . over."

"Why? Because you don't know how to let someone love you?"

"You don't know everything, Eli."

"I know that he loves you enough to deal with your bullshit, and that whatever you've done to push him away, you could fix. Talk to him."

"No. He deserves more than what I can give him. I want him to find the woman who can be his forever."

"And you?"

She dropped into a chair and rested her cheek against her bent knees. "I'm going to live alone with a hundred cats. We'll eat ice cream and curl up on the couch together. No talking about feelings required."

"You're allergic to shellfish and cats, and ice cream makes you gassy."

"Hey, the ice cream thing's a secret."

"It's no secret."

She sighed.

He laughed and then, with a quick but warm hug, left her alone.

 CHAPTER 21

At work the next day, a bunch of supplies got delivered to Brynn's classroom. Construction paper, colored pens and pencils, tissue boxes, tape . . . literally everything she'd had on her wish list. There was no note, but she knew it was from Eli. She called his cell at lunch, and Max answered from a boat in the marina, telling her that Eli was on a dive.

When she got home, she slid out of her car to find Eli and Mini waiting for her, and several reactions hit her at once. Affection. *Deep* affection, the kind that comes from knowing someone to the core over a long period of time. And there was definitely comfort in that. But it wasn't comfort racing through her veins. Nope, it was hunger and need, both of which made her ache.

But there was also a little bit of hesitation.

She understood what he'd done, and she could also admit that if she'd been in his position, if it'd been her closest friend's sister who'd shown up, she would've let it play out between them too.

So she thought maybe she'd have to revise her new one-strike rule slightly.

He was leaning against the porch railing, arms and feet crossed, but he straightened when she walked up to him.

Mini leapt to her feet, tail going back and forth with such force it could've generated electricity for the entire state. Because the dog was so cute, Brynn bent low and hugged her, getting her chin licked for her efforts. Because the man was so hot, she straightened and gave him a kiss on the cheek.

"Have a good day?" he asked, his hands going to her hips.

"Yes, since it was Christmas."

He cocked his head.

"Don't look so surprised. *Santa.*"

He still didn't say anything, and she shook her head and smiled. "Thank you," she murmured, going up on tiptoe to brush another kiss to his cheek. But he turned his head and their mouths met. "It was really sweet," she whispered against his lips.

"I don't know what you're talking about."

She smiled. "No?"

"No. I'd never try to bribe the woman I'm falling for into falling for me too."

Her breath caught. "Falling?"

"Fallen." He pulled her into him, threading a hand in her hair, palming her scalp, lightly kneading. Comforting. "All you have to do is let it happen."

"But . . . there's stuff to consider."

"Stuff like . . . I screwed up," he said, nodding. "I know. My plan is to never hurt you again and also to be as irresistible as possible."

She looked up at him. "I like that plan. But . . . I don't think it's all you. I've failed at every relationship I've ever had."

"Me too. But when you think about it, it only takes one time. The right time. Brynn . . . you're so good at caring for others. You're even better at keeping all your wounds buried deep. But you don't have to do that with me. Ever. I like *all* your pieces."

"Even the odd ones that don't quite fit?"

He lowered his head and rubbed his jaw to hers. "*Especially* the odd ones."

"I like all of your pieces too," she whispered, and held her breath. It was a safe admission as admissions went, but it was still a big admission for her.

Looking genuinely touched, he stroked a finger along her temple, tucking a stray piece of hair behind her ear, watching the movement. "I'm not sure anyone's ever felt that way about me before."

Her heart squeezed, but then his smile faded. "There's something else."

She inhaled a breath. "Something's wrong."

He gave a slow shake of his head and reached for her hand, slowly pulling her into him, giving her plenty of time to resist. She didn't, and ended up against him for a warm hug that stirred all her emotions into a complicated mass. Affection. Desire. Hope.

Because in spite of all that had happened, she really was falling too. "Tell me."

"In this instance, showing is much better than telling."

"That sounds promising."

He laughed softly. Sexily. "That too hopefully, but this first." He opened the front door and took her inside. There were three boxes stacked in a corner, with Kinsey and Max standing next to them, looking unusually nervous.

The boxes were labeled with her name. She stared at them, the room suddenly so quiet she could hear her heart pounding in her ears. "What is this?"

"Your stuff," Kinsey said. "Or what's left of it anyway. Your landlord apologized for not realizing what had happened."

Brynn stared at her, feeling her face heat. They'd found out her things weren't in her trunk. "You drove the three hours to Long Beach and retrieved my stuff."

"I wanted to also hunt down Asshole, but someone stopped me," Kinsey said, looking at Eli.

"Not worth the jail time," he said.

Brynn hadn't taken her eyes off the boxes. "All of you went?"

"Yes," Max said. "I'm sorry I lied to you when I said Eli was in the water. He was dealing with your landlord."

Watching her carefully, as if maybe she was on the very edge, Eli nodded, still holding on to her hand. "Before you got up this morning, we decided to do something for you. So we . . . borrowed your keys to get your boxes from your trunk."

Where they'd found no boxes, because she'd lied. She'd lied outright—when she'd flung their lies back in their faces.

"When we figured out that you couldn't unpack because you didn't have your stuff," Kinsey said, "we wanted to fix it. Your moms gave us your old address. I really wanted to punch your ex," she said with feeling, still sporting the bruise in the center of her forehead where Brynn's serve had smacked her. "But I controlled myself."

"With some help," Max said mildly.

Brynn stared at Kinsey's bruise, at the fury on her face, both of which were because of her. She took in Max's stance. He'd been really quiet, but he also looked pissed off, though not at her. He'd taken hours and hours to help her out, and he wasn't getting anything out of it except her friendship.

And then there was Eli, who she had a feeling had been the captain of this mission. Like others before him, he'd claimed to care about her, but unlike the others, he didn't seem to want anything from her that she wasn't willing to give. That was very new, and very . . . discombobulating.

His eyes were warm on hers, still worried, watching as she slowly came undone by their gesture. "Brynn? You okay?"

In her mind, she answered with sincere gratitude.

In reality, she burst into tears.

Kinsey's face fell. "Wait. What is she doing?"

"I believe she's crying," Max said, looking pained.

Brynn was so mortified, she let herself be pulled into Eli's arms. "You've got all the power here," he murmured, mouth to her ear. "We just want to help."

This only made her cry harder.

"Stop that," Kinsey said. "There's no crying here."

"Right." Max was awkwardly patting Brynn on the back. "Because telling someone not to cry *always* works."

Kinsey blew out a breath. "Brynn, that asshole doesn't deserve your tears."

"I'm not crying cuz of him!" she sobbed. "I'm crying cuz of you idiots. I can't believe you did this for me."

Kinsey huffed out another sigh and slowly joined the hug.

Brynn lifted her head in shock. "Are you . . . *hugging* me?"

"Yeah, and if you tell anyone, I'll . . ."

Brynn sniffled. "You'll what?"

"I don't know, I can't think of anything that won't permanently scar or maim you."

"Good to know you have some boundaries." Brynn sniffed and then stared at Kinsey some more. "Why do you smell like my mom's dry-skin salve?"

"I don't."

"You do. You smell just like it even though you said it smelled like dirt."

"It's turmeric, not dirt," Kinsey said with a straight face.

Brynn shook her head. "I can't with you. And why is your hand on my ass?"

"That's not me."

"Oops," Eli said.

Brynn laughed through her tears and knew that's what he'd intended all along. So she hugged him again, keeping one arm around Kinsey. "Thank you," she whispered.

Kinsey untangled herself. "Okay, well, this has been fun and all, but I've gotta go be with people who aren't crying right now."

"She's allergic to hugs," Eli said. "Watch." He snagged Kinsey around the neck with a long arm and pulled her in tighter.

Kinsey screeched and smacked at his head until he let her go.

"See?" he said to Brynn. "Allergic to hugs, kindness, and cats."

"Wait. You're allergic to cats?" Brynn asked. "You never said a word at my moms' house, either time."

"She took two Benadryl pills before we got there for dinner," Max said. "The other time, that first time, she came home all swollen and slept it off."

"Oh my God." Brynn's eyes filled again. "That was so sweet."

Kinsey looked at Eli while pointing at Brynn. "She's doing it again. I'm going out." She headed to the door.

"Is that a euphemism for going to Deck's to get laid?" Max asked.

"Shows what you know," Kinsey said. "Deck and I aren't doing that anymore."

"Since when?"

Eli was doing an across-the-throat-with-a-finger gesture to his brother, but Max wasn't getting the hint.

"He's not home," Max said. "I got a text from him a bit ago that he's at the bar and grill with Sam from his work, and that I should join them."

Kinsey whipped around from the door. "Sam? Sam's a *woman.*"

Max, who'd finally caught onto Eli's warning, grimaced.

Kinsey slammed out of the house.

Eli gave Max a look.

"Right," his brother said, grabbing his keys. "I'll go after that and try to settle it down."

When they were alone, Eli turned to Brynn.

"Why would she leave Deck? He loves her so much, and I know she loves him too."

"People do stupid things when they're scared."

Very true. She was a perfect case in point. She looked at her boxes. "I still can't believe you guys did this for me."

"We wanted to help."

"I'm not good at letting people help me."

"I've noticed." He gave her a small smile. "But there are people here who care a whole lot about you, Brynn, and just want to be there for you."

Her stomach did a flip-flop. So did her heart. "I don't know how to let that happen. What you did for me today . . ." She shook her head. "No one's ever done anything like that, and I'm not sure how to thank you."

"You just did."

She gave a small smile. "Doesn't seem like enough. You brought a piece of myself back to me. How do I thank you for that?"

"My thanks is you speaking to me."

"We're more than speaking."

His gaze locked on hers. "Are we?"

"I understand why everything went down the way it did," she said. "I do. But I'm going to tell you the same thing I told Kinsey. No more holding back. No more lies."

He opened his mouth, and she put a finger on his lips. "I can't be in this otherwise, Eli."

He took her hands in his, kissed each palm, and then wrapped her arms around his own neck. "You're in this?"

Her heart, going against everything she'd ever taught it, took a huge leap of faith. "Yes," she whispered against his lips, and then she kissed him. The rough male sound of pleasure that came from deep in his chest rumbled through her. She pushed his T-shirt up his abs and chest, and when he tugged it the rest of the way off, she reached for his zipper.

Letting out a choked laugh, he grabbed her hands again.

"You said I had all of the power," she teased.

His eyes heated. "You do. But I need privacy for what I intend to do to you."

"And vice versa." She took him by the hand and led him to her room, playfully pushing him down onto her bed, then slowly crawling up his body. "Do you want me to be gentle?"

"Not even a little bit," he said, his hands going to her hair, holding it back from her face. "Just don't let me go."

They made love like they had all the time in the world. He brought out a side of her that she hadn't known existed before him, before his touch and his want of her. And then she did what she'd never been able to do with anyone else. Comfortably all tangled up in him, she slept that way for the rest of the night.

BRYNN SAT AT her moms' kitchen table eating the best banana bread on the planet for breakfast. She'd stopped by on her way to work to visit, and they'd talked about what Eli, Kinsey, and Max had done the day before, and how much it meant to her.

"So you and Kinsey are going to be okay?" Raina asked.

"Yes. And oh my God." She couldn't stop stuffing her face. "This banana bread."

"I know." Raina grinned. "Right? Olive won't even try it."

"Because you use a pound of butter," Olive said.

"Not a *whole* pound."

Olive rolled her eyes and turned to Brynn. "Sweetheart, we know you. Really well. You've clearly got more on your mind. Let's hear it."

Brynn stuffed another bite into her face. To stall, but also because seriously, best stuff on the planet. When she reached for another slice, Raina took the platter away. "Answer your mom."

Brynn sighed. "Okay. I want to know about my dad."

Raina and Olive exchanged long looks.

"What?"

Olive put her hand over Brynn's. "We knew after that family dinner you'd be back here asking about him."

Brynn was relieved that they didn't seem upset. "What can you tell me?"

"You know we've tried to talk to you about this over the years," Raina said. "Many times. You always said you didn't want to know, that you had zero interest."

"Things change."

Olive squeezed Brynn's hand gently. "Does your not wanting to know back then have anything to do with the bullying you faced at school before we homeschooled you here?"

"No." Brynn paused. "And you knew about that?"

"Honey, when are you going to realize? We know everything."

"We went to the administration right away, of course," Raina said. "But they were useless. The fuckers."

Olive nodded tightly. "I'll never forgive that principal you had. He was such a bigoted asshole."

"We tried to get you to change schools," Raina said. "You flat out refused."

"You didn't want our help," Olive said.

"It wasn't that," Brynn said.

"Then what?" Olive asked.

She'd avoided this conversation for years, and for a very good reason. She hated to say or do anything that would hurt them, and this would hurt them. "It wasn't just me having a hard time. You two faced criticism and shunning for bringing a child into your world."

Olive and Raina looked stricken. "You knew?" Raina whispered.

Brynn nodded. "I hated what you were going through because of me, and didn't want to add to it. Changing schools wouldn't have helped any of us. It would've felt like giving in."

"First," Olive said, "you were never at fault. Never, baby."

Brynn held her gaze and felt the love. So much that she couldn't speak.

"Can you tell us what the real reason was that you didn't want us to help you get info on your father?" Olive asked.

Brynn let out a breath. "I didn't want you to think that you weren't enough. Or have any regrets about having me."

Raina burst into tears. Olive's voice sounded thick with emotion as well. "I never regretted a single thing about you," she said with the intensity of a mama bear.

"You're our whole world," Raina said. Or at least that what's Brynn thought she said, though it was hard to tell, because when Raina cried, only dogs could hear her.

"I finally let you try my magic mascara this morning and you're crying it all off," Olive said, not sounding all that steady herself. "Stop."

Raina swiped at her tears. "You can't just tell someone to stop crying. It only makes them cry harder."

Olive hugged her and looked over her head to Brynn. "I'm so sorry you felt you had to protect us. We should've been the ones protecting you. It was our life choices that led to this happening to you."

"How you choose to live shouldn't matter to anyone else," Brynn said fiercely. "You are who you are, and I love you both so much."

At that, she had *all* of them crying, and no one cared very much about their mascara. Finally, Olive got a box of tissues and pulled out more banana bread. "I'd get out the gin, but it's seven in the morning."

"You've spent too much of your entire life trying to please everyone," Raina said to Brynn. "And that's got to be exhausting. I think it's time to please yourself."

"What would please me is to find my father. Not for me. I mean, let's be realistic. He didn't sign up to be a dad, and

I don't need one. But Kinsey needs a donor. I'm going to get tested too."

"I've still got a friend at the fertility clinic," Olive said. "I'll see what I can find out."

"Thanks," Brynn said gratefully. "I was so afraid I'd hurt your feelings."

"Never." Olive cupped Brynn's face. "But that's not all that's weighing on you. There's something else."

Wasn't there always . . . "I'm . . . having a lot of feelings that I didn't intend to have."

"Well, that's normal," Raina said. "Kinsey's your sister. No matter how complicated your relationship has been over the years, blood ties bind us." She smiled. "Even when we don't know they're there."

Olive was watching Brynn's face, and she slowly shook her head. "She doesn't mean just Kinsey. She also means Eli."

"How do you know?"

Olive smiled. "Hard to miss the chemistry between you two. When you look at each other, the air crackles."

"He's wonderful," Raina said.

Olive nodded. "But he's also a man. And where there's a penis, there's trouble."

Brynn choked on her banana bread.

Raina laughed so hard she just about had a coronary.

When Brynn left for work a few minutes later, her lunch bag was bursting with leftovers. Her heart felt just as full, because, one, she was going to find her and Kinsey's dad, and, two, she'd called and gotten an appointment tomorrow to get her blood test. Life was looking up.

BRYNN'S MORNING IN the classroom didn't go quite as smooth as visiting her moms. Suzie had "borrowed" her best friend's pencil box, broken it, and then lied about it. Matt pushed his best friend into the sprinklers on the playground grass, and then told everyone he peed his pants, and so on. Also a new girl joined the class after moving into town. When Brynn asked her if she wanted to tell everyone her name and share anything, she'd said: "Hi, my name's Charlotte and my daddy has a baby that my mommy didn't have and now we're living in Wildstone with my grandma."

Right before lunch, already exhausted, she and the kids made a big sharing circle. "Okay," she said, holding the talking stick. "So we had a bit of a rough morning, testing some of our friendships, but I think we overcame it. The thing about friends is that you have to treat someone the way you want to be treated. There's a message in the way you treat people." She thought about how Kinsey had treated her back at summer camp compared to how they were now.

Okay, so there wasn't all that much difference. The difference was in Brynn. She was far less willing to put up with crap. "If someone hurts your feelings, it's okay to tell them. A good friend will apologize. Be friends with someone who can admit their faults and tries to be the best friend they can be to you."

Everyone nodded sagely.

She smiled. "Okay, let's switch gears to share time. Who's got something they'd like to share with everyone?"

A few minutes later, after some cringe-inducing sharing, Brynn became aware of someone in the doorway, and knew by the little quiver deep in her belly that it was Eli.

"Hi," he said as all thirty-three heads turned his way.

"Hi!" all thirty-three heads said cheerfully.

"Class," Brynn managed, focusing on the guest pass pinned to his shirt instead of his eyes. "This is Eli Thomas. He's a marine biologist."

They all just stared at him, not sure what "marine biologist" meant.

"It means I get to play in the water with the sea lions," Eli explained.

The kids all boggled at that, and oohed and aahed. Eli grinned, and Brynn found herself doing the same. "I don't want to interrupt," he said. "I was just trying to leave lunch for Ms. Turner." He had a pizza box from her favorite pizza place.

The kids cheered over this, and Brynn couldn't help but both salivate and smile. "I already brought my lunch. Leftover enchiladas."

"Raina's?" he asked hopefully. "Because maybe we could arrange a trade."

"A deal?" she asked playfully.

His eyes darkened. "Yes."

"If you want to join us in share circle, we can swap after we finish here." She scooted over to make room for him. "Where were we?" she asked the kids.

Carly raised her hand for the talking stick. "Tabitha called me the b-word."

Brynn looked at Tabitha. "Did you call Carly the b-word?"

Tabitha shook her head. "'Motherfucker' doesn't start with a 'b.'"

After a stunned silence, during which Brynn didn't dare look at Eli or she might laugh, she reprimanded Tabitha's use of bad words, and then they all had a long conversation about acceptable words and unacceptable words. Brynn said one more person could share if no unacceptable words were used. That was a new and very hard-and-fast rule.

Carly raised her hand for the talking stick. "My mommy made a new rule too. Now we have to knock *and* wait before entering her bedroom on account'a sometimes my daddy's giving her special medicine in the morning."

Brynn grimaced and risked a glance at Eli, who looked like he was choking on the laugh he was clearly holding back. "Maybe that's enough for today," she said.

"Ms. Turner!" Suzie was bouncing up and down. "You share something. Like yesterday, when you told us the reason that you smile more now. It's cuz you like someone."

"Okay," Brynn said, blushing, standing quickly, back to avoiding looking at Eli. "I think we've *definitely* shared enough for today—"

"One more!" Cindy yelled enthusiastically. "From the sea-lion man!"

Eli looked down at the talking stick after it was passed to him. "Okay, something to share . . ." He looked around at the kids. "Well, I've got a new friend. And at first it was really scary because making new friends can be scary . . ."

Everyone nodded. They completely understood this.

It was adorable.

So was Eli, sitting on the floor in the sharing circle, holding the talking stick.

No, wait. He wasn't adorable. He was . . . amazing.

"Does your new friend hold your hand when you get scared?" Suzie asked. "Because that's what a good friend would do."

Eli looked at Brynn. "Yes."

"Do they want to eat with you and share their stuff?" Suzie asked. "Because that's what *my* best friend does."

Eli smiled into Brynn's eyes. "Yes."

The lunch bell rang and everyone sprang up. They ran, jumped, skipped, raced to their cubbies for their lunches, then headed out to the cafeteria with an aide. Brynn took the pizza box to her desk, turned to the small fridge she had behind it, and pulled out her lunch box for Eli.

He set it down, took her hand, and tugged her around the desk so they were toe to toe. Cupping her face, he gave her a soft, sweet kiss. "Hi."

She smiled. "Hi back."

"You've had a day so far."

"It's better now. Thanks for the pizza. And thanks for letting me be your new friend."

"Thanks for always treating me like I'm important to you."

"You are," she said, and surprised them both. She thought maybe he'd say it back, but he didn't. In fact, he didn't say anything for so long that she sucked in a nervous lungful of air.

"I think," he finally said, voice serious, "that you're more important to me than you can possibly imagine."

Warmth and affection hit her, as well as a whole bunch of other things, things that shouldn't be happening at work. "It's not been very long," she said softly.

He gave a low, wryly amused laugh. "It's been years. Lots of years."

She shook her head. "Come on. We both know those don't count."

"They do." He took her hand, brought it up to his chest, right over his heart. "I didn't deserve you then. Still don't, but here I am, standing in front of you, just a guy who wants to date a girl. *His* girl." He paused. "And also eat her enchiladas."

Her mouth must've dropped open because he used the fingers on his free hand to catch her chin and gently lift it as he smiled. "Scared? Or on board?"

That made her smile. Hell yes, she was scared. But looking into his eyes, which were filled with an easy warmth along with a much deeper emotion, made her feel . . . exhilarated. "I didn't expect you, you know," she said. "You sneaked up on me and somehow, when I wasn't looking, you became the thing I didn't know I needed, but now can't live without. So . . . definitely on board."

That earned her a good-bye kiss to rival all the other kisses in the land. When he'd finished, she staggered back, having zero operating brain cells left.

He flashed her a grin. "Have a nice rest of your day."

# CHAPTER 22

Later that day, Brynn got a group text, including Eli and Max, from Kinsey. She wanted to know if she'd be home after work. Brynn confirmed that she would, and assumed that meant a barbeque, or maybe game night.

But with Kinsey, it could be anything.

When Brynn parked and walked into the house, her boxes were no longer stacked in a corner. They were front and center in the living room, next to the huge bag of Chinese takeout on the coffee table.

And once again, Eli, Max, and Kinsey were waiting for her.

"What's going on?" she asked, feeling a little panicky. Did they want her to leave?

"We thought it felt like a great night to unpack," Kinsey said. "To make this place home for you."

"It *is* home," she said.

"Not until you unpack, it's not."

Okay, so yeah. She was still afraid to unpack. Afraid if she got too comfortable, it'd all fall apart somehow, like it always did.

"You've helped all of us in one way or another," Kinsey said. "So now you're going to let us help you."

"You're supposed to ask, not tell," Max said.

"She knows what I mean." Kinsey looked at Brynn. "You know what I mean."

"I do," Brynn said. "But I don't need help."

"But . . . you're going to let us help anyway, right?" Kinsey asked. She slid a look to Max, like, *See? I asked, not told.*

Max smiled.

Eli took Brynn's hand. "Only if you want," he said.

All of them waited for her response. Against her better judgment, she nodded.

So . . . they unpacked her boxes. Max put her approximately one billion books on the shelves in her room. Kinsey pulled out the clothes from her duffel bag and either hung them in her closet or folded them and put them away in the dresser. Eli hung up her pictures on her walls.

At first, Brynn was . . . embarrassed. Why couldn't she have done this for herself? But then Eli looked at her, saw everything she was feeling, understood it, clearly also understood everything behind it, and hugged her. And that's when she got it. It was about love, about acceptance.

When Max found her CD collection and made happy love noises, she made the executive decision to let the rest of the embarrassment go.

Eli had opened a bottle of wine with the Chinese food. By the time they finished, they were on their second bottle. And at the end of the night, Brynn was fully, one hundred percent moved in. No one had pushed her to do anything she didn't want to do. No one had judged her. Well, Kinsey had not approved of her collection of three pairs of shoes—flip-flops, sneakers, and flats—but that had been expected. No one had made her feel bad for not being able to unpack herself. They'd simply recognized she couldn't take the final step even though she wanted to, and then come forward to help her.

They were her personal superheroes, sweeping into her life, accepting her as she was. Loving her as she was. She'd come to them, ashamed and enforcing her own helplessness. She'd felt unworthy. But they didn't care, didn't judge any of that. They showed up for her. Always. Without her having to ask.

She looked around at her stuff now integrated with everyone else's. She hadn't known where she wanted home to be, but she was starting to realize home wasn't a place. It was a *where*, a where her people were. And her people were here, in Wildstone. Some of them right here in this house.

That made it home.

They'd made it home.

Even better, every last corner of the place now had a memory attached to it, a group memory with the four of them, laughing, joking, teasing . . .

This was her family, the very best kind of family.

THE NEXT MORNING, Brynn woke wrapped up tight in Eli's arms, held against his warm, firm body in a way that gave hers some serious ideas. It was his fault, she decided. He was such an incredibly intuitive, generous lover in bed.

And out of bed . . .

He had a way of taking her outside of herself. She never knew what she was going to get with him; gentle and tender, rough and erotic, all of it intimate and seductive.

She'd never been with anyone like him. But she had to go. She did her best to slide out of his arms as stealthily as she could. Which apparently wasn't that stealthy at all because his arms tightened around her.

She let out a low laugh, her hands skimming up his back and then down again, taking hold of two handfuls of the best buns in Wildstone. Maybe in the whole world.

He nearly purred like a big, dangerous, playful cat, and began kissing and sucking and nibbling his way down her neck.

"Gotta get in the shower," she whispered, and kissed him softly. "I've got an early morning."

His mouth was at her breast now. "I'm good in the shower," he said huskily.

Which was why it took her forty-five minutes to get out the door instead of her usual fifteen. But Eli had been right—he was very good in the shower.

Body still humming, she drove into town for her appointment. In the waiting room, she grabbed a magazine, but at her every move, the scent of Eli's soap—which he'd used liberally all over, *twice*—teased her nostrils. She smelled like him, and her mind kept drifting to the way his eyes had been so intense and focused on her as he'd moved inside her, hands everywhere as he'd whispered naughty, wicked nothings in her ear . . .

When her phone buzzed, she wasn't surprised to see him calling her. He'd gone back to bed after their shower, saying he had thirty minutes before he had to get up and he needed his beauty rest. So she answered her phone, "Sleeping Beauty arises."

He laughed softly. "You've got no idea."

She laughed softly. "Did you call for anything in particular?"

"Maybe I just wanted to hear your voice."

"What did you want to hear?"

"That sound you make when I—"

"Stop," she said on a laugh even as she blushed. "Besides"— she lowered her voice—"I'd need assistance to make that sound."

"I'm available when you are."

Her body got very happy, but someone was calling her name. "Gotta go." She slid the phone away and was surprised to find Deck standing there in the doorway waiting on her. He was in midnight-blue scrubs and looking badass official with his credentials hanging around his neck along with a stethoscope, and an iPad in his hand.

He remained utterly professional as he brought her to the back and gestured to the chair she was to sit in.

Once she had, he set down his iPad and looked at her.

"I have to do this," she said.

"So she doesn't know."

When she shook her hand, he looked pained but also relieved.

"You're worried about her too," she said.

"Only every single second of every single day."

She smiled sadly at him, and he nodded before pulling on gloves and then getting out the supplies he needed to do her blood draw. He eyed both of her arms, clearly looking for the best vein. As he wrapped a rubber tourniquet around her biceps, she inhaled a deep breath, and his gaze went to her face. "You have a needle phobia too?"

"No, it's just not my favorite thing to do," she admitted, and then sucked in a breath. "Wait—Kinsey has a needle phobia?"

He swiped the spot he'd chosen on her arm with an alcohol pad. "Along with a phobia of men's toes, people throwing up, and getting dirty, yes. Worst one is the needle phobia, though. It's bad."

She gaped at him. "But she gets stuck every week."

"Three times a week, two pokes each time. Make a fist, darlin'. Little pinch, that's all."

She made a fist, so distracted by the thought of Kinsey suffering through a genuine phobia of needles and how awful it must be for her that she barely felt the needle go in. "She never complains."

Deck's gaze lifted briefly to Brynn's. "She does this thing where she protects everyone she cares about from worrying about her. Something you two seem to have in common. That's it, all done." He pressed a cotton ball to where the needle had gone in. "Hold on to that for me."

"That was fast."

"I'm good."

"I barely felt it."

"Not my first time."

She smiled at him.

He smiled back, but it wasn't full wattage.

"You haven't been around," she said.

"She kicked me to the curb."

"I was hoping that was more like a temporary thing."

"Nope." He turned his back to her and began writing on labels to attach to the vials of her blood.

His broad-as-a-mountain shoulders seemed relaxed and his tone had been mild, but she wasn't buying it. She'd seen the way he looked at Kinsey. She'd felt how much he loved her. "Are you okay?" she asked.

He pulled off his gloves, tossed them into the bin, and turned to her. "You should get the results within a week."

Code for *no*, he wasn't okay. "I'm sorry," she said softly. "I don't know what happened. She's very clearly head over heels for you."

His smile was small and dry. "She's the bravest woman I know, but she's also a huge chicken when it comes to certain things."

"Things like telling someone they're related to her?" she asked wryly. "Things like letting someone into her heart? Like facing any emotion other than amusement or bad temper?"

He touched his finger to his nose.

She sighed. "If it helps, I'm pretty sure she has no idea what she's doing."

"Makes two of us."

She turned to go, but stopped. "Do you think you could rush the blood work?"

"I'll put in for a rush, but don't hold your breath. The fastest I've ever seen this test come back was three days."

She drew a deep breath. "I'm putting out feelers, looking for our dad."

Deck went still. "She know that?"

"There're so many definitions of 'know' . . ."

"Shit," Deck said.

"I told her the morning after I found out we were sisters, but she didn't like it. I don't care. I happen to think sisters should be open and honest with each other, but still be their own person."

"I agree," Deck said. "And while Kinsey's honest about who she is and makes no apologies for it, she's not exactly an open book."

Brynn sighed. "Yeah. But, hey, maybe there's a silver lining. Maybe I'll find our dad and he'll be a match *and* a great guy who wants to save his daughter's life. And maybe I'll *also* be a match. Maybe she'll have choices."

"That's a whole lotta maybes," he said.

Yeah. It was. "Well, while I'm wishing on stars, maybe Kinsey will be grateful that I'm doing these things."

His mouth twitched. "Wouldn't bet my life on that, cute stuff."

She blew out a rough breath. "Yeah, so 'grateful' is a little much, I agree. I'll settle for her not killing me."

"It's been good knowing you."

She laughed. "Okay, you're doubtful, and I get it. But I think she's . . . changing. Slowly."

He didn't say anything to this, which probably meant he thought she was foolish.

"Look," he finally said. "I'm going to give you some advice

you didn't ask for. You should talk to her about this stuff. *Before* you find your dad, because it might be there's a good reason for her to feel the way she does."

Wait. Did he know something she didn't? His voice had been his usual calm, not giving anything away, but she searched his face. "Is there something you want to tell me?"

He didn't say anything to this, just busied himself gathering the vials, setting them in a holder.

"Deck."

He pulled her out of her chair. "This is between you and her. She's made it clear where I fit into her life, which right now is nowhere. Sorry, but you're on your own with this one."

She shook her head. "I don't believe that. You care about her too much. You love her."

"I do," he said, and that this big, huge guy who looked so tough could so easily admit his feelings made her throat tight.

He tilted his head back to look at the ceiling, and then met her gaze. "I also got tested. I'm not a match," he said.

And he clearly wanted to be a match, badly.

"But it wouldn't have mattered if I was," he said. "She wouldn't take a kidney from me. And not from you either."

She took his hand. "I'm sorry. But if I'm a match, she's damn well going to take it if I have to shove it down her throat myself."

He looked at her and then gave a small smile. "I like you. You're going to give her a good run for her money. She needs that. Don't let her push you away too."

"I won't."

"And watch your six. If she figures out what you're up to, it won't be pretty. She seems like a curmudgeonly grump, but it's coming from a place of wanting to protect those she loves."

Brynn's phone buzzed with an incoming call from Raina.

"Take it," Deck said. "I've got to get to my next patient."

Brynn hugged him hard. "My sister would be an idiot to let you go. She's not an idiot." She kissed him on the scruffy jaw. "She'll come to her senses."

He nodded, but she could tell he didn't believe it. Hurting for him, for Kinsey, she walked out and answered her phone.

"Guess what?" Raina asked.

With Raina, it could be anything. "I don't know, Mom. I need a hint."

"Oh, for God's sake," she heard Olive say. "Give me that phone." There was a tussle and then Olive said two words into the phone. "Found him."

"What?"

"We found your dad."

Brynn's heart flung itself against her rib cage. "Tell me everything."

AT SUNSET, KINSEY was standing alone on the beach, feeling sorry for herself because she wasn't out on the water with Deck. Or out to dinner with Deck. Or in his big, amazing bed with Deck doing big, amazing things to her body, the same body that only felt alive when he was working his magic.

And whose fault was that . . . ? a little voice asked.

God, she was such an idiot. She hadn't gone to the bar the other night. Max had stopped her, and that was for the best. After all, she'd been the one stupid enough to let Deck go.

When her phone rang with an incoming call, she almost didn't answer it. But she didn't have that luxury. It could be her doctor, or the hospital telling her there was a donor. It could be about Deck; maybe his motorcycle had finally done what she sometimes had nightmares about and he'd been in an accident.

She was a glass-half-empty type of girl.

But it wasn't her doctor, the hospital, or Deck, who'd probably removed her as his emergency contact since she was such a bitch.

Best Sister on the Planet was calling.

She stared at the phone for another full ring, not sure she was up for this. Because her sister was definitely a glass-half-full kind of girl. She swiped to answer, but before she could say anything, Brynn beat her to it.

"I found him," she said, voice shaking with excitement.

"Who?" Kinsey asked.

"Dad."

She froze.

"Kinsey?"

"I must be hearing things," she said in the voice she used to warn people she was considering committing murder, the same voice that said she already knew where she was going to hide the body. "Because I distinctly remember telling you we *weren't* going to look for him."

"Yes," Brynn said, using the same voice right back at her. "But since you're not the boss of me, I figured it was better to ask for forgiveness instead of permission." She laughed. *Laughed.* "Come on, Kins, this is great news. Admit it."

She would do no such thing. "I have to go."

"Okay, but don't you want to know *where* I found him? Bakersfield! Can you believe it? This whole time he's only been a few hours away."

Not only could Kinsey believe it, she'd been to his place in Bakersfield. And she didn't want Brynn there. She didn't want Brynn anywhere near him.

"It's Thursday," Brynn said. "You know what that means, right?"

"That tomorrow is Friday?"

"Yes, smart-ass. We'll leave right after work. We'll drive out there, and if he's not home, we can get a hotel and make a night of it, then try again on Saturday morning. We have the whole weekend to catch him. *Road trip!*"

Kinsey stopped breathing. "No. Brynn—"

"I wish I had called one of those reality shows that track people looking for their birth families. We'd make such a good episode, don't you think? We're going to get our happy ending, Kins! Anyway, I'm hanging up now, before you can tell me all the reasons why this is a bad idea." And then she did just that and disconnected.

Kinsey carefully sat on the sand, pulled her knees to her

chest, dropped her forehead to her knees, and . . . missed Deck. Missed his comforting presence, his calm, his adventurous spirit, but most of all she missed how he made her feel safe. She needed him right now. He would know what to do.

She also loved him, almost beyond bearing. And that was her own burden to bear.

 CHAPTER 23

For the first time in Kinsey's life, she woke up the next morning *wanting* to feel sick so that she could postpone the stupid road trip.

So of course she felt great.

Karma was such a bitch.

The problem was that she knew that with or without her Brynn was going.

And Kinsey couldn't let her do it alone.

She had a text from Brynn saying: *Pack before work, we leave right after!*

Whatever. She purposefully didn't pack a bag until she got home from work. Opening an overnight duffel, she started with pj's. She'd been sleeping in a shirt she'd pilfered from Deck, one she hadn't washed because she was pathetic and wanted to have his scent on her. Carefully folding the T-shirt, she tucked it into the bag like it was her finest possession. Which it was.

With a big exhale of grief, she did as she'd done a hundred thousand times since she walked away from him. She picked up her phone and brought up his contact info, her thumb hovering over his number.

She wanted to hear his voice more than she wanted her next breath.

Then she thought about why she'd let him go. Because as much as she loved him, as much as she ached to be with him, she *knew* he felt the same about her. So in the only way she knew how, she was protecting him, she reminded herself. Only one of them needed to feel this heartbreak.

Slinging her bag over her shoulder, she headed down the stairs. Through the living room window she could see Eli and Brynn by her car. They stood close, barely any space between them, but Eli pulled her closer still. They kissed, his hands slowly sliding up her slim thighs, vanishing beneath the hem of her sundress. With Eli's mirrored shades and Brynn's brightly colored clothing, they could have been on the cover of any summer magazine in the land and sold a gazillion copies.

Kinsey wanted to be totally and completely annoyed by the PDA, but even from here she could see how much Eli adored her sister. With a sigh, she strode out the front door.

They were still kissing, and now Brynn had wrapped her arms around Eli's neck and appeared to be trying to climb him like a tree. "Thought we were on a schedule," Kinsey called out, waving her phone. "Ticktock."

Brynn broke free with a grin, so blissful it almost hurt to look at her.

Eli was much slower to pull back, gazing down at Brynn like maybe she was the most important thing on the planet to him.

"We'll need to stop for snacks." Brynn smiled up into Eli's face. "Lots of snacks."

"I thought *I* was your snack," he said.

Kinsey rolled her eyes, but Brynn laughed, a low, husky sound that spoke of sexy memories and an easy, natural connection.

Eli laughed too, in a way that Kinsey hadn't seen him do in a while. He was . . . happy, she realized. Her sister and her best friend were clearly in love, and something deep, deep, deep inside, so far in there that Kinsey hadn't even known that corner existed, both warmed and got worried at the same time. Why were they doing this? Didn't they know the danger? And how was it possible to be genuinely happy for two of the best people on the planet, but also at the same time to be just a little jealous? But then her heart squeezed. Because it wasn't jealousy. She loved Eli, but she wasn't in love with him. She *wanted* him to be happy. He deserved it. He deserved this.

A part of her recognized that she'd pushed away the same thing for herself, on purpose, and that she wasn't going to get another chance. Hardening her heart, she moved to the car. "Let's go, dammit."

Brynn started to get behind the wheel, but Kinsey gave her hip a bump. "I'm driving," she said. "It'll be dark before we get there and you can't drive at night."

"Neither can you," Eli pointed out.

Brynn's mouth fell open as she stared at Kinsey. "How did I forget that? You're as blind as I am at night."

Kinsey shrugged. "Makes sense we'd have at least one thing in common."

"Oh, we've got more than that in common," Brynn said.

"No we don't."

Brynn ticked the points off on her fingers. "We both work with kids, love our unit, have the same hair—"

"Hey." Kinsey touched her hair. "Mine's not frizzy like yours."

"Because you buy ridiculously expensive product for it that I can't afford." She grinned and hugged Kinsey tight. "Shotgun!" she yelled and dove into the passenger seat.

Eli flashed Kinsey a grin and slid in behind the wheel.

Kinsey climbed into the back, grumbling, "You're both children."

"Sticks and stone," Eli said mildly. "Destination?"

Kinsey gaped at him. "You don't know?"

"I didn't tell him the amazing secret yet," Brynn said. "I wanted it to be a surprise." She turned to face Eli. "I found our dad. He's in Bakersfield."

Eli flicked a glance Kinsey's way, his brows up.

"Exciting, right?" Brynn was practically bouncing in her seat. "Let's get going. I'll get the GPS programmed."

With Brynn's attention turned to the navigation system, Eli craned his neck to look right at Kinsey, a look that said: *We need to talk.*

No shit. "The weather app says it's going to be a hundred and five in Bakersfield. I vote we wait for it to cool off."

Brynn stared at her like she was a nut. "It won't cool off until October."

Exactly . . .

"I'm not waiting that long," Brynn said.

Again Eli flicked a glance at Kinsey in the mirror. *What else do you got?* his eyes asked.

"I'm pretty hungry," Kinsey said. "Let's stop at a restaurant."

"I'm too excited to eat first."

By now they were leaving the lush, green coast and heading into the high desert landscape of the middle of the state, and Kinsey was still doing her best to ignore what was happening, which was that she and her life were both circling the drain because she had no idea how to make this little impromptu re-union *not* happen. "The car's making a funny noise," she said. "We need to try again another time."

"I'll buy us bus tickets if I have to," Brynn said.

Okay, who was this ballsy, brave chick and what had she done with her sister the mouse? Fuck it. Just fuck it. "So . . . there's some stuff I should tell you."

"Hell no."

"Excuse me?" Kinsey asked.

"You think I don't know how much you don't want to be on this trip? You're trying to make it not happen, but it's happen-ing, Kinsey. Deal with it." As she'd been speaking, Brynn had been searching for a radio station, finally settling on country music, which always made Kinsey's teeth grind. "No one listens to the radio anymore," she said. "If you turn it off, I'll bring up my Spotify—"

"Road trips require the radio," Brynn said. "It's part of the adventure, not knowing which song is going to come on."

"You've got an odd sense of adventure," Kinsey said, having to automatically disagree with everything. It was how she was wired. Especially when secretly, deep down, she envied Brynn's sense of ease in winging things like road trips and . . . *life.*

The song was some guy wailing about his tractor, his dog, and the woman who'd left him. "My ears are bleeding."

Eli caught her gaze in the rearview mirror. "Doesn't Deck love country music?"

"Yeah, that's why I dumped him."

Brynn turned to face her. "He seems really sad about the break up."

Kinsey blinked. "When did you see him?"

"I ran into him at the clinic the other day while I was getting tested." Brynn paused. Grimaced. "Um, so that was supposed to be a surprise."

Kinsey stared at her for a full ten seconds before words came to her. "A surprise," she repeated carefully.

"Yes."

"That's not a surprise," Kinsey said carefully. "That's a damn secret. A surprise and a secret are two *very* different things. A surprise is something done out of affection and is based in love. A secret is a *lie,* based in fear."

"That's . . . not how I see it."

"Okay, so tell me this," Kinsey said. "Do you have the results yet?"

"No."

"So if you'd found out you weren't a match, would you have ever told me?"

Brynn hesitated.

Kinsey's brows shot up.

Brynn sighed. "I don't want to answer, on the grounds that it'll incriminate me."

"See?" Kinsey said. "*Secret.*"

At this, Brynn did something that would've made Kinsey laugh under just about any other circumstance. She rolled her eyes so hard they probably almost fell out of her head. It was a move Kinsey recognized on a soul level, as she herself had taught it to Brynn. She actually felt proud, but also furious. And a little terrified. "I'm not ever going to take a kidney from you."

"Deck and I had this conversation, and yes, you will," Brynn said. "If I have to shove it down your throat myself."

Kinsey jabbed a finger in her direction. "We're not doing this, not here, not now. Not ever." Shaking her head, she pulled out her phone.

"What are you doing?" Eli asked.

Getting myself a one-way ticket out of here. "Calling Deck to come get me. This was a bad idea." She hit Deck's number, realized what she was doing just as he answered in that low baritone, and quickly hit disconnect.

Dammit. She was *such* a chickenshit. She wanted to see him. She'd been wanting to since the day she'd walked away, but she hadn't known how to reach out. Now, because she was a dumbass who'd acted on sheer emotion, she'd called and hung up. She might as well have shown up on his doorstep and thrown herself at him. Same thing. Worse, she knew Deck, who knew her just as well. He'd consider the hang-up a call for help. She'd just single-handedly set feminism back a good decade by playing the damsel in distress.

This wasn't the right way to reach out to him. It wasn't fair and she knew it. So when her phone began ringing with an incoming call—which she knew was him without even looking because her nipples got hard—she sent him to voice mail.

Yeah. A dumbass through and through. At least she was consistent in her failures.

"Sometimes," Brynn said quietly, "people keep secrets because it's easier than the hurt and disappointment that knowing those secrets will lead to."

Knowing Brynn as well as she did now, how badly her sister had been hurt, from childhood bullying to her ex destroying her confidence and self-esteem, most of the fight left Kinsey. She couldn't help but wonder if she'd known back in summer camp the things she knew now, how everything might've gone differently. She'd like to think she'd kick the ass of anyone who was mean to Brynn.

And yes, she got the irony of that statement. But to be fair, she'd been kicking her own ass plenty lately. "Since we're all mad at each other, we should go home."

Brynn shook her head. "This is happening."

Oh, goodie. Her sister really was as stubborn as she was, maybe even more, and that was saying something.

The next hour of the road trip was quiet. Kinsey knew why she was quiet. She was still trying to figure out a way to end this crazy trip. Eli was in his driving zone. And the only reason Brynn was quiet was because she'd fallen asleep.

Clearly *she* wasn't burdened with a nightmare trip of her

own making. She had no secrets; her life wasn't exhausting in the way Kinsey's was.

When Eli pulled off the freeway in Bakersfield and into a gas station, Brynn sat up, rubbing her eyes. "We here?"

Eli pushed her hair out of her face. "Getting gas," he told her, and got out of the car.

Kinsey followed him. Eli stood at the pump, watching her come around the car toward him.

"So," she said quietly. "Guess we're in a bit of a pickle."

Eli shook his head in disgust. "There's no 'we' in this pickle, Kins. This is all on you."

"You think I don't know that?"

"You've got to tell her. Before we fucking get there."

"Hello, I tried."

He rolled his eyes.

"Fine," Kinsey said. "I know. I will, I promise."

"And then what?"

"And then what *what*?"

"Do you have a plan? She's going to be devastated," he said.

Like she didn't know that. "I'm just trying to protect her."

He didn't bother with words: he didn't need to. It was all in his eyes. He was pissed off at her. Well, he could join the club. She was pissed off at herself too. "There hasn't been a moment to tell her," she said.

"There's been more moments than you deserve."

Absorbing the unexpected hurt of his barbed words, she let out a low, hurt, "Wow."

Eli slid angry eyes her way and then softened slightly. "Look,

I get it," he said quietly. "You don't want her hurt. But you went about this all wrong, and now *she's* going to pay for that."

"Don't even try to tell me that this is just about that," she said. Huh, look at that, *she* could get angry too. Actually, she was already angry. "For you, this is about you two."

"Hell, yeah, it is. You already nearly derailed us once and now you're at it again, all because you refused to tell her everything she needed to know."

Brynn got out of the car. "What are you guys arguing about?" Kinsey froze.

Eli did not freeze—he never did. "Kinsey's being Kinsey," he said.

He had an answer for everything. Kinsey strode off, heading for the convenience store. She heard Brynn say, "Take it easy on her, okay? She's probably really nervous about meeting up with our dad."

And Kinsey's heart, the one she'd thought dead, slowly rolled over in her chest and exposed its underbelly. Frustrated, scared, she loaded up on goodies. Some days, sugar was better than any anxiety med out there. She'd been working hard at finding a reason to be mad at Deck, at Eli, at Brynn . . . all of them, simply because they'd had the misfortune to be the people she cared deeply about. Like it was *their* fault that her heart beat for them. She knew this was stupid and irrational. She knew none of them had done anything wrong.

But she couldn't help herself. She self-detonated her happiness on a regular basis, but this time was different because she was doing it to keep them safe.

From loving her.

And now her own inability to adult was going to cost more than just her own burgeoning relationship with Brynn. It was affecting her and Eli as well.

She was going to need more chips, and grabbed additional bags. Five should do it.

Eli walked into the convenience store to pay and stopped short at the sight of her, arms loaded. Switching directions, he picked up a shopping basket and gestured for her to dump her load into it.

Her eyes filled with tears.

Eli didn't sigh. He didn't look pained. He set the basket on the ground and wrapped an arm around her, kissing her on top of her head. And then, like always, he went right for the heart of the matter. "You've got the chance to get what you've always wanted, Kins. She clearly loves you. She's not going to blame the fact that your dad's an asshole on you. But you know her. You know she worries about failing those she loves. She'll feel like bringing you here was her bad."

Kinsey sniffed. "I know! But I can't tell her now that we're here. And yet I can't take her there either. He's going to be awful. It'll break her."

"Is that the reason you haven't told her? Oh, Kins." He hugged her. "Just *talk* to her about it. Talk about real expectations, how you're feeling, and where you're both at."

"I'm sorry, have you met me?"

"I just don't want to see you get hurt, and if you don't tell her, I can promise you that you will hurt her."

She sighed. "I just want . . ."

"What?"

"I want her to like me." There she said it. She closed her eyes. "I know I'm not all that likeable, E. I'm cold. I'm selfish. And such a bitch."

He gave her a quick squeeze. "We all get over it. I did."

This had her choking out a rough laugh. She wrapped her arms around his waist and set her head on his chest. "You know what I love about her the most? She's not afraid to be happy."

"You could be happy. If you let yourself."

She sighed. "Don't you ever get tired of being my person?"

"Never. And for the record, I might not always like you, but I always love you. *Always*, Kins."

She sniffed and buried her face in his shirt.

"You're not snot-rocketing me, are you?"

She just hugged him harder. He was still letting her do that when Brynn came in and smiled. "Group hug!" She squeezed herself in between the two of them and added her love to the mix.

Over her head, Kinsey's gaze met Eli's, and she knew there was only one thing to do.

Make sure they didn't get to her dad's house.

 CHAPTER 24

B rynn's nerves were dancing as Eli finished gassing up the car. She'd been trying to put on a brave front because Kinsey had been getting quieter and quieter the closer to Bakersfield that they got, going more and more into her own head with every mile.

She hadn't even sung along to the '80s rock station Brynn discovered. Who didn't sing along to "Livin' on a Prayer" when it was blasted out the window at full volume on a long stretch of highway with no traffic, the wind blowing back your hair? But Kinsey was still pale, almost green, really, and she seemed tense enough to shatter.

"Do you need food, maybe?" Brynn asked her, not sure how she could with the sheer amount of crap food in a bag in her arms. Brynn herself couldn't have eaten a bite to save her life, but Kinsey nodded.

"Do you want to eat before we go see him?"

"*Yes,*" Kinsey said, almost gasped, and so quickly that Brynn was bummed she'd made the offer.

"You sure you'll be able to eat? It might just be nerves, and the only thing that's going to be able to fix that is going to see him."

"Doubt that," Kinsey muttered.

Eli gave her sister a long look, but said nothing. They got back into the car and ended up at a pancake house. "Yeah?" Eli asked Brynn.

"Yeah." She leaned over and gave him a soft kiss. "Thanks."

He slid a palm to the nape of her neck and kissed her back.

"Oh my God," Kinsey muttered, and got out of the car, slamming the door. She strode into the restaurant.

When Eli and Brynn entered, Kinsey was nowhere to be seen.

"I'll get her," Brynn said. "You get us a table." She then walked through the restaurant and checked the bathrooms. No Kinsey. She walked back through the huge place, which wasn't overly crowded. No Kinsey. And no Eli either.

Then she heard a familiar voice in her sister's I'm-going-to-kick-ass tone, so she headed that way, finding them in a back corner at a booth facing away from her.

Arguing.

A bad feeling came over Brynn, and she marched over there. "Okay," she said. "Spill it. Tell me what I'm missing."

Kinsey looked up, eyes filled with remorse and guilt.

"Goddammit." Brynn shook her head. "No puppy eyes. I want the truth. All of it. What are you still hiding?"

"Tell her, Kins," Eli said. "The truth, all of it this time, starting with the fact that you know who he is, and you also know where. She deserves to know."

"You think I don't know that?" Kinsey asked. She scrubbed

a hand down her face and looked at Brynn. "I have one more secret. I held it too long, and then tried to tell you in the car, but—"

"Don't blame this on her," Eli said quietly.

Kinsey closed her eyes. "You're right. This is all on me." She opened her eyes again. "Here's the thing. I . . . love you."

"Uh-huh," Brynn said. "Tell me what you're not telling me or I walk out of here."

"Harsh," Kinsey said.

"Love isn't about being gentle. Or protecting people. It's about being there to pick up the pieces when everything falls apart. Right now, I'm not feeling loved, I'm feeling managed. *Mismanaged*."

Kinsey nodded. "I know where our dad is."

"Yeah. Because I told you."

"No, I mean I knew before. I've . . . always known," Kinsey said very softly, clearly ashamed of the words.

Brynn stared at her, then Eli, who'd clearly known as well. Gripping her purse, she considered chucking it at them both. But she loved her purse and didn't want to get it dirty. Besides, the one funny thing was that it wasn't anger coursing through her veins. Nope. It was hurt and betrayal, and there was nothing she could throw at them that would take away either of those things. "I asked you for one thing. The truth from here on out."

Kinsey closed her eyes, looking exhausted and sick.

Brynn tried to harden her heart to that. "Did you give him

a head's up that we're coming? Did the two of you have a great laugh about me butting in?"

Eli shook his head. "That's not how it was." He looked at Kinsey. "Tell her."

"She won't understand."

"I understand plenty," Brynn said. "And you know what? I've changed my mind. Don't tell me. I wouldn't believe you anyway." She turned to go. Where she planned on going, she had no idea, but Eli stepped in front of her.

"Give her a minute," he had the nerve to say to her.

Brynn shook her head. "She's used up all her minutes with me. The meter's empty." She realized it wasn't just hurt and betrayal pummeling her, but also humiliation. "Do you want to know why I jumped at the chance to live with you guys?"

"Well, 'jumped' is a bit of a stretch," Kinsey muttered.

"Because I wanted to belong. For once. I never have, you know. I've got no idea how to be . . . *normal.*"

"You're kidding me, right?" Kinsey said, standing now to go nose to nose with her. "You think *you're* not normal?" She spread her arms. "You don't know the meaning of *not* normal!"

Brynn stared at her, once again feeling like that stupid little kid, alone and scared at summer camp, homesick, and trying to deal with the mean girl. "Why did I think you'd changed? Why the hell didn't I remember how awful you were?"

Kinsey sighed and deflated like a birthday balloon. "Oh, you remembered," she said quietly. "I told you I'd changed, and you believed me."

"Well, that was stupid of me."

"No, it was hopeful," Kinsey said. "And I love that about you. You're always willing to believe the best in people, and I took advantage of that because I wanted you to be in my life so badly."

"Are you kidding me right now?" Brynn asked in disbelief. "You *hated* that Eli brought me home. You went kicking and screaming into this so-called relationship. You wanted nothing to do with it, or me."

Eli made a sound low in his throat—regret?—but he didn't speak. In fact, she realized, he'd stepped back, making sure that this moment was about her and Kinsey, not him. But the look on his face was remorse and sorrow, and if she hadn't been so upset it'd have actually stolen her breath. But she *was* upset, devastated actually, so much so that she could hardly even see.

Kinsey looked down at her own shoes, like she needed a moment. They were pretty great shoes: strappy high-heeled sandals in a label Brynn couldn't afford. Kinsey didn't have that much more money than her; she just shopped like a pro when Brynn couldn't be bothered. Brynn preferred the easy route. Kinsey wouldn't know easy if it hit her in the face.

Her sister looked up then, her eyes suspiciously shiny. Which was odd, because Kinsey didn't often show her true feelings. "Fine," she said. "I lied to you. I didn't want to do this. I wanted to *never* have to do this. But don't stand there and say you've never lied."

"We made a pact to be honest with each other," Brynn said.

"No, that was you, not me. I never promised that. I *couldn't* have promised that. Because this is bigger than whatever you think of me right now, Brynn. I'm a walking, talking expiration date. Do you realize that? I try to stand back, keep myself distanced so I don't hurt someone when my time's up."

Brynn's chest tightened unbearably, and hell if her own eyes didn't well up. "That's bullshit. People want to love you, Goddammit. It's not fair of you to hold back from the people you care about when those fears of yours about the future might never happen."

Kinsey stared at her, shook her head, and turned to Eli. "Talk some sense into her. Tell her."

He gave a slow shake of his head. "She's right, Kins."

Oh, no. Hell no. He didn't get to side with Brynn now. Taking a big step back from them, she said, "I can't do this. I came back to Wildstone to . . . heal. I'd been naive. Stupid. And so I made a pact with myself. I would still try to see the best in people, but only until they revealed otherwise, and then *poof*, I'd be gone. But once again, I failed myself. You lied and I stayed. *Twice.* So really, this is my fault. I mean, I can't even remember why I'm doing this, fighting for these relationships. And I sure as hell don't know why I moved in, or why I wanted to make this work. Coming home was the biggest mistake of my life, and believe me, I've made some doozies." And with that, she turned and started walking.

ELI JUST MANAGED to catch Brynn at the back door of the restaurant, *barely*. He put a hand over her head on the wood and held it shut with one hand, using his other to turn her to face him.

She leaned back against the door and glared up at him from eyes broadcasting pain and betrayal and a sadness that grabbed him by the throat.

Oh, and fury. So much fury, she almost blew him back from the force of that anger alone.

Which made two of them. Because she was going to walk away like everyone else. She'd just said coming home was her biggest mistake—which clearly included him. She was more concerned about storming out and being mad at Kinsey than dealing with the fact that she was blowing him and her up as well when, as far as he could tell, his only sin had been attempting to stand between someone he considered his sister and the woman he loved. "So what, you're just going to walk away?"

"Yes."

"Coming home was your biggest mistake?"

She yanked free. "I need to be alone. I'm tired of this fight."

"You're not even in this fight."

"I am," she said. "I'm totally in it."

"Babe, you're not even in the ring."

That must've been true because she wouldn't even look at him. "Let me go."

"Brynn—"

"Good-bye, Eli," she said, then whirled and slipped out the door.

Gone.

He stood there, his hand on the door, not even sure what the hell had just happened. Then he slowly turned back to Kinsey.

She raised her hand for a waitress. "I'd like the special, please."

A waitress hurried over. "The double-double pancake special, the triple-triple pancake special, or the quadruple?"

"Yes," Kinsey said.

The waitress looked at Eli.

"Nothing for me."

"You used to be in my corner," Kinsey said when they were alone.

"I'm *always* in your corner. But not even you can make me choose between you two. I love her."

Kinsey dropped her head to the table. "I'm sorry," she whispered. "I'm so sorry I ruined it for all of us."

"It wasn't all you," he said, looking at the door where Brynn had gone. "Each of us made some questionable choices."

"Think she's coming back?"

"No."

Kinsey nodded. "Which probably makes her the smart one."

That might be true, but it didn't make the hole in his heart that she'd left in her wake any easier to take.

KINSEY WAS SITTING on a bench outside the restaurant, waiting for Eli who was paying for the food they'd not eaten—and hopefully leaving the waitress a big, fat tip—and frustrated.

Brynn had vanished.

Well, not completely, because Kinsey had that stupid Find Your People app now, so she and Eli had opened it and stared at the screen.

Brynn had gotten into either an Uber or a Lyft, and was heading for their dad's place. When the phone in Kinsey's hand rang, she jumped and looked hopefully at her screen.

Not Brynn. But her heart still took a big old leap.

Her Biggest Regret was calling.

She stared at the screen before she answered. "Deck."

"You called."

His voice. God, that low, gruff voice. "I did," she admitted.

"Then you hung up on me. And didn't answer your phone."

She squeezed her eyes shut. "Yeah."

Out of all the things he could have said, what came out of his mouth both surprised her and warmed her cold, dead heart.

"Are you okay?"

God. Even now, when she'd screwed up so badly, he cared. "No," she whispered.

Someone sat next to her, and she lifted her head to glare at them, but instead she stopped breathing.

It was Deck, still holding his phone to his ear, just looking at her.

"How did you find me?"

"Your sister." He pulled his phone from his ear, hit disconnect, and waited as she did the same. "Why did you call me, Kins?"

Tell him. Don't blow it with him like you did with Brynn. Get something good in your life. "Because I was wrong."

"About . . . ?" he asked.

Okay, he wasn't going to make this easy, and she got that. "I was wrong to push you away, wrong to let you think I didn't have feelings, *deep* feelings, for you."

"So why did you?"

"Because I couldn't admit I was scared." She took a breath. "Scared to be alone. Scared to blow it. Scared to face my questionable future." She paused and met his gaze. "Scared to admit the things I feel for you."

"Newsflash, babe. You're going to face the medical shit whether you like it or not. And you are alone. You did blow it. Because I'd have been there with you if you'd let me. Every step of the way."

"I know." She closed her eyes. "I'm sorry I've been such a coward."

He lifted her chin with a finger and waited until she looked at him. "You're anything but a coward, Kinsey. You're one of the bravest women I've ever known."

Her throat tightened. "But I'm not normal."

"Look at me. Do I look normal? Do I look like I want normal?"

"But I'll never be the woman standing at the door waiting for you at the end of the day wearing heels and pearls. I mean, unless we're playing some kinky sex game."

He snorted. "I'm putting that into the queue. Also, you've been watching old sitcom reruns again."

She lifted a shoulder, and he bumped his broad-as-a-mountain shoulder to hers. "All I want is for you to do you, and let me be a part of your life while you're doing it."

"You said you wanted more."

"Yes," he said. "More being more *you* in my life. More you sharing yourself. Letting me in."

"I want that too."

His eyes never wavered from hers as he took a beat. "Why now, after all this time?"

Fair question. "Because I'm slower than most when it comes to matters of the heart? I think I'm getting caught up though."

He didn't smile, didn't move a muscle. "I was starting to think maybe I was wrong on how you felt about me."

"Yeah," she said, not proud of this. "I'm pretty good at evading, misdirecting, and avoiding the truth."

"You mean lying."

She had to take a deep breath. "Yes. That."

"So my question stands. Why now?"

Get this right, Kins, or lose him forever. "People don't . . . see me. Not all of me anyway."

"What does that mean?"

She shook her head, trying desperately to find the words. "You're the kind of person who walks into a room and everyone notices you."

"Yeah, because I'm as tall as the green giant and covered in tats. It's hard to miss me."

"That's not it," she said. "You change the light, you change the energy, without even knowing you do it. But someone like me walks into a room and no one . . . sees me. You're so much more than me, Deck. You could do a lot better."

He stared her, and finally shook his head. "The first time I saw you was in the ER. You'd collapsed from dehydration from the flu. It was two in the morning and you were trying to tell the on-call doctor about your medical history and he wasn't listening. You got up off your cot, hospital gown flapping open as you laid into him about patient rights and the skill of listening." He smiled. "That doctor was an asshole, and I fell in love with you right then and there. I saw you then, and I've seen you every second since. Now say 'Why, Deck?'"

"Why, Deck?" she whispered.

"Because Kinsey Teresa Davis, you light up my life."

She blinked. "That's a song. A very old song. And if you say it again, it's going to get stuck in my head."

"You light up my life."

"Oh my God," she said, but inside she was thinking, *Oh my God . . .*

"Need me to say it another way? You had me at hello."

She fought a half-hysterical laugh. "I never said hello to you that night."

"I know." He smiled as if the memory were precious. "You said, 'What the hell are you staring at? Never seen a girl's ass before?'"

Another laugh bubbled out of her. "And you said, 'Oh yeah, I have. What I haven't seen before is a woman so beautifully unafraid to speak her mind.'"

He nodded and then his smile faded. "I never knew you felt that way. That you don't feel seen."

"People who know me see my disease. People who don't know me just see a cold, unreachable woman."

He smiled. "You like that though."

She managed a small smile in return. "Yeah. Like I said, good at misdirecting."

He ran a thumb along her jaw. "What is it? Something's still wrong."

"You're not the only one I blew it with."

"Brynn?"

She nodded.

"She found out you knew where your dad was before you told her yourself," he guessed.

"Just like you said would happen."

Not one to say "I told you so," he shrugged. "So go fix it."

"It's not that simple."

"Family is family. You can be annoyed, irritated as hell, fight with them . . . whatever you want, but you don't just let them go."

She stared up into his face, cupping his jaw in her hands. "How did you get so wise?"

"The love of a good woman."

She sucked in a breath. He meant her. He thought she was good for him. He thought he loved her. So who was she to argue with him? "I thought it was only sex with us," she admitted. "But it turns out, that's just how you hooked me."

He snorted.

"I mean it," she said. "With you there's an emotional, intimate connection that scares the shit out of me. But . . . it's what makes it impossible to walk away from you."

"And yet you managed," he said lightly.

"No, I didn't. I tried, believe me I tried, but I couldn't." She turned to fully face him, meeting those warm, dark eyes. "I need you in my life, Deck. I'm sorry it took me so long to figure it out. And I get that you might not even want to take another chance on me, but if I don't at least try to fix what I messed up,

I'll regret it for the rest of my life. And I don't know how long that might be, but—"

He kissed her softly, then not so softly, pulled back and pressed his forehead to hers. Given the look in his eyes, she figured he was about to say something incredibly sweet.

"Did that hurt?" he asked.

She laughed.

He watched her like she was the best thing he'd ever seen. Clearly not caring that they were on a public bench outside a pancake house in Bakersfield—which by the way looked a little bit like Mars and was hotter than hell—he hauled her onto his lap. "You called me," he said. "Do you know what that means?" He cupped her face and made her look at him. "It means you want me in your life. You've known for a long time that I love you," he said seriously. "I'm keeping you now, Kinsey. No take backs."

Her heart was pounding in her chest as she slid her hands into his hair. "No take backs."

His eyes were still very serious as he raised his hand to touch her cheek. "A long time," he repeated, softer now.

She let that soak in. Love had never done much for her except hurt. She'd always believed that *that* was what love was, a way to hurt someone. "What if I die?"

"You do realize you're not the only mortal here, right? I could get run over by a bus tomorrow."

"Deck."

"Or you could dump me and rip my heart out. Again. Either

way, we could lose each other. But why are you wasting what time we *do* have? I know you love me back, Kins."

She nodded slowly. "I do. I love you, Deck. I love you so much."

His breath whooshed out. "I've always known you'd walk when things got too heavy, that you'd push me away, especially if your health took a turn for the worse. That you'd steal time away from me. But when it happened, it still nearly killed me."

"You still might lose me," she said. "But I can promise you, it won't be because I choose to walk away. Not ever again."

This time it was the six-foot-five tough guy whose eyes went shiny. "Forever then," he whispered against her mouth.

"Or for as long as you'll have me."

"Forever," he repeated. He met her gaze, fingers in her hair. "But I know you, babe. We can't do this, we can't do us, until you do what you've gotta do with Brynn."

That he so thoroughly understood her brought tears to her eyes. "I know. I'm going to try to fix that. And then Eli. And then you and me. But that does *not* make you my third priority."

"I know. And we're already fixed, babe. Go do what you have to do. I'll be there when you're done."

The words he didn't say, didn't have to say, were that he always would.

 CHAPTER 25

B rynn got out of the Uber at the address she had for her dad
and took in the apartment building in front of her. It was
utilitarian, with no landscaping other than the weeds growing
through the cracks in the asphalt parking lot. The neighbor-
hood looked sketchy at best, and she turned back to the Uber to
ask him if he'd wait for her, but he was already gone.

Okay, then.

All she had to do was go knock on a door and meet her past.
And her present. And maybe her future.

But that didn't feel true. It felt like her present and future were
back at that pancake house, and she'd walked away from them.

Kinsey.

And Eli . . . God, Eli.

Unable to process that right now, she stared at the building,
anxiety and panic and sadness all stirred up inside her so that
she could hardly breathe. She would've called ahead, but she'd
only had the address, no number. Her mom had been able to
get it through her contact, but no other information.

But as it turned out, she could've gotten it from her very own sister. Furious all over again, Brynn headed up the walk, took the stairs to the third floor, and knocked on the door.

A woman answered. She looked to be about Brynn's own age and was wearing cutoff short shorts and a clingy white tank top, with higher heels than Brynn could've managed on her best day.

"Um, hi," Brynn said. "Does a Kenny Vega live here?"

"Who wants to know?"

"That's . . . a bit complicated."

The woman narrowed her eyes. "You're not his ex, are you? He told me you two weren't seeing each other anymore. I'm his new girlfriend, Karen, and I don't share."

"I'm not his ex. I just really need to talk to him."

Karen looked past Brynn to the hallway. "Are you one of those server people for the courts?"

Brynn blinked. "No. I'm . . . his daughter."

Karen's entire demeanor changed. She straightened and smiled. "Oh my goodness, of course. I can see it now, you look just like him. Kinsey, right? Hang on, I'll get him—"

"No, wait—"

Too late. Karen turned and yelled at the top of her lungs, "Kenny, get your ass up, your daughter's here to see you! And don't forget pants!"

A man came up behind Karen, thankfully wearing pants. In his early fifties, he was tall, lean, and his girlfriend had been right. Brynn recognized herself in his face. Same eyes, same nose, same mouth.

Same not-quite-tamed hair.

"Honey bun, look," Karen said. "Kinsey came to visit you. Thought you said you two were on the fritz."

His eyes were friendly, but confused. "This isn't Kinsey."

Brynn swallowed back the renewed pain of the betrayal that he knew Kinsey. "Nope, not Kinsey." Her smile faltered because she'd already blown it. She hadn't planned to burst out with the information of who she was. For one thing, he'd clearly never meant to be in her life, so she couldn't just step in and blow up that life. That wasn't fair and not what she wanted.

As for what she *did* want, suddenly she was short on the details of her own plan. She hadn't thought this through. At all. Which meant Kinsey was right, a fact she hated. "I'm Brynn Turner. I was born thanks to . . . a fertility bank in Santa Barbara."

He raised his brows and gave her a second look over. "No shit?" He grinned and looked at Karen. "What do ya know?"

She smiled at him. "I'm going to give you two a minute."

"Thanks, honey." He gave Karen a sweet kiss and then slapped her on the ass. "I'll tell you all about it later, okay? Why don't you open my laptop and see what I've been shopping for. Hint: it's gold and sparkly, and it's for you."

With a delighted squeal, Karen twirled and vanished into the depths of the apartment.

"Sorry," Brynn said. "I really didn't mean to spring this on you."

"Look at us. We've got the same eyes. Same expression. I bet you've got the touch."

"The touch?"

"The charisma, honey. You've got it in spades, I can tell. You come by it naturally, you know, and you are welcome." He flashed a charming smile and stepped aside for her to move inside.

The place was small and spare, with worn furniture. No personality, which was the very opposite of its two occupants. In the living room, he gestured for her to have a seat. Then he turned to a bar and splashed something into two shot glasses before turning to hand her one. "Vodka—"

"Oh," she said, automatically taking it. "Vodka and I aren't really friends—"

"To a new father-daughter relationship," he said, and clinked his glass to hers before drinking.

And because he hesitated, seemingly waiting for her to drink as well, she took a small sip. And then nearly coughed up a lung.

"So," he said. "Tell me all about yourself."

She searched her brain for something exciting to tell him and came up blank. "I went to summer camp with Kinsey."

He looked astounded. "Small world."

"It was the only summer camp in the area where we grew up, so not really all that surprising. We didn't know we were related then."

"What do you do?"

"I'm a teacher."

He flashed a grin. "I've got smart kids."

"Do you have any more? Kids?" she asked tentatively, not wanting to be rude, but desperately curious.

"Not that I know of." He paused. "In hindsight, it was all pretty stupid on my part, really."

"Stupid?"

"Yeah. I mean, people could start knocking on my door, suing me for paternal support, right? Dumb mistake. Should never have done it."

"I . . . don't think anyone can sue you for paternal support."

"That's good, then. I only did it because I needed money. The clinic had ads out in the local paper, and I thought, Why the hell not? A quick buck, you know?"

Brynn's heart skipped a beat. "A quick buck."

"Yeah. But when Teresa—Kinsey's mom—found out about it, she was pissed. That was the first time she kicked me out, but not the last."

"You were together with Kinsey's mom?"

"On and off, but it's been years. How's Kinsey doing anyway?"

"You don't know?"

He shook his head and spread his hands. "We don't see eye to eye."

This was nothing like she'd expected. "You know she's . . . sick."

"Yes." His smile was gone. "It's awful. Tragic. She needs to buy a kidney."

"Well, not buy," Brynn said. "She's on the list for a donor."

"Yes, but I told her she'd get it faster if she bought it. Kidneys fetch a pretty penny, you know."

"Did you ever get tested?"

"Did you?" he asked.

"Of course." She set down her still-full shot glass, not liking the odd feeling deep in her gut. "And if I'm a match, I'm going to give it to her. For free."

He gave a slow shake of his head. "Maybe not a chip off the old block after all."

While she was sitting there, feeling like throwing up, his cell phone rang and he pulled it from his pocket. "Hey, honey," he said, voice oddly low as he turned to eye the hallway. "I thought I told you *not* to call me during the day. Texts only." He listened for a beat, then whispered, "Yes, we're still on for tonight, but I've gotta go." He disconnected and caught Brynn looking at him.

He smiled. "Prank call."

"Uh-huh."

His smile faded some. "Look, it's not what you think."

What she was thinking was that he was a whole lot like Ashton. Charming, charismatic, but also a snake. Which was funny, since they said a girl always goes for someone like her dad.

Luckily, she'd learned that she deserved more. She stood. "I'm sorry, I have to . . ." She gestured to the door and then headed that way.

He was right behind her. "Already? We were just getting to know each other. Let's keep in touch. Where do you work? Where did you say you were living?"

Shaking her head, she opened the door and practically ran out, crossing the street to the next block with absolutely no destination in mind. Her eyes were blurry with unshed tears, her heart was pounding in her ears, her chest felt like she'd been stabbed with a hot poker, and she couldn't breathe.

The man was cheating on his girlfriend. He wanted Kinsey to buy his kidney.

And he was her father.

For a second, she really did think she was going to be sick right there on the street, and she sank down to sit on the curb, head to her knees.

That's when she heard what sounded like high heels coming at her. From the corner of her eye she saw those heels appear.

Black, strappy, high-heeled sandals.

Her humiliation was complete. She closed her eyes. "If you're here to yell at me, you'll have to wait until after I throw up."

Brynn expected this to send Kinsey running. Instead, she stepped off the curb, inspected it with a wrinkled nose, and then carefully, gingerly sat down.

Brynn lifted her head and stared at her in surprise. "You're going to get dirty."

"Not my biggest problem."

Since Brynn was pretty sure *she* was Kinsey's biggest problem, she dropped her forehead to her knees again. "What are you doing here?"

"What do you think?"

"Where's Eli?"

"Are you kidding me? You dumped him. Even knowing all he's been through and how he would take it, you walked away from him. And I thought I could trust you with him."

"It wasn't like that."

"Wasn't it? Because all Eli's guilty of is putting the two of us together. To him, family isn't about blood. It's about who you choose. And he chose me to be his sister, and you to hold his heart. To him, our unit is everything. And you tossed it aside like it was nothing. You tossed him aside like he was nothing."

Brynn closed her eyes. "Please just go away. I'm still mad at you."

"Yeah, well, I inspire a lot of that. It's a talent." Kinsey eyed her own feet. "You should know I had to park three blocks away, and these shoes, while doing amazing things for my calves, are *killing* me. What did the asshole do this time?"

Brynn turned her face away, not wanting to do this right now, but knowing there was no choice. "You should've told me about him."

"That's the general consensus," Kinsey said grimly.

Brynn sighed. "I couldn't not come."

"I know." Kinsey paused. "And I'm sorry. Truly. I really was just trying to spare you, but I know now I can't make decisions for you, that it isn't fair to you. Are you going to throw up or not?"

"Not."

"One good thing about today, then." Kinsey stood, grabbing Brynn's hand while she was at it, tugging her to her feet as well. "Let's get out of here."

They walked back to the car in silence. Brynn didn't say anything about what she'd learned about their dad. She figured she didn't have to; Kinsey clearly had known.

And Kinsey didn't say anything further about Brynn going off half-cocked, though she did continue to mutter about her feet and blisters, and possibly something about ungrateful sisters and no effing parking spots.

Brynn was pretty sure they still had a big fight coming, but it'd have to wait until she was done shaking.

Something she figured Kinsey also knew.

Brynn desperately wanted to hold on to her anger, but she was having trouble with that. Because clearly, neither Kinsey nor Eli had hidden this from her just because. They'd done it to protect her. Because sometimes you did bad things for a good reason, for the people you love . . .

Halfway back to the car, Kinsey stopped, swore, and slipped her heels off.

"Whoa," Brynn said. "Your bare feet are touching the street."

"No, they're not. I'm wearing invisible shoes."

"But—"

Kinsey's head spun like in a horror flick as she leveled a look at Brynn. "*Invisible* shoes, Brynn."

They got to the car and once again both of them went to the driver's side.

"You smell like vodka," Kinsey said.

"One sip."

"And I had zero sips. It's also almost dark. You can't see in the dark."

"Again, neither can you!"

"Look, you might've gotten the good moms, the good kidneys, and that guileless smile that makes people love you, but I got the better eyes. Slightly, but still."

"Yeah, well, you're pale and look like shit."

"Aw, sweet of you to say." Kinsey shook her head. "Just get in the damn car."

When Brynn did, Kinsey tossed something into her lap.

Brynn looked down in shock. "Your journal from summer camp? You kept it?"

"Read it," Kinsey said. "Or at least skim for the good parts."

"Which are?"

"About you."

Brynn stared at her, then opened the journal. She read about Kinsey's increasing health problems, which had led to her not going back to camp, and then to the fated phone call to Brynn.

Who'd hung up on her.

She read about the surgery, about the kid who died giving Kinsey his kidney, about her rough relationship with her father.

Brynn's father.

She closed the journal and her eyes. Twenty minutes of silence had gone by, and though Kinsey had started the car for the air-conditioning, she hadn't left their parking spot. "You still should have told me," Brynn said quietly.

"Obviously." Kinsey pulled into the street before tossing her heels out of the car.

Brynn whipped around to watch them go flying into the air. Kinsey turned the corner before she could see where they landed, and she twisted to stare at Kinsey in disbelief. "Those cost you a fortune."

"Yeah, but they also suck. Look . . ." Kinsey kept her eyes on the road. "I know you think I'm the problem in this relationship, but—"

"Hold on," Brynn said. "Did you just admit we *have* a relationship?"

Kinsey slid her a look. "We're related. We're in a relationship whether we like it or not."

"You never have, though."

"Never have what?"

"Liked it."

Kinsey had the good grace to grimace. "So, I've had my doubts we could make this work. We both know that. We're polar opposites. You're . . ."

"A pain your ass?" Brynn asked mildly.

"Nice. Sweet. Kind."

Brynn blinked. "I can't tell if you're complimenting or dissing me."

Kinsey sighed. "Complimenting. See? I can't even do that right. My point is that I'm not nice, sweet, *or* kind."

"You are," Brynn said, feeling the need to defend her sister, even if it was to . . . her sister.

Kinsey raised a brow. "Look at you, lying right to my face. I feel very proud. If Eli were here, he wouldn't believe it."

Eli. Brynn slumped in her seat as her chest seized up.

"Look," Kinsey said. "I know who I am and who I'm not. I'm loyal and protective of those I love, however that looks to the outside, which I don't care about. What I *do* care about is being there for you."

Still mired in pain, Brynn gave a soft snort. "Why did you come after me?"

"Because that's what sisters do." Kinsey paused. "I'm going to say it again, because I know it bears repeating. I'm sorry. From the bottom of my black heart. I was wrong not to tell you, to think I knew what would be best for you. It was so wrong and rude and . . . possibly unforgiveable. And if I could go back and change it, I would. I promise you."

Brynn just stared at her. "I'm going to need a favor."

Kinsey glanced over at her, wary.

"Stop trying to protect me. We can't have the relationship I want to have if that's how it's going to be."

"And what kind of a relationship do you want to have?"

"A real one."

Kinsey's expression said she was afraid to hope that was true. But it was. In spite of everything, maybe *because* of everything, Brynn *did* want a relationship with her. Badly.

"You're sure?" Kinsey asked.

"Very."

Kinsey gave a single nod. "Okay, but in the spirit of not protecting you, I'm not the only one who messed up today. You also did, with Eli, big time."

"He lied to me."

"No. He didn't tell you something. Because I asked him not to, and I'm very sorry. I shouldn't have done that."

"He didn't have to do what you asked. He chose to keep up your lie."

Kinsey didn't look impressed. "Okay, pot, meet kettle."

"What the hell does that mean?"

"You lied to your moms for *years* about being bullied because you didn't want to hurt their feelings."

Dammit. True story. Which meant she was a hypocritical asshole.

"Eli's a good guy, Brynn. One of the best guys I know. And all he's guilty of is giving me time to figure out how to tell you the truth, which, for the record, he hated every moment of."

He was the best guy she knew too, and the only guy she'd ever wanted to keep.

Forever.

Kinsey was quiet a moment, concentrating on the road. "You know his biggest fear is not being chosen. You know he was a throwaway, like me. That's why we connected all those years ago at summer camp. His mom was done with being a mom. His dad had moved on with a new wife and new kids, and Eli was left in the dust. If it hadn't been for me and Max, he'd be without family at all."

Brynn's heart hurt, worse than during her last panic attack. "I know. I screwed up."

"Yeah, you did. You took those fears of his and turned them into a reality for him. You made it very clear to both of us back there at the pancake house that you were done, and why? Because things went a little pear-shaped. Well, guess what, sis? When things go bad, you don't just walk away. You fight it out. But that's not what you did. You told us we were your biggest mistake. Now, me? I couldn't give a shit. I'm a *lot* of people's biggest mistake. But Eli. Jesus. How could you think that wouldn't hurt him?"

Brynn had no idea. She hadn't been thinking. She'd been hurt and angry and embarrassed, and she'd reacted.

Badly.

"A long time ago, he decided the hell with getting hurt and stopped letting people in. Until you." Kinsey looked over at her. "He let you in, Brynn."

And she'd walked away from him. He hadn't been a mistake. Not even close. And it'd never been her intent to hurt him, ever. He was the only guy who'd ever really entrusted her with everything, and what had she done? She'd thrown it away like it hadn't meant anything to her. "Where is he?"

"I don't know. He told me that he'd find his own way back and to leave him alone for a bit."

Brynn stared at her. "Why would he leave without you?"

"Because he saw me with Deck."

"Deck?"

"Remember when I called him earlier and then hung up on him? Long story, but he felt sorry enough for me to come. And to take me back."

Brynn shook her head, full of too many questions. "You let Eli leave? And Deck actually came for you? Did you grovel? Is there video?"

"Yes, yes, yes, and thank God no. And I let Eli leave because he *wanted* to be alone. Plus, *I* wasn't the one who broke his heart. Deck came for me because, although it defies believability, he loves me. And I admitted I loved him. And then I asked him to wait at the pancake house for me while I came to get you." She smiled. "Did you know loving someone is better than pancakes?"

"Yes," Brynn whispered. It was. And she'd blown it. She pulled out her phone and called Eli.

He didn't pick up, and she felt her chest pinch tight with worry. She looked at Kinsey. "I'm happy for you. Really happy. But I need to get to Eli."

"Agreed. But he's not picking up my phone calls either. You should have put him on your Find Your People app."

Brynn watched the high desert landscape go by, feeling worse and worse by the mile. "What do you think my chances are of fixing this with him? Honestly."

"Honestly? Probably zero."

"Not helping."

"You asked."

Brynn was still looking out the window. She saw something. Someone. She squinted at the guy walking down the highway, heading away from them. He was in faded jeans and a loose T-shirt, and Brynn's heart skipped several beats. "Oh my God, pull over!"

"What? Why?"

"It's Eli!"

"How can you tell from that distance? You can't see anything past your own nose."

She'd have known that sexy butt anywhere. Her heart was in her throat, because this was all her. She had to make this right, and historically, she wasn't all that great at that.

Kinsey slowed, flipping off the car behind her when it honked at her. "Don't screw this up."

Brynn nodded and hopped out before the car even came to a full stop. "Eli!"

He didn't look, just kept walking.

Dammit. She'd taken off her shoes with Kinsey, and the roadway was hot. "Ouch, ouch, ouch . . ." she muttered as she jogged to catch up with him.

At that, Eli turned to look at her. He wasn't smiling. He looked cool and calm and distant. *Very* distant. She drew a deep breath, knowing that this could go only one of two ways. Easy. Or hard. And given the look on his face, she figured she knew it wasn't going to be easy. But she had to try. "Can we give you a lift?"

"No."

"So you're just going to walk the one hundred and thirty-five miles home?" she asked.

"I'm not in a hurry."

Okay, the hard way it was, then. She came closer, wincing at the hot asphalt, thinking *ouch, ouch, ouch* with every step.

Eli shook his head. "What the hell are you doing?"

"Stepping into the ring."

He just looked at her.

"Look," she said. "I warned you I was bad at this. But I'm working on it. Do you know why I came to Wildstone?"

"To turn me upside down and inside out?"

She let out a wry smile. "That was an unintended side effect, for the both of us. It started out as just me needing a safe place to lick my wounds, a place to get a fresh start to prove I wasn't a total loser. Because that's always been my biggest fear, that I'd fail, or that I'll disappoint the people I care about."

His eyes softened. "Brynn—"

"I needed to figure out who I was."

He nodded. "Did you?"

"More than." She reached for his hand. "Turned out I also needed people to believe in me before I could believe in myself. Steady, reliable, loyal connections who made me feel safe, and I found that, thanks to you."

"You and Kinsey made up."

"More than. She's important to me. So is Max, and Deck. But you . . ." She took his hand in hers and brought it to her chest. "You're everything, Eli. I'm sorry. I screwed up. You're angry, and I get it. Past Brynn wouldn't have, but I think Present Brynn's gotten smarter and learned a whole lot. And hopefully Future Brynn will get even smarter, quicker." She put her hands on his arms, shifting her weight from foot to burning foot.

Taking a deep breath, he said, "Put your feet on mine."

Grateful, she stepped onto the tops of his shoes. "I'll never throw you out, Eli. I'll never get tired of you. And I'll never send you away."

He looked at her then; the intensity of her words had obviously reached him, as his arms came around her to help her keep her balance. "Better?"

"Getting there."

With a shake of his head, like he couldn't quite believe what a pain in the ass she was, he lifted her up and twisted, nudging her behind him so that he was carrying her piggyback as if she weighed nothing. He carried her that way to a small wild-grass patch under a tree for shade.

She slid down his back onto the grass, dug her toes into the coolness for a minute, and then lifted her face to his. "You're not my biggest mistake. I'm so sorry I said that. I was angry and hurt, but coming home *wasn't* the biggest mistake of my life. Hurting you was. Finding you again, having you in my life has been the very best thing to ever happen to me. I choose you, Eli, and I always will. Even when I'm being a dumbass."

He looked at her for a long minute, his thoughts veiled from her thanks in part to his dark sunglasses. "How do I know you won't run off again?"

"Honestly? You should be the one running from me." She pulled those glasses off his face and looked into his stormy eyes. "But I'm not budging. Not ever again. I realized something when I was trying to spin my dad into something I needed him to be . . . You can't *make* someone be your person. You can't make them love you. You can't hurry love up, or even set it aside. I know, because I've spent too much of my life trying to do just that. And standing there in my dad's apartment, I finally understood that. I got it." She drew a deep breath. "I love you, Eli."

Whoa. That last part had just slipped out, and, startled to the core, she staggered back a step, and bent over, hands on her knees, before lifting her head to send him an apologetic grimace. "Sorry. I've never said that to a man before. But I mean it, even if I'm scared." She straightened. "Terrified, actually, and I think that's been evident," she said wryly. "But I've never been more certain of anything in my life. So if you're going to run, you should do it now."

He cupped her face, his thumbs gently rubbing her jaw, his fingers sinking into her hair as he stared into her eyes. "I don't run from love. And I do love you, Brynn. I think I always have. I knew I was in trouble that day we ran into each other at the vending machine, from the moment you pretended not to remember me. So be sure. Because I'm playing for keeps."

"Me too."

He let out a breath. "Then there's something you need to know."

She stopped breathing. "Okay," she said with what she thought was great bravery.

"I was going to come after you and figure out a way to get you back."

Relief had her sagging, but he had a good grip on her. "Yeah?"

"Yeah," he said quietly, looking right into her eyes. "I don't want to scare you even more, but you should know that I'd have followed you anywhere."

"Right back at you," she said softly, and smiled. "Maybe it's time for a new deal."

"Conditions?"

She shook her head. "No conditions."

He looked surprised. "That's a lot to promise."

"Yes, but I'm good for it. And *your* conditions?"

"Same as you." He searched her gaze. "A forever deal, Brynn, yeah?"

Brynn smiled through her tears, everything but Eli fading away. "Yeah." Going up on tiptoe, she kissed him, while from the car Kinsey yelled out the window, "You two about done yet?"

Eli lifted his head and looked into Brynn's eyes, his own steely gray gaze no longer stormy, but warm and filled with so much promise, she could hardly believe it. "Never," he said.

"Never," she repeated fiercely. "You're mine now."

"I am, and right back at you." He hugged her close. "Now take me home to seal the deal."

She smiled as her heart swelled. "We should probably seal it twice. You know, just to make sure it sticks."

"As many times as it takes," he said, holding her hand in his as they headed to the car.

And to the rest of their lives.

 EPILOGUE

Two years later

Kinsey pulled her phone from her pocket and called Deck. "My sister's boring me. She's in the bathroom. *Again.*"

"Babe, that's because you insisted on your weekly girls' night out even though she told you she wasn't feeling well."

"Well, she's gone from not feeling well straight to living in the bar bathroom."

"I'll come down."

"No, you don't have to, you're having a you-and-Toby night."

"That got canceled. He's got a cold, so he stayed with his mom. I was surfing with Max, we just got done. We'll come keep you company."

"Good, because this is her fourth time in there."

Max came on the line. "Call Eli too."

"She'll kill me if I call and worry him."

"Call him anyway."

So she called Eli. "Your wife's being a pain in the ass." She moved from her high-top table at the Whiskey River Bar and Grill to the hallway so she could hear if Brynn needed her.

"Define 'pain in the ass,'" Eli said. "Is this like the time last year when you were both still in the hospital after the kidney transplant and you got mad because you thought she stole your red Jell-O?"

"She *did* steal my Jell-O."

"Yes, and when you got home, I had a year's worth of red Jell-O waiting for you."

"It's not about the red Jell-O!" Kinsey was fighting back panic and anxiety and worry while Eli wanted to talk about the fucking red Jell-O. She eyed the bathroom door.

The locked bathroom door.

"Look," she said. "This isn't about me, okay? We both know I'll never be able to repay her for what she did for me."

"She doesn't want you to."

Kinsey drew a deep breath, her throat tight. With terror. "I think she's sick, Eli."

"Wait, what?" His voice got a whole bunch more serious. "You said 'pain in the ass,' not sick. She's been fine, recovering with no problems at all."

For which Kinsey had been forever grateful, but now she was afraid she'd jinxed it. "Come get her before she hurts herself."

"What makes you think she's sick?"

"She's thrown up like three times."

Eli disconnected.

Kinsey shoved her phone away and stood guard right outside the bathroom door, knocking on it. "Hey, let me in."

Brynn unlocked the door. She was green. She held up a finger and turned back to the commode, sinking down in front of it.

Kinsey's heart officially stopped working as she moved in close to hold back her sister's hair. Five minutes later, Eli was rushing through the door, dropping to his knees beside his wife, hugging her.

At the sight of him, Brynn starting sobbing—no, wait, she was laughing. Laughing *and* sobbing.

Eli looked stunned as, right there on the floor of the bar bathroom, he pulled her into his lap. "Yes?" he asked her.

Brynn nodded, looking equally stunned. "Yes."

"What the hell is going on?" Kinsey demanded, hand on her heart to keep it from leaping out of her chest. "Is she going to die? Goddammit, if you die, Brynn, I swear, I'll follow you and strangle you—"

"I'm not dying," Brynn said, eyes on Eli.

"Why didn't you tell me?" he asked her incredulously.

"*Tell you what?*" Kinsey yelled.

No one looked at her.

"I didn't know what to say!" Brynn said to Eli. "It's not like we planned it, and then last week . . ."

"What?"

"You don't even remember? You came to our end-of-the-year classroom party, and little Maxie peed on you and you said something like 'I never want one. Ever.'"

"I wasn't talking about kids in general. I meant I didn't want *that* one."

"He's cute."

"He peed on me."

Kinsey was putting the pieces of the puzzle together, and got weak in the knees, so she dropped to the floor and joined them, her heart in her throat. "Are you saying . . . ?"

Brynn smiled and set her head on Eli's shoulder. "We're going to have a baby."

Kinsey felt her eyes fill. Sure, the floor was undoubtedly covered in germs, but . . . pregnant? "We're having a baby?"

Brynn smiled at her through her tears, and then they were hugging too, Kinsey holding on tight, eyes closed, feeling more love and affection than her heart felt like it could possibly hold.

"You're going to be the best auntie on the planet," Brynn said to her, eyes fierce and full of a matching love and affection. In five or ten minutes, that would most likely switch to irritation more than once, but Kinsey had never been as happy in her life as she'd been the past two years with her sister at her side.

Deck and Max appeared together in the doorway and stared down at the three of them on the floor.

"Are we okay?" Max asked worriedly.

"We're pregnant," Kinsey said, like her sister both laughing and crying. "We're pregnant!"

Deck hit his knees and pulled his wife into him, fist-bumping Eli over Kinsey's head, leaning in to press a kiss to Brynn's sweaty temple as well.

"I don't know anything about babies," Brynn said to the room. "Do any of us know anything about babies?"

"Deck does," Kinsey said.

"I winged it," Deck said.

Eli pressed his forehead to Brynn's. "Winging it, it is. With all of us, how can we go wrong?" He stood and helped Brynn to her feet. "You okay? How about some soda water, or crackers? Something to settle your stomach?"

"I'm better now."

Max handed her some wet paper towels. "Can we name the baby Max?"

"Of course not," Kinsey said, trying to smooth Brynn's hair back down. "She'll be Kinsey."

Brynn looked into Eli's eyes and smiled. "Feels right, doesn't it?" she asked softly.

He pulled her into him again. "With you, *everything* feels right."

"Yeah, yeah," Kinsey said as they all followed the couple out of the bathroom. "But about her name . . ."

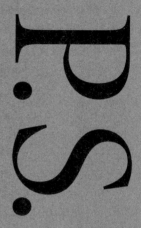

About the author

About the book

Read on

Insights,
Interviews
& More . . .

Meet Jill Shalvis

Susan Zweigle, ZR Studios.com

New York Times bestselling author JILL SHALVIS lives in a small town in the Sierras full of quirky characters. Any resemblance to the quirky characters in her books is . . . *mostly* coincidental. Look for Jill's bestselling, award-winning books wherever romances are sold and visit her website for a complete book list and daily blog detailing her city-girl-living-in-the-mountains adventures. ❧

Reading Group Guide

1. Brynn is given a real shock when she learns the truth of her connection with Kinsey. What did you think of her reaction? How do you think you'd react if you were told a similar life-altering fact?

2. Kinsey has been dealing with illness her whole life. How do you think that's affected who she has become? In what ways do you think difficulties shape our character?

3. Families come in many different forms and in this novel, Brynn and Kinsey are struggling to decide if they are family or if they are just biologically related. How would you define family? What makes a family unit?

4. If Kinsey had told Brynn the truth about their connection when she first moved in, would Brynn's reaction have been different or would she have believed she was only wanted for her kidney? Was Kinsey right to try to build a relationship first?

5. If you were Eli, would you have made the decision to keep Kinsey's secret?

6. Kinsey sees herself as selfish. Do you agree? ▶

Reading Group Guide *(continued)*

7. Keeping a secret to protect
   another happens more than
   once in *The Summer Deal*, from
   Brynn not telling her moms about
   the childhood bullying to Kinsey
   not telling Brynn about their father.
   Is this kind of secret worth it or is
   it a type of lie? Would you keep
   this kind of secret? ❧

Coming soon . . .
An Excerpt from
The Forever Girl

**Keep reading for a sneak peek at
the next heartwarming novel from
JILL SHALVIS**

The Forever Girl
Available January 2021

Prologue

Three years ago . . .

Maze Parker was good at playing
a role, so good she'd have sworn she
couldn't access a real emotion even if
she wanted to. So she was shocked to
find herself stopping twenty-five yards
short of her goal, unable to so much
as swallow past the lump stuck in her
throat.

For ten years now, since she'd
been fifteen, she'd made this annual
pilgrimage, but her legs refused to go
another step. As far as her eyes could
see, green grass spread out in front of
her like a blanket over gently rolling
hills, dotted with aged sweeping oaks.

And a myriad of gravestones.

Above her, the sky above churned
moodily. Thunder crackled, and a part ▶

An Excerpt from *The Forever Girl*
(*continued*)

of her heart smiled because Michael had
always loved a good storm.

Buoyed by the idea of her onetime
foster sibling sitting on a cloud creating
weather to amuse her, she managed to
coax herself closer and let the strap of
her beach chair slip off her shoulder.
She tried to open it, but it was more
stubborn than . . . well, her. "Not today,
Satan," she muttered. She'd paid too
much for this damn chair at the touristy
general store in Wildstone for it not to
work, and finally, after a two-minute
battle of wills, swearing the air blue
the whole time, she got the thing open.
Feeling righteous, she plopped down—
only to have the chair jerk beneath her
weight, making her gasp dramatically
and throw her hands out, braced to fall
to her ass.

She didn't.

Letting out a long breath, she pulled
a can of soda from her purse, cracked it
open, and toasted to the grave. "Happy
birthday. Hope that was entertaining."

"Oh, hugely," said an amused female
voice behind her. "*And* you beat us here."

"Of course she did," a second female
voice said. "Maze's far too perfect to
be late. There's a reason I always wanted
to be her when I grew up."

Maze snorted. *Perfect*. Right. Just one
of many roles she'd played. She looked
up as Caitlin and Heather moved into
her view, two of the only people on
earth who could both make her laugh

and drive her insane—almost as if they were a real family.

Which they weren't. Caitlin and Michael had been the only actual blood siblings. Maze and Heather, and a whole bunch of others, had been just the foster kids.

Caitlin and Heather began taking things from a big bag: HAPPY BIRTHDAY streamer, balloons, and a small cake—all superhero themed, of course.

Tradition for Michael's birthday.

Maze stood, pulled a Deadpool action figure from her pocket, and set it on Michael's headstone.

Heather smiled at her and produced a Thor.

Cat had—no big surprise—Catwoman. She and Heather got *their* beach chairs open without incident, setting them up in an informal semicircle facing Michael's grave. Maze noted Caitlin had left space between them for a fourth chair.

The last member of their ragtag group hadn't yet arrived. Hell, maybe he'd be a no-show this year. The thought made her chest go tight. She'd thought about not showing up either, but guilt was a huge burden, and no one felt the weight of it more than she—seeing as she was the one responsible for Michael's death.

"Stop," Caitlin said, cutting the cake in her lap into three pieces. "I can hear ▶

An Excerpt from *The Forever Girl*
(continued)

your self-destructive thoughts from
here."

A lot Caitlin knew about self-
destructive thoughts; she'd never
had a moment of doubt in her life.
Caitlin was the perfect one, the *real*
deal perfect. Two years older than
Maze, Cat had her shit together.
She'd been *born* with her shit together.
Her hair was a long, shiny, blond silk
that never frizzed, her smile could
draw in even the most hardened soul,
and she had the sort of willowy body
that looked good in every damn thing—
even though her idea of exercise was
lifting her Starbucks coffee cup to her
lips. Maze could hate her for that alone,
except . . . Cat was one of the most
intensely loyal and fiercely protective,
caring people that had ever come into
her life.

"You can't just tell someone to stop
angsting," Heather said, taking a piece
of cake. Heather was petite, barely
coming up to Maze's chin. But what
she lacked in height, she made up for
in grit. Today her black hair had bright
magenta highlights that gave her an
implied attitude to mask the fact that
she was the sweetheart kitten of the
group, one who never used her claws.

She didn't have to. Maze used hers
enough for everyone. People said it was
her red hair. It wasn't red, it was *auburn*,
thank you very much, but still, there
was no getting around the fact that her
hair—a bunch of uncontrollable waves

and the bane of her existence—did
tend to match her bad 'tude. She hadn't
needed the shrinks that CPS had sent
her to to tell her that because she'd never
really had a sense of belonging. That's
what happened when you were raised
to be a wild tumbleweed in the wind,
tossed in directions against your will.
Whatever. She was long over it, and took
another long pull of her soda to hide all
the feels annoyingly bombarding her.

Caitlin handed her a piece of cake.
She'd just taken her first bite when she
felt it, awareness tingling at the back
of her neck. Her body knew what that
meant even if her brain pretended not
to, and the frosting went down the
wrong pipe. While she went about
choking up a lung, Heather pounded
her on the back until she could suck
in air again.

Walker Scott hadn't made a sound in
his approach. No footsteps, no rustling,
nothing. The man was silent as the night.

Walker the boy hadn't been silent.
He'd been feral, and there'd been
nothing calm or quiet about him.

But things changed, and so had he.
She watched as he set out his chair.
It didn't dare misbehave, opening for
him with a flick of a forearm. He then
set a Batman action figure next to the
others on the gravestone, and with a
hand braced on the stone, stood still
for a moment, staring down at Michael's
name.

When he finally turned to them, ▸

An Excerpt from *The Forever Girl*
(continued)

both Caitlin and Heather lifted their
arms in greeting, and he obligingly bent
to hug them one at a time, murmuring
something too low for Maze to hear.
Whatever it was seemed to comfort
them both, and it did something deep
inside Maze to see their honest emotion,
something she herself had a hard time
revealing on the best of days—of which
this wasn't. Didn't stop her from soaking
up the sight of Walker. He wore dark
jeans, work boots, an untucked blue
button-down stretched taught over
broad shoulders, and . . . a sling holding
his left arm tight to his body. Dark
aviator sunglasses covered his eyes,
but she didn't need to see them. That
sky-blue gaze of his was burned onto
her soul.

There'd been a time when he'd
smiled at her with warmth, affection,
and hunger. There'd been even more
times when he'd made her laugh, made
her *feel*—back in the days when she
still could. All of it was long gone now
as around them the air went thick with
memories, some of the best and worst
memories of her life.

Maze did not lift her arms in
invitation.

And he did not reach for her.

"Maze," he said simply and gave her
a single curt nod. She got it, but even
after all that had happened between
them, a little tiny part of her yearned to
see that old spark of pure trouble in his
eyes, accompanied by that bad boy smile,

the one that promised a thrill and had never failed to deliver.

Caitlin pulled something from her bag.

A bran muffin.

Walker didn't do cake, or any junk food for that matter, never had. He ate to fuel his body, which of course showed since he looked like a lean, hard-muscled fighting machine. Food wasn't a pleasure button for him like it was for her. Nope, Walker had other pleasure buttons, something she sometimes relived in the deep dark of the night.

Taking the muffin, he let out an almost inaudible sound of amusement before turning to stare at the gravestone while slowly, and clearly painfully, lowering himself to the chair.

"What happened to you?" Maze asked him softly.

He shrugged with his good shoulder and took a bite of the muffin.

She turned to look at Heather and Caitlin.

Caitlin looked pained, but said nothing.

Heather was biting her lower lip like she was trying to hold back, but finally burst out with "He got shot." Then she slapped her hand over her mouth.

Maze sucked in air. *"Shot?"*

"On the job," Heather said from between her fingers. "He's on leave."

Walker sent Heather a long look, and she tossed up her hands. "Whatever, ▶

An Excerpt from *The Forever Girl*
(continued)

Walk. You all know I don't keep secrets anymore, not for anyone." She began to chew on her fingernails, painted black and already bitten down to the nubs. She switched to waving a hand in front of her face. "And now I'm sweating."

Maze, Heather, and Walker had all come from vastly different but equally troubled backgrounds by the time they'd landed in the same foster home—run by Caitlin and Michael's parents—that long-ago summer. After The Event, the one that had unintentionally scattered them all far and wide, Maze and Heather had been fostered into new, fairly decent families within a few months of each other. Walker had ended up in a group home, ageing out of the system less than a year later. From there, he'd gone into the military and then the FBI. The rigorous discipline had molded him, given him a sense of purpose and a way to channel his demons. It'd toughened and hardened the already toughened, hardened kid.

But Maze knew him better than most, or at least she had. Very few understood that beneath the edgy shell he wore like armor beat a heart that would lay itself down for the people it beat for. Once upon a time, she'd been one of those people.

"The leave is temporary," Walker said. "I'm going back next week."

Heather's eyes filled. "You almost died."

"But I didn't."

Maze's gut clenched. As kids, they'd all had hopes and visions of what they wanted to be when they grew up. Walker had wanted to run a bar or restaurant. He'd wanted to be surrounded by friends and be able to take care of them by feeding them. Simple dream, really, but it spoke of his deep-seated need to have those few trusted people in his life close to him. That was all that mattered.

He'd ended up going in a very different direction. Maze wasn't sure why exactly, but her working theory had always been that he figured giving a shit had never gotten him anywhere, so why try.

"You almost died?" she asked softly.

He looked pained as he swallowed the last of his muffin. "I'm fine."

"But—"

"Drop it, Maze," he said in a warning tone that she imagined probably had all the bad guys' gonads retreating north.

Good thing she didn't have gonads. She opened her mouth to tell him that very thing, but Heather pointed to the carefully tended gravesite and said quietly, "I love the wildflowers you planted last year, they're all blooming now." Ever their peacemaker. At nineteen, Heather was the youngest, and therefore remembered the least about that long-ago night. She'd never been able to process bad stuff, and the rest of them always shielded her the best they could. ▶

An Excerpt from *The Forever Girl*
(continued)

Caitlin smiled her thanks at Heather, but it wasn't her usual two hundred watt. If Heather was the group's soul, Caitlin was their heart. "I was out here last week to pull the weeds." She paused. "*Without* using Daddy's tractor."

Everyone looked at Maze, who sighed. "One time. Jeez. You *borrow*"—still holding her fork in one hand and the paper plate in the other, she managed to use air quotes for the word *borrow*— "a guy's tractor one time, and no one lets you forget it."

"That's because thanks to you, it's now illegal to drive a tractor without a permit in the state of California," Walker said.

Eyes narrowed, Maze searched his gaze, because she'd have sworn she'd heard amusement in his tone, but his expression was completely blank. "That's a total exaggeration. I didn't even get arrested." Not that the implication that she'd been wild and impulsive was wrong. Still wasn't. She'd merely learned how to fake being mature.

Caitlin smiled and reached out for Heather's and Maze's hands, waiting for Heather to take Walker's so they were all connected. "I love you guys."

"I love you too," Heather said.

"Love you," Walker said quietly in his low baritone without a single beat of hesitation.

There came a beat of silence, and when it wasn't filled, once again everyone looked at Maze.

"Me too," she said.

Heather shook her head.

Caitlin rolled her eyes.

Walker didn't react at all.

"*What,*" Maze said defensively.

"You never say the actual words," Caitlin said.

"Of course I do."

"Never," Heather said.

Okay, so they were right. But as far as she was concerned, those three little words held *way* too much power.

Caitlin had been eyeing her watch and craning her neck to look behind them at the parking lot a good hundred yards back.

"What are you looking for?" Maze asked.

"Mom and Dad should've been here by now."

Maze's stomach dropped. "You invited them?"

Heather raised her hand. "Actually, that was me. I was checking in with them the other day and I mentioned our annual thing."

"You mean our *secret* annual thing?" Maze asked.

"Again," Heather said slowly and clearly. "I don't keep secrets anymore. And you know why."

The cake soured in Maze's belly. Yeah, she certainly did know why Heather no longer kept secrets. She turned to Caitlin. "Why didn't you tell me Jim and Shelly were coming?"

At the use of her parents' first ▶

15

An Excerpt from *The Forever Girl*
(*continued*)

names, annoyance flickered over
Caitlin's face. She probably thought
Maze was trying to get back at them for
the last time they'd spoken, which hadn't
gone well to say the least. But that wasn't
it. Well, at least not all of it. It was more
that Maze felt like she didn't *deserve* to
call them Mom and Dad.

"Today would've been Michael's
nineteenth birthday," Caitlin said
quietly, and Maze's heart clutched.
Michael had loved birthdays. And
he'd only gotten nine of them.

"I didn't tell you they were coming,"
Cat went on, "because I knew you then
wouldn't."

"It should've been my choice to make,
not yours." And great, now Maze's voice
was trembling. "You don't get to make
choices for me anymore." It was a low
blow and she knew it. But she wasn't
sweet like Heather, and she sure as
hell couldn't be rational like Caitlin.

"Michael was their son, their baby,"
Caitlin said.

See? Rational. "Believe me," Maze said
tightly. "I get that."

Disappointment joined annoyance
on Caitlin's face. "You know that's not
what I meant. I'm just saying that they
have every right to be here at their son's
grave."

While Maze did not. Right.
She started to stand up, but Caitlin
tugged on her arm. "Don't go. They'll
want you to be here. And Michael
would want that too."

"Did you ask them?" Maze met her gaze. "Or is this a complete surprise for them as well?"

Caitlin winced, giving herself away. Dammit. Maze shook her head. "See, *this* is why it's easier to not be part of a family."

"*A* family?" Caitlin asked. "Or *this* family?"

Contrary to popular belief, Maze did have a few social skills and could read a room. She knew she was treading in dangerous territory here, and was about to seriously piss off the only people who'd ever remained at her back. But a funny thing happened to her when she felt cornered. It made her . . . *feel*, which also made her even more stubborn than usual, and that was saying something.

Heather was already crying. But to be fair, Heather cried at the drop of a hat.

Maze closed her eyes. "Heather . . . don't."

But then Caitlin sniffed too, and when a tear ran down her perfect cheek, it shook Maze because Caitlin almost never cried. "Stop that. You're all just proving my point."

Caitlin swiped angrily at her face. "Let me guess. You suck at meaningful relationships, so why bother, right?"

"Something like that." But the real truth was, Maze didn't just suck at them, she destroyed them. That was what she did, self-destructed her happiness. And she was good at it. ▶

An Excerpt from *The Forever Girl*
(continued)

"Bullshit," Caitlin snapped. "You just don't like needing anyone."

Maze drew a deep breath. "Look, I didn't come here to ruin this for you guys. But we all know that we're here because of me. I'm the one. This is all my fault."

Caitlin stood, vibrating with fury. "No. You don't get to own this, Maze." She began shoving everything back into her bag, her movements jerky with anger. "We all made decisions we regret that night."

Maze was vibrating too, with sorrow and angst. "I'm not a kid anymore, Cat. You don't have to protect me, and I don't need your misplaced sympathy. You should hate me."

Heather was still crying and Caitlin put her hand on her shoulder as she stared at Maze. "Is that what you want? Us to hate you?"

Okay, so she'd backed herself into a corner, and as always she was going to start swinging, taking out only herself. "Yes," she said. "That's what I want."

Everyone stared at her in shock. Except Walker. He was still showing nothing.

"I refuse to believe that," Caitlin finally said. "You're part of this family, whether you like it or not. You can't just run away. Love doesn't work like that and I thought you knew it." She nodded to Heather. "Come on, honey, let's go wait for Mom and Dad in the parking lot."

Maze didn't watch them go. She closed her eyes and tried to think of something else. The ocean. Puppies. Thai takeout. But it didn't work. She strained to hear their retreat, but they must've been already gone because all that came to her was the rumble of not-too-distant thunder.

Good to know she could still clear an area without even trying. Feeling sick that she'd just destroyed everything—once again—she opened her eyes and stared up at the churning, turbulent sky, which was in exact accord with her mood. Telling herself to get over it, she swiped her own tears on the hem of her shirt before reaching for her chair to try to close it. When it fought back and pinched her finger, she gave it a good kick.

A low male snort came from behind her and she froze. Why was it that Walker of all people always got to witness her most humiliating moments? Was it karma? Had she once forgotten to say thank you, or maybe very slightly cheated on her taxes? *Lied about not wanting to be a part of the only family she'd ever wanted as her own?*

Walker gave her a slow clap. "Well done, Mayhem Maze."

Rolling her eyes at the old nickname, she glared down at her chair, now upside-down on the grass but still fully opened.

When Walker reached for it, she ▶

An Excerpt from *The Forever Girl*
(continued)

stopped him. "No, I've got it," she said, practically choking on her stubborn pride. The theme of her life, of course: being stupidly, doggedly stubborn, because being perceived as helpless or needy made her nuts.

Walker pushed his sunglasses to the top of his head and eyed her. "You going to kick it again?"

"Probably."

There was a small smile on his mouth, but not in his eyes, those sharp blue orbs that saw everything and revealed nothing. "You never change."

Aware that this wasn't exactly a compliment, she looked away, because facing Caitlin's parents was nothing compared to facing Walker. Forget the chair. She needed to be anywhere but here. Even a root canal without meds would be preferable.

"Walking off for the win," he said to her back. "Shocking."

She whirled around. "*You're* the one who's always gone."

"For work. Not because I'm running scared."

A direct hit. She barely managed to get the words out. "Your work doesn't deserve your dedication. It nearly killed you."

"What do you care? These days all I see you is once a year, here, and you ignore me."

"Well, I'm *trying*," she said, tossing up

her hands. "For all the good it's done since you're still *right here*."

He just looked at her for a long moment, then folded her chair with annoying ease—one handed—and set the strap on her shoulder. "Always good know I still irritate the shit out of you, Maze."

He was favoring his shoulder, and her heart hurt. "It's time for a new job," she said quietly. "You know that, right? At some point, you're going to run out of your nine lives."

He just shook his head, either at the truth of her statement or because he just didn't want to hear her opinion. Both were entirely possible. "There are lots of other jobs," she said. "You don't have to put your life on the line for a paycheck."

His smile was grim as another rumble of thunder sounded. Ignoring the rain as it started, he shook his head. "It's what I know. I can't jump around like you do. What is it this week, business school?"

The rain cooled her skin, but not her anger. Yes, she'd jumped around, doing a huge variety of jobs before landing on bartending while working her way through business school, but she felt she finally had it right. Not that that was any of his beeswax. "Still a total asshole, I see."

"Maybe I just care."

And maybe once upon a time, she'd believed that to be true. "Screw you, Walker." ▶

An Excerpt from *The Forever Girl*
(continued)

"You already did that. Didn't work out so well for me."

Since that was the shameful truth, she should've been wise and kept her mouth shut. But when had she ever been wise? "Just . . . stay the hell away from me." Then, as she had the morning after they'd gotten hitched by an Elvis impersonator on one shockingly memorable drunken night in Vegas a few years ago, she turned and walked away. ᥫ

Discover great authors, exclusive offers, and more at hc.com.